T0121606

"Take your hair down for me, Hattie."

His words were barely a whisper, but something in his voice was so demanding, she felt compelled to obey. "It's a lot of foolishness," she said tartly, but began removing the pins that held her hair in place.

Reed turned sideways, and his new position gave him an unrestricted view of Hattie as she sought the pins in her hair. When she held them all in her hand, she unwound the coil so that the braid lay over her shoulder.

In the dim light of the moon, she could barely see Reed's eyes, but she could feel his hot gaze on her. As an uncomfortable heat shot through her, she resolved to finish the task as soon as possible and hastened to undo the plait.

"Let me," Reed whispered, and before she could respond his hands were there.

He gently began separating the three strands as his hands edged up the front of her body.

"Reed . . ."

He heard a thread of fear in her voice and carefully continued his task, freeing her hair from the tight bonds.

"It's beautiful, Hattie," he told her.

Refusing his flattery, she replied, "You'll have it wild, running your hands through it like that."

"Wild? Is that a promise?" He leaned closer to her, his breath soft on her cheek. She jerked back, but he stayed her with his hand, and his voice was comforting, his lips only inches from hers. "Remember what I told you when I gave you this swing? As long as you stay on the porch swing, a man can only go so far."

"How far is that?" she asked, her voice quivering with both excitement and anxiety.

"Not nearly far enough," he answered as he barely touched her lips with his own.

Bantam Books by Pamela Morsi

HEAVEN SENT

COURTING MISS HATTIE

COURTING MISS HATTIE

PAMELA MORSI

BANTAM BOOKS
NEW YORK · TORONTO · LONDON · SYDNEY · AUCKLAND

COURTING MISS HATTIE
A Bantam Book

PUBLISHING HISTORY
Bantam edition / October 1991
Bantam reissue / October 1994

All rights reserved.
Copyright © 1991 by Pamela Morsi.
Cover art copyright © 1994 by Gabriel Molano.

No part of this book may be reproduced or transmitted in any form or by any means,
electronic or mechanical, including photocopying, recording, or by any information
storage and retrieval system, without permission in writing from the publisher.
For information address: Bantam Books.

ISBN 978-0-553-76195-5

Published simultaneously in the United States and Canada

Bantam Books are published by Bantam Books, a division of Bantam Doubleday Dell
Publishing Group, Inc. Its trademark, consisting of the words ''Bantam Books'' and
the portrayal of a rooster, is Registered in U.S. Patent and Trademark Office and in
other countries. Marca Registrada. Bantam Books, 1540 Broadway, New York, New
York 10036.

PRINTED IN THE UNITED STATES OF AMERICA

145038997

For Kevin,
my friend, my cousin, and my fellow librarian.
Who, for my sake, learned more about rice
than he ever wanted to know.

Snap, Crackle, and Pop say, "Hey!"

COURTING MISS HATTIE

Prologue

A NCIL DRAYTON is thinking to court you!"

"What?" Hattie Colfax stood next to her buggy in the shade, unsure she had heard the excited whisper of the Reverend Mr. Jessup's wife, Millie, correctly.

"It's the truth," Millie said.

Hattie lifted her head and scanned the crowd of people milling outside the church, searching for the man in question.

"Don't look!" Millie urgently waved her hands downward as if the action would lower her companion's eyes. "You don't want him to think I've told you."

"I don't want him to think you've told me what?" Hattie asked. "You haven't told me anything yet."

Millie was obviously beside herself with the news. She beamed at Hattie and leaned forward, as if sharing word of a conspiracy. "He came to speak with the Reverend about it last night."

Millie Jessup always referred to her husband as "the reverend," even though everyone else in the county called him Preacher Able.

"Why would Ancil Drayton ask Preacher Able about courting me?" Hattie asked skeptically.

"For permission! Well, not permission, exactly," Millie corrected herself. "With his wife passed on so recent, he wanted the reverend's opinion about remarrying."

Hattie nodded, remembering that Lula Drayton had been put to ground only early last winter.

"The reverend told him," Millie went on, "that with all those children of his to care for, God and everybody else would understand about him starting to look for a helpmate a little earlier than usual."

Hattie surveyed the crowd again, but she still didn't see him. "Just 'cause he's looking, Millie," she told the other woman, "doesn't mean he's looking for me. Sure, he and I are of an age, but most men have no qualms about marrying a bit younger."

This was obviously Millie's most thrilling piece of news, and she delivered it with giggling delight. "He specifically told the reverend that he wanted to start courting Hattie Colfax."

A surge of blood pounded through Hattie's veins, and an embarrassed flush stained her neck as she realized Millie might not be mistaken. Glancing up once more, she finally saw Ancil Drayton plainly. He was standing behind his wagon giving a leg-up to his youngest little towheaded boy. As if sensing her gaze, he raised his eyes and caught her looking at him. Smiling broadly, he offered a friendly wave that shook Miss Hattie to the toes of her brown high-buttons.

Could it be true? she wondered. After all these years, was someone finally going to court Miss Hattie?

"Have you heard about Old Horseface?"

Reed Tyler looked up from the chicken leg he was eating and gave Bessie Jane Turpin a stern look. "Bessie Jane, I've told you not to call her that." The young couple were having an after-church picnic on a little hill that overlooked a low-lying field next to the river. "When I buy the Colfax farm," Reed continued, "no matter where we build our place, Miss Hattie's going to be our closest neighbor. She's a good friend of mine, and I think you ought to be thinking of her the same way."

Bessie Jane made a little pout that was not an apology but was pretty enough to diffuse his anger.

As he turned back to his chicken leg, he asked, "What about

Miss Hattie? What could anybody possibly find to gossip about her?''

"Ancil Drayton wants to court her!" Bessie Jane laughed as if that were the funniest joke ever told.

Reed stared open-mouthed, not believing his own ears.

"Can you imagine?" Bessie Jane continued, giggling. "That smelly, balding old man and that dried-up old spinster on a sparking bench! Oh, I'd love to be a little fly and hear what those two have to say to each other." Her eyes sparkled with an amusement that was hard for Reed to resist. "They'd probably trade recipes for lumbago salve!"

Reed managed with effort to hold back his laughter at the image. But then he tried to picture for himself Ancil Drayton courting Miss Hattie. Drayton wasn't exactly what came to mind when one thought of a courting gentleman. Far from fastidious in his clothing, he typically garbed himself in worn overalls that were less than clean. He wasn't the one to call on for help, and Reed thought him plain lazy. Oh, he worked. He plowed and planted and brought in a crop, but he wasn't much of a farmer. He was certain Miss Hattie felt the same. "Well, that piece of news will go out of style soon," he said to Bessie Jane. "Miss Hattie will send old Drayton packing in a minute, and that will be the end of it. She's not the type that will take just any man as long as it's a man."

Bessie Jane raised her eyebrows skeptically. "Seems to me that she ought to consider herself lucky to have even the chance to turn him down. I heard in church today that she's never had a caller, not even one!" Shaking her head in disbelief and widening her eyes in false innocence, she added, "Why I've had so many, I'm sure I've lost count."

Reed silently admitted that was probably true but disliked having her point it out. Half the single men in the county had shown up at Bessie Jane's door at one time or another. Bessie Jane was so pretty, it was hard for a man to take it all in. Her hair was corn-silk blond and fell in a mass of ringlets down her back. Her eyes were big and blue, and coyly concealed by the longest, thickest eyelashes he'd ever seen on a human. Her head came up just high enough to rest against Reed's chest, and her minuscule waist and generous bosom caught the eye of every man in the county between the ages of twelve and ninety. And when she smiled that sweet dimpled smile, Reed knew, he went just as calf-eyed as the rest of them.

Was it true that Miss Hattie had never had a beau? he wondered. He tried to think back to when Miss Hattie was younger. He'd been the plowboy for the Colfaxes since he was eight, so he'd known her since she'd first put her hair up. He couldn't remember any men paying court, but he'd not been much interested in that sort of thing then.

Miss Hattie had never been particularly pretty, Reed supposed, but surely there were men who had looked beyond that. "It doesn't matter to me whether she's had callers or not," he said finally. "I don't think you should be gossiping about her, Bessie Jane. She's doing real good by us, waiting to sell her farm until I've got the money to buy it. And if anyone should be standing up for her good name, it should be my betrothed."

One

THE stillness of the gray morning was abruptly shattered as the barn door flew open, slamming back on its hinges. Peering out as if to see if the coast was clear was a handsome, well-groomed nanny goat. Her barley-colored coat was accented by white markings on her face, and her intelligent eyes and twitching pointed ears were evidence that this was no typical barnyard dweller.

Daintily seeking her way across the yard, she headed directly to the sturdy white clapboard farmhouse. She ignored the twisting honeysuckle vines and the crape-myrtle bushes, and climbed up the two small steps of the back porch. Lowering her chin, she butted the screen door in a rhythmic fashion, not unlike any caller knocking when paying a visit.

" 'Morning, Myrene," a voice called from inside. "I'm up before you are today." Hattie appeared at the door, pail in hand, and paused to pat the goat on the top of the head before assessing the new morning.

It was still quite cool, but spring was just around the corner. It was her favorite season, all green and new. It was the renewal of life, the promise of another chance.

She walked across the barnyard to the milking platform, and the goat followed in her wake. The area, swept only the day before with a yardbroom, was as clean and orderly as the woman who cared for it. Even at this early hour, her faded cotton work-dress was neatly pressed, and her mass of dark blond hair was pulled circumspectly into a coiled plait at the nape of her neck.

With an ease born of habit, she led Myrene onto the platform, guided her head through the round slot, and lowered the crossbar to secure the goat in place. Adjusting the stool, she seated herself for milking.

Hattie Colfax was a strong farm-muscled woman of twenty and nine. Her figure was unremarkable, but she did have the requisite number of feminine curves. Her eyes were an in-between color—not green, not quite blue. And her hair, she joked to the ladies at the church, was the exact color of possum fur.

Hattie was blessed, or cursed, with a quick and easy smile. She was faster than most to see the humor in things, and the sound of her laughter was familiar to all who knew her. Her friendly open smile, though, displayed her very straight, very white teeth. Unfortunately, they were also large and numerous, and they gave her a rather equine appearance. She had been born on the Colfax farm, the only child of Henry and Sarah Colfax. Since her mother's death two years earlier, she'd lived there alone. But at least she wasn't lonely.

Gazing down the road into the fleeting darkness, she saw Reed Tyler striding toward the house, and a smile automatically curved her lips.

Unhitching Myrene from the milking platform, she patted the nanny on the rump. "Have a good day, Myrene, and stay out of my canna bulbs."

Hattie carried her pail of milk back to the house and poured it through a towel to strain it. Setting the quart of fresh milk on the counter, she checked the fire in the stove, stoked it a couple of times with the poker, then began mixing up the morning biscuits.

A knock on the back screen signaled Reed's arrival. " 'Morning, Miss Hattie.''

She heard him opening the door and glanced up with a welcoming smile. " 'Morning, Reed. Looks like a good day for plowing.''

"Yes, ma'am," he answered, seating himself at the table.

"I saw your garden on the way in. For shame, Miss Hattie," he scolded in mock horror, "You've been plowing on Sunday."

Hattie dismissed the teasing with a shrug. "I had some things on my mind yesterday," she said. "It's always best to get yourself to work when you start ruminating about something. The good Lord understands that I'm thinking."

As Hattie put the bacon on to fry, she glanced over at the young man she knew so well. At twenty-four, Reed Tyler was one fine specimen of male humanity. He was right at six feet in height, and every inch was covered with the rangy muscles of a hardworking farmer. His hair was as black as good Arkansas dirt, and his eyes were the warm color of cinnamon. In the morning light of the kitchen she could see the faint pale lines that forked out from his eyes. They were a sure sign of a farmer who plowed with a smile on his face.

"You want coffee or buttermilk this morning, Plowboy?" she asked.

A smile spread across his face, livening his features. "I believe I'll have buttermilk this morning," he said. Hattie immediately set a cup of coffee down in front of him.

It was an old joke between them, one that continued to bring smiles to their mornings. One breakfast years ago when Reed was little more than a cockerel of sixteen or seventeen and going through that time of learning to fit into the world of men, he'd suddenly raged at her. "Damnation, woman! Why are you always serving me up this buttermilk like I'm some pap-fed baby? I'm a man, and I want coffee!"

Hattie had walked over to the table, picked up his glass of buttermilk, and threw it in his face. "You want coffee, Plowboy? Then you ask for it, but don't you ever curse at me again."

Since that day, Hattie had served him coffee every morning, and Reed kept his more expressive language for the menfolk on Saturday night.

Setting their plates on the table, Hattie reminded herself that Reed Tyler was no longer the plowboy. He was a man now. A well-respected man, which was not a typical circumstance for a sharecropper. In this sparsely populated farm country, a man without his own land was often a source of ridicule. But Reed was strong, hardworking, and ambitious, and he was going to be somebody someday. Not a soul in the county doubted it for a minute.

Joining him at the table, Hattie watched with pleasure as he devoured the bacon, eggs, grits, and biscuits she'd made for him. "So, what you planning today?" she asked.

Reed took care to swallow before answering. "I'm going to walk the west field by the spring. I suspect that's where I'll be plowing first. I'm going to put the corn and wheat over there this year. Heard they've had a real mild winter down south. Their cotton won't make much. That's good news for us."

Hattie nodded in agreement, then said, "I'm going to spread some manure on my garden today. We got any fresh, or should I get some from the heap?"

"There's plenty of fresh," he said, then added with a look of good-natured censure, "But I'll be doing the spreading, Miss Hattie. There's no call for ladies to be out spreading manure."

"Ladies, Plowboy, can do anything that is necessary," she said emphatically.

Reed couldn't help but grin. He loved it when Hattie got up on her high horse. "I agree completely," he said. "But in this case it's just not necessary. I'll spread the manure before I head out to the fields."

She thanked him and got up to the take their plates. As she poured him another cup of coffee, she urged him to sit and drink it while she did the dishes.

Reed took a sip of his coffee, then leaned back in his chair and watched Hattie work. Her movements were smooth and efficient. Remembering Bessie Jane's piece of gossip, he began studying Hattie in a way he never had before. Facing toward the sink, she offered a view that might be considered her best. Her hair was parted in the middle and carefully wound into a neat little bun at the nape of her neck. Although not petite and curvaceous like Bessie Jane, Hattie was definitely built like a woman. She was tall, maybe standing as high as his chin, and her shoulders were broad for a woman. But her waist was nicely differentiated, and he suspected it was no larger than Bessie Jane's. Allowing his gaze to drift downward, he didn't fail to appreciate her behind. It wasn't lush and tempting like Bessie Jane's, but even decently covered by her shapeless calico dress, he could tell it was high and well rounded. Had Ancil Drayton noticed that too?· he wondered.

The idea didn't sit well with Reed. Shaking the thought away and transferring his gaze to the fields outside the window, he reminded himself that Miss Hattie would have nothing to ·do with old Drayton, and it was none of Reed's business anyway.

"Suspect I'd better get out there, Miss Hattie," he said. "Those fields aren't going to plow themselves."

Hattie heard the scrape of his chair and turned to him as he rose. With his arms high over his head, he stretched languidly, a yawn escaping his lips. Her gaze was drawn irresistibly to his broad, hard chest.

He smiled at her as he reached for his hat. "I'm going to spread that manure for you first thing," he said. "Don't you be forgetting that you have a man around this place."

Preacher Able arrived very near to dinnertime with the official word that Ancil Drayton wanted to court her.

He was mounted on the Tennessee walking horse that was his pride and joy. If the preacher had one weak point where temptation was apt to get him, it was his love of good horseflesh. Although spiritual guidance was something Hattie reserved for Sunday reflection, she had a goodly respect for Preacher Able. Her trust of the tall, lanky man, though, was based more on his fine care of his livestock than his hellfire-and-damnation preaching.

"I was just sitting down to dinner, Preacher Able," she said, smiling. "But I suspect you know that, having timed your visit so well."

The preacher couldn't help but laugh at being caught red-handed finagling himself an invitation to dinner.

"I can't lie, Miss Hattie," he said as he dismounted. "I always say that you set one of the finest tables in the county, and truly I don't get asked to it near often enough to suit me."

Hattie laughed, then apologized for her tardy invitation. "I never have a soul over to break bread with me, excepting Reed of course, and I truly never think of it. You're going to have to get Millie to remind me that having the preacher to dinner once a month is part of my Christian duty, as well as my pleasure."

The goat trotted up and butted the preacher lightly on the side.

"Myrene!" Hattie scolded, grasping the nanny around the neck and pulling her away. "This goat just doesn't have any manners, Preacher. She's thinking you've got sugar or something sweet in your coat, like most of the peddler men that stop by this way."

The preacher reached down into the long pockets of his black coat and pulled out a sugar cube. "Indeed I do, Miss Hattie," he said, laying the sweet in his palm and offering it to the eager animal. "She must have magic eyes, this goat, to be able to see what is in a man's pocket."

As the goat thoroughly cleaned his hand, Preacher Able glanced around the Colfax homestead. As usual, it was fastidiously clean. The little four-room clapboard house was neatly painted white, and a trellis of budding vines shaded one side of the long hardwood front porch. The washporch stood on the near side of the house, and all the tubs and brushes, brooms and buckets, were neatly hung. A place for everything, and everything in its place. The T-shaped clothesline poles stood perfectly straight at either end of the backyard, and the three lines of cord were pulled taut between them and tied with precision. Up the slight slope to the south, he could see the carefully laid-out garden plot next to the whitewashed chicken coop. To the west, the barn, sheds, and pigsty were all in the kind of shape to make any farmer proud. Even Miss Hattie's privy, discreetly nestled between two lilac bushes, was freshly painted. He shook his head in admiration. Miss Hattie had a fine homeplace, and she'd done it all on her own. It was the kind of success many a farmer in the county would envy.

The conversation centered on plowing and livestock as Hattie fried up side meat and stirred it into some beans and eggs. Served with corn bread, it was a tasty dinner that stuck to a man's ribs. She entertained the preacher with stories of Myrene's exploits and her plans for breeding her Hampshires. She wanted to raise the finest hogs in the county, and Preacher Able could easily understand that ambition.

After Hattie had sat down and thanks was offered for the meal, Preacher Able came directly to the reason for his visit. "Ancil Drayton has come to see me, Miss Hattie," he began, then gave her a long, thoughtful look, as if expecting her to make some comment. She didn't, and he continued. "It seems that you have caught his eye and he wanted to get my opinion on him courting so soon after his wife's death, and to ask me to approach you with his suit."

Hattie swallowed convulsively and tried to maintain a facade of polite interest. It would be highly foolish for a woman of her age and circumstances to act as eager and giddy as she felt.

"You understand, Miss Hattie," the reverend went on as he heartily partook of Hattie's fine cooking, "under usual conditions, I wouldn't hear of a man setting out courting so soon after his wife's death.''

Hattie nodded and waited, making it a point to continue to eat, although she found herself dreadfully nervous and without appetite.

"I've known Ancil Drayton for a lot of years,'' Preacher Able said, ''probably as many as I've known you. He is a decent, God-fearing man who loved his wife and grieved when he was forced to put her to ground.''

Remembering the funeral calmed Hattie's nervousness somewhat. Ancil had truly been hurting, and the tears shed by those little children were the like to break anyone's heart.

"But with seven young ones to attend,'' the preacher continued, ''well, a man pretty much has to have a wife of some sort.''

Hattie felt a prick of annoyance at the slighting remark. Any wife, even Miss Hattie, was better than nothing.

"Now I know,'' he continued, overfilling his mouth with corn bread, ''you've been a spinster lady for a lot of years now. A woman gets set in her ways, and there just ain't no getting around that.'' He punctuated his words with stabs at his pork. "If you're thinking that you just couldn't abide all those children or being under the rule of a man, well, truly, Miss Hattie, I'm not one of those preachers that thinks all women are meant for marriage. Obviously some females, like yourself, are just natural spinsters.''

Almost stunned with disbelief, Hattie stared at her long-time friend and fought the urge to box his ears.

"I'm not sure that I think of myself as a 'natural spinster,' Preacher Able,'' she said civilly.

"Well,'' he said, swallowing as he pondered. ''I suspect it wasn't all your choice. Your daddy dying when he did, you were in mourning for a good long while, and then taking care of your mother. I guess you could say that your prime marrying years just sort of passed you by.''

Hattie felt a strange hollowness growing inside her. She knew that what the preacher said was true, but somehow she had always managed to keep the truth at bay. Her youth, her prime, her chance for love and marriage, had simply slipped away without her even noticing it.

Preacher Able believed she was over the hill, that her good years were all behind her.

He thought she was past wanting and needing a man. But did a woman ever really get past that? Hattie wasn't entirely sure. Maybe some women did, but she never had. Her childish fantasy of love and romance had faded through the years, but she had never in her heart of hearts given up the dream.

Trying to give the reverend the benefit of the doubt, she admitted to herself that she had never, by word or deed, acted as if she were interested in having a man. Her disinterest was a deliberate defense. She would not be one of those pitiful females who spent her life pining after some prince who never came. No one would ever feel sorry for her.

She was surprised to find she had played her part so well. Could the whole community not see that underneath all her contentment and satisfaction with her life she wanted the love, companionship, and yes, even the romance, that she believed other women enjoyed?

"Now, don't you give a thought about hurting Ancil's feelings," Preacher Able droned on. "I told him I didn't believe for a minute that you'd be interested, so he is pretty much primed for a letdown."

Hattie opened her mouth to protest, but the man continued on his painful, thoughtless course without hesitation. "I told him he ought to be heading over to Carson's Flat. The widow Blackburn has four little ones still to raise, and I'm sure she would be grateful to team up with a good steady man like Ancil."

Preacher Able washed down a bite with a good gulp of coffee, then added, "She's already been married and knows what to expect. I'm thinking that you're probably not going to be interested in learning how to raise up another woman's children, not having any of your own, nor even little brothers or sisters to have concerned yourself with."

Hattie felt near to panic. After twenty-nine years, a man had finally shown a bit of interest in her, and Preacher Able already had practically sent him to some other woman's front door. This might very well be her last chance. And it surely would be if she refused to see Drayton. The whole town would believe she was exactly what the preacher thought she was, a natural spinster with no interest in men or married life. No lonely bachelor or hardworking widower would ever give her a thought because it would be the official word in the county that Hattie Colfax wasn't interested.

Gathering together all the courage that had helped her face

so. many long years alone, Hattie risked the humiliation of having her secret heart exposed to all. "Please tell Mr. Drayton that I would be pleased to have him and the children over for Sunday dinner," she said calmly, without a word of explanation.

Preacher Able's spoon stopped two inches from his opened mouth as he stared at her. "What was that you said?"

Hattie hid her nervous smile behind her hand. "I'll fix Sunday dinner for Mr. Drayton and his children. That will give us an opportunity to have a word or two together, and then perhaps I can make a more informed decision about whether or not I would like him to court me."

Two

REED sat on the porch swing at the Turpin place with Bessie Jane snuggled up tightly beside him. He'd offered his sweetheart not much more than a peck on the cheek so far that day, and as Bessie Jane's delicate little fingers explored his shirt-front, it was obvious she wanted more. Now that dinner with her parents was finally over, she was undoubtedly expecting a romantic walk in the woods with him. He wasn't sure that was such a good idea, so he continued to sip lemonade on the veranda.

Stretching out his long legs in front of him, he contemplated his current predicament. Porch swings had been invented, he was sure, by a careful father who wanted to ensure the chastity of his daughter. This particular porch swing sat immediately in front of the parlor window and squeaked with rhythmic regularity.

When Reed had first begun courting Bessie Jane, he had sneaked over in the middle of the night and oiled the hooks on the swing. The next time they had sat to spark, he'd been able to make progress theretofore impossible with the noisy hinges broadcasting his every move. The oil had since worn off, though, and with his arms folded across his chest, he ignored

Bessie Jane's chatter and listened instead to the creak of the chain scraping across the hanging hook.

"Reed, honey," she whispered against his neck, "what are you thinking about?

Glancing down at her, Reed was startled anew at how truly perfect she was. A man could get lost in those big blue eyes and that tiny little mouth, its full lower lip giving the impression of a permanent pout. "Just thinking about farming, sweetheart," he answered lightly.

Bessie Jane didn't seem to like his answer at all, but with good grace she tried again. "You want some more of my mama's pie? It's always sweet."

"No thanks," he answered distractedly.

"I want something sweet," she said squirming slightly. "But I wasn't thinking of pie." She leaned closer and took a tiny bite out of the exposed flesh on his neck.

"Bessie Jane!" he whispered harshly, trying without success to move farther away.

"This is plenty sweet for me," she said. "I don't think I'll ever get my fill."

Grasping her shoulders, he deliberately put her from him. "Bessie Jane, we will not start something we can't finish."

"Who says we can't finish it?" Her eyes were wide with innocence, but her voice was clear with understanding.

Reed had been completely stunned one night last fall when, after months of rather lackluster interest in him, Bessie Jane had simply failed to call a halt to his sparking. He'd had no intention of actually having her without benefit of marriage. Once he'd gone so far, though, he just hadn't been able to stop himself.

He was still confused about why she had allowed it to happen. It was obvious she hadn't enjoyed it. Although he was not totally inexperienced, he'd never been with a virgin before. He had tried to be gentle and careful, and felt sure he hadn't hurt her. He felt no tearing flesh, noticed no restricting barrier. But if tears were proof of lost virginity, it was beyond doubt that she had lost hers. He held her in his arms as she sobbed her sorrow, her delicate frame shaking with the intensity of her grief.

He'd felt closer to her in those sad aftermoments than at any time before or since. Immediately, he asked her to marry him. But even as she accepted his proposal and its accompanying declaration of love, she'd continued to cry as if her heart were breaking.

Reed didn't regret what had happened between them. Regret was a useless emotion best employed by sinners on their deathbeds. Still, he was determined that such a foolish lack of control would not happen again. For the last five months he'd kept his ardor in check, despite Bessie Jane's undisguised attempts to overcome his wiser judgment.

"Bessie Jane," he said quietly, "you need to stop that, sweetheart. Why don't we take a walk down to the pond? We could see if the water level has risen much, and we could check on the ducklings."

"There aren't any ducklings yet," she replied, deliberately ignoring his hint. "I'm just content as I can be right here."

She tried to snuggle closer again, but Reed wouldn't have it. Standing up, he offered his hand to her as he called into the parlor window, "Mr. Turpin, Bessie Jane and I are walking down to the pond."

As they strolled away from the house, her hand tucked carefully in the crook of his arm, Reed attempted to keep the conversation on safe subjects. "I've got some good news for you, Bessie Jane," he said, and he watched her face change.

"Good news for me?"

"Good news for us, I guess would be the better way to put it." He was smiling now, that smile that caused heart flutters in half the women of the county. "I think this year is going to be good for cotton. If I'm right, then even if next year is only moderate, I'll still have enough to buy out Miss Hattie."

"That's nice, Reed," she said casually.

He was surprised at her lack of excitement, then quickly decided she didn't understand the significance of the news.

"That's only a year and a half, Bessie Jane." His voice was soft, loving. "Eighteen months, and we can finally marry up proper. It's not so long to wait. It'll pass quickly, I promise."

Sighing, Bessie Jane turned to look at him. There was no pretense or coyness in her expression.

"I don't want to wait, Reed. I see no need to wait. Surely you know by now that I don't need you to own that piece of land before I marry you."

"I need to own it, Bessie Jane. I don't want you to ever think that you married down."

"I would never think that," she said with exasperation. "All Daddy talks about is how wonderful you are and what a bright future you have. He really believes in you, Reed. He'd loan you the money to buy that land in a minute if you asked him. And I know he would let us live here until we got on our feet, because he told me so himself.''

"I could never live off your father, Bessie Jane.''

She didn't answer. She walked beside him for a few moments, lost in thought, then slowly she increased the pace until they were practically running to the woods.

"What are you up to?'' Reed asked, laughing as they rushed into the shelter of the trees.

Out of sight of the house, she stopped suddenly and wrapped her arms around his neck, pressing herself against his body. He lowered his head for a kiss. His lips were warm and gentle, and Bessie Jane moaned low in her throat. She tried to deepen the kiss, but he broke away from her abruptly.

"None of that,'' he scolded. "I won't have you tempting me beyond what I can bear.''

"How much, exactly, can you bear, Mr. Tyler?'' she asked, walking away from him toward the pond with an exaggerated sway in her hips.

Reed followed her, far enough back to enjoy fully her teasing display. When she had almost reached the water's edge, she stopped at the sight of a small wildflower bursting through the soil. Bending down to pick it, she deliberately thrust her bottom in the air in a very unladylike fashion. Smiling, Reed walked up and took the offered bait, laying a large tanned hand on her slim-hipped backside.

Bessie Jane straightened immediately as a sultry exclamation of feigned surprise escaped her lips. Turning, she moved eagerly into his arms, her eyes darkening with smoky invitation. "Reed! I don't want to wait a year and a half. I don't even want to wait until dark.''

"Sweetheart! What if your daddy should see us?''

"He's back at the house.''

"I really shouldn't take such liberties with you before we're married.''

"Then let's get married. Let's get married today, Reed. I don't think I can wait any longer.''

Reed was not immune to the feel of her warm, sweet-smelling body against his. He ran his hand down her spine and splayed his fingers over her buttocks.

"Yes, Reed,'' she whispered. "You want me, you know you do.''

"I do want you, Bessie Jane," he said in a tortured voice. "But I can't have you. Not now, not before I've bought my land, before we're married. I can't risk giving you a baby."

She pulled away from him angrily. "That's exactly where I stand in your plans. First your land, then your marriage and children. Bessie Jane comes in a distant third."

"Sweetheart, that's not so. Everything I do, I do for you, for us." He reached out to touch her, but she turned from him. "I know it's hard for you. It's difficult for me too." He stood behind her, his hands gently massaging her shoulders as if to make his words easier to bear. "Believe me, Bessie Jane, I understand about *needs,* and I've told you I can help you with that. I've heard things and read things. I can give you a woman's pleasure without having to risk a baby."

"Don't talk to me about *needs,*" she snapped. "What I need is to be married!"

He set his jaw firmly. "Now you're being unreasonable."

She whirled to face him, her arms folded across her chest. "My mother told me, you let a man have his way with you, and he'll never marry you. He'll make up every excuse under the sun, but he'll never walk you down the aisle. I would never have believed it of you, Reed Tyler, but it's apparently the truth."

"It is not the truth," he snapped, annoyed with such nonsense. "I have every intention of marrying you. Everybody in the county knows my intentions. Do you think your father would let us come out here alone if he doubted my sincerity?"

"It's not my father's doubts you have to worry about—it's mine. I'm already seventeen. Most of my friends are planning weddings right now, and I, the most sought-after girl in the county, I can't even set the date!"

Shaking his head in exasperation, Reed tried to make her see reason. "It's our future I'm thinking about, not what some other girls in the county might do. I want to give you a good life, Bessie Jane. I want us to start out ahead, not trying to work ourselves out of a ditch."

"Mr. Tyler, I will not have my wedding decided by the fate of a crop! You either intend to marry me this fall or you do not."

"I have explained that to you time and time again, Bessie Jane," he said, straining for patience. "If I can't provide for you, if I don't own my own land, I will not marry you."

•   •   •

With her arm threaded through the handle of her egg basket and a pan of shelled corn in her hand, Hattie made her way to the chicken coop, scattering feed as she went. She paused outside the door of the henhouse to wave to Reed, who was sharpening the plow near the barn. Even in the coolness of the spring day, sweat plastered his shirt to his body and made his thick black hair gleam with lights. Things were going to work out for Reed, Hattie was sure of it. He was like a brother to her, she told herself, and he deserved to be happy. If she could help that along, well, there was no law against it.

Walking into the henhouse, she found two hens still sitting. " 'Morning, Hazel, Earline," she said cheerfully. "You girls got me some eggs this morning?"

Only the laying hens and her rooster, Jackanapes, had names. She wasn't about to get so personal with some broiler she'd be putting in the frying pan. As it was, when one of the old hens stopped laying, it was mighty hard to send her to the stew pot. Hattie usually resolved the quandary by finding out who was ailing and fixing them a nice chicken soup. As long as she didn't have to eat those old friends herself, it was all right.

She remembered when she was a girl—their old cow Sally had run dry, and her daddy had said he was going to send her to the slaughterhouse. Hattie had cried and pleaded with him until her mother had taken a switch to her and sent her to bed. The next morning at breakfast her father had said, "Hattie, I've been thinking all night about old Sally. This is a farm, and when an animal eats and don't produce, we just got to be rid of it. But Sally . . . Well, she birthed three good calves for me and been providing the milk on this table for nigh onto ten years. I don't expect that old cow owes me nothing."

Hattie had cried for joy, sobbing in her daddy's arms, though her mother had called it a "sentimental bit of foolishness." Old Sally was put out to pasture, and she was probably the only milk cow in the history of Arkansas to die of old age. Sally and Hattie's daddy had died the same summer, both of them going while they slept with not the slightest warning.

As Hattie carefully checked through the hay in the nesting boxes for hidden eggs, she thought about that first summer without Daddy. Her mama had never been a strong woman. She had been dependent on someone all her life, and her husband's death

had left her in a void of uncertainty. She'd been so bowed down
with grief that she spent most of those first few months in bed.
She leaned heavily on Hattie, a frightened and sorrowing teenager who day after day saw her mother weaving through anger,
bitterness, and tears. Mama could no longer carry on a conversation without crying.

Hattie had to finish the crop that year, something she had
never done. And she wouldn't have made it without Reed. He
was only fourteen at the time, wasn't even shaving, but he was
there every day for her. He pulled his weight, and more. When
they finally got that cotton in, they just looked at each other and
started laughing. Hattie couldn't remember ever feeling so tired
or having such a sense of accomplishment. She and Reed just
kept laughing, tears running down their faces, aching-in-pain
type of laughing.

The next three years she leased the land to Hiram Weger,
and he hired Reed to tend it. When Weger gave it up, Jack
Coats leased it for a year. He had his own boys to work it, so
Reed was out of a job. He'd gone down to his uncle, south of
Helena, to work in the rice. The next year he came to Hattie
and asked if he could lease it himself. The way Hattie figured
it, Reed had been working the Colfax land for fifteen of the last
sixteen years. It seemed to her that after that long a time, a man
deserved to own it.

She squinted at the sun as she let herself out of the henhouse.
In a couple of years Reed would own this land. She would miss
farming it, but a little knot of anxious enthusiasm stirred inside
her. Maybe she'd continue farming somewhere else with another
man at her side.

Reed adjusted the blade carefully back on the plow, satisfied
with the job he'd done. He pulled off his old straw hat and
wiped the sweat from his brow with his sleeve. Gazing up at
the sun to gauge the time, he flopped the hat back on his head.

A high-pitched squeal caught his attention, and he looked
across the barnyard to see Miss Hattie washing down her pigs
near the hog wallow. She set quite a store by those black-and-
white Hampshires of hers, he thought, as well she should. The
sow must weigh seven hundred pounds, and she'd had thirteen
shoats at her last farrow. Miss Hattie was some farmer. Her

pigsty was cleaner than some women's houses, and her animals were among the healthiest in the county.

"What's ailing that old sow, Miss Hattie?" he called across the yard.

She looked up from her task and smiled. From this distance, all he could see was the dipping brim of her sunbonnet and that row of gleaming white teeth. Miss Hattie did have one amazing smile.

"This old sow's just dirty and lazy these days," she called back, laughing.

He walked over to the pigsty and leaned against the fence. "You going to breed her this spring?"

Hattie nodded. "In another week or so, I suspect she'll be ready."

"You want me to ride over to Britts Hollow and see if they'll let us use that old Hampshire to stud again?"

"Nope." Hattie smiled broadly once more. "Remember that fine-looking young boar I sold to Mose Whimsley? He's going on ten months now, so I'm going to breed him back."

It was obvious to Reed that Hattie was absolutely delighted with her livestock's prospects, and he readily agreed to get the young boar for her when the time came.

Despite Reed's smile, Hattie saw something strange in his expression. "What's ailing you, Plowboy? I've been thinking all day that you might be needing a spring tonic."

His answering chuckle was genuine. "No, thank you, Miss Hattie. I just had a bit of a spat with Bessie Jane. Nothing too serious, I suspect."

"A spat?"

"Bessie Jane and I have a misunderstanding about calendars. Mine has four seasons; hers only has today, tomorrow, and next week."

Hattie's eyes lit up with humor. "They say sweethearts and squabbles are like flowers and rain. Takes both to make it springtime."

Reed shook his head as if to belittle any problems he might have. "I expect you're right, Miss Hattie. And it's surely nothing for me to be wasting my morning worrying about."

"I saw you two at church last Sunday," Hattie said, smiling like a proud parent. "Can't think of a more attractive couple that I've ever seen. You're so big and dark, and she's so tiny

and blond, you're just a sight walking across the churchyard
together."

Reed smiled at her fanciful description. "I only wish it were
that easy." He jerked off his hat and ran a hand through his
hair, as if the motion might make his thoughts clearer. "She
doesn't understand all that it takes to make a go of things. She
thinks we should just get married and everything will work itself
out."

Hattie pondered that for a moment, then nodded. "Sometimes it's that way. People do marry without having much of a
plan for things, and most times it works out just fine."

" 'Just fine' isn't enough for me, Miss Hattie. You know
about my dreams for this place, for growing rice and all. That's
just not going to happen if I take on a wife I can't afford." He
sighed disgustedly, trying to gather his words. "Bessie Jane
likes pretty things. I expect she wants a fine house and all the
best. I want her to have those things, but the farm has to come
first."

"She's young, Reed," Hattie said. "It's hard for her to see
past the wedding day. Once you're married and she takes on her
responsibilities, she'll be able to understand better."

He grinned wryly. "You're right about her not seeing past
the wedding day. That's all she thinks about, and she was hop-
ping mad when when I said we'd need to wait out two crops."

Hattie nodded, seeing the younger woman's point. "That *is*
a long time for a woman to wait."

"Not you too!" Reed cried in exasperation. "You think I
should marry her when I'm no more than a sharecropper with a
few dollars in the bank? A man's got his pride, you know. I
don't want anyone thinking she's marrying down."

Hattie knew about male pride, especially Reed Tyler's vari-
ety. His family lived just over the next ridge. They were good,
hardworking salt-of-the-earth people, but the Tyler farm was
only one rocky little hill. With nine children to feed, it was no
wonder they sent out their children to work when they were still
young enough for the schoolroom. Hattie knew that Reed wanted
better than that for his children, better than that for himself.
"Why don't I go ahead and sell you the land, Reed?" she
suggested. "You've got most of the money already saved, and
you can pay me off when you can. I trust you for it."

He sighed and shook his head. "You may trust me, Miss
Hattie, but how can I trust myself? What if I have a bad year?

Two bad years, or a whole slew of them, is not unheard of. I'll
have Bessie Jane and probably some children, and I might have
to let you down."

"I'd understand that."

"You might understand it, but understanding don't pay the
fiddler. This farm is all you've got, Miss Hattie. Your daddy
would roll over in his grave if you trusted it to anybody who
wasn't family."

"You're like family to me, Reed, you know that."

Her words were almost painful in their sincerity. Reed knew
that she had no one. "No, Miss Hattie," he said. "The answer
is no." His voice was stern, his decision final. "When I can
get the money together to pay for this land, then I'll buy it. As
long as I don't have it, it'll be your land."

Hattie knew there was no sense in arguing *that* any further.
Once Reed set his mind to something, he could be as stubborn
as a Missouri mule. She searched her brain for another way for
him to raise money. She made all the cash she needed selling
her eggs and hogs, but those were hers, and she knew Reed
wouldn't accept so much as a piglet in charity. He just had to
make more money on the farm.

As the solution came to her, her eyes brightened with excitement. "How about a second crop?" she said.

"What?"

"If you raise a second crop to sell, you'll make more money
this year. Maybe enough to pay for the farm."

"What kind of second crop are you talking about, and where
would we raise it? We're using every piece of good ground on
the farm now."

"Not *every* piece of good ground." Her voice was almost
teasing now. "A farmer, for whom I have great respect, told
me that those wasted acres out by the bluff could be planted in
rice."

Three

THE breeze that ruffled Hattie's skirts as she sat nervously in her buggy was a chilly one from the north. She gathered her shawl more closely around her shoulders and chanced a self-conscious glance at the man sitting next to her.

Ancil Drayton smiled broadly, his ruddy face beaming with obvious delight. "The weather is plumb dandy these days, eh, Miss Hattie?"

She nodded in agreement and tried with some success to gather up a bit of her misplaced gumption. At church, Ancil had suggested he drive her buggy while the children follow in his wagon. It was a perfectly reasonable idea and would give them time alone to get acquainted, but Hattie had found driving away from the church, with every eye in the place focused on her, extremely disquieting. Now, after traveling at least a mile, she had been unable to string three words together in respectable order.

"If this sunshine keeps up," Ancil continued, "I may be able to start plowing next week sometime."

"Reed's already started," she managed to say. At least if

she could keep him talking about farming, she thought, she'd be able to offer something to the conversation. She had no idea what courting couples talked about, but she suspected that farming was not a choice subject. It was, however, the only subject, other than the Bible, that she felt she could discuss with any semblance of knowledge.

"That Reed Tyler is a good boy," Ancil said. "You've been real lucky having him work your place. He's going to make a good farmer one of these days."

Hattie smiled proudly. "Reed is already a good farmer. And you know, he doesn't work for me anymore. He's leasing that land on a sharecrop."

Ancil nodded. "It's a shame old Clive Tyler didn't make much of his place. All them kids going to have to make their own way, get their own land. I'll be wanting to give my own boys a start when it comes time for them to be out on their own."

"I suspect that's what all parents want," Hattie said. "To give their children a better chance than they had."

Taking a deep breath for bravery, she worked up the courage to look Ancil full in the face. He was smiling and unthreatening. He was tall, maybe too tall, and that gave him a lean and gaunt look. His thinning reddish-brown hair began far back on his forehead, and he'd parted it low on the right side and combed it up and over. Hattie suspected that the fringe of well-oiled hair used to cover his shining head had to be a foot long. His red mustache was neatly waxed and curled only slightly on the ends. His big brown eyes, twinkling with just a hint of the devil, were his most attractive feature, shaded by eyelashes that were long and thick and amazingly red. His pleasant and friendly smile, the slight gap between his two front teeth, appealed in a boyish way. He was clean and neat in his Sunday suit, and Hattie had to admit she was favorably impressed.

Dressed in her own best ivory lawn shirtwaist with a green gabardine skirt, she hoped his opinion was similarly positive. She knew her shoulders were a little broad, but that gave the impression that her waist was smaller than it actually was. Bonnets were her preferred headdress, but that morning she wore a little round straw hat with an excessively wide brim, to which she had pinned a large bow of Irish lace.

"Hope cotton will make something this year," Ancil was

saying. "You know, Miss Hattie, it's not just whether you can
get a good crop but how much they're paying for cotton that
makes a good year."

She resisted the temptation to tell him that she knew as much
about farming as he did. She should show him how capable she
was, she reasoned, not take to bragging on herself. "They've
had a real mild winter down in the Deep South," she said.
"That won't be good for their cotton, so perhaps prices will he
higher this year."

Ancil's eyes widened with surprise and a hint of appreciation.
"Is that so? Well, that is good news for sure, Miss Hattie."

Arriving at the Colfax farm, Ancil drove the buggy right up
to the front door. After securing the handbrake, he hurried
around to help Hattie down. Unused to such gallantries, she was
almost down by herself before he could reach her. He offered
his hand, and she placed her own in his. A little thrill coursed
through her at the sight of her hand looking so small and feminine within his.

"The boys and I will take care of the horses," he offered
politely as he escorted her to the front porch. "Mary Nell and
the girls can help you get the dinner on the table."

"That will be nice," she said, hoping it was true. She called
his three daughters to join her in the house as she watched Ancil
tell his sons to lead the horses to the barn. Ancil's daughters
were attractive girls, although a bit pale and quiet. Mary Nell,
the oldest child, was thirteen, and Hattie already knew that the
majority of the housework and the raising of the children had
fallen to her. She assumed she and the girl would have a good
deal in common, both having taken on adult responsibilities at
an early age.

She smiled a welcome at the girl, but it was returned by a
look of sullen dislike that surprised Hattie in its intensity. She
quickly opened the stove and stoked the fire, making mental
excuses for Mary Nell's behavior. "What would you like to do
to help, Mary Nell?" she asked, determined to ignore the young
lady's bad manners.

"I wouldn't like to do nothing," Mary Nell replied. "I been
cooking all week for this bunch, and I thought I'd be getting
the day off coming here." She glanced at the stove where most
of the cooked meal sat waiting to be reheated. "It don't look
like you need my help much anyway. I'm going out to sit on

the porch." Turning her back on Hattie, she flounced out to do exactly that.

"Oh, don't mind her, Miss Hattie," the second of Ancil's daughters said. "Mary Nell's just an old sour persimmon. We don't pay her no mind nohow."

Hattie smiled with relief at this girl. "Would you like to help me? You are Cylvia?"

The girl offered Hattie a hand to shake, smiling a gap-toothed smile like her father's. "Just call me Cyl, like everybody else. This here is Ada," she said, indicating the pretty little cotton-haired child at her side. "Ada's four her next birthday, and I'm nine, so I sorta take care of her."

Shaking Ada's hand also, Hattie greeted them both with a polite howdy-do. "Would you two like to roll out the biscuits for me?" she asked, picking a task that had been her favorite when she was young.

"I sure would!" Cyl answered. "I ain't never done it before. Mary Nell did it for Mama afore she died, but since then, Mary Nell says corn pone is easier, so we never have no biscuits."

"It's really easy," Hattie said. "I'm sure both of you will be able to do it. Why don't you just wash your hands at the sink?"

Cyl turned hers over and looked at them critically. "Mine ain't hardly dirty, ma'am. Papa made us all take a bath last night. Mary Nell like to had a fit about it, saying it weren't necessary."

Hattie was horrified, but she reminded herself that these poor motherless children probably had little direction at all. "I always wash my hands before I touch the food," she said quietly. "If you're clean, then the food you cook is also clean, and cleaner is healthier on a farm."

Cyl shrugged in genial acceptance, and with Hattie's help both girls had soon washed their hands at the kitchen pump.

As Hattie directed them in the rolling and cutting of the biscuits, she hacked the chickens apart and put them to frying in the big iron skillet. With pleasure she listened as Cyl talked a blue streak. The youngster seemed to have something to say about pretty near everything, and Hattie found her delightful and entertaining.

Little Ada was allowed to have the last bit of biscuit dough to play with, and the child was positively gleeful.

"She don't talk much," Cyl explained. "But she's real pleased with that dough. She don't got much toys, only her paper dolls."

"Do you collect paper dolls, Ada?" Hattie asked, hoping to draw the pretty child out. Ada only smiled and nodded.

"I cuts them myself, from the Sears and Roebuck for her," Cyl said. "She must have near a hundred that she keeps in an old cigar box under the bed."

"How nice for you," Hattie said to Ada. "I would love to see your collection sometime. Would you show me?"

The little girl's eyes gleamed with pleasure as she nodded vigorously, her white-blond curls bouncing.

The biscuits were a perfect golden brown when the Drayton family found their places around Hattie's dinner table. Cyl bragged about how she and Ada had made the biscuits, and Mary Nell kept her nose in the air, not about to speak to anyone.

Ancil's boys had to be prompted to wash their hands, and Ancil followed them with an apologetic smile for Hattie. She smiled back, hoping to convey that she understood how difficult it was for him raising seven children on his own.

Mary Nell obstinately ignored the direction to wash, and Hattie just let it go. If the girl was willing to eat with dirty hands in the hopes of causing trouble, Hattie thought, she was just going to have to be disappointed.

The four boys had the look of hardworked farm children. Ancil, Jr., "A.J.," was the oldest, only ten months younger than Mary Nell. Luke was ten but was already taller than his older brother and had the look of Ancil more than any of the other children. Fred was seven. Most of his front teeth were missing, and that brought him a good deal of teasing all around. Buddy was barely two. His little blond curls and bright brown eyes captivated Hattie. This child would never remember his natural mother, she mused. More than any of the others, she could become the little boy's mother.

Quickly putting a stop to such errant thoughts, she glanced up at Ancil, grateful that he couldn't read her mind.

"Fried chicken is my absolute favorite," he said, surveying the spread. Along with chicken, there were mountains of mashed potatoes, candied carrots, field peas, turnip greens, and a big bowl of pickled beets.

"In another month I should have something fresh from the

garden," Hattie said, a note of apology in her voice. "This late in the year, we just have to take pretty much what's left."

"That's what Mary Nell tells us," Cyl said. "We've been eating nothing but corn bread and black-eyed peas for nigh onto a month."

Ancil laughed as if Cyl were exaggerating, but Hattie could tell by his flushed face that there was a good deal of truth to the story.

"Well, I certainly have more than my share," she said casually. "I always put up more canning than I can eat. Before you leave, Cyl, I'll take you down to the cellar, and you can pick out whatever you want."

"Me too?" young Ada piped up.

It was the first words Hattie had heard the little girl speak, and she was delighted. "I'm thinking, Ada, that I still have a couple of pints of plum butter down there. Would you be interested in taking home some plum butter?"

All around the table faces lit up in anticipation, and Hattie knew she'd said the right thing. Even Mary Nell seemed to perk up.

Ancil said grace, and at his "amen," it was as if a gun had been shot off for a race. Every child instantly reached across the table for something.

Attempting to maintain a semblance of order, Hattie picked up the platter of chicken and handed it to Ancil, on her left. He easily mimicked the method, and with a little coaching for the boys, the dishes were soon passing clockwise around the table in a civilized fashion.

"This is fine cooking, Miss Hattie," Ancil said, pointing to his plate with his chicken leg. "Preacher Able told me that you set quite a table, but I never imagined anything so downright tasty."

Hattie demurred with an embarrassed thank-you and tried to control the stain of flushed pleasure in her cheeks.

"Is this goat's milk?" Fred asked.

She nodded, and the boy made a face. "I hate goat's milk!"

Hattie struggled to think up an appropriate response, but Cyl took care of it for her. "Taste it, Freddy. It ain't nothing like the milk we get at home. This is plumb good."

The boy picked up the glass, still unsure, and took a tiny sip of the despised liquid. His eyes widening in pleasant surprise, he gulped down half a glass. "This is good!" he exclaimed. "You sure this is goat's milk?"

Smiling, Hattie assured him. "I milked her myself."

"It sure don't taste like the milk we get," Luke said.

"Yeah," Fred said. "The milk we get tastes like snot!"

Hattie nearly choked on her biscuit.

"Fred!" Ancil's stern admonition wiped the smile off the boy's face.

Covering her shock with a slight cough, Hattie tried to diffuse the embarrassment at the table. "Is your goat's milk getting ropey, Mr. Drayton?" she asked, hoping to bring the conversation back to practical farming concerns.

"I don't really know, Miss Hattie," he admitted. "I guess it is. I don't drink the stuff myself, and Mary Nell takes care of the milking, of course."

Turning to the older girl, Hattie was careful to keep a friendly smile on her face. "Are you having trouble with your milk, Mary Nell? Is it coming out stringy?"

"It ain't made nobody sick," the girl said defensively.

"Oh, no," Hattie said. "Ropey milk won't hurt you, but it doesn't taste all that good. It happens when the place where you're keeping the goat has gotten dirty. Goats are naturally clean animals and won't eat from a dirty trough or a fouled floor if they have any choice at all. Once you get the goat cleaned up and her quarters whitewashed, that stringiness will go away in a week's time."

Mary Nell raised her chin in defiance. She was definitely not taking any advice or instruction from Miss Hattie. "I got six children to clean after, and I sure to the Lord don't have time to be cleaning after some goat."

"Mary Nell!" Ancil raised his voice for the second time during the meal and gave Hattie a look of genuine discomfort at the poor behavior of his offspring.

Hattie smiled reassuringly at him, while thinking that this courting business was a bit trickier than she had expected.

"When Ancil Drayton helped Miss Hattie into that buggy, I swear Reed's jaw dropped nearly down to his belt buckle." Cal Tyler's description of his brother brought a round of laughter to the dinner table.

Andy, the Tylers' youngest at fifteen, had his own comment. "Reed just wanted Bessie Jane to see for sure that he still had all his own teeth!"

Even Bessie Jane, sitting a little self-consciously amid the boisterous Tyler clan, giggled at that.

"Watch it, squirt!" Reed said, giving his youngest brother a look of unspoken menace.

"I told Reed that Miss Hattie would jump at the chance to have a man court her," Bessie Jane said, "but he was sure she wouldn't look twice at Ancil Drayton."

Reed turned to his father. "Have you seen the silt that comes off his stretch of the creek?"

The elder Tyler nodded gravely. "Muddy runoff is a sure sign of poor planting and sick soil."

"You're not telling me nothing," said George, the brother just older than Reed. "I have to live downstream from that cracker. His best topsoil floats into my drinking water. And the fishing from that creek gets worse every year he lives there."

"Be careful who you're calling a cracker, young man," Mary Tyler admonished. "There are those who say the same thing about us."

"Yeah, Mama," Cal said. "But the boys and I make sure they only say it once."

Everyone laughed again. Laughter was not an unusual occurrence at the farmhouse Clive and Mary Tyler had built on the small rocky rise on their forty-acre cotton farm. Six of their nine children were there that day for Sunday dinner. The long pine table was crowded with the grown Tyler children and their wives and husbands. Outside, the grandchildren, who'd been fed first, were running and screaming in a game of tag.

The three absent Tylers were Clifford, who had headed off to Texas five years earlier; Betty, the oldest girl, who was married to a druggist in Cape Girardeau; and young Harry, who'd died of diphtheria when he was eleven. Only Reed, Andy, and Marybeth still lived at home. Andy was too young to be on his own, and Marybeth was simple in her mind. She would probably never leave Mama and Pa. Cal, who ran the Tyler farm these days, had built his wife a little house of their own at the foot of the hill. George and his wife, Clara, had a place near Clara's folks. Emma's husband, Sidney, owned one of the biggest farms in the area and had a part interest in the local cotton gin.

Reed would be leaving home soon. That was why he'd brought Bessie Jane to dinner with him that day. But he was still so surprised about Miss Hattie, he could hardly speak of anything else. "She's twice the farmer he is," he said. "It's just impossible for me to understand what she could see in a man like Drayton.''

Emma laughed at her brother's dismay. ''I agree with Bessie Jane. What she sees is a chance to have a husband and children.''

''That's what all women want,'' Bessie Jane said firmly.

Reed shook his head, clearly convinced Bessie Jane had it all wrong. ''Miss Hattie would never be interested in a man like Ancil Drayton,'' he said with absolute certainty. ''Miss Hattie would never really be interested in any man. She's not like you or your friends, Bessie Jane, and she never was. She's always been self-sufficient and independent.''

''You men are so silly,'' his fiancée said. ''Of course she wants Ancil Drayton. She wants any man she can get!'' Bessie Jane shook her head in dismay at the thickheadedness of men ''She *is* different from me and my friends. She's ugly. She's so ugly, no man would ever give her a second look. Now finally, old snuff-smelling Drayton with his seven brats has taken an interest in her, and she'll jump at the chance to marry him if he offers.''

''You don't know Miss Hattie.''

''I know Miss Hattie a good deal better than you do, apparently. Why, that old maid would stand on her head on Main Street if she thought it would get her a man!''

''Bessie Jane!'' Reed's voice rose in anger.

''I think we've had enough of this,'' Mary Tyler said. ''Miss Hattie's business is certainly none of ours.''

''What puzzles me,'' Clive said, looking curiously at his son, ''is why you find it so difficult to believe she would take up with Drayton. Your own sisters used to bring around every worthless, no-account dandy in the county, and it didn't surprise you a bit.''

Reed stared thoughtfully at his father for a moment but was saved from having to answer when Cal piped up, ''Thank God only Emma married one!''

The dinner progressed cheerfully, each brother and sister eager to tell the latest news and hear what was happening with the others. Dessert was being passed around when the conversation drifted back to Reed.

''Well, I've got a new project going this year,'' he told the group. ''You'd better listen up, Sid.'' He nodded to Emma's husband. ''Miss Hattie and I are putting in rice down near Colfax Bluff.''

''Rice?'' Cal repeated. ''Reed, what are you talking about?''

"You know that rice field I've been thinking about since I got back from that year with Uncle Ed? Well, we're going to give it a try."

Clive smiled broadly. "Why, son, that's the best news we've had all day! You get a good crop of rice this year, as well as the cotton, and you'll be able to buy that place, won't you?"

"Yes, sir," Reed answered. "That's what I'm hoping."

Sid raised a hand to disagree. "I admit to knowing absolutely nothing about rice," he said. "But it's sure not like corn, where you just throw a couple of seeds in the ground and get out of the way while it grows. It takes a lot of trouble to grow rice."

"True," Reed said. "That field by the river is a natural, but growing rice means controlling the water. We'll have to drain it before we sow it, then flood it until the grain's near big enough to cut, then drain it off again."

"That's going to mean a lot of fancy equipment," Cal said.

"We'll need a pump and at least two floodgates. I'd want it to be divided into at least four cuts. That means levees and locks."

"Can't those things be built?" Clive asked, though he knew the answer.

"Not without money," Sid interjected, then added pompously, "And I hope you're not thinking to use any of mine, 'cause I'm not interested in any crazy farming schemes."

"Sidney Tucker, don't you speak to my brother in that manner," Emma fussed at him.

"It's okay, Emma," Reed said. "I won't need any of your money, Sid. Remember, I'm the sharecropper. It's not my farm. Miss Hattie's got her own money."

"It's your idea, Reed," his father said. "It always has been. Are you telling me that Miss Hattie's going to pay for all of it?"

Reed fidgeted in slight embarrassment. "It wasn't my idea to do it this year. Miss Hattie says she wants to do some more farming before I buy her out. She says she's going to miss it and wants a real challenge before she gives it up completely."

"Do you believe that?" Clive asked.

Reed shook his head. "Truthfully, I think she's doing it as kind of a wedding present for me and Bessie Jane."

"I'd rather have a quilt," Bessie Jane said.

"Seems like a pretty expensive present to me," Sid commented.

"I told her I couldn't let her do that," Reed said as a smile stole across his face. "She told me that I can't *let* her do anything, and that I would do well to remember that it's her land and her money."

Mary nodded. "Hattie's independence has always been something she valued."

"You could have just refused to do it," Cal said.

Reed laughed at that suggestion. He remembered their argument distinctly.

"Listen, Plowboy," Hattie had said to him, "I want a rice field. I've been hearing you talk for years about a rice field, and I've decided that I want one." She folded her arms across her chest, her stance and expression saying that she could be just as stubborn as he was. "You're not the only farmer in this county who believes that cotton is not the most dependable crop to market. If we can grow rice on this ground, I'm for growing it."

Reed tried to interrupt her, but she held up her hand, determined to speak her piece.

"You're planning to buy me out in a crop or two. I won't be getting any chance to farm after that. I'll be spending my time tending livestock. I think before I give it up completely, I'd like to know what it feels like to have my own rice field."

"I don't believe you, Miss Hattie," he said, the sincerity in his tone underlined with disapproval. "You would have sold this land years ago if you hadn't known that I wanted to buy it. You've been more a friend to me than a business partner, and I know you could have leased this land to a half-dozen other men for cash money, not a share of the crop. You've done a lot for me, Miss Hattie—really too much."

"I haven't done anything that I didn't want to do," she insisted. "Now what I want to do is grow me a rice field. And for the life of me I can't understand why you're against it, since it's you that put the idea in my head in the first place."

"You're just doing this for me and Bessie Jane."

"I *was* doing it for you and Bessie Jane, but I'm so blasted mad about it now, Plowboy, that if you don't build me a rice field, I'll find somebody else who will!"

Smiling at his family, Reed said, "Miss Hattie has her way of getting what she wants. It's not a sweet and winsome way, like a lot of ladies, but it seems to work just as well."

Four

THE south field of the Colfax farm overlooked the homestead, and as Reed walked the ground he intended to plow, he couldn't seem to stop his gaze from returning to Miss Hattie's house. She was hanging clothes on the back line. Although at this distance he couldn't see anger in her movements, he feared it was there.

Catching his shoe on a sharp edge, he knelt beside the piece of limestone that had worked its way to the surface. As he began to pull the craggy intruder out of the topsoil, he remembered asking Hattie's father, "If we plow this ground every year, how do these stones get in here?"

The older man's eyes had lit up like sparklers, and he'd smiled his big, toothy smile, just like Hattie's. "Why, they grow here!" he'd answered. "Bad boys come by here in the fall and sow these fields with gravel. By spring, we've got full-grown rocks!"

It was the thing that Reed had most appreciated about Old Man Colfax—his sense of humor. He remembered that long-ago day when he was just eight years old and Henry Colfax had come to the Tyler farm. He'd eaten dinner with them and told so many funny stories, the family could hardly eat for laughing.

When he got around to business, the talk had been a bit more serious. "My little gal, Hattie, now she's a fine worker," he said with obvious pride. "But she's thirteen now, and I'm thinking that it's time she stayed about the house and took to perfecting her woman's work. When a man comes looking for a wife, he don't usually ask how well she can plow."

Everyone laughed at that, and Reed's father easily picked up on the direction of the conversation. "What you're needing is a plowboy," he said as he glanced around the table at his sons. "A youngster that's willing to work for meals and a bit of pocket money could learn a lot about farming, I suspect."

"I'm talking more than pocket money," Colfax corrected him. "For a steady, hard worker I'm thinking fifteen cents a day. Not a man's wages, but enough for a boy to lay aside something to buy his own piece of ground sometime."

To Reed it sounded like a fortune. He looked around the table and watched as his older brothers considered the idea. He saw no need to hesitate. "I'll do it, Mr. Colfax," he said, causing everyone to look at him in surprise. As the next to youngest of the Tyler boys, Reed was not exactly what Colfax had in mind.

Before anyone could say so, he quickly continued. "I know I still don't have my growth," he said evenly, "but I'm strong for my size and a hard worker. I'll be there every morning at sunup without fail, and Mama can tell you I ain't never sick."

Mr. Colfax studied him for a moment as if trying to size him up. Reed felt a nervous sweat bead on his upper lip. He was not as big or as experienced as his brothers, but he managed to be accepted as an equal by using his brain. He searched it now for assistance and found a way to prove himself. "I'll tell you what, sir," he said. "You let me work for you for a month for no wage at all. If you think I ain't strong enough or I don't suit, you just say the word, and I'll be up and gone, no hard words or bad feelings. You won't lose nothing, and I'll get the chance to show you I can be a good hand."

The silence at the table seemed to extend forever, and Reed surreptitiously wiped his palms on the thighs of his denim overalls.

His father finally smiled and nodded. "My boy Reed is smart as a whip," he told Colfax. "He's not too big yet, but he's growing, and he's a quick study. I suspect he'd make you a good worker.''

Colfax considered it for a minute longer, then offered his hand across the table to Reed. "You come on over in the morning," he said. "None of this working for free, though. I'll pay you your wage and try you for a couple of weeks. If you can't do the work, then I'll be looking elsewhere, and you can come ask me again next year when you've got a bit more meat on you."

"Thank you, sir," Reed said, shaking his hand in what he hoped was a manly and businesslike manner. "I don't think you will ever be sorry."

Reed smiled as he laid the piece of limestone at the edge of field with the rest of the rocks he'd found. He was sure Old Man Colfax hadn't been sorry. No boy had ever worked as hard as Reed that summer, or tried so hard to remember everything he was told. He always recalled that blissful summer without the strain and sweat, but with that surge of self-satisfaction that comes with accomplishment.

From the first day, Mr. Colfax and young Miss Hattie had treated him like family, praising him when he did well and straightening him out when he needed a setdown.

As he finished his survey of the ground, his gaze strayed again to the house. It was still hard for him to believe Hattie was actually interested in Drayton. He was not exactly a ne'er-do-well, but Reed thought him a poor farmer. He had a good piece of land, but he worked it to death—taking, taking, taking from the soil and never giving a thing back. He'd heard that cotton yields were down on Drayton's place, and he wasn't a bit surprised. He had warned Drayton that if he didn't start rotating his crops, he was going to wear out the soil. Drayton had dismissed scientific fact as "newfangled ideas."

Hattie could never put up with a backward ignoramus like that, Reed was sure. Thinking that, it was understandable that he had taken the first opportunity that morning to tease her about her bald, dimwitted, snuff-dipping beau. He cringed at the memory of his callousness.

"Mr. Drayton is a fine Christian man," Hattie had said, her cheeks blazing with fury. "I should think you would have better things to do with your time than investigate my personal friendships."

Reed had taken the setdown with good grace. Of course, he

had no cause to intrude in Hattie's personal life, but Ancil Drayton? He just couldn't see it.

Spring was definitely upon them. The trees were heavy with new buds, and little patches of green were determined to take over the tired straw-colored landscape. Birds were chirping, frantically trying to organize their building projects so that their eggs would have a place to rest. Bees droned softly in the noonday sunshine, looking for the first blossoms of the wildflowers.

Walking up the path to where Reed was plowing, Hattie studied the man as she drew nearer. His loose brown trousers couldn't disguise his long, thickly muscled thighs that made his walk a study in controlled power. His faded calico shirt was tucked loosely into the narrow waistband of his trousers, and the suspenders that crossed his back and lined his chest emphasized the breadth of his shoulders. A well-worn, wide-brimmed straw hat shaded his flashing eyes and welcoming smile.

He stopped plowing and came to meet her, quickly relieving her of her bucket and offering his arm as she picked her way through the coarse furrows at the rim of the field.

"You being so close to the house today," she said in explanation, "I brought you a bit of hot food."

He nodded his thanks. "Why don't we see what my mama packed in this dinner pail?" he said, grabbing his lunch from the side of the plow seat where he'd secured it. "Between the two of these, there ought to be enough for you to join me."

Hattie recognized an olive branch when she saw one, and with a nod of acceptance took him up on his invitation to lunch.

There was no picnic tablecloth or romantic view. Reed led Hattie to the shade of a small blackjack tree that had managed to flourish at the edge of the field. Seating themselves, Hattie opened his lunch while he opened hers. With exclamations of appreciation and expectation, they shared Hattie's warm pork chops and gravy and his mama's cold fatback and greens. Both women had packed pickled okra, and Reed declared it an abundance of riches.

"I was out of line this morning, Miss Hattie," he said as they settled down to eat.

She waved his apology away. "Don't go trying to make up to me like I'm some fragile flower," she said. "I jumped off the handle this morning for no good reason. Truth to tell, I suspect it is a mite funny about Mr. Drayton coming round to court me. I'm not exactly a winsome girl these days."

Her smile was bright, but Reed knew she wasn't feeling as charitable as she made out. "I think I didn't express myself too clear, Miss Hattie," he said seriously. "It's not that I think it funny that a man would want to court you. I was just surprised that you'd be interested in a man like Drayton. I wouldn't think you two would have a thing in common. He's not the kind of farmer your daddy was, and he has all those children."

"I like children."

"Of course you do. I just didn't imagine you'd want to take on seven of somebody else's."

Looking into his eyes, Hattie could see only sincerity and concern. There was no teasing now. He was giving her his honest opinion, and she felt obliged to respond with equal truthfulness. "I don't know if we have anything in common or not," she admitted. "I thought that was the purpose of courting, for a couple to get to know each other."

Reed nodded, although he wasn't sure he or most men would concur with that assessment.

"The children," she went on, "well, I don't really know. Like most other women, I always imagined myself with a family. Somehow it never worked out that way."

Picking a piece of nonexistent lint from her skirt and straightening her already perfectly straight collar, Hattie gathered her thoughts. "I realize there may be a bit of good humor and gossip about my interest in Mr. Drayton. However, I feel that I owe it to myself and to him to find out if we would be compatible."

Reed leaned back against the tree and studied her. She was obviously shy about discussing her tender feelings, and he wished he could say something to put her at ease. The sunshine filtering through the tree dappled her complexion but didn't disguise the embarrassed flush on her cheeks.

She was not so much older than himself, he realized. Five years was a lot at ten or fifteen, but once people reached their twenties, the differences in age seemed to shrink. It was not really so strange that the things he wanted—a home, a wife, children—would be the same things she wanted.

In her faded calico workdress she was neat and clean, and not totally unattractive, he thought. Shifting his gaze to take in the specifics of her anatomy, he noted that her bosom was full enough that a man would have no trouble finding it in the dark.

Her waist was decently narrow and curved nicely into hips that hinted at womanly excess. Her muscled arms and tanned skin were definitely not in fashion, but few men would find fault with her warm curves if they were offered.

As if sensing his scrutiny, she turned to look at him, smiling her usual open, friendly smile. He smiled back and decided that if it wasn't pretty, her wide smile was definitely appealing. A man might have his preferences, Reed thought, but Hattie should not have languished for lack of beaux. If she wanted a man, she ought to have one.

"What are you thinking with that strange look on your face?" she asked.

Hesitating a minute to try to gather all his thoughts into a coherent statement, Reed shook his head. "I'm thinking," he said finally, "that Ancil Drayton is a lucky man to have caught your eye, Miss Hattie."

Her jaw dropped open as she stared at him, then the noonday quiet was broken by her deep, rich laughter. "You'd best be practicing that smooth talking with Bessie Jane," she said, her eyes sparkling with amusement. "This courting business is new to me, and I'm liable to get my head puffed up like a cottonmouth!"

The uneasiness between them vanished as he joined in her laughter, and in a few moments the guilt in Reed's heart and the hurt in Hattie's vanished like salt in a stewpot.

"When are you going to have all this planted?" she asked him, correctly assuming that the south field was the last to be plowed.

"If the weather holds out, I hope to have most of the seed in the ground by next week sometime," he said.

"Then it's about time we start talking more seriously about the rice."

He nodded, grinning with eagerness. "I've been thinking about it and making some lists of the things we're going to need."

"Are we going to have to send off for equipment?" Hattie asked, knowing that even the fastest shipments could delay them past time to plant.

Reed shook his head. "I'm going to try to get away for a few days and go down to visit Uncle Ed. I'll let him have a look at my plans and see if he thinks there's something else we're going to need. I think I can get ahold of a pump around here somewhere. That's the most crucial piece of equipment. The rest I can probably piece together with scrap.''

"Good," she said, her face serious with concentration. "Do you know how much money you're going to need? We can go to town when you're ready and draw out whatever cash you think it's going to take for lumber and seed.''

He twisted slightly, rising to his knees as he drew a piece of paper from the back pocket of his trousers. "I've worked up a kind of estimate of what I think we'll need and what it's likely to cost," he said, placing the worn paper in her hand. "I think you should look it over and think about it, to make sure you really want to spend this kind of money on something that's pretty much a gamble.''

Hattie unfolded the paper and read the carefully penciled list of what they'd need, the amounts added together on the side. After only a couple of moments, she handed it back to Reed. "I have thought about this rice field," she said, "and I know it's a gamble. It's the same kind of gamble I took when I decided to raise those purebred Hampshires. People round here said a pig is a pig, but I knew better, and I was willing to take a chance that I might be wrong. If we lose this money, neither of us will starve. If we don't lose it, well, we will really have proved something.''

A smile of genuine approval and appreciation spread across Reed's face.

Hattie beamed at his obvious pride in her, and she felt a bit of pride herself. She had earned this money on her own. Now she was investing it in a new venture that could make the Colfax farm one of the most profitable in the county. A woman had a right to feel a bit of a high step about that.

Five

ON Saturday, Hattie was surprised to see that Reed had loaded up the wagon instead of the buggy for the ride to the bank in town. Dressed for company, he obviously planned to go with her.

"This may be your rice field, Miss Hattie," he said as he seated himself beside her and took up the reins. "But I don't intend to allow any other plowboy to talk you into letting him build it."

Hattie widened her eyes in feigned astonishment. "Do you think any other plowboy would be fool enough to do it?"

"Not likely," Reed said with a laugh as he gave the horse a click of the lines. "I'm going to talk with Harmon Leege about a pump," he went on as they drove through the cool morning. "I heard he's got an old twelve-horsepower crankstart that he picked up for a song. If I could get us a good deal on that, it could help out a lot with expenses."

"That would be good, Reed," she said, her tone business-like. "But I've got the money in the bank, and I don't see any need to stint on an investment. If Leege's pump won't do, we'll order a brand-new one out of Memphis."

Reed gave her an approving smile. "I've a mind to try to get by as cheaply as we can," he said. "But you're right. There's no reason to spend money on equipment that won't do the job."

"When do you think to get started?"

"I'm going to head down to Helena the first part of the week. I'll spend a couple of days there, buy us some seed, and be back here to start digging on Friday or Saturday."

"Digging?" Her tone was incredulous. "It's rice I want in this field, not potatoes!"

He chuckled at her teasing sarcasm. "This first year, it will take a bit more than just plowing. I'm going to have to build levees all around the field. The plot is just about big enough for four cuts, so I'll run a long embankment down the center and another crosswise against it. The cutbanks between the plots don't have to be as strong as the ones around the field, but all of them will take a heap of dirt, and the only way to get it is to dig it up."

"Are you going to need another man to help you, Reed? It sounds like there's going to be a lot of work involved."

He shook his head. "I can always get one of my brothers to give me a hand if I need it. Truly, Miss Hattie, I've been wanting to do this so long, I suspect I won't even notice the work."

"You'll notice, all right," she said. "You'll just be too self-satisfied to complain."

The small county seat was a collection of low-lying buildings fanning out in four directions from the big brick courthouse that sat in the middle of the square.

The Farmers' Bank dominated the north side of the square, and Reed eased the wagon up next to the boardwalk in front of it. Securing the horse, he helped Hattie down and rescued her handbag from the seat. "Do you want me to go with you to see the banker?" he asked.

"No," she replied as she straightened her bonnet and tried shaking a bit of the dust out of her skirts. "You go on and see about that pump. I can take care of my own banking business."

Reed tipped his hat, and Hattie headed into the imposing gray stone building with the bars on the windows. She would meet Reed at Turpin's Dry Goods in an hour. Heading the wagon down the street, Reed had a word and a glance for everyone he met, carefully remembering to lift his hat for the ladies. Getting into town was strictly a Saturday occurrence for most farmers, and as the multitude of wagons and rigs tied along the street suggested, nobody wanted to miss it.

On the far end of River Street, in the midst of scarred, scraped, and broken-down farm implements, rusted chicken wire, and assorted trash, Harmon Leege had his place of business. At one time, Leege's shack had been just another shanty by the river. Now the town had grown up around it. At nineteen years old, Harmon made his living repairing and selling overhauled farm implements and used hardware of all kinds. Reed saw him working on something out in the yard as he drove up. He hailed him, and the younger man returned Reed's wave with a halfhearted one of his own.

"Good morning, Harm," Reed said, jumping down from the wagon and walking up to meet him. Harmon Leege was big, almost brawny. His bare arms, bulging with muscles, were deeply tanned, though they retained a hint of redness that was typical of blonds. That is, Reed thought, if one could call Harm's hair blond. Actually, it was just plain yellow and curled up tightly against his head in waves and ridges.

"Tyler," the young man said briskly in greeting. "Something you wanted, or you just stop by to socialize?"

Reed nearly smiled at Leege's rudeness. It was rumored that Harm Leege was sweet on Bessie Jane. Talk was that he'd asked to court her back before she took up with Reed. The two were worlds apart, and Arthur Turpin had put a stop to that in a hurry. His daughter was far too good for the likes of Harmon Leege!

Old Man Leege, Harm's father, had a fondness for liquor. When his wife walked out on him years ago, he'd resigned himself to his position in the community as town drunk. Harmon himself never touched a drop. That was well known. He'd established his own reputation and his own position. Folks called him the junkman. He was not a bad sort, most agreed, but Reed knew few parents would welcome him as a suitor for their daughters. He could almost feel sorry for Harmon, but he, too, couldn't see Harmon courting Bessie Jane.

"Heard you got a little twelve-horse pump that I might be needing," Reed said as the two men stood eye-to-eye.

Harm nodded. "It's here in the backyard."

Following Harm, Reed thought that "backyard" was not a good description of the trashy overgrown area behind the shack.

Stepping carefully to avoid the loose pipe, metal fittings, and tin shingles that composed some of the items hiding in the knee-high grass, he shook his head in disgust. "Harm," he asked, "did you never hear of a place for everything and everything in its place?"

Harm looked around curiously. "I know where everything is," he said. "I like it spread out so I can see it."

Reed couldn't hide a slight grin.

"Here it is," Harm said. As Reed joined him, the two squatted next to the small motor. Watching as Harm primed it and got it ready to run, Reed couldn't help but be impressed with the young man's easy handling of the motor.

"You know a lot about machinery," he said by way of a compliment.

Harm shrugged. "More than I know about people, that's for sure," he said, and quickly changed the subject. "What are you planning to do with this little pump?"

"I'm finally going do something I've been thinking about for years. I'm going to drain that field down by Colfax Bluff and plant it in rice." Reed was unable to keep the pride out of his voice.

"Rice?" Harm repeated, scoffing. "Rice is something they grow in *J-pan*. It don't have nothing to do with Arkansas!"

"We've already got rice growing in the lowlands. I just want to bring it up here."

Harm shook his head in disbelief. "You're really thinking about growing rice? Everyone knows this is cotton country. If you want to raise rice, you'd best move yourself on down toward the Mississip."

"I tell you, Harm," Reed said, his enthusiasm sparked by the younger man's skepticism. "We can grow rice here. The ground is good for it and I'm sure it can be a better crop for us than cotton."

"Hey, I'm no farmer, and that's for sure," Harm said, "but if this land had been meant for rice, our great-grandpas would have planted it when they got here. They came out here and tried pretty near everything on this ground. They found that what grows best is cotton and corn. I don't see no need to test it out again."

"You're right, as far as it goes," Reed said. "The ground they found out here was just good for cotton and corn. But it ain't the same ground anymore, Harm."

Harm frowned. "What do you mean, it ain't the same ground?"

It was obvious the younger man's curiosity was piqued, and Reed continued on, determined to convince at least one person that planting rice there was a fabulous idea. "Those big earthquakes of 1811 and 1812 sank all the land in this part of Arkansas several feet at least."

Harm pulled off his straw hat and scratched his head thoughtfully. "Why, that's ridiculous. An earthquake can't sink half a state. It just ain't possible."

"And a big river like the Mississippi can't flow upstream for days at a time, but it did. It's a fact, recorded. An earthquake that's big enough to do that wouldn't have any problem letting a little Arkansas dirt settle."

Harm raised his hands, conceding the point. "All right, I admit it is possible that the New Madrid Quake might have had some effect on the land hereabouts. But that was nearly a hundred years ago. Things are bound to be getting back to normal by now."

Reed shook his head at the other man's ignorance of science. "I'm *talking* about normal. Earthquakes are a normal thing that happen, just like changes in the weather. Dirt isn't like a holy book. It changes every year, and you've got to farm according to the condition of your soil. If you've got marshy wetlands, the thing to do is raise rice. Not try to drain the land and change it to make it fit for cotton."

Harmon looked clearly interested. "You grow cotton, too, Tyler?"

"I do. And I plan to keep growing it, especially on the high ground. But if I can make Miss Hattie's rice field prosper like I think it will, in the next ten years, I'm moving into rice in a big way."

Harm listened intently as Reed talked of his vision of the future, the things he had seen in the lowlands and in Louisiana, and the prospects for rice as the major Arkansas crop. The young man saw the enthusiastic eyes of a dreamer and heard the carefully thought-out arguments of a practical, intelligent man. Harmon was young enough still to have dreams himself and smart enough to weigh the words he heard. "Growing that rice," he said, "it takes a good bit of equipment, don't it?"

Reed was startled by the question. "Well, a lot more than cotton, I guess. It's different equipment. Preparing the ground, planting, harvesting . . . It just can't be compared with cotton. The growing's not the same, either, and the milling is totally different from a cotton gin."

"If you're right and this rice really does grow here, where are you going to get your equipment? How you going to mill it?"

Reed looked at the other man curiously. "Well, I thought to send it down the river. There are dozens of rice mills in New Orleans."

"But there ain't no rice mill hereabouts." Harm's words were a statement more than a question. "If this were to catch on, the man who owned the rice mill, who could provide the equipment for growing and harvesting, might do mighty good for himself."

Reed nodded, surprised by Harm's insight. He hadn't thought about that part of it at all. The challenge to him was the growing, actually producing the crop. Sure, the rice would need to be milled, and a local mill would save time and money for the farmer and make the miller a lucky man.

"You know anything about rice milling?" he asked.

Harmon's mouth curved in a wide handsome grin, and his blue eyes sparkled with excitement. "I don't know nothing about nothing," he said. "But I ain't opposed to learning anything. And there ain't nothing about machinery I can't figure out."

"Maybe you could be a help to me," Reed said. "I'll be needing some advice about the engineering of this crop. A man who understands engineering and the workings of gears and machinery might come in pretty handy. Don't know that I'd be able to pay much."

Harm remained silent for a minute, then offered his hand to Reed. "I'm not selling you this pump. I'm giving it to you as an investment. You teach me what you know about the rice business and help me get a jump on Turpin's Dry Goods for supplying the hardware and machinery, and I'll help you however I can."

Reed hesitated. "This isn't a sure thing, Harm. You may have to wait for a cold day in hell to get your money back."

The younger man shrugged. "Maybe it'll be worth the wait."

Reed accepted his handshake.

"I'm out!" Preacher Able said gleefully.

Everyone else groaned, and Hattie picked up the piece of

paper sitting on the corner of the table. "That's a fifty for going out, and twenty-five off me. How much are you holding, Mr. Drayton?"

Flattening the rather large collection of dominoes in front of him, Ancil said sourly, "Seventy."

"Ten for me," Millie piped up.

Hattie quickly made her calculations. It was practically unnecessary. Preacher Able had soundly trounced them.

"If you ask me," Ancil said, his mouth drawn into a long unhappy line, "there's something not particularly comforting about a preacher who is so good at table games."

The preacher laughed, not taking Drayton's discontent seriously. Hattie could see, however, that Mr. Drayton was quite unhappy. He obviously was not a man who liked to lose.

Hoping to smooth things over, she reached out and touched his sleeve. "Perhaps the preacher has called for divine intervention," she said. "I wouldn't put it past him."

Her gesture had two effects—the one she'd hoped for, a lightening of the mood and a bit of laughter all around, and one she hadn't expected. Ancil glanced down at her hand on his arm, and a strange light came into his eyes. He laid his hand on hers and smiled.

Not knowing what to do, Hattie longed to jerk her hand away but restrained herself. She couldn't quite meet anyone's eyes, though.

"You got any more of that apple pie, Miss Hattie?" the preacher asked fortuitously.

"Don't you dare get him another piece," Millie said. "The reverend has had more than enough, and it is past time that we ought to be heading home."

"Oh, you needn't go so soon," Hattie said, hoping that Ancil would leave first.

The Jessups could not be dissuaded, and a few minutes later, Hattie and Ancil were standing in the yard as the other couple climbed into their buggy.

"We'll have to do this again," the preacher said. "Next time at our house."

"How about next week?" Ancil asked, causing Hattie to turn her head sharply and stare at him.

"Sounds fine." The preacher nodded toward them both. "Millie and I will be expecting you two next Saturday."

As they drove off, Hattie found herself slightly piqued that neither Ancil nor the preacher had asked her if she wanted to go. She hated it when men just assumed women would go along with their plans. Shaking the errant thoughts away, she reminded herself that having a man of her own was worth sacrificing a bit of autonomy.

"Well, Miss Hattie," Ancil said quietly, "it's been a real nice evening."

"Thank you, Mr. Drayton," she answered.

He was standing so close, she actually had to tilt her head back to look up at him. From the light shining through the front screen, she could just make out his face and the hopeful smile beneath his mustache.

"I was wanting to have you out to my place for Sunday dinner," he said, sounding somewhat uncomfortable. "But a company dinner is a lot for my little Mary Nell and I—"

"Don't think another word of it," she interrupted.

"I would like you to come out to my place sometime," he said. "Just so you could have a look around, see the house and everything."

She didn't know what to say. It was too fast. She wasn't ready to think about his house, his life. She was scrambling for a way to tell him that when she felt his hands on her shoulders. His eyes were closed, and he was leaning toward her with the intent to touch his lips to hers. Like a shot, she was out of his arms, stepping back a good three paces.

"Good night, Mr. Drayton," she said primly.

He stared at her for a moment, obviously displeased with her reaction.

"Good night, then, Miss Hattie," he said at last, his voice glacial. Carefully placing his bowler on his head, he nodded politely and mounted his horse.

Six

"I APPRECIATE your enthusiasm, son," Arthur Turpin said, looking from his rocking chair to the couple occupying the settee. "But rice will never make it around here. We don't know how to grow it or what to do with it. We don't even eat it."

"But we're going to learn, Mr. Turpin," Reed said. Dressed in his best white shirt, the tiny front pleats neatly pressed and his sleeves unrolled despite the heat, he looked exactly what a young gentleman come calling was expected to look like. "In the next ten, maybe twenty years, this whole county is going to be planted in rice. I'm sure of it."

The older man laughed. "Well, I'm not sure of it. And I can promise you, I'll never invest one cent in that kind of prospect. I can't imagine a down-to-earth woman like Hattie Colfax risking her hard-earned money in such a scheme."

Bessie Jane giggled. "Maybe being courted by old Ancil Drayton has addled her mind."

Reed looked sternly at her, and she immediately straightened her mouth into a more serious expression. Her eyes, however, continued to dance. She always felt slighted when her father sat up for hours talking business with Reed, and she knew a surefire way to get Reed's attention was to make fun of Hattie Colfax.

"I expect a lot of people will have their doubts about our new crop," Reed continued. "But I don't intend to let any naysayers make me nervous."

Turpin rose with a little chuckle. "That's what I like about you, boy. You're not just smart, you're determined. You're going to be somebody in this town. I've never doubted it. That's what I told little Bessie Jane." He smiled at his daughter. " 'That Reed Tyler's the one you ought to be setting your sights on,' I said to her. 'He's the best one of the lot.' "

"Oh, Daddy," Bessie Jane said, a blush staining her cheeks.

"All right, all right, honeybunch." He chucked his daughter under the chin. "I'll be letting you two have a bit of sparking time. Not much, mind you, young man," he added, pointing a finger at Reed in a joking imitation of an overly prudent father. "I'll be leaving the door open. Don't stay too late."

"Yes, sir," Reed answered dutifully.

The older man was hardly out of the room when Bessie Jane scooted closer to him, and with a slight smile he wrapped his arm around her shoulders.

"I hope Daddy didn't make you mad," she said, pouting prettily. She was wearing a cerise muslin dress ornamented with tiny white dots. The gown flowed from her shoulders like a confection one might purchase at the soda fountain, and the sweet loveliness of her mouth and eyes had Reed almost forgetting what she'd said.

"No, I'm used to it by now," he answered after a moment, grinning. "It amazes me that he likes me so much and thinks that all my plans are so foolish."

"It's just that he has his own plans for you, Reed." She inched a little nearer, so that he could feel the warmth from her knee as it almost, but not quite, touched his. "He doesn't mind your interest in farming. He just hopes that you'll give it up when we wed and come into the business with him."

He looked at her and ran a finger gently along the side of her face. Her skin was pale and flawless, and the slight roses high in her cheeks never came from a paste bottle or coloring paper. "I hope you understand, Bessie Jane, that I have no intention of doing that."

She lowered her chin, then looked up at him coyly through

her lashes. "It doesn't matter to me what you do, Reed. I just
want to be your wife. That's all that's important to me."

He smiled. Pulling her into his arms, he kissed her softly,
sweetly. She sighed, and he released her to gaze lovingly into
her face. "You are so beautiful," he whispered. "When I'm
not with you, I forget how really pretty you are."

"Thank you, Reed," she answered, but there was a strange
distance in her eyes. Reed didn't understand it. He always wondered if she doubted his sincerity, or if his compliments seemed
lame when compared to those other beaux had given her. He
quickly pushed her lack of response from him and set about
trying to cheer her. "I got some good news today in town," he
said.

"What?" she asked, always eager for the latest gossip.

"Miss Hattie and I have a new partner in the rice."

Bessie Jane opened her mouth with surprise, and a delighted
giggle escaped. She'd already anticipated that Reed's extra crop
would cut into the little time they usually had to spend together.
Another man to share the work would be a welcome addition.

"Who in the world did you find to go in with you?" she
asked, leaning forward.

"One of your old beaux, actually."

"Who?" Overwhelmingly curious now, she mentally ran
through the long list of gentlemen who had found their way to
her door.

"I can see it's hard for you to guess," Reed said dryly.
"You've had so many beaux, you can no longer remember them
all!"

She laughed, enjoying the game. "I've had a good many,"
she admitted. "But only one that I can recall who ever bored
me to tears by talking about rice."

"Bored you to tears!" He tweaked her nose. "You should
have been taking notes, young lady. Every word from my mouth
is an oracle most profound!"

Her eyes widened in a semblance of awe. "Oh, do forgive
me, Herr Professor. In the future I'll consider every foolish
remark you make as if it were written on the stone tablets from
Mount Sinai."

"You're getting downright sassy," he said, shaking a finger
at her in teasing reprimand. "I've half a mind not to tell you."

She giggled. "Come on, Reed. Confess. Which of my beaux
have you recruited to work for Horseface Hattie?"

"Bessie Jane."

She raised her hands in a gesture of supplication. "Sorry, let me try again. Who is helping you out in Hattie Colfax's rice field?"

"Harmon Leege."

Bessie Jane froze, and she was momentarily stunned into silence. Her face paled as she stumbled over words of reply. "Harm—Harmon Leege never called on me!"

Reed was startled at the vehemence in her voice. "Well, I didn't mean—"

"Do you think I would have allowed a *junkman* to call on me?"

He could feel her trembling beside him, and worriedly tightened his arm around her. "Bessie Jane, I—"

"My father sent him away immediately. I never . . ." Her eyes suddenly grew round with horror. "Did he say something to indicate he had spent time with me?"

"No, Bessie Jane, he—"

"What did he say about me?"

"Nothing. We didn't even speak of you."

"Oh." Flushing with guilt, she licked her lips nervously, as if suddenly realizing she had made too much of nothing. She attempted to counter her overreaction. "I wouldn't want any gossip being spread about me," she explained. "Sometimes gentlemen whose suits are not well received say terrible things to ease their pride. Just because I was not willing to walk out with a man who is obviously not my type, I shouldn't be the subject of slander."

Reed patted her shoulder. "Of course not, sweetheart. And I would never let any man speak a word against you. I wouldn't worry about Harm, either. He seems like a very decent and upright fellow. I'm sure he would never spread untruths about you."

" 'Decent'? 'Upright'?" Her tone was genuinely puzzled. "Daddy says he and his father are the most worthless excuses for human beings in this town."

"Your father," Reed said, his jaw set firmly, "is sometimes harsh and a bit hasty to judge."

Bessie Jane was surprised at this criticism of her father. She didn't always like Daddy's decisions, but she never considered that he might be wrong.

"Certainly Old Man Leege is no sterling citizen," Reed went

on. "But he's never harmed anyone but himself. And Harmon works hard and has managed to keep them both fed since he was a boy. I would say there's a lot to admire in him."

"Do you really believe that? Do you really think there might be something to admire about that junkman?"

Reed couldn't fathom her puzzled expression, and put it down to his comment about her father. "Yes," he answered, "I do think Harmon is admirable. You're very young, Bessie Jane. Try not to judge people so quickly. Just because Harmon Leege is poor doesn't make him any less important or worthy of our respect or our friendship. Only children and the narrow-minded measure the whole world by themselves. It's time for you to grow up a bit, sweetheart. Try to learn to look a little deeper into the people you meet. Treat Harmon Leege as you would any other man."

He watched with curiosity the strange series of emotions that raced across Bessie Jane's face. He was about to question her further when the young woman got a grasp on her wildly scattering thoughts. In a ploy to distract him, she reached over and undid a button on his shirt, allowing her small hand to seek his tingling flesh. "Let's not talk about Harmon Leege," she whispered. "Let's not talk at all."

She raised her face to his, and he slanted his mouth across hers, taking the sweet warmth she offered. Forgetting the odd expression on her face, forgetting his intuitive awareness that something was amiss, he was aware only of the hot tenderness of her mouth.

Slowly, steadily, the kiss deepened. As Bessie Jane wrapped her arms around his neck, Reed pulled her closer. He could no longer seem to think. Through the layers of clothing, he could feel the hard points of her nipples and couldn't resist the entice-ment. Rubbing his chest against them, he reveled in the fire that burst inside him.

Taking his hand in hers, Bessie Jane brought his eager fingers to her breast. "Touch me," she murmured. "Don't you want to touch me?"

"Bessie Jane!" he hissed. He freed his hand and set her a respectable distance from him. "Your parents are in the next room."

"Daddy's snoring. Can't you hear him? It's safe, Reed. Please touch me. Please love me."

"Sweetheart, we can't," he said, his voice hoarse, his breathing rough.

"We can. Please, we must," she said, and laid her hand in his lap, touching him intimately.

Reed jumped up as if he'd been shot from a gun. Turning away from her so that she wouldn't see the evidence of his desire, he strode across the room and shut the door. Leaning his forehead against it for a moment, he strove to catch his breath. When he was in control of his body once again, he faced her. "Bessie Jane, you must stop this constant assault on my better judgment." He spoke resolutely, like an irate father or a disapproving older brother.

She bowed her head, not willing to look at him.

"I am as eager to . . . to consummate this relationship as you are," he went on. "But there are proprieties—and dangers."

He ran a hand through his hair and began pacing in front of the settee. "I realize that if I'd practiced more self-control that evening in the barn, you would not be aware of your 'woman's needs.' " He stopped, disconcerted by the expression and its implication. "Without knowing how it is, waiting until we're wed would be easier for you." Halting directly in front of her, he gazed down at the pretty little princess in the frothy pink dress and felt infinitely older and wiser. "Truly, Bessie Jane, I do blame myself, but I cannot undo the past."

He seated himself on the settee at a respectable distance from her. "I'm trying to control my feelings for you," he explained, carefully avoiding words like *lust* and *desire*. "But you will also have to try to help me if we're to make it through the next several months." He leaned over and cupped her chin gently in his hand. "If you continue to lure me and tempt me at every opportunity, I will have no choice but to avoid being alone with you as much as possible."

Bessie Jane lowered her eyes in shame. Folding her hands primly in her lap, she whispered, "I'm sorry, Reed. I just want to make us closer. I want to show you I care for you."

Feeling like a heartless cad, Reed patted her hands gently. "I know, sweetheart. But there'll be plenty of time to love each other after we're legally wed."

She nodded, but wouldn't meet his eyes.

A silence fell between them, a silence that embarrassed them both.

• • •

Hattie shaded her eyes as she stared in surprise down the road. Trotting toward her was a large rather grim-looking Hampshire boar, his head held high as if he were the undisputed ruler of the universe. In his wake was Reed, urging him on with angry words, looks of exasperation, and a solid willow switch.

Reed had returned from Helena the previous morning with seed and equipment and so many plans, one head couldn't hold them all. Harm Leege had gone with him, and the two of them had sat at Hattie's table for nearly three hours last evening talking about everything they had seen and learned.

Hattie had never spoken more than a couple of words to young Leege before, but she'd been favorably impressed with the handsome man. He'd seemed as excited and hopeful about the rice as Reed, and he quickly grasped the engineering concepts necessary for a successful rice-farming venture.

"What they're doing now," Reed had told her, eagerness flooding through his voice, "is drilling wells and cutting irrigation canals so they can utilize the acres that don't sit next to a river or stream."

He glanced quickly at Harm for confirmation. Their matching smiles made them look like schoolboys who'd found themselves locked in the candy store. "Do you know what that means, Miss Hattie?" Reed said. "It means we could eventually put most all of this farm into rice, acres and acres of rice."

Hattie tried to imagine it. Acres and acres of rice growing where they now had cotton. It was difficult to believe.

"And with the move toward irrigation and more mechanization," Harm went on, "it means more rice per man-hour. Miss Hattie, it's actually possible to have two, maybe three hundred acres under cultivation without needing fifty men to work it."

"And there's more," Reed said, sliding his chair closer to Hattie as if letting her in on a well-kept secret. "Farmers' down there are talking about building their own rice mills. They're saying that the mills in New Orleans are a monopoly and that it's possible to build a small mill close to home that can do enough business to make a profit."

"And marketing," Harm added. "The farmers are thinking of doing away with the rice broker and selling their milled rice directly. Using the railroads for shipping is just a task to be learned. You needn't pay someone to do it for you."

Hattie listened in awe and fascination at the exciting new business she had surprisingly found herself a part of. It was exhilarating to be on the ground floor of a commercial venture. "So are we building our own mill?" she asked the two young men.

They stared back at her, dumbfounded. After a moment, Harm looked at Reed as Reed settled back in his chair. He paused to get a grip on the facts of the situation. "It takes money to build a mill, Miss Hattie," he said, trying to hold their collective ambitions within the realm of reality.

"I've got money saved, Reed. You know that."

"I've also got some money," he said. "And I suspect Harm has a bit put by too."

"Not much," the younger man admitted.

Reed continued. "I need mine to buy this land, and you're already risking a good portion of yours, Miss Hattie, with the crop." Smiling at his partners, Reed spoke optimistically, but kept one foot firmly planted in pragmatism. "There's no sense in us getting ahead of ourselves. We won't need a mill unless we can grow a crop."

Harm chuckled, nodding in agreement.

"Of course we can grow a crop," Hattie said, scoffing at the suggestion of failure. "We have two very bright, hardworking young men who are carefully doing their homework. And one very thrifty older woman who is going to be out there every day nagging you both to blue blazes!"

That was exactly how it was, Hattie thought as she watched Reed and the strutting boar approach. She was certain that the rice field would succeed, and she intended to be a part of it.

They were all eager to get started, but Hattie's sow had come fertile. She was not about to miss the extra cash they could make from a litter of shoats that summer. Reed had readily agreed with her, and that morning he'd headed over to Whimsley's place to get the young Hampshire boar she wanted to breed back to her sow.

"I thought you were bringing him in the wagon," she called as he neared the yard.

"Miss Hattie, this has got to be the stupidest, most stubborn pig that God ever put on this earth." Reed punctuated this harsh appraisal with a sharp snap of the willow switch on the boar's foreflank. He was attempting to turn him into the yard, but the recalcitrant animal was determined to resist his best interest.

Hattie went to Reed's assistance, and the hog was finally persuaded to enter the yard.

"There were five grown men," Reed said, "trying to get that stupid hunk of spoiled sausage into the wagon, and he just refused to go." Reed's temper was so near the surface, Hattie found it amusing. "So I made him walk the entire way. And serves him right, I think," he added, as if he had actually won a battle of wills with the large male swine.

The boar began running up and down the outside of the pigsty fence, slobbering, snapping his jaws, and making strange barking noises.

"He sure is ranting," Hattie said. She had little experience with boars and generally disliked them. They were lazy, difficult, and usually bad-tempered. But unfortunately, they were essential for pig breeding.

Reed shook his head in exasperation. "I swear he smelled that sow two miles up the road."

"Reed!"

"Excuse me, Miss Hattie," he said politely, "but it's the truth. I thought I was going to have to shoot that crazy boar before I got him to understand we were heading in the right direction."

Hattie felt suffused with embarrassment, but she tamped it down for the sake of expediency and practicality. "Well, let's get on with it. Anything to stop that caterwauling."

"Is the sow ready?"

She pointed toward the far end of the pigsty. "I've got her tied up between the other side of the hoghouse and the fence."

Reed nodded and, brandishing his willow switch, headed for the boar. "Come on, Romeo, your dreams are about to come true."

" 'Romeo'?"

He raised his hands in a helpless gesture. "That's what Whimsley calls him." A naughty smile spread across his face. "This is, however, his first opportunity to prove it."

Hattie attempted to maintain a calm expression, but she was unable to control a blush.

Reed saw it and couldn't resist teasing her. "Why don't you go tend to yon Juliet, and we will chaperone the courting couple."

Lifting her chin, Hattie replied in a similarly prim and haughty tone. "The young lady's name is Mabel, and I will thank you to instruct your protégé in the proper decorum of a gentleman.''

Reed's laughter followed her as she headed for the love nest she had prepared for Mabel.

Because domesticated boars had been bred so large, the mating of purebred hogs literally required outside support. Hattie had tied Mabel into a corner of the pigsty and surrounded her on three sides with hay bales. With this protective buffer, no matter how boisterous the huge, ungainly boar might become, Mabel would be safe from being tipped over and trampled, a fate that had befallen more than one unlucky sow.

Making the loud, sad love-grunts of a sow in heat, Mabel was a pitiful creature to behold. Hattie stroked her silky black snout and scratched her gently behind the ears. "Now, Mabel, everything is going to be fine," she said. "Reed has brought you a nice young friend, and he's going to give you lots of little piglets.''

The racket of the boar making his less than graceful entrance into the hogpen captured her attention.

"Dammit, Romeo, get in there!''

Hearing the frustration in Reed's voice, Hattie looked up to see him trying valiantly to lead Romeo in the right direction. "This is the stupidest pig I've ever seen in my life!'' he called to Hattie. "Come on, Romeo, she's over this way, you dumb porkchop!''

Hattie couldn't help but smile at the clumsy, reluctant lover and his exasperated tutor. "Over here, Romeo," she said. "Your ladylove is this way!''

As if suddenly getting the picture, Romeo made a mad dash toward Mabel. He squealed horrible bass sounds as he sniffed and rooted the ground around her, then gave what could only be described as a cry of triumph as he violently mounted the sow.

"No!'' Reed yelled, and ran forward.

Mabel squealed wildly and struggled, desperate to get away. Her cries were obviously from pain, and Hattie was frightened at their intensity. "What's wrong?'' she asked.

He didn't even look up as he furiously slapped Romeo's back with the willow switch. "Get down! Get down!''

"Reed, what is it?'' she shouted over the plaintive wails of the sow.

Looking up at her, he was at a loss for words. His face and

neck turned bright red with embarrassment. Without answering, he continued his angry assault on the young boar.

"What is going *on*?" Hattie's voice clearly expressed panic as Mabel's cries continued unabated.

"He's—" Reed hesitated, looking back down at the pigs, "he's got his . . . He's not . . ." Speechless, he turned away from Hattie and continued trying to get the boar's attention.

Frightened for Mabel, Hattie quickly climbed over the fence to see for herself what was amiss. An outraged glance at the entangled swine revealed the problem. In his urgency and inexperience, Romeo had embedded himself deeply into poor Mabel's rectum.

Gasping with shock, Hattie stood immobile for an instant, then rushed to the edge of the pigsty where the yardbroom was propped against the fence. Grabbing it, she raced back to Mabel's rescue. Raising the broom high over her head, she brought it down with a sharp crack across the shoulders of young Romeo.

Squealing with pain and surprise, the boar retreated momentarily before the need to mate overcame his fear. It was enough. This time he found the proper geography, and Mabel's screams of terror changed, if not to sighs of contentment at least to grunts of appreciation.

Standing near the copulating swine, Hattie took a deep breath. She was almost painfully aware of the indelicacy of what had just occurred and of Reed standing beside her. Deciding that the less said about the incident the better, she turned to him, intending to ask him to watch over Mabel while she attended to other tasks in the house.

She never uttered the words. Reed was obviously not flustered and shamefaced as she was. He was clutching his sides, trying to hold in the hilarity that threatened to burst out of control. Seeing her staring at him wide-eyed, he lost the battle and howled with laughter.

"Stop it!" Hattie told him. "Stop it right now." Still, she couldn't control the smile that curved her own lips.

Laughing so hard he could barely stand, Reed drifted backward until he was leaning against the fence. He bent forward as he struggled for breath.

"Reed! It is not a bit funny," Hattie said, but found herself beginning to succumb to unbridled amusement. "That stupid pig could have injured Mabel. He . . . Well, he . . . Oh, Reed, shut up!'' Her face as red as a tomato in summertime, Hattie fought in vain against the irresistible impulse to laugh. After a moment, the sound of her warm throaty giggles brightened the barnyard.

Every time she almost had control of herself, she would look at Reed and begin again. Staggering to the fence, she, too, braced herself against the wood slats, her ability to stand now dangerously in question.

It was only natural that when Reed opened his arms, she stepped into his embrace, and they held each other as they laughed. Trying to restore order time and time again, Hattie would take a deep breath and struggle for control, only to have Reed say one word—''Romeo,'' ''stupid,'' or ''yardbroom''— and the hysterical laughter would begin again.

Finally, as their laughter dissolved to giddy smiles, Hattie became aware of her arms on Reed's shoulders and his hands clasped at the small of her back.

Reed also noticed their position. As he gazed down into her laughing eyes, an unexpected feeling of rightness and contentment swept through him.

Hattie, now aware of the inappropriateness of their embrace, shrugged slightly to loose herself. To her surprise, Reed pulled her tightly against him. He released her immediately, but her eyes widened in shock. Had Reed hugged her? Glancing at his face, she couldn't read his expression at all. Surely not, she told herself. She had imagined it.

Of course, she must have imagined it. But was she imagining the zing of fire that now surged through her veins?

Seven

HATTIE wasn't sure about the dress. It was a light summer lawn with a blue organdy-and-lace insert at the yoke. The sleeves were wide and fluffy with lacy double cuffs, and the skirt sported three rows of stiff organdy ruffles at the hem. It was a delicate feminine dress that made her eyes almost true blue and emphasized her tiny waist. She wanted to look her best, and as far as her apparel went, this dress was it. But it was not her typical wardrobe for an evening with friends, and she hoped she did not appear too eager.

She was ready a good half hour before Ancil was supposed to call, and the waiting made her extremely nervous. Unused to idle time, she walked out onto the front porch. Standing there a moment, she worried that Ancil might come down the road and spy her waiting. Stepping down to the ground, she strolled toward the elm tree at the end of the drive.

A small bush of four-o'clocks had bloomed, and she stopped to admire the blossoms, gently caressing the soft inner petals and breathing in the delicate scent. The white blossoms would look perfect against the blue organdy on her dress, she thought. Carefully pinching off three of the little blossoms, she pinned

two at the collarbone of her bodice and added the other to the
knot of hair she'd set high on her head. The flowers were probably silly, she told herself, and undoubtedly made her appear
frivolous, but she couldn't deny herself the small vanity.

As she walked around to the back of the house, she admired
the spring evening and the neat, well-kept place she called home.
There was a lightness to her heart that made her almost giddy.
Having prided herself for so long on not caring about her old-
maid status, she was surprised to find the adventure of being
courted oddly pleasant.

As she rounded the back corner of her house, the goat ambled
up to her to check out the new gown. Hattie petted her long
sleek neck and scratched her playfully behind the ears. "Well,
what do you think, Myrene?" she asked, swirling her skirts.
"Do you think I'm too gussied up for this occasion?"

"I think you're liable to pop old Drayton's eyes out."

Hattie glanced up quickly at the words. She hadn't known
Reed and Harmon were still there. They were sitting near the
back steps, scrunched down like boys playing marbles as they
studied a sketch in the dirt of their plans for the rice field.

Chagrined that they'd heard her foolish conversation, Hattie
was reassured by their warm smiles. "You startled me," she
said, not quite able to meet their eyes.

"You look right good, Miss Hattie," Harmon said, rising to
his feet and politely doffing his hat.

She inexplicably giggled at the young man's sincerity. "I
hope I don't look the fool," she said, glancing at Reed for
approval.

"No, Miss Hattie. You look real nice," Reed said honestly.
In fact, he was somewhat startled. Seeing Hattie all dressed up
on a Saturday night made him feel he should be squiring her
someplace, not Ancil Drayton. Unwittingly, he remembered that
moment in the hog pen when he had held her close. As he had
done on previous occasions when that memory flitted through
his mind, he quickly cast it out, unwilling to dwell on its meaning. "I've never seen you in that dress before," he added.

She shrugged. "It's not the kind of thing you wear to wash
down the hogs."

"And your hair's different too." He walked up to her and
gestured with his finger for her to turn around.

Hattie felt disconcerted at slowly revolving herself for his
display. Inexplicably, she trembled under his scrutiny.

"Those flowers look real fine," he said quietly.

Her brow furrowed in self-doubt. "Do I look like a plowhorse pretending to be a high-stepping filly?"

His smile was warm and reassuring. "You look, Miss Hattie, like a woman expecting a gentleman to come courting."

Shyly lowering her eyes, Hattie was inordinately pleased. She could feel Reed's gaze on her, and the trembling he'd caused made her suddenly aware of her flesh and the magical sparks that seemed to be skittering across it.

Eager to change the subject and regain her composure, she inspected the drawing scratched out in the dirt. "So this is my rice field?" she asked Harmon, seating herself on the porch step.

"Yes, ma'am," he said with a wide grin, eager to show off the design. "This is the main levee between the field and the river." He pointed to a wide line carved into the dirt. "The floodgates will be here and here." He indicated two green cottonwood pods at either end of the line. "These horizontal lines are the levees for the cuts, and this rock is the pump."

Reed squatted beside her and began to illustrate how the system would operate. "The pump works on either side of the levee," he explained, "so we can use gravity when it favors us. That'll save on fuel. When the river is higher than the field, we won't need the pump to flood it, and if the field gets higher than the river, we can drain it easily."

Excitement rippled through Hattie. "I can hardly wait," she said. "You've been talking about this so long, Reed, I guess I never believed I would actually see it. When are we going to be able to start?"

"Monday morning!" he announced without hesitation. "I'm going to try to get everything ready tonight, so we can start turning dirt at daybreak."

The three exchanged delighted glances. Reed saw his dream about to be realized, Harmon saw his opportunity to make something of himself, and Hattie saw herself back in farming at last. Words were unnecessary, until the sound of an approaching rider interfered with their reverie.

"I believe Romeo has arrived," Reed joked, offering his hand to help Hattie rise. It irked him more than it should that she would be spending the evening with Drayton.

"Not Romeo!" she said with mock sternness. "Mr. Drayton is nothing like that foolish pig."

Reed's smile was positively wicked. "I guess that means you won't be needing to take the yardbroom with you."

Hattie's mouth dropped open in speechless shock. With a tender touch of his knuckles, Reed chucked her on the chin, effectively shutting her mouth. "I'd best hitch up the buggy for you, Miss Hattie."

Harmon Leege watched Miss Hattie's buggy drive away with Ancil Drayton at the reins. His partner—well, maybe even his friend—Reed Tyler, sat silently beside him and didn't even glance up at the departing couple. It was obvious Reed didn't like Drayton, but he seemed more bothered by his presence than necessary. Drayton wasn't much, Harm had to admit, but Miss Hattie was real sweet, and it was nice she finally had a man of her own.

Gazing back at the crude drawing he'd made in the dirt, Harmon couldn't help but feel pride in what he'd done. He was no engineer, no builder, but he knew his design was a good one. "I think we've about got this thing together," he said.

Reed nodded. "I can't think of a thing we've forgotten, but there's always something."

Harm silently agreed. It was impossible to prepare for all the things that could happen. In his short life, he'd already learned some hard lessons about how plans can go awry. "The way we've set up the equipment ought to work," he said, "no matter what the conditions."

Reed nodded again. "We've done all the usual things we saw in the rice fields around Helena."

"Barring some act of God, I think this thing should work."

Reed gazed off to the horizon as if trying to see the future. "The rest we'll just have to figure out by trial and error."

"I'm glad you decided to go ahead with this," Harm said, leaning back to get a better look at his partner. "I was sure when your uncle said he would help you buy out that old man on the place next to his, you would jump at the chance."

Reed shrugged. "I promised Miss Hattie."

Harmon chuckled. "I suspect she would have understood about you leaving. That was a chance of a lifetime, Reed. As soon as I heard your uncle's offer, I figured you'd be packing your bags."

"I don't know about that," Reed said lamely. It wasn't the first time his uncle Ed had found him a good deal on some rice ground. Reed had always found an excuse to reject the idea, though. "Just buying a place that's already planted in rice isn't the challenge we've got here," he argued irrationally. It wasn't very good reasoning, but it was all he had. He didn't know why he'd felt compelled to turn down every offer, but the idea of leaving Colfax Farm was abhorrent to him.

Harm snorted. "It sure isn't the challenge. Not the challenge, not the risk—hell, this isn't even your land. You were a damn fool to turn your uncle down." Two big dimples appeared in Harm's cheeks as he smiled. "But I'm sure glad you did."

Reed laughed. He genuinely liked Harm and felt a kinship with him. Shaking his head, he said, "It's all that rice pudding Aunt Nell made us eat. I think it must rot the brain."

"You better hope it doesn't, 'cause I'm planning to be eating nothing else in the next few years."

"Me, too," Reed said, then more seriously added, "That is, if this rice will really work here."

"You losing your nerve?" Harm teased. "When something finally begins to go right, you start borrowing trouble?"

"Not usually. But usually when I'm set on a gamble, it's my own money on the table."

"Miss Hattie don't seem to be worried."

"That's 'cause she trusts us," Reed said, slapping the dust off his hat. "I just hope she's right."

"How can we lose?" Harm asked. "Miss Hattie had to have it right. The ground is good for rice, the equipment will work, and she's got two strong backs that both want to succeed real bad."

"Because we're both landless and broke with something to prove," Reed said truthfully, and turned to look at the other man. "You keep this up, Harm, and you're going to get where you actually like me."

Harm immediately shuttered his expression. "I've never said a word agin you," he said flatly.

"I suspect you haven't, but you don't like me. And it's because of Bessie Jane."

"Bessie Jane Turpin is nothing to me." Harmon's denial was quick and curt. Reed nodded and opened his mouth to say more, but Harmon forestalled him. "She's your woman, and that's the end of it."

The two were silent for a moment, allowing the tense feelings to pass. It was Harmon who forced the return to normal conversation. "As for Bessie Jane," he said, "it *is* Saturday night. Hadn't you better head off to see her?"

"I'm not going over tonight," Reed said, rising to his feet. "I'm going to try to overhaul that plow a little. I don't want it bogging down in the wet ground. I'll be seeing Bessie Jane tomorrow at church."

Harmon nodded, but he didn't quite understand how anyone could prefer the company of a plow to being close to Bessie Jane Turpin.

It was after ten when Hattie and Ancil stepped out onto the Jessups' front porch.

"I swear, Preacher," Ancil said, "there is something positively sinful about the way you always win."

Preacher Able laughed good-naturedly. "I suspect that's why I was called to preach. The good Lord didn't want me making my living skinning boys at the Domino Parlor."

"Able!" Millie's voice was horrified. "The reverend didn't mean a word of that," she quickly assured her guests.

"Of course not," Hattie said, then gave the preacher a teasing wink.

After saying their good-byes, Ancil handed her up into the buggy. Hattie seated herself on the far right side, modestly arranging her skirts. To her dismay, Ancil, rather than making himself comfortable on the left side of the buggy seat, sat squarely in the middle.

He unhitched the lines from the brake handle, gave a cluck and a shake, and headed the buggy out to the road. He was sitting so near that Hattie was very aware of his person. His clean white Sunday shirt seemed close and threatening, and the smell of hair tonic mingling with the faint odor of snuff was overpowering.

She tried discreetly to move a little farther away, only to discover that he was sitting on her dress.

"So, Miss Hattie, ma'am, did you have a good time tonight?" he asked hopefully, his smile gleaming in the moonlight.

"Yes, thank you," she replied, attempting to lean casually away from him.

"I never realized you were such a cutup," he said.

"A 'cutup'? Oh, I enjoy a bit of fun, just like everyone else, I guess."

Ancil seemed to approve of that answer and began to lean in her direction. "Yes, ma'am," he said. "I guess we all just enjoy a bit of fun." Transferring the reins to his left hand, he adjusted his hat with his right, and then, his gesture overly casual, brought his arm down to rest on the seat behind her.

Hattie eased forward, away from his arm. She hoped he would recognize her disapproval of his initiative and make a polite and hasty retreat. Ancil, however, seeming unconcerned with her opposition, matched each inch of her withdrawal with an inch of advance.

"How are your children?" she asked as she again shifted away from him.

"Children? Oh, they're all right, I suppose." He smiled quickly as if a new idea had just proposed itself. "Lula really did the raising of the children, you know," he said gravely. His voice was amazingly close, and she skittered another inch away. "I'm a fair hand at teaching the boys what they need to know—plowing and working and such. But them girls, they sure do need a woman's hand, and that's for sure, Miss Hattie."

"They seem like lovely girls," she said, trying to maintain the facade of simple communication. "I was especially taken with Cyl and little Ada. Such a lively twosome."

"Too lively," Ancil said, shaking his head. "Mary Nell tries to keep them straight, but I swear every time you look up, they're off somewheres a'playing."

"But they are children. They're supposed to play."

He nodded. "Once the day's work is finished and their chores done, I've nothing against it."

Hattie continued to lean away, but was interested in his views on childrearing. "I understand Ada has a collection of paper dolls," she said.

He frowned at her, seeming surprised. "Don't know where she got them," he said with a shrug. "She had an old cornhusk doll someplace, but I think Buddy was sick on it or something, and Mary Nell threw it in the fireplace last winter."

Ancil scooted the last quarter inch possible, and his thigh sat squarely against Hattie's.

"Did Mary Nell make her a new doll?" she asked, determined to ignore his shocking behavior.

He shook his head, chuckling. "Now Mary Nell is a good girl, but she don't waste her time on anything but the necessities. She'd no more make a doll than she'd take up crochet. There's a good bit of work for a woman on the farm—not much time for foolishness."

Hattie meant to tell him that a child's doll was not foolishness, but he set his hand that held the reins on his thigh next to hers and slipped his arm off the back of the buggy seat so that it touched her.

Leaning forward and to her right, Hattie found her position was so precarious, she grabbed the hinges on the buggy top and positioned her feet carefully to maintain her balance. As if on cue, Ancil hit a rut, and it was only his grasp of her waist that kept her from a headlong plunge onto the road.

"Whoa there, Miss Hattie." He pulled her snugly to his side. "You best stay here right close where I can keep you safe."

"Thank you," she said, shaken by her near calamity. Realizing that Ancil had not released her but kept his arm proprietarily around her, she sat up straight and spoke with a hint of hauteur. "I am perfectly all right, Mr. Drayton. You may release me now."

His grin was wide, his chuckle lazy. "Now, Miss Hattie, once a fellow's got his gal in a snuggle, you don't expect him to just let her go that quick, do you?" He punctuated his remark with a rather too friendly squeeze.

Her face paling, then suffusing with color, Hattie was not sure quite what to do.

"Do you recollect when we was younguns?" he asked her.

She stiffened more, if that were possible, appreciating memories of her childhood even less than his arm around her.

"We sure done some wild things in them days," he continued, chuckling at his own memories. " 'Course, you didn't do much too wild, but we sure was into teasing you."

She squirmed slightly to try to get him to loosen his grip on her waist, but to no avail.

"You was a funny little thing in them days," he said. "Almost like a growed woman dressed up like a child. We sure did give you a lot of grief, I'm thinking."

"I don't recall," she lied primly. "It was a long time ago."

"It surely was. It's funny, but I remember it like it was yesterday. All us boys playing tag and rope-the-goat and you girls sitting round giggling over button-button."

It was not exactly how Hattie remembered it, but she declined to comment.

"Were you sweet on me then, Miss Hattie?" he asked her, his face uncomfortably close and his smile unreasonably smug.

"I certainly was not."

"I thought you was. Yes, I thought you was plumb taken with me. But then, a lot of them gals was back then, afore I lost my hair."

"Mr. Drayton, I'd like for you to release me," she said, her voice carefully controlled.

"Hattie-hon, you need to loosen up a bit," he told her, ignoring her complaint. "It's a pretty night, we got a nice big old moon up there, and we're due some sparking." He squeezed her again. "Ain't nobody to see and none to know."

"I believe I am already sufficiently loose," she said.

Ancil laughed loudly. "Now that, Miss Hattie, I ain't heard. But I'm willing to test it out." He pulled her tightly against him and leaned down in an attempt to kiss her.

She squealed in terror. "Don't you dare!"

"It's just a little smoochy-smooch, Miss Hattie. There ain't no call to be getting yourself all riled."

"I have not given you permission to kiss me, Mr. Drayton."

If his scowl was any indication, Ancil was clearly displeased. "These days, a man don't need to ask permission," he said. "Everybody knows that courting couples kiss. Why, how else are they going to be able to tell if they like each other?"

"Prior to marriage, a kiss might be appropriate," Hattie said, her chin high. "However, I do not believe any dalliance at this point in our courtship is proper." Her words were as cold as icicles and had the desired effect.

Moving away, Ancil flicked the reins sharply. The horse immediately quickened its pace.

"At your *age*, Miss Hattie, I'm thinking you'd be better off trying to be pleasing than proper."

She turned to him, her mouth open in shock.

"You'd best do some thawing out," he added. "A bit of kissing ain't going to ruin you."

• • •

The moon came out from behind a cloud, making the white paint on the Turpin house glow with silvery highlights. Harmon Leege approached the house by the road, but before he reached the yard, he veered to the left, into the woods.

It was well after midnight, and not a lamp showed inside the house. As he quietly approached on the back side, his stealth disturbed neither the chickens in the nearby pen nor the lazy dog asleep on the back porch. He stopped underneath the huge elm tree on the south side of the house. Leaning against it, he watched the curtains of one second-story window wave lightly in the breeze. His stance was calmly determined and patient, as if he had been on this watch many times. Even in the anonymity of the darkness, he did not allow his expression to reveal his inner thoughts. He merely observed the tantalizing play of the curtains and cursed the fates for destroying what might have been.

Reed was not so bad. Harm had finally had to admit that. The time they'd spent together in Helena and working at Miss Hattie's place had taught him that the man was fair and could be trusted. The way he treated Miss Hattie was surely evidence that he would be neither cruel nor thoughtless as a husband. Even his sense of humor encouraged Harm. A man who was willing to enjoy the vagaries of life, rather than set himself against them, would find a pleasant future.

Harm's own future seemed infinitely more bleak. He had known from the time he was small enough to walk upright under the buckboard that he was "trash." Worthless white trash, not fit to consort with decent folks. Hearing it over and over, he'd come to accept it as a part of himself, like his hair and eye color. But that was before he'd known what acceptance meant, known what he would have to learn to live without.

He couldn't stop the sigh that blew through him like grief. He pushed away from the tree and turned to go, then he stopped. Like Lot's wife, he couldn't resist. He looked back and was lost. Cupping his hands around his mouth, he gave the call of the mockingbird, then waited. His eyes focused on the upper window, he gave the call again, and this time his message was answered.

A slim delicate hand whisked the curtains away, and Bessie

Jane Turpin looked down at him. Her hair was tousled from sleep, but her eyes were opened wide, revealing both surprise and fear. They stood staring at each other, able to see perfectly clearly, yet the distance between them was far more than could be measured in miles. They watched, waited. Finally, Harm turned, glanced back once, then walked into the night.

Eight

FROM the moment Reed put his plow to the earth, he knew he was right. The blade cut through the blue prairie grass and turned the topsoil, revealing water just inches below the surface. As he sliced through the thick layer, the disruption created a thick mud soup that was ideal for rice.

"This is it," he told Hattie. "If I had any doubts, they're all flying in the breeze this morning."

Monday had dawned warm and bright with just a hint of wind. Reed had been so anxious, he'd barely managed to gulp down his breakfast of grits and eggs. But he did take three biscuits with him before he hitched the mules to the plow.

As he headed out to the field, he chanced to look back. Hattie stood on the porch watching him go. She looked more than a little disappointed and very left out. "It's your rice field, Miss Hattie!" he called to her. "Don't you want to come down there with me? Watch the first cut in the soil?"

Her eyes lit up momentarily until discipline and good judgment overruled. "I've got chores to do yet this morning," she said. "I'll be down a little later."

Reed stopped and gazed at her, considering.

"I said I'd come down later!" she called more loudly, apparently assuming poor hearing had caused his hesitance.

Looking at the mules hitched to the plow and ready to go, he said to himself as much as to them, "It just wouldn't be right for Miss Hattie not to be there." He led the team to a shade tree and started back to the house.

"With both of us working," he said as he stepped up onto the porch, "we'll get through your chores in a gnat's age."

Hattie's smile spread delightfully across her face at his words, and was followed by laughter when he added, "But I am *not* milking that goat!"

"Guard your tongue, Reed Tyler," she said. "If you hurt Myrene's feelings, there'll be nothing but sour-milk biscuits for a month."

Reed said he'd take the hogs and chickens if Hattie milked Myrene and handled the house and garden.

Jerking her straw hat off the wall, Hattie bolted from the porch so quickly, she startled the goat. "Don't a one of you give me a lick of trouble this morning," she warned the occupants of the barnyard. "These are going to be the fastest chores ever done."

Reed laughed at her threats to the dumb farm creatures, but remembering his own remark to the mules, thought it best to refrain from comment.

Hattie showed she was as good as her word, gathering eggs and straining Myrene's milk with her usual efficiency. Like her partner, though, her mind was down at the rice field.

Within an hour the two were walking side by side, leading the team to the bluff. The sun wasn't yet hot, and Hattie carried her straw hat, letting the wind blow through the wisps of hair that had escaped the proper knot at the nape of her neck. With the sky a bright blue and the bees droning their sweet summer song, she felt as carefree as a girl. Reed's smile didn't hurt the situation one bit.

"Look at that cotton, Miss Hattie," he said, pointing to the fields as they passed. "It's already knee-high. I tell you, it's going to be a good year for farming."

"I suspect so," she said, then added with a mischievous smile, "but I'll always remember this year as the year we started the rice."

At first she stood at the side of the field and watched Reed follow the plow in mud up to his calves.

"Gee! Gee!" he called to the team repeatedly. Disliking the strange new experience of plowing in mud, the animals took direction only sporadically.

Listening to his constant commands and the slapping of the leather reins against recalcitrant rumps, Hattie quickly realized that leading the mules in this mud would be the right idea. She hitched her skirt up to the tops of her boots, tying a big knot in the excess to keep it out of the way, and waded down into the boggy bottom.

"Miss Hattie!" Disapproval vibrated in Reed's voice. "You get out in this, you'll have mud clean up to your eyeballs."

Grasping the lead on the cheek of the left mule, she retorted smugly, "It's my ground, Plowboy. If I'm thinking to take a bath in it, it's none of your concern."

Looking at her over the backs of the team, Reed raised an eyebrow. "You'd best be careful about calling names, *Plowwoman*. You're the one that's got that mule's lead."

She squinted her eyes in a mock threat. "Perhaps we'd better change places, then. I don't want you to be thinking you're the boss here."

He shook his head. "I think your choice shows you know just which end of these beasts a lady best attend to."

The plowing was not done in straight furrows for planting. The purpose was to break up the soil so that the levees could be built. The rice would grow in standing water, and in order to control the water, raised embankments would be built all around it. The going was slow, and the plow got bogged down in the slippery mud, further disturbing the animals.

By noon, Reed and Hattie were both tired, sore, and very dirty. Before attempting to eat the food they'd brought, they made their way to the river to wash off the worst of the mud.

Scrubbing his hands and arms, Reed glanced over at Hattie squatting beside him. The knot that had held her skirts out of the mud had ridden up slightly, and the knee of her white cotton drawers was clearly visible. Around the gathered flounce that covered the knee was a tiny trim of delicate pink rickrack. Reed's eyes honed in on that little piece of femininity, and he was startled at his reaction. Straightening abruptly, he wandered down the bank away from her, adjusting the fly on his trousers and mentally chastening himself.

It had been a good long time since he'd been with a woman, he thought. Not since that sad-sweet night with Bessie Jane.

Still, he was a man who generally maintained control of his baser nature. And surely at twenty and four, the sight of some old maid's underdrawers shouldn't have him sprouting like a cucumber in the middle of the day.

But, he admitted, Miss Hattie wasn't just some old maid. He'd never thought about her much in the past, but since Drayton had started to court her . . . well, he had started to look closely at her. He'd held her too, he reminded himself, thinking of her soft warmth and the sweet clean smell of her.

Reaching down, he jerked up a long sprig of Johnsongrass. With reflex motions from childhood memory, he held it between his thumbs, lifted it to his mouth, and blew across the edge of the blade. The shrill whistle distracted him from the strange feelings for Hattie that plagued him.

Hattie was like a sister to him, he assured himself. The fact that he was aware of her as a woman was just a combination of her new status as Ancil Drayton's lady-friend and his misdirected desire for Bessie Jane. He would simply have to be more careful about his urges. He sure didn't want to ruin a good friendship with Miss Hattie over a scrap of pink rickrack.

"I heard you whistling that Johnsongrass," she said, coming up behind him. "You calling for help or just making noise?"

He turned to look at her cheerful face, her big horsey smile. The knot in her skirt was gone and the fabric now flowed modestly to the tops of her mud-covered boots. "I guess I was just seeing if I could still do it," he said.

"It seems like a lifetime since I heard that sound."

He nodded. "It's because there aren't any children around here. Once you pass through those child things, it takes new little ones to remind you of them."

"I guess you're right," she said thoughtfully. "It's funny how the good Lord and nature take care of us. It's the cycle of life. Just when we're getting old enough to forget all about the fun and foolishness of play, we start having little ones of our own, who are close enough to the ground to see the simple joys of the earth."

Reed gazed at her with almost tender compassion, and she realized immediately why his expression bespoke pity. Despite the laws of nature, she still had no babies to conjure up such remembrances.

"I mean for most," she corrected herself hastily with studied nonchalance. "Not everyone wanders the same path."

Her smile was brave, but not totally convincing. Silence fell between them as they avoided each other's eyes.

"I'm about starved, Miss Hattie," Reed said at last, breaking the tension. "Why don't we get those dinner buckets and have us a feast."

They walked back along the shoreline, Hattie in front. She turned frequently to comment on the prolific tendencies of her laying hens and exclaiming about the exceptional quality of her new radishes.

Just before they reached the picnic spot under a low-hanging willow, she tripped on a root. She might have fallen, except for Reed's arm grasping her around the waist and pulling her against his side.

"Are you all right?" he asked, not letting go of her.

"Yes, I'm fine," she answered, though she did feel foolish. She was perfectly capable of standing on her own two feet, but for some reason, she wasn't eager for Reed to loose her.

She looked up into his eyes. Their cinnamon-brown color was only a tiny rim circling a deep blackness as he stared at her. She felt a peculiar pulsing inside her, as if her blood were suddenly electrified. Her gaze dropped to his lips, slightly parted as his breath rushed quickly through. A sudden startling desire to taste those lips assailed her, and she ran her tongue across her own lips in anticipation.

A choking sound forced itself from Reed's throat, and he released her immediately. "Be careful, Miss Hattie." His voice had a strained, distant quality.

"Yes, of course," she answered, not even aware of the drift of conversation.

"There's always something around here to trip you up." From Reed's tone, it was hard to tell if he was speaking to her or himself.

It was near dusk when Reed and Hattie brought the team back to the house. Both were disgracefully filthly—despite washing off in the river—incredibly tired, and foolishly happy. They separated at the barn, and Reed led the mules to the trough to water them for the night and clean the mud and grime from their hooves. As the mules drank, he watched Hattie continue on to the back porch. Myrene trotted up to her, and she gave the goat a friendly pat, but she didn't linger. Without even hanging up her hat, she grabbed the big copper bathtub leaning against the outer wall and carried it through the back door. Reed smiled, then turned his attention back to the mules.

Hattie couldn't remember ever having felt so grimy. She had washed off the best she could at the river, but after a full day in the muddy field, she was soaked to the skin. Her hair had partially dried and was caked to her head as if styled by a dirt dauber, and the smell and taste of mud assailed her senses. She pictured Reed and herself slipping and sliding in the thick black mud, often falling, and she couldn't help but smile. The residual dirt on her face cracked, which made it seem even funnier.

As she put the water on to heat, she found herself dwelling on the pleasantness of the day. From the moment Reed had agreed to help her with the chores to the parting at the barn that evening, it had been an adventure.

She set her hat on the counter. It was still damp and covered with the black dirt. After it dried, she thought, she could brush the worst of the soil out of it. It would never be quite the same, but she figured the fun was worth at least one old workhat.

Peeling off her mud-soaked clothes and putting them in the washtub for the morning, Hattie continued to think about all that had been said and done. She felt such a part of the rice now. When it succeeded, it would truly be her success as well as Reed's. She was inordinately pleased that she shared something with him. Every year when he sold the cotton and paid her her share, she was proud, but it wasn't her cotton. The money was hers by right, yet it didn't give her a feeling of accomplishment. She hadn't felt that with Reed since the summer her father had died. This year, she vowed, when that rice headed to the mill on a flatboat, it would be her achievement too.

By the time she was stripped to her camisole and drawers, the water was boiling. Protecting her hand with a pot holder she had knitted for her mother on some long-ago occasion, she carefully poured the steaming water into the tub. She added cold water from the pump by the bucketful until it was just the right temperature, then drew another kettle for rinse water. She put it on the stove and quickly discarded the last of her clothes. Modestly covering herself with her hands, she gratefully stepped into her bath.

With her knees up, she could lie back almost to her neck and feel the muscles in her back and shoulders relax. She closed her eyes and moaned with pure pleasure. She was warm. She was comfortable. She smiled languidly and thought of Reed.

Reed! Hattie sat up immediately as if the house were afire. What was she doing thinking about Reed? It was Ancil Drayton who was courting her. If she was going to sit in the bathtub and dream up fanciful thoughts, it should be Ancil Drayton who played the central role.

What nonsense, she thought, to be picturing Reed Tyler smiling down at her. Reed was like a brother, a younger brother. She'd known him since he was wiping his nose on his sleeve. She loved Reed, of course. She would never deny that. He was the closest thing to family that she had left. She wanted the very best for him. He'd have this land and a pretty little wife in Bessie Jane. Someday she'd bounce his children on her knee, and maybe they'd call her Aunt Hattie. But she could not, would not, have foolish schoolgirl daydreams about him.

Grabbing the washrag and soap, Hattie began scrubbing herself with a vengeance as her mind raced on. Reed was her best friend, her business partner. Getting skittish notions about him would be a disaster. What if he suspected? She stopped and covered her face with the washrag. If he thought she was pining after him, he would think her pitiful. He'd probably tell Bessie Jane how sorry he felt for his sad, besotted old-maid friend. And Bessie Jane would tell every living human in the county! Hattie's heart began palpitating with anxiety. She would die of humiliation! Just the idea had her face flaming with shame.

Trying to get hold of herself, she purposely slowed her fevered brain. She had to be calm and rational, she thought. Concentrating on taking deep healthy breaths, she washed herself thoroughly and systematically. There was no need to go off half-cocked. She simply needed to figure out what had happened and whether she had actually done anything stupid. If she had humiliated herself, she wanted to be the first one to know.

She mentally retraced her steps, carefully, methodically. She had not acted any differently that morning than usual. Reed didn't make her nervous, as Ancil did. She never had trouble talking to him or feeling relaxed in his company.

They had talked and worked together just like always. There had been those few strained moments at noon but nothing that would indicate any change in her relationship with Reed. Perhaps she shouldn't have drawn attention to her childless state, but it was a fact, and both of them knew it.

No, this day had been just like every other day, she assured herself. Then her brain focused on the instant when she'd tripped on the root. The memory of his arm around her waist and the intensity of his eyes was vivid. What had it meant? Had she revealed something, some inner longing of which she was unaware?

She sat up in the tub, resting her elbows on the rim and holding her chin in her hands. His arm had felt safe and pleasant around her waist. The memory of Ancil's arm in the same place popped up then, like a garden weed. Her brow furrowed as she compared the two episodes.

Reed's touch had made her feel warm, secure. She had not attempted to move away from him but had welcomed his strength. Ancil's touch had made her uncomfortable and wary. When he had tried to hold her close for longer than she liked, she had become very annoyed.

"Well, of course," she said aloud, a relieved smile brightening her expression. A brother's touch would make a woman feel protected. She wouldn't run from it or be fearful of it. But the touch of a man who was courting her . . . Well, a woman would feel a good deal different about that. Hattie knew enough about gentlemen to understand that the woman was supposed to be always on her guard in case his feelings got out of hand. Even with a man that she loved, a woman maintained a healthy distance. It was why all brides were nervous, she supposed. Courting was a strange and frightening experience to get through.

There was nothing frightening about Reed Tyler, though. He was no mystery to Hattie Colfax.

Lying back comfortably again, Hattie sighed. She was pleased with her insight. It was such a disadvantage to start courting at twenty-nine, she realized. Why, the girls Bessie Jane's age could talk about these things and figure out what their feelings were. If the courtship became really confusing, they could always go to their mothers or an aunt. Hattie couldn't confide in a soul—she'd feel like an utter fool. It was a little like putting up preserves without a recipe, she mused. She knew it would take sugar and cooking, but beyond that, she'd just have to find things out as she went along.

It was natural that she would think about Reed, she assured herself. She'd just spent a very pleasant day with him. He was charming and a fine looker too. A woman couldn't fail to notice that, even if he was practically her brother.

· · ·

Harmon had been in bed a little more than an hour when he heard the stumble on the porch, followed by a racking cough and the heaves of retching. Rolling out of bed, he grabbed the lantern that hung on a hook near the door and fumbled for the matches. When the lantern's light illuminated the dilapidated shack, the two rough cots, the worn table, and the two remaining spindle-back chairs that served as the furniture in the Leege household, Harm adjusted the wick and headed out onto the porch.

Raising the lantern high, he glanced around. "Pa? Where are you, Pa?"

A cough from the edge of the porch answered his question, and Harm went over to investigate. Jake Leege lay on the ground next to the house, not more than a foot from where he'd vomited.

Harm set the lantern on the porch and squatted down to help his father. "Come on, Pa. Let me get you inside."

"I'm sick," the old man said, his voice raw and hoarse from the fiery liquid he'd consumed.

"That stinking rotgut will make you sick,' Harm said, trying without success to get his father on his feet.

"Don't tell your mother I'm drunk again," Jake beseeched his son.

Harm ignored the statement. He'd never told his mother, not once. That hadn't kept her from knowing. It hadn't kept her from leaving, either. She'd just walked away and never looked back, fifteen years ago. Harm wondered what strange quirk of his father's whiskey-soaked mind always made him forget that she was gone.

Finally seeing that Jake was not going to walk into the house on his own power, Harm lifted his father as if he were a child and carried him into the shack. It wasn't much of a chore. His father, who had once been as big and muscled as Harmon, was now little more than skin stretched over brittle bones. He rarely bothered to eat, though Harm cooked every day. Each morsel had to be forced down his father's throat. Jake cared nothing for it. It was only whiskey he wanted. Whiskey was everything—wife, child, home, work. Whiskey was life.

"Where did you get the money, Pa?" Harm spoke softly, no hint of anger or threat in his voice.

Still, the old man looked nervous. "I'm sick," he repeated querulously.

"Did you steal from somebody, Pa? I got to know so I can pay for what you took so the law won't come get you."

Jake turned his head toward the wall, not willing to look his son in the eye. "I didn't steal from nobody."

"Then where did you get the money if you didn't steal it?" Harm asked, then immediately knew the answer. "You found my stash." His voice was flat with finality. Saving nearly every penny he got was almost a compulsion with Harm, just as spending every penny on drink was Jake's. Drunks were clever people; Harm knew that for a fact. He constantly had to move his money to new hiding places to keep it out of his father's hands. Sometimes, like now, even the most ingenious secrets were breached.

"Did you take it all?" he asked quietly.

Jake nodded. "I'm sorry, Harm." He began to cry. "I know you been saving that money to get away from here, to make something of yourself. I told myself I'd never take it. But I got me such a thirst yesterday morning, and I just kinda started looking around, and when I found it, well, I clean forgot that it was yourn, not mine."

Harm nodded and turned away. Walking to his bed, he doused the lantern, then lay down, flinging an arm across his eyes. He hoped to hell Miss Hattie's rice field panned out. They would dang sure need that money before winter.

"I'm sorry, Harm." The sound of his father's bitter, choking sobs filled the room. "I'm so sorry."

Harm barely listened. He'd heard these apologies before.

Nine

HATTIE was late for church, a calamity that rarely befell her. It was exhaustion and nothing less, she told herself. Making a rice field out of a piece of fallow ground was hard labor.

Harm had come the last three days to help with building the levees and leveling the field, but even with the two men doing most of the heavy work, Hattie had pushed her physical resources to the limit.

It had been worth it, though. The three sides of the field away from the bluff now had high embankments to trap the water. The largest of these, the levee on the river, had two fancy mechanized floodgates. They leveled the field by attaching two-by-fours to the grader and slowly smoothing them across the ground.

"Smooth as a pool table," Harm declared, complimenting his partner on his farming skill.

Reed had been buoyant and happy every day, constantly teasing both Hattie and Harmon, neither of whom could resist his good humor. For all the struggle and effort, Hattie wouldn't have traded the experience for anything. She couldn't remember when she had enjoyed herself more.

Arriving at church, she maneuvered her rig among the others.

There were no shady spots left, but the weather wasn't too warm yet, and there was just a bit of a breeze blowing.

She set the handbrake carefully, then took her parasol and handbag and stepped down from the buggy. As she walked toward the church, the singing of "Shall We Gather at the River" wafted through the windows. After checking the angle of her hat and smoothing down her skirts, Hattie opened the door as quietly as possible and slipped inside.

The congregation was on its feet for the hymn, and Ancil stood next to the aisle in the last pew on the left side. As if he had been waiting for her, he smiled and moved slightly aside, indicating she could join him in his pew.

The children, well scrubbed and wide-eyed, were all watching her. She nodded to them in what she hoped was a friendly fashion. It wasn't their fault their father was such a clodhopper.

Her gaze returned to Ancil, and she froze him like a masher, then calmly continued on toward the front of the church. The Colfaxes had always shared the second pew on the left with Milt Tuttle and his wife, right behind the preacher's family and Deacon Eschew. Hattie saw no reason for this morning to be any different.

She nodded at the Tuttles as she stepped into the pew, then glanced to her right. As usual, the Tylers took up the front three pews on the right side. Clive and Mary Tyler nodded to her. Reed was in the front pew with Bessie Jane and had apparently missed her entrance.

Not needing a hymnal, Hattie sang the final chorus in her strong alto as Marybeth Tyler, Reed's simpleminded younger sister, played the tune unerringly on the piano.

> "Yes, we'll gather at the river,
> The beautiful, the beautiful river.
> Gather with the saints at the river,
> That flows by the throne of God."

As the last strains of the music faded, Preacher Able rose from his seat behind the pulpit and nodded to Marybeth. The young woman twirled around on the piano stool, her proud smile precious in its honesty, as she jumped up. She joined her family in the first pew. The Tylers shifted, making room for her, and Reed draped his arm along the back of the pew behind Bessie Jane. As he did, his glance caught Hattie's. He smiled and mouthed, "You're late."

Hattie gave an almost imperceptible shrug in reply. Reed let his gaze wander to the back of the room toward Ancil, then looked back at her, raising his eyebrows meaningfully. His expression insinuated that Ancil Drayton might have precipitated her tardiness.

It was almost impossible for Hattie to resist Reed's teasing. Especially, she thought, when he was dressed up for Sunday. With his brawny masculinity cleverly disguised in a broadcloth coat and his thick black hair, usually controlled by his old straw hat, waving enticingly, he looked just about as handsome as Hattie had ever seen him. With a thrust of her chin, she managed to ignore him and turn her attention to the preacher.

Within a few minutes, though, her gaze was drawn unwillingly to the right. Reed was looking at the preacher, and she had a moment to study him. The sunlight shining through the window beyond him gave a glow to his lustrous hair, the back, she saw, beginning to creep over his collar. She had a sudden desire to reach over and stroke the errant black mane.

Reed would never attempt to take liberties with a woman as Ancil had, she told herself loftily. Reed would court with respect and would seek honesty, common goals, and love. Then, grudgingly, she conceded that this was one aspect of Reed's life she didn't know at all, one part of him that even as a close friend she could never share.

She had no idea about Reed's expectations of a wife. Surely he'd chosen Bessie Jane for her beauty and wit, but he'd never divulged to Hattie any tender feelings for her. Actually, more often than not he spoke about Bessie Jane's lack of knowledge about farm life. Her curiosity aroused, Hattie wondered how *their* courtship had proceeded.

As a woman unblessed with a pretty face, she always assumed that life for those with comely looks was easier. Perhaps it wasn't so. Prettiness might attract a man, but what was necessary to hold one? Of course, she mused, for a man like Reed a woman would be willing to do most anything. That thought flittered through her mind before she had a chance to guard against it. Forcing herself to concentrate on Preacher Able's sermon, she put such fancies behind her. The meaning of them did not bear close scrutiny.

•   •   •

Reed stopped the buggy near the cottonwood tree at the top of
Colfax Bluff and helped Bessie Jane down. The rice was so
important to him he had to share it with her.

"You won't believe how much we've done," he said excitedly. He looked out over the huge expanse of plowed acreage
and gestured with his arm. "Come this time next week, all of
this will be planted in Honduras Red, and Miss Hattie and I will
really be in the rice business." Pride resonated in his voice.
"This is just the beginning for us. Someday most of this farm
can be put in rice, and we'll be headed to the bank. Let the
other farmers worry about weevils and cotton prices. Rice is the
crop of the future."

Glancing back at Bessie Jane, Reed saw that she was not
admiring the black beauty of his well-designed field but was
staring off at something down near the river. Following her gaze,
he saw Harmon on the river levee, working on the pump. Cupping his hands around his mouth, Reed called Harm's name.
When the other man looked up, he waved an arm in a gesture
of welcome.

"Let's go down and see what he's doing," said Reed, reaching for Bessie Jane's hand.

She hesitated. "I'll just wait here."

His smile faded into annoyance, and he grasped her hand
firmly. "He is *my* friend, Bessie Jane," he said, assuming her
reticence was more of her ill-conceived concept of superiority.
"You will treat my friends with due respect, young lady. I will
not accept anything else."

His authoritive voice was so like her father's, she immediately obeyed and followed him down the tricky slope to the rice
field. As they gingerly made their way across the new levee,
Bessie Jane concentrated on putting one foot in front of the
other.

Harm had seen them coming. Reed and Bessie Jane together
was not an unusual sight, but he wasn't used to speaking to
them as a couple. Bessie Jane looked beautiful, he thought.
Dressed all in gauzy white, she was like an angel against the
dark background of Arkansas soil. The vision captivated him
even as he tried not to look at her, tried not to think about her,
tried not to allow a light-headed feeling overtake him and make
him say something foolish.

Why had he come here today? he asked himself. He should
have guessed Reed would bring her out to see what he was

doing. Why hadn't he had the sense to stay away? Well, it was too late now. He stood, wiping his hands on his trousers. He would not make a fool of himself or worse yet, embarrass or discomfit Bessie Jane.

"Don't you know Sunday is the day of rest?" Reed asked as they drew near.

Harm shrugged. He strove to keep his gaze on Reed and not look at the lovely young woman following him. "I just wanted to come out and have a look at things," he said as Reed stopped in front of him. "I guess you'll be planting next week."

Reed nodded, obviously pleased at the prospect, then turned to draw Bessie Jane up beside him. "Sweetheart, you remember Harmon Leege, don't you? Harm has furnished us with the pump and drawn up the plans for the levee system. He's a partner with Miss Hattie and me."

Bessie Jane was well aware of these facts, but having Reed related them forced her and Harm to acknowledge this new bond between them. She still had not looked at him, and Harmon felt protectiveness well up inside him. He held out his hand to her, determined to set a polite tone.

"It's nice to see you again, Miss Turpin." He smiled, first at Bessie Jane, then at Reed. "Miss Turpin and I were in grammar school together," he explained, as if that were the last time the two had met.

"Good afternoon, Harmon," she said in an even voice. "Reed has spoken well of the work you've done here."

Her formal words were off-putting, but Harm didn't fail to note that she still had not looked him in the eye. Was that how far she had gone? Was he now unworthy of even a glance?

"I came out here to show Bessie Jane how much we've done," Reed said. "I guess I've talked so much about this rice field, I just wanted her to see it."

Harmon nodded his understanding but couldn't help noticing that Bessie Jane continued to concentrate on the ground immediately around her shoes. She seemed to have not the slightest interest in the rice field.

"It's really taking shape," he said. "It's something you can be proud of, Reed. Even if you don't get one grain of rice to grow, just taking the chance is impressive."

"It'll grow, all right," Reed said with an easy smile. "This dirt was sent from heaven just for rice growing, I'm convinced of it."

Harm smiled at his little joke, and Reed glanced over at Bessie Jane to see if she was amused. She was studying her fingernails and had apparently not heard a word.

"I'm about done here," Harm said, making a couple of final adjustments on the pump. "I suspect I'd better head for home."

"We've brought a picnic lunch, Harm," said Reed. "Why don't you join us?"

Bessie Jane finally looked at him. Her head snapped up in surprise. Harm gazed into her eyes, her beautiful deep blue eyes, and saw stark terror.

"My pa's not well," he said. "I got to be getting back home to check on him."

Reed nodded, and Harm chanced one glance at Bessie Jane. Her relief was a tangible thing.

"I hope it's nothing serious," Reed said.

He shrugged. "He seems kind of off his feed these days. Guess he's just getting old."

Reed didn't press for details, and Harm was grateful not to have to give any. The drink seemed to be dragging his father down these days, but he didn't want to discuss that with Reed. Strangely, he did want to pour his heart out to Bessie Jane. She was beyond listening, though.

They walked with him down the levee to where he'd tied up his boat.

"Where'd you get this little bucket?" Reed asked, examining the small wooden craft.

"I traded for it down at St. Francis," Harm answered. "It was in pretty bad shape, but I put a little time and some new lumber in it. I take it out fishing most mornings."

"What do you catch?"

"Drum and carp mostly, but occasionally a channel cat. It ain't much, but it's pretty good eating."

"I haven't been fishing in a month of Sundays," Reed said wistfully. "Some morning you'll have to take me with you."

Harm stepped into the boat. "Sure," he said, wondering at the strange twist of fate that had made Reed Tyler the nearest thing to a friend he had in the county. Reed Tyler, who had all that Harmon wanted.

Reed helped to push the boat into the river, then watched Harm maneuver it with the paddle until it was headed downstream. Harm was a different kind of man, Reed thought, so private and brooding. When the younger man glanced back for a moment, Reed wondered at the intensity of his expression—until he turned and saw the pale face of the woman beside him.

Hattie invited Ancil to come over for pie after supper. Although she was not sure it was quite proper for the two of them to be alone, she knew that another Sunday meal with his children would not allow them an opportunity to talk. Plying him with her best strawberry pie couldn't help but smooth things between them.

True to her expectations, Ancil gobbled down his first slice of pie, then licked his lips, his fork. Fearing he might go after his plate, Hattie graciously served him seconds.

"You are a mighty fine cook, Miss Hattie," he said, smiling at her from across the table. "I've been hearing that about you for years, and now I can sure testify to it myself."

"Thank you, Mr. Drayton." She did not blush at the flattery. She knew she was a good cook, and she worked hard at it. Her mother had impressed upon her the importance of good food to a working man.

The silence grew between them, and Hattie was not sure exactly what she should say to break it. She looked over at him as she pondered the situation.

Ancil was slightly red-faced himself, as if ill at ease, but he managed to choke out a few words. "My Lula was a pretty fair cook, but with all those children and her being in the family way most of the time, she just kinda let things go."

Hattie nodded, thinking of Lula Drayton. For years she'd looked tired, even old. Maybe the work had been too much for her. Hattie would have thought her a hardy soul, but some of the most robust-looking women could be delicate.

"I ain't complaining about her," Ancil added quickly. "She was a right fine woman, and I feel real bad about her dying. I'm thinking the whole county thinks I worked her to death." His eyes were wide with distress. "I didn't, Miss Hattie, I swear it. I never pushed her or made a fuss about nothing, especially when she was carrying. I don't know why her heart give out like it did, but I never made her work when she weren't fit for it."

His confession touched Hattie deeply. She had never thought Ancil particularly sensitive or softhearted. Was it possible he could be a gentle and caring man? A wave of tenderness flowed through her, urging her to reach out to this poor tortured man who blamed himself for his wife's death. "Ancil, there has not been a word said against you," she said. "Everyone knew that you cared for Lula. No one blames you for her death."

"Mary Nell does."

Hattie's jaw dropped in surprise. "No, she doesn't. I'm sure you're mistaken." But she remembered vividly the anger and waspish behavior of his oldest child.

"It's the truth. She told me so herself. She told me not to expect her to kill herself to please me, the way her mama did."

"She's so young and so confused," Hattie said, generously defending the spiteful girl. "She doesn't know what she's saying. When children get that age, they just say things to hurt their parents. There is no rhyme or reason to it. You know that."

"No, I don't. I don't know nothing about raising younguns." He shifted in his chair, again uncomfortable. "My stepdaddy put me in the fields as soon as I was old enough to walk. The only time he ever paid me any mind was when he took a strap to me." He raised his chin up quickly, as if to counter any pity that might be forthcoming. "Not that it hurt me none," he went on gruffly. "It taught me how to work and how to take care of myself. I was no sugar-fed mama's boy. I was doing a man's full day when I was still in kneebritches."

Hattie nodded, thinking of Reed. He too had been working from childhood. It hadn't made him hard or unfeeling, though.

"Lula tried to teach me about being a father to my own, but I ain't no good at it."

Hattie impulsively reached across the table and laid her hand on his. "I understand, Ancil. I do truly."

As he stared at her, she drew her hand away, trying to bring her thoughts into words. "Sometimes the bad that happens to us," she said slowly, "is just as important as the good. You may not be the best father in the county, but you're a sight better than your stepdaddy, and your sons may be better than you. That's how it works, you know. Through the generations, easing out the choler in the blood."

"You think so?" Ancil's voice was surprisingly hopeful.

She nodded. "Your children are a fine bunch," she said truthfully.

"That's Lula's doing. She tried to give 'em love and manners and the like."

"But you've given to them what you could," Hattie insisted.

"You keep clothes on their backs and food on the table. That's a lot in itself."

Ancil looked down as if he couldn't agree with the excuse she was giving him. "You're a good woman, Hattie Colfax. Not just a good cook and good housekeeper. You're plainly a good person."

Hattie blushed at this. It was the kind of compliment that could never be taken for granted.

Rising from the table, Drayton reached for her hand. "I think there's a good-sized moon tonight," he said, leading her outside. "It's a shame we cain't see it."

The night was shrouded in a fog so thick it made everything seem close and stifling. They stood on the steps of the front porch, the light from the doorway shimmering around them.

Ancil turned to her. "Do you remember when we were kids, Hattie?" he asked, laughter in his voice.

"Of course," she said, wondering what he was getting at.

"Childhood, that's the best time of life. You know who you are and where you're going, and all the things that you want seem possible. Sometimes I'm jealous of my own younguns. They got all their lives ahead of them to do whatever they want. I don't know if I've got anything ahead of me."

She squeezed his hand. "You've got your next crop and the winter coming and heaven someday, just like the rest of us. Even more, you've got those children of yours to watch grow. You've done your best at raising them. You have cause to be proud."

"Children need love, Hattie," he said quietly. "I know that as well as you. And I think women are better at giving it than men."

"Not always," she said, thinking of her embittered mother.

"Maybe not, but for sure, most women could give it better than me."

"That's why you've decided to marry again so soon?" she asked. "To find someone to give love to your children?"

He shrugged. "That's part of it, for sure. I need a woman to work and to take care of the younguns. Everyone in the county agrees with that."

He looked at her, shifting from one foot to the other before continuing. "But that ain't the half of it, Miss Hattie." He stared out into the obscuring haze. "I need a woman of my own."

He dropped her hand and began to slide his arm around her waist. "Come eveningtime, a man cain't help but think how good it would feel to have a woman beside him."

Hattie stiffened as she felt his hand crawling along the small of her back. "Mr. Drayton, I don't think that you should—"

"Awhile ago, you was calling me Ancil," he interrupted, moving closer, intent on a kiss. "I like hearing you speak my name. It sounds kinda special comin' off your lips."

"I think I told you the other night—"

"You told me you don't want no sparking, that's true." He smiled down at her. "But I's thinking that you being innocent and all, you probably think you got to say that." His hand caressed her spine, and she jumped slightly at the unwelcome touch. "I won't be doubting your virtue, Miss Hattie, so there's no need for us not to satisfy our curiosity."

His lips swooped down to take hers, and Hattie swiftly turned her head away. "Ain't no need to tease me, honey," he said, his arm tightening around her. "I intend to get my kiss tonight."

Desperately, Hattie tried to pull away, but found herself held fast. "Let me go." Her tone was more plea than demand.

"Don't go all starched on me, woman," he said, hauling her up against the front of his body. "I ain't trying for nothin' but a little kiss. That's not much to ask for the man who's courting you."

"I don't like you holding me so close," she said, continuing to struggle against him.

"Well, to tell the truth," he said with a naughty chuckle deep in his throat, "all this squirming of yours, ma'am, I like it a bit too much."

She froze like a statue. "Mr. Drayton, I'd like to suggest that we go back in the house." Her voice was prim, demanding, and prudish.

The smile she received in reply was less than gentlemanly. "Miss Hattie, the only reason I can see for goin' back into that house is if you're inviting me to your bed."

With a gasp of mortification, Hattie began struggling again. When she sharply kicked his shin, he released her.

"Dammit, woman! I ain't stealing your virtue, just a kiss."

Hattie replied smartly, "Kisses, like all other favors, should be given freely. Only thieves try to steal."

Livid with rejection, Ancil puffed his cheeks out like a toad. Stomping back into the house, he retrieved his hat and slapped it on his head. As he stepped off the porch, he looked back at Hattie. " 'Kisses, like all other favors,' " he mimicked her angrily. "Kissing that toothy mouth of yours wouldn't *be* no favor. Hell, I'd rather kiss a mule!''

Harmon eased the last of the crawdad soup down his father's throat. The old man was not at all well, and Harm knew it wasn't just whiskey shakes. He was weak as a newborn calf, and although he claimed to be cold, he sweated profusely. As he laid his father back on the cot, Harm sighed heavily at the wreck of a man before him.

At forty-three, his father looked eighty. His formerly blond hair was thin and lifeless, hanging around his shoulder like a worn gray mop. The arms that had once hoisted Harmon into the air were now only bones with the hide on, their strength long drowned in a whiskey dream. His flesh hung with the same ill fit as his clothes, only his distended belly a mockery of his once robust health. His skin was yellow. It had started in his eyes, spreading to his fingers and toes. Now he was mostly yellow, the color of sickness, the color of death.

Harmon watched as the old man's eyes closed and he drifted into sleep where, his son hoped, he was happier.

Settling himself in a chair, Harm wished there was a place where he could be happier. He had dreams, of course, a million of them. Dreams of engines and motors and fancy black-glazed machinery. He'd design something unique, something modern and miraculous, something that would make him rich. On nights like this he'd dream about going off north somewhere, where there were modern factories and heavy-duty equipment, where his knowledge of mechanics would be useful, where folks had never heard of drunken Jake Leege or his worthless son. On his own, Harm was sure he could make it. Hadn't that trip to Helena proved it?

None of the Delta planters had known a thing about him except what they saw, and to a man they'd liked him. They'd actually liked him. It had been an experience not to be taken lightly. He'd said what he knew and asked questions about what he didn't understand, and those men had taken him for an equal.

"Because I am equal!" he said under his breath.

In his dreams of triumph he would go anywhere he wasn't known and make a success. He'd have money and respect and friends. Then he'd come back to town. Everybody in the county would turn out to see him, and all the young girls would swoon and sigh behind their hands. He'd return in triumph in a snappy new rig or maybe even one of those noisy little roadsters. He smiled to himself. *Imagine Bessie Jane's face if I drove up in one of those.*

He shook his head as if trying to discard the thought. When he came back, Bessie Jane would be married to Reed Tyler, the man who had turned out to be his friend. When he returned rich and worthy, Bessie Jane would be lost to him forever.

He glanced at his father. He couldn't go anyway. He could never run out on Jake the way his mother had. He would have to be there for him from now on. Harm knew that. That's why he hadn't left already. He wasn't free to go.

He doused the lamp, pushed open the screen door, and stepped out onto the porch. The fog was thick, oppressive, constricting. He wanted to get out, get away. To go someplace where he could breathe.

After one hesitant backward look into the shack, Harm jumped off the porch and loped down the path toward town. He didn't need a lantern to find his way. He'd traveled this route so many times, so many nights. He followed his heart, which led him unerringly to Arthur Turpin's big white house on the other end of town.

When he reached the foot of the giant elm, he gazed up at the curtains at the second-story window. In the dense fog he could barely make them out, but he knew they were there. She was there. He gave the call of the mockingbird and saw her face immediately at the window. She'd known he would come. She'd been waiting.

They stood looking at each other, both trying to read the other's thoughts and still the pounding of their blood.

"Go away!" Bessie Jane's hushed plea filtered down through the strange thickness in the night air.

She was right, Harm thought. A man with any sense at all would simply go away. He jumped to catch the first limb on the elm and pulled himself up. Using a familiar route, he climbed to her bedroom window. She watched him in silence, and on her face he saw dread warring with jubilation. When he reached her, standing on a limb that was a mere step from the window-sill, she seemed frozen, unable to speak.

"Shut the window, sweet Bess," he whispered. "Shut the window and go to bed. Forget that I came here tonight. Forget that I still want you."

"I can't," she said in a choked voice.

"I know." He stepped onto the windowsill, then sat down as her eyes seemed to devour him.

"Why did you come?" Bessie Jane asked, blinking back tears. She ached to reach out to him, touch him.

"I've come many times," he said. "Dozens of nights I've watched this window and dreamed of climbing that tree again."

She wiped away a stray tear and swallowed with difficulty.

"I want to come in, sweet Bess," he whispered. "Say that you've changed your mind, that you can't live without me. Break it off with Reed, and I'll take you in my arms again."

Her arms were trembling with the need to hold him, but she straightened her shoulders and stiffened her spine. "Nothing has changed, Harm," she said, ignoring the errant tears that continued down her cheeks. "Daddy still does not like you. He says you can't provide for me. If I married you, the whole town would be laughing up their sleeves. 'Bessie Jane and the junkman.' "

Harm's jaw tightened, and his lips thinned into one dangerous line. "Quit listening to your daddy, Bess, and listen to your heart." With effort, he softened his tone. He understood how frightened she was. He didn't know how he'd provide for her either, but he wanted to and was certain he could. "I've got no land, that's a fact. I live in a shack and have my father to care for. But I am the man you love."

Hearing the words out loud set Bessie Jane to trembling. She had fought against this so long, fought against the weakness in herself, the weakness for this man. She could not give in, not now, not ever. "I love Reed Tyler."

"You're lying, Bess. We don't need to argue that, we both know it." She opened her mouth as if to disagree, but he stopped her. "I've seen you together. He's fond of you, all right. He thinks you're sweet and pretty, but he doesn't love you. I don't know how you managed to get him to propose, but it wasn't 'cause he's in love. I don't think he even knows what love is."

"I can be a good wife to him," she insisted.

"Maybe, but you can never love him. You love me."

"No! The real world is not some romantic fantasy with brave knights and castles in the air. These days, a woman has to think of the practical things."

"Who's speaking now, Bess? Not the sweet girl I once knew. It sounds more like a tired old shopkeeper who sees life more in dollars and cents than hearts and flowers."

"My father only wants what's best for me."

"Reed has no more than me, Bess. He's a sharecropper for Miss Hattie. Sure he wants to make something of his life, but so do I. I have plans too. Would you listen to my plans? Share my dreams?"

"Reed comes from a good family," she said, as if by rote. "Good stock makes a good herd."

"You know nothing about herds, Bess," he said gently, knowing it was her father speaking, not herself. "Your daddy judges a man like he would a hog, but it's not the same. It's love a woman needs, and Reed Tyler can never love you like I do."

"He does love me!" she said angrily. "He loves me more than you can ever imagine."

"Then why isn't he here?"

"Because he has more respect for me than to risk my reputation."

"When a man and a woman love each other, reputation is an afterthought for the both of them." Reaching out to touch her face, he caught a tear on his finger and held it up to her. "Is this how happy your good reputation has made you?"

He laid the tear against his own cheek. "Sweet Bess, I would take your tears as my own for a lifetime."

"It can't work," she insisted. "We're too different."

"Different? Yes, but do you forget we are one?"

Her eyes widened. "Don't speak of that! You promised not to speak of it, ever."

"I don't speak of it, sweet Bess. But do you think on nights like this, nights like we've shared, I could forget how it was with us? What we've been to each other?"

Bessie Jane stiffened her resolve and hardened her heart. "What we have been to each other is two naughty children caught up in a game we didn't understand. I am a woman now. I will not sell my life so cheaply."

Carelessly flinging a hank of fine blond hair behind her shoudler, she continued with sudden disdain. "I want more for myself and my children than a dirty shack and a heritage of family disgrace. You have nothing else to offer me, Harmon Leege.''

"I have love, sweet Bess," he replied. "It's all I have, but it's worth more than all else you crave.''

"It's not enough." Her words were brusque, unyielding. "Now I would appreciate it if you would leave the premises and stay away for good. I'm to marry Reed in the fall, and I don't want the slightest rumor to besmirch my reputation.''

Harmon looked at her, his longing and frustration roiling into anger. He had loved her since they were children. No other woman had ever captured his heart. Her games and teasing had taunted him throughout adolescence, but their love had been worth every second of waiting, every unfulfilled ache of desire. Now she had thrown it away like soiled linens.

"I hope your reputation and respect will make you happy, Bess," he said in a cold voice, "because you are sending love away.''

With that, he slipped off her windowsill and vaulted down the tree, dropping to the ground. As he walked casually toward the woods, this time he didn't look back.

Ten

THE sound traveled strangely in the fog, not muffled or hushed but in little pockets of sound, as if on water. To Reed, as he walked to Miss Hattie's barn to check on the swollen knee of one of the mules, the sound was as distinct as if it came from his own head.

Immediately realizing that the woman weeping so mournfully was Hattie, he quickened his step, ultimately breaking into a run to get to her house.

Illuminated in the light from the doorway, Hattie sat on the front porch step, her arms crossed on her knees, her head on her arms, crying as if her heart were breaking. Standing beside her, like a friend offering solace, was the goat, Myrene, whose big-eyed expression was almost as dismal as Hattie's sobs.

Without hesitation, Reed walked up to the step and seated himself at Hattie's side.

She jumped, startled at the intrusion. "Reed!" she exclaimed, her voice raw from crying. Hastily she choked back the sobs and tried to wipe the telltale wetness from her face. "I didn't hear you come up."

"What's wrong, Miss Hattie?" He handed her a worn blue kerchief from his back pocket. "Has something happened?"

"Oh, no, nothing," she said. "I'm just being foolish." She attempted to laugh, but it failed when she couldn't stop the flow of tears from her eyes. "It's nothing really."

Reed was not an expert on crying women, but he'd seen his share, and without hesitation offered the only surefire cure he knew. Slipping his arm around her back, he pulled her to him, nudging her head down onto his shoulder. "Come on, Miss Hattie," he coaxed. "Tell me what's wrong."

His sympathy met with a new torrent of tears mixed with words as sorrowful as they were unintelligible. Reed rocked her back and forth, holding her close as she cried her misery into his shirtfront. He remembered another time when he had held her like this, the day her father was buried, but he didn't remember being aware of the softness of her body or the sweet smell of herbs in her hair.

As she quieted, he continued to hold her, rocking gently and humming a child's lullaby. It was a warm, comfortable moment encased in the privacy of the night fog. Innocent yet pleasurable.

It was Hattie who moved away first, as embarrassed by her contentment in his arms as she was by her loss of control. "I'm sorry, Reed, I—"

"Shhh," he interrupted, smiling at her with tenderness. "What are friends for but to hold you when you cry."

His sincerity was real, and Hattie looked away, timid in the face of it. He reached over and lightly grasped her chin, turning her back to him. "None of this hiding, now, Miss Hattie Colfax," he said. "You tell me what awful calamity brought you to such a sad state that it took me and Myrene both to dry your tears."

Hattie glanced from him to the goat, who now that the excitement had passed, was calmly nosing around in the tall grass near the porch. Trying to ignore his request, she shrugged and leaned forward to stroke Myrene's long silky neck. "It's so silly, it's not even worth telling."

"If it made you cry," Reed said, raising an eyebrow slightly, "it's worth telling."

Hattie hesitated, crumpling his blue handkerchief in her hands. Swallowing back the residual sorrow that still clogged her throat, she gave a halfhearted sigh. "Well, Mr. Drayton was here this evening," she began. With her attention focused on the handkerchief, she missed the hard expression that streaked across Reed's face.

"Was that son of a bitch fast with you?" he asked.

She jerked her head up, startled. "Reed! Your language."

"Damn my language! If that no-account laid a hand on you, Hattie, there won't be enough of him left to scrape up and bury!"

"Don't be ridiculous," she said. "It was nothing like that. I mean, nothing like that, exactly."

Reed gazed at her speculatively, not quite willing to let it go. "What do you mean, 'nothing like that exactly'?"

Hattie looked at everything around her, except Reed before finally replying with a slight cough to muffle her words. "He tried to kiss me."

Involuntarily, Reed's gaze dropped to the bodice of Hattie's thin summer gown. "Where?" he asked impulsively.

Following the imprudent direction of his eyes, Hattie gasped in shock. Not too casually, she crossed her arms over her chest. "On the mouth, of course," she whispered, mortified.

"Of course," Reed said immediately, silently cursing himself as twenty kinds of fool. Drayton had upset her, and he was making it worse.

They sat silently side by side, neither quite ready to look at the other. Taking a deep breath, Reed finally broke the spell. "So Drayton tried to kiss you, and you didn't like it," he said.

Hesitating over her answer, Hattie found herself not totally comfortable talking with Reed about her feelings.

"It wasn't that I didn't like it," she began.

"You liked it." It was a statement rather than a question, and its brusqueness surprised her.

"Well, no. I mean, well—" She broke off, disgusted by her missishness. "I don't know if I liked it or not. I didn't let him kiss me."

"Because you don't want to kiss him," Reed prompted, turning to face her.

"No." She sat up straight and tall with an air of independence. "I do want to kiss him, but I don't know how."

"What!"

"You heard exactly what I said," she replied, stiffening her resolve. "I wanted to kiss him, but I didn't know how."

Reed shook his head in disbelief. Carefully pulling one leg

up and draping his arm over his knee in a relaxed pose, he studied Hattie. "What are you talking about? There's no *how* in kissing. There's just kissing."

"That's easy for you to say," she said, obviously miffed. "You probably kiss Bessie Jane every week, and maybe even other girls before you were engaged to her."

Reed declined comment and adjusted his position until he was leaning against the porch pillar facing Hattie. He continued to study her, wondering why a kiss had caused her such distress. Unless . . . "Surely kissing today is not much different from when you were a schoolgirl."

Staring down at her hands as they continued to twist his handkerchief in knots, Hattie confirmed his suspicion with a shrug. "I never kissed anybody in school," she said quietly. "I've never kissed anyone, ever, except Mama and Daddy, and I know that's not the same."

He nodded. She chanced a look at him and felt herself blushing under his unrelenting regard.

Throughout the years of their friendship, Hattie had never cause to feel naive. She was older, after all, and Reed had always looked up to her. He respected her judgment and valued her ideas. Now she felt the sudden powerful need to explain herself, clarify her past, vindicate her lack of experience.

"You don't know how it was for me in school," she said. "You've always seen me as the older sister who knew what she was about. But I haven't always been that way."

His silence encouraged her to continue. "Living out here as an only child, I just didn't play much, didn't know much about other children and the kinds of games they enjoyed. When I went to school, I was frightened of the other children at first. They were so noisy and messy. Mama would have never put up with that, and I was afraid the teacher would be as angry as my mother would have been. So I stayed away from them. Since I was by myself most of the time, the other children began to tease me."

She looked quickly to see Reed's expression. It revealed nothing, and she gazed off into the obscurity of the fog, as if seeing the past. Reed steepled his hands together, touching his fingertips to his lips as he gazed intently at her. This frightened, lonely child was a Hattie he'd never known. She intrigued him.

"The other children made me the joke of the school," she went on. "For years, all a child had to do to get the admiration of the other children was to tie my pigtails to the back of my chair or paste the pages of my reader together."

She smiled slightly as if the nightmares of childhood were not wistful memories. "I grew out of it finally," she said with a hint of triumph. "By about ten or twelve, I was making friends and learning to get along. I was still a bit of a joke, but I made a place for myself." Her tone was more confident now. "I was very good in school, which pleased my teacher, and I tried to be the first one to make fun of myself so that no one else could. Most of the children liked me if it were just me and them. But when the group got together, I was still 'odd man out.' "

She shook her head as if tossing away the worst of the memories, then looked at the man beside her. "So you can see," she said, "I probably wouldn't have been the boys first choice as a sweetheart. And then, of course," she added vaguely, "there was the other."

"What 'other'?" he asked immediately.

She looked down, unable to hold his gaze. "My looks," she said quietly. Then she lifted her head, refusing to cower. "The young men didn't favor my looks."

Reed opened his mouth to say something, but no words came. He stared at her, his brain searching for the right words, the honest and allaying words, but they couldn't be found.

Painfully aware of his silence, Hattie focused once again on the handkerchief. She could feel Reed's eyes upon her and fought the desire to jump up and run.

"There is nothing wrong with your looks," he said finally. His tone was matter-of-fact, as if to emphasize the truthfulness of his conclusion.

"You're sweet," she said, easily disregarding his statement. "But you see me through the eyes of a friend, or a brother." Not wishing to prompt him to further undeserved compliments, she hurried on, struggling to explain. "You may not believe this, but when I was a young girl, the boys had a name for me." She swallowed hard, screwing up her courage to reveal a truth she'd spent a good deal of time ignoring. "The boys called me . . . they called me Horseface Hattie."

Years of pride and success couldn't completely override the remembered pain of childhood. As Hattie heard her own words, her bottom lip trembled, and the tears she had so carefully controlled filled her eyes once more.

Reed watched her emotional struggle as the echo of her words rang in his ears. He could hear the cruel name on Bessie Jane's lips, and instinctively he reached out to take Hattie in his arms and comfort her. "Shh . . . Hattie, no," he whispered into her hair.

"It's true," she said, her voice muffled against his chest as her tears dampened his shirtfront again. "No man in the county would ever look twice at Horseface Hattie."

"Don't say that, Hattie," he admonished her tenderly. "Boys are cruel and stupid, but that was a long time ago."

"Not so long as I thought," she said. "The other day, Ancil was talking about when we were children, about the rotten jokes they used to play on me. He was one of the ones who always called me that. I remember his face as he said it to me. I remember it so clearly, it hurts me still."

Tightening his arms around her, Reed would have held her all night if need be, but Hattie pulled away from him, wiping her eyes with the much abused kerchief.

"So Drayton needed a lesson in manners," he said, "preferably applied with a razor strop. So did most boys at his age. But he's changed his tune these days. Now he's wanting to court you and trying to kiss you. He's forgotten all about his childish teasing, and you should too."

With a shrug meant to imply more nonchalance than it did, Hattie admitted it might be true. "But the thing is, Reed, I remember. I know how it was, and I don't want to be humiliated again."

"You think Drayton would try to humiliate you?"

"No, I don't think he would try. But I'm afraid I might humiliate myself."

Reed smiled, unable to imagine sensible, practical Hattie Colfax making a fool of herself. "You could never do that," he told her with certainty.

"Oh yes, I could," she insisted. "Maybe I already have. You should have seen his face when I refused to kiss him."

Waving her concern away, Reed didn't question his pleasure at Drayton's lack of success. "Plenty of women make a man wait for a kiss. It won't hurt him a bit.

Hattie smiled at his protective attitude. "But how long can I make him wait? If he continues to court me, sooner or later I'll have to kiss him. And when I do, he'll know I've never been kissed before."

"What's wrong with that?" His voice softened with sincerity. "Most men would be honored to be a woman's first kiss."

"Maybe I don't want to 'honor' him."

Reed leaned forward genuinely intrigued. "I don't understand."

"When he realizes that nobody has ever kissed me, it will just remind him that I'm Horseface Hattie, the woman nobody wanted."

Reed frowned. "Don't call yourself that name. I hate it, and I don't want to hear it."

"No more than me," she replied curtly. "But it's not so much the name anymore as what it represents."

"It represents a passel of rude children that needed a switch taken to them. Children are so cruel, Hattie. It doesn't mean anything."

"I've got a mirror, Reed, I know exactly what they were talking about."

He touched her chin, turning her face toward him. "What do you see in that mirror, Hattie?" he asked softly. "I see a kind, loving face with a strong jaw and a big smile. It's a good face, Hattie, with the right number of eyes and noses."

She pulled out of his grasp pridefully. "I'm not fishing for compliments, Reed. I've lived in this face for twenty-nine years, and truth to tell, I'm kind of used to it."

"Then what is it?"

"I'm not sure," she said. "I was always shy with the boys when I was young, because I knew they thought I wasn't pretty. But now that Ancil and I are both older, both farmers, both a little bit work-hardened, we're more equal. I still get a little shy and nervous around him, but I don't let him impress me, and I don't feel the need to try to impress him."

"You don't need to *try* to impress him, Hattie. You outfarm the man seven days a week."

She was pleased with this compliment but didn't dwell on it. "I'm afraid I'll lose that equal footing. And if I did, I'd never be able to get it back. I don't want a man who thinks he's doing me a favor."

"And you think your lack of kissing experience is going to make that happen?" Reed asked.

"It's just not fair for a grown woman to have to act like a schoolgirl," she said with a sigh of disgust. "I should have learned all about this years ago, like everyone else my age."

Reed couldn't help smiling at her seriousness about her predicament. "Kissing is not really such an amazing thing, Hattie. And there is nothing difficult about it."

"That's easy for you to say."

"It's easy for you to say too," he teased. "Say it. 'Kissing is easy.' "

"That's ridiculous. I'm not going to say that."

"Say it!" He grabbed her hands, retrieving his bedraggled handkerchief in the process.

"No." She was giggling now.

"Say it."

"Oh, for heaven's sake, all right. Kissing is easy."

"Very good. You sound just like a woman of the world."

"Oh, hush up," she snapped with mock fury. She started to move away but found that he had not yet relinquished her hands.

"Now," he said with a modicum of solemnity, "there are a few facts about kissing, which is very easy, that every woman should know."

"What kinds of facts?" she asked suspiciously.

"Just a few facts. Nothing very secret."

"Okay."

"First off, kissing is like plowing, or, well . . . maybe planting, or . . . sewing."

"Sewing? What are you talking about?"

"I'm talking about kissing. In kissing, as in plowing or sewing, you just have to get an idea about how to do it and then do it. The first time you plow a row, it may not be as straight as the hundredth time, but it's still plowed, and if you don't like it, you can do it again."

"I may not know anything about kissing, Reed Tyler, but I'm no fool. How can you take a kiss back and do it over?"

"But that's exactly what you do," he claimed. "You practice it until you get it exactly like you want it."

"What about the other person? What's he supposed to do while I'm practicing?"

Reed's eyes sparkled with mischief. "I suspect he'll be enjoying it some." At Hattie's blush, he added, "And remember, he'll be practicing himself. Kissing is not a one-person job. It's like working a lumber saw. You got to have someone else on the other end."

"Plowing? Lumber saws?" Hattie laughed out loud this time. "Leave it to a man to mix romance and farm equipment! This is the most ridiculous nonsense I've ever heard."

"That's because nobody's ever explained anything to you about kissing."

"All right, explain to me about kissing."

"There are three kinds of kisses."

"Right," she said skeptically. "Don't tell me, they're called hook, line, and sinker."

"That's fishing. This is kissing. I know a lot about both, and if you want to know what I know, listen up and mind your manners."

He'd released her hands, and she folded them primly in her lap, sitting up straight like a good pupil. Her expression was still patently skeptical, though. "Okay, three kinds of kisses," she repeated, as if trying to remember.

"There's the peck, the peach, and the malvalva."

Hattie didn't bother to control her giggle. "The mal-whata?"

"Malvalva. But we haven't got to that one yet."

"And with luck, we never will. This is pure silliness," she declared.

"You admitted yourself that you know nothing about kissing," Reed said. "It's easy, but you've got to learn the basics."

"I'm all ears."

"Ears are good, but I think we ought to start with lips."

"Reed!"

There was laughter in his eyes as a flush colored her face, but he continued his discourse matter-of-factly, as if he were explaining a new farming method. "Okay, the peck is the most common kiss. It's the kind you're already familiar with. That's what you gave your folks and such. You just purse your lips together and make a little pop sound, like this." He demonstrated several times, his lips pursing together seductively, then releasing a little kiss to the air.

Hattie found the sight strangely titillating. "Okay, I see what you mean," she said.

"Show me," he instructed.

She made several kisses in the air while Reed inspected her style. "I feel like an idiot!" she exclaimed after a moment. "I must look so silly."

"Well," he admitted, "kissing the air is a little silly. But when it's against your sweetheart's lips, it doesn't feel silly at all."

She made several more self-conscious attempts as he watched her lips. "Is this the way?" she asked.

"I think you'll do fine with that." He shifted his position a bit and looked past her for a moment. "That's a good first kiss

for someone like Drayton,'' he said seriously, then grinned.
''Don't let him get the good stuff until later.''

She opened her mouth to protest, but he cut her short. ''Now,
the second kind of kiss is called a peach. It's a bit different
from the peck.'' He reached out and grasped her shoulders,
scooting her a little closer. ''This is the one that lovers use a
lot.''

''Why do they call it a peach?'' she asked curiously.

His smile was warm and lazy. '' 'Cause it's so sweet and
juicy.''

''Juicy?'' she repeated worriedly.

''Just a little. First, open your mouth a little, about this
wide.'' He demonstrated.

''Open my mouth?''

''Yes, just a little. So you can taste the other person.''

''Taste?''

''Just a little. Try it.''

She held her lips open as he'd shown her. He nodded encouragement. ''That's about right,'' he said. ''Now you need to suck
a bit.''

''Suck?''

''Just a bit.''

She shook her head, waving away the whole suggestion.
''This is ridiculous, Reed. I can't do it.''

He slid closer to her. ''It only feels ridiculous because you're
doing it without a partner. Here . . .'' He again grasped her
shoulders and pulled her near. ''Try it on me. You won't feel
nearly as silly, and it'll give you some practice.''

''You want me to kiss you?''

''Just for practice. Open your mouth again.''

She did as she was told, her eyes wide in surprise. Reed
lowered his head toward hers, his lips also parted invitingly.
''When I get close like this,'' he said, his breath warm on her
cheek, ''you turn your head a little.''

''Why?''

''So we won't bump noses.''

Following his lead, she angled her head. ''That's right. Perfect,'' he whispered the instant before his lips touched hers.

It was a gentle touch, and only a touch, before he moved
back slightly. ''Don't forget to suck,'' he murmured.

''Suck.''

''Like a peach.''

"Like a peach."

Then his mouth was on hers again. She felt the tenderness of his lips and the insistent pressure of the vacuum they created. She did as he'd instructed, her mouth gently pulling at his. A little angle, a little suction, a little juicy, and very, very warm.

"What do you think?" he whispered against her mouth.

"Nice" was all she got out before he continued his instruction.

They pulled apart finally, and Hattie opened her eyes in wonder. The blood was pounding in her veins. Staring at Reed, she saw mirrored on his face the same pleased confusion she felt. "I did it right?" she asked, but she knew the answer already. Kissing might be new to her, but it was impossible not to believe that what she felt was exactly why courting couples were always looking for a moment of privacy.

"Yes," Reed answered. He slid his arms around her back and pulled her more firmly against his chest. "Do you think you can do it again?"

This time when their lips met, Hattie was confident and curious. She ran her hands across his strong shoulders, then wrapped her arms around his neck, pressing herself to him. Inexplicably, her nipples had hardened, as if from the cold, and somehow she'd known they'd feel better against his chest.

Reed felt the eager little nubbins and moaned deep in his throat. He was turgid and eager against her. She felt so good, so soft, so sweet, so right. He intensified the kiss, then opened his legs, wanting to pull her against his aching erection.

"Oh, Hattie," he whispered, and the sound of her name on his lips reminded him of who she was. He immediately released her and slid back slightly. Her lips were still open, inviting, and her eyes were wide with innocence and desire.

Choking down his own need, he cursed himself. This was not the woman he was sworn to marry. This was Miss Hattie, his best friend and business partner. "I think you've got the hang of it," he said, readjusting his legs to hide the effect she'd had on him. "You have a lot of natural talent."

Smiling and pleased at what she took for a compliment, Hattie nervously straightened her hair as she allowed her breathing to return to normal. "Do you really think so?" she asked finally, with careful nonchalance.

He nodded, and she asked another question, "You don't think Ancil will find my peach lacking?"

Reed's mouth thinned into a stern line. "I think the peck will do nicely for Drayton for a while, Hattie. And I doubt he will ever find anything amiss."

She giggled, delighted as a child. "You're just like a brother, saying I should only give him a peck. I've already figured out that the peck is for your maiden aunt. For the man who courts you, it's the peach every time."

"That's not so. Actually, you use the peck a lot."

Hattie shook her head in disbelief. "I wouldn't. Why would you ever peck when you can peach!"

"You do both," he said. "You mix your pecks with peaches, so you get all different kinds of textures and feelings."

To the surprise of them both, Hattie leaned toward him, her hand trembling as she touched his cheek. "Show me," she whispered.

Their mouths met with practiced perfection. The peach was hot this time, hot and juicy and illicit. Reed added pecks to the side of her mouth, her eyes, her throat, returning again and again for more peaches. As their bodies pressed together, his blood was pounding with a furious insistence. He eased his chest from left to right to feel her nipples rub against him. Needing, wanting, he heard the tiny cries deep in her throat. Answering them, he thrust his tongue into her mouth.

"*Oh!*" With a cry of surprise, Hattie pulled back. She hadn't expected the wild intrusion of his tongue or the desires it provoked.

Reed sat beside her, his lust overriding his common sense as he watched the rapid rise and fall of her bosom. Of its own volition, his hand lifted and cupped her breast. Her firm warm flesh filled his hand, and he felt the hardened nipple against his palm.

Hattie only looked at him, and in the bright glow of the doorway light, she was beautiful. Her eyes were wide and anxious, but she was not afraid. She trusted him. He could see it in her face, and at that moment, he was not a man to be trusted.

"Dammit, Hattie. Slap my face!"

She did. Bringing her right hand up, she struck him a stinging blow. The hand that had so tenderly caressed her breast now covered his cheek. Stunned by what they had both done, she turned away from him. They sat silently, staring into the foggy cocoon that surrounded them and trying to adjust to the abrupt change in their long friendship.

Hattie spoke finally, her voice firm and controlled. She would not allow herself the luxury of embarrassment. "Was that the third kind of kiss, Reed? When you put your tongue—"

"Yes," he interrupted, not wanting her to describe it further. "It's a lover's kiss, Hattie. Not one for courting. Certainly not one from a friend."

She nodded, still not looking at him.

"I just want to tell you how—" he began, but she cut him off with a gesture.

"I think it's best that we not speak of it again, Reed. Thank you for teaching me about kissing." She stood up to go into the house.

When he spoke her name, she finally looked back at him. "You are a very sweet and desirable woman, Hattie," he said, his voice as gentle as a caress. "Please don't let Drayton take advantage of your innocence."

Gazing at him for a moment, she tried to memorize how he looked, as if she would save the image for a lifetime. "I've also learned how to slap a man's face," she said quietly. "Good night, Reed."

Eleven

HATTIE plucked a ripe red tomato from the vine and set it carefully in her basket. Her garden was doing exceptionally well, and if its growth was indicative of that of the field crops, this was going to be a good year.

At the end of the last row, she turned back to survey her work. After pulling out one stray weed, she declared her gardening done and headed back to the house. As she walked, she glanced around the fields, unconsciously looking for Reed. Earlier that morning he'd been chopping cotton on the lower ridge, but he was nowhere in sight now. She felt a pull of disappointment and immediately chastised herself. After her behavior last Sunday evening, she had absolutely no business thinking about Reed Tyler.

However, telling herself not to think about Reed and what had happened and not thinking about what happened were two entirely different things.

The week had been a hectic one, and both she and Reed had been busy. He'd shown up at breakfast Monday morning as usual and hadn't mentioned a word about the kissing lesson. She in turn had shown up at the rice field to help sow the seed and studiously avoided any subject but farming.

Reed had wanted to drill the seed instead of broadcasting it, in the hope that the birds would be cheated out of their share. It took more time, but Hattie was willing to help. She hoped the familiarity of working together would erase the disquiet that had sprung up between them. It did, and as the week passed, they slowly recovered their lighthearted working relationship. They went on just as before, Hattie told herself, but occasionally she was weak enough to remember the fire in his kiss and the warmth of his hand on her breast.

As quickly as the thoughts returned, she shook them away. She'd been invited by Preacher Able and Millie for dominoes again that night, and of course they had included Mr. Drayton. He would be driving her in her buggy. Anticipating some time alone with him, she imagined how different this evening would be. She wouldn't have to run like a scared rabbit when he tried to kiss her. Smiling to herself, she wondered what the kiss would be like. If she could make a man like Reed tremble, she thought, she had no cause to be apprehensive about Ancil Drayton.

She would never have admitted it to anyone save her confessor, but she'd found kissing an activity entirely to her liking. It was downright scandalous for an aging spinster to think that way, but Hattie knew the truth when she saw it.

She untied her work bonnet and hung it on the nail just inside the kitchen door. After carefully setting her tomatoes bottomside-up on the windowsill, she checked the chicken stew simmering on the stove. Reed had told her Harmon's father was sick, and she'd decided to drop off a healing chicken broth for him on her way to the Jessups'. Most folks had no use for Jake Leege, but Hattie had already decided that a man who had fathered a fine boy like Harm must have plenty of good inside.

Harmon had been out several times to check on the pumps at the rice field. Hattie had been favorably impressed by his ability and his manners. "Where'd you learn how to work on these motors and such?" she'd asked him one day.

He shrugged his broad shoulders. "I don't know, really. I'm just kinda curious about the way things work. Machines pretty much work like they're supposed to. It's just common sense putting them together."

"Seems like uncommon sense to me," Hattie told him. "All these little gears and belts and the like. I expect there aren't many men who have an understanding about them the way you have."

The handsome young man actually blushed at the compliment. "It ain't really nothing," he insisted. "I don't know a blasted thing about farming."

"Not everybody's supposed to be a farmer," she said. "And thank the Lord for that. It's differences in folks that keeps life from boring us to death."

He laughed, and Hattie couldn't help but notice the perfection of his smile and the rough masculinity of his laughter. This young man was a heartbreaker, she thought. She suspected half the girls in town secretly swooned over his smile. "How come a hardworking man like you isn't married?" she asked, teasing him.

To her surprise, the smile was immediately wiped off his face. "I'm not the marrying kind," he said.

His voice was so curt, Hattie suspected there was more to it than that. "When the right girl comes along," she said lightly, "all men are the marrying kind."

If possible, Harm's expression became even more bleak. "Sometimes," he said quietly, "the right girl is looking for something other than what the man's got to offer."

Hattie nodded her understanding, feeling an affinity with Harmon. Being judged on things you couldn't control was the cruelest fate.

Thankful for the slight breeze outside his father's barn, Reed set up sawhorses and carefully used a chalk string to measure a couple of two-by-fours. His father came out of the barn and stared curiously at him.

"What are you putting together there?" Clive asked.

"It's a swing for Miss Hattie's porch," Reed replied.

As he picked up the saw and set the blade against the mark he'd made, his father added the weight of his foot to the far end of the board. "That's real nice of you to take the time, son," he said as Reed began sawing. "But knowing Miss Hattie's pride, I'd be thinking she would have paid a carpenter to build her a swing if she'd been wanting one."

Reed flushed slightly at the truth of his father's observation. "She didn't ask me to build it," he admitted. "It's a present."

Clive's eyebrows rose, but he made no comment.

Though he didn't want to examine his motive too closely, Reed still felt a strong need to explain himself. "It's a courting swing. If she's going to be sitting out on the porch with a beau, it had best be the most uncomfortable seating arrangement in town!"

His father laughed. "I remember feeling that way when the boys started coming out here to see Emma." He looked more closely at his son and added speculatively, "When did you become Miss Hattie's guardian?"

"It's just that now she's being courted . . . ," he began clumsily. "I know if her father were alive . . ." With a sigh of self-disgust, he turned to his father and said almost angrily, "Drayton comes out to her place to see her without a chaperone within five miles!"

His son's disapproval was so vehement that Clive had to chuckle. "I can't seem to recall any complaints from you about lack of chaperones when you go courting," he teased.

"This is entirely different," Reed said. "Miss Hattie is no match for Ancil Drayton. It's like a wolf paying call on the lamb."

"That tends to be the way it is between a man and a woman," Clive said as he helped Reed match the cut boards. "He chases her till she catches him, is how your mama says it."

Reed wasn't reassured. "The differences between those two aren't like the usual. Drayton's got seven children, and Hattie might as well be a green girl."

Watching his son pound nails with a vengeance, Clive speculated on Reed's feelings. "Hattie may not be worldly," he said after a minute, "but she's not ignorant. She's quick-witted and practical. If you're thinking that Drayton's intentions aren't what they should be, I'd say you're dead wrong."

"Drayton is a lazy, slipshod excuse for a farmer!"

Clive grunted. "I have to agree with you there, son. I've known Ancil all his life, and I wouldn't give two cents for any piece of land he's held for more than a season." Before his son could feel justified in his disapproval, Clive added, "But I do think he intends to marry Miss Hattie. I don't think he's courting her to make her fast and loose. There are plenty of flashy skirts around both younger and prettier if that was what he wanted."

Reed pounded the last nail in with a burst of fury. "There is absolutely nothing wrong with the way Miss Hattie looks," he said. "She's got nice thick hair that kind of glows in the sunshine. Her eyes just light up like sparklers, and she's always smiling. Her waist's small, and any fool can see that she's plenty curvy—and it ain't from starching the ruffles on her camisole!"

The elder Tyler rocked back on his heels and studied his son. "It seems she was pretty enough to catch your eye," he said.

Embarrassed at his father's canny observation, Reed turned back to his work. "She's like a sister to me," he said. "You know I'm not interested in her that way."

"I know that she's been a friend of yours for a lot of years," Clive said. "And I also know that you never gave a thought about the courting of your sisters. You sound almost as jealous as protective."

Reed's head jerked up at his father's words. "Pa, you know that Bessie Jane is going to be my wife. I'm not the kind of man who'd be false to his betrothed." Yet as the memory of Hattie's face in the shadowy fog skittered across his vision and he saw again her eagerly parted lips and felt the warm firmness of her breast in his hand, Reed paused, angry at his own duplicity.

For days the remembrance of his vile behavior had stalked him. Hattie had been hurt and vulnerable that night. She had trusted him as a friend, and he had allowed his baser nature to override decency and good sense. Still, he couldn't quite bring himself to wish it hadn't happened. No kisses had ever been so sweet, no innocence so appealing.

Clive Tyler didn't miss the swiftly changing expressions on his son's face but thought better of questioning him about it. "You and Hattie have been friends for a good long while," he said. "It wouldn't be against nature for that friendship to deepen. Hattie would make a good wife for a farmer. It's not strange you should notice that."

Reed shook his head. He forced himself to think not of Hattie's kisses but of Bessie Jane's tears the night he'd spent his passion inside her. "Bessie Jane and I are to be married in the fall," he said adamantly. "Do you think I should forget that?"

"I don't think you'd play Bessie Jane false," his father said. "I do know that every man may have occasion to notice another woman. Once you're married, you just ignore it and go on with your life. When you're still single, a man would be a fool not to at least ask himself what it is that got his attention."

"I'm already as good as married," Reed said. "I've made

a promise, and I intend to keep it. Besides," he added, attempting humor, "I've got trouble enough with one stubborn woman. Two would put me in an early grave!"

Clive laughed, as his son had intended, but he couldn't quite forget the expression on Reed's face.

The Jessup parsonage was only a stone's throw from the church. Preacher Able, like his congregation, was a farmer. It was all good and well to have a church for Sunday morning, but a man's family had to eat.

Seated in the fancy parlor, Ancil contrived to have the couples play bridge or Parcheesi, hoping to change his luck. He was sure that losing at dominoes was not helping him impress Miss Hattie.

The reverend would have none of it, however. "Don't even suggest such a thing, Ancil," he said emphatically. "Games with cards or dice are the devil's handiwork."

Watching Ancil shift uncomfortably, Hattie hurriedly changed the subject. "Preacher Able, I think you should make a point to go by and see Jake Leege. He is not looking well at all."

"Where did you see Jake Leege?" Millie asked, astounded that her friend would take note of such a derelict.

"I had Ancil drive me over to his place," Hattie explained. When the preacher and his wife looked at Ancil, he shrugged, indicating the excursion had not been his idea.

"The man is turning yellow," Hattie said in a horrified whisper. "I've never seen such a thing in my life. His skin looks like a summer squash."

"My heaven!" Millie exclaimed. "Do you think it's contagious? I've heard tell of yellow fever down in the bayous. Do you think it's that?"

Hattie shook her head. "Harmon says it's from the whiskey he drinks. It stirs up the biles in his system, and they just give him the jaundice."

"Leege is a sad case, for sure," Preacher Able said. "He's been a slave to corn liquor nearly his whole life."

"Well," said Ancil, "if the old man is turned yellow, his days of slavery are about over." He glanced at Hattie and offered an offhand explanation. "My stepdaddy drank himself to death. He turned yellow before the end. It was a sight to see, I remember."

Shuddering at the thought, Hattie gave Ancil a comforting smile, reminding herself that his life, too, had been difficult.

"I don't understand how you got interested in Jake Leege," Millie said. "I almost never see him myself."

"I really didn't get interested in Jake," Hattie admitted. "But his son, Harmon, is working with Reed on the irrigation for the rice field."

Ancil gave a slight snort of laughter. "Have you been out to see Miss Hattie's experiment in agriculture, Preacher Able?"

"No, I can't say as I have," the preacher answered, and smiled at Hattie. "I have heard talk all over town that you and Reed have got it into your heads to grow a patch of rice."

Before Hattie could reply, Ancil said, "A patch of trouble is what they're about to grow. I tried to tell Hattie not to let that boy talk her into such nonsense, but you know how partial she is to him."

"It's not a patch of trouble," Hattie replied evenly. "Actually, rice is much easier to grow than cotton. There isn't all that chopping and picking. All that's really required is a constant and dependable water source."

Ancil shook his head disparagingly. "It does take water. Preacher, they flood those fields and keep that water standing inches deep all summer." At Drayton's words, the preacher looked askance. "What they'll most likely grow," Ancil continued, "is the biggest crop of mosquitoes this county has ever seen."

Hattie felt her temper rise at Ancil's criticism and the preacher's nod of concurrence. "Rice is the future," she declared. "Look at all the land around here that's too wet for cotton. Unless we find a way to get some use out of that land, most of our young people are going to have to move west to farm. There are acres and acres here that are just going to waste."

Preacher Able admitted that was true, but Ancil had another solution. "We've got to drain that land," he said with certainty. "In the next ten years, the government is sure to come in here with one of those drainage projects and get us all fixed up."

"We don't need it drained," Hattie said with just as much certainty. "That's not good for the ground. We just need to control the water."

Ancil smiled tolerantly and patted Hattie's hand. "I do admire a woman that takes an interest in the crops. But cotton is still king in the South, and I think most of us like it that way."

Bristling at his attitude, Hattie couldn't help but retort, "The boll weevils will be very pleased to hear that."

Finally aware of the Jessups' embarrassed silence, Hattie glanced around and caught sight of Millie's wide worried eyes.

Rising to her feet, Millie gave Hattie a signal to follow her. "Come and see the new curtains I've made for the kitchen, Hattie. I've been dying to show them off."

Following Millie through the neat little parsonage, Hattie couldn't help but reflect on the nice home and family Millie had, comparing it with her own life of loneliness.

"Here they are," Millie said, gesturing to the one large kitchen window that offered a nice view of the plowed fields of cotton surrounding the house.

"They're lovely, Millie," Hattie said, admiring her friend's ability to make something so attractive and useful from the cheap cotton sacking material.

"Hattie," Millie said slowly, as if speaking to someone simpleminded, "you really mustn't dispute Mr. Drayton's word."

"I'm not disputing his word," Hattie replied. "I'm just telling the truth as I see it. I know a good deal more about farming than he does."

Millie shook her head gravely. "Knowing more can't be helped. But you need to at least pretend that you value his judgment."

"Millie, he's wrong about the rice. I'm as sure of that as I'm sure the sun is going to rise tomorrow. He says in ten years we'll be getting a drainage project. I believe that ten years from now this whole county will be planted in rice."

Millie smiled, but obviously didn't believe her. "That won't happen, Hattie. All these men know about is cotton, and they'll keep on raising it."

"You're wrong," Hattie said flatly.

"Maybe so. And it's not much problem for you to say so to me. But, Hattie, women just do not contradict their menfolk."

"Ancil Drayton is not *my* menfolk!"

"And he never will be if you get on your high horse about such nonsense," Millie warned. "If you're right, fine. Time will tell. Ten years from now, do you want to be right and alone or right and married?"

Hattie blushed. Millie had a point, but Hattie hated to admit it. "I can't start acting like an empty-headed miss. Nobody would believe such a change."

"I'm not suggesting you pretend to be something that you're not. I'm just saying that when the man you want says something stupid, bite your tongue."

"You mean I'm not supposed to think for myself?"

"You can think all you want. Just be sure to keep your thoughts to yourself."

Hattie stubbornly crossed her arms. "Is that how you got Preacher Able, by not speaking your mind?"

Millie flashed a wicked smile. "That and an occasional well-calculated glimpse of my ankles." Raising her skirt a few inches, the preacher's wife boasted, "The reverend still says they're the trimmest ones in town!"

Reed had finished the courting swing for Miss Hattie and was in the shed sorting through tins of nails and lengths of chain, trying to find the right hardware.

His father's idea that there was some kind of attraction between him and Hattie was completely wrong, he assured himself. Hattie was his friend. He'd been going over to her house, talking and laughing with her for years, and not once had even a whiff of desire been present. Honesty forced him to correct that. There had been no desire until recently.

It was almost as if seeing Miss Hattie with another man had brought home to him that she was a woman. But she wasn't *his* woman. He shouldn't be thinking about Hattie. Bessie Jane should be occupying his mind. In truth, he'd been avoiding Bessie Jane, avoiding her eagerness, her sensuality, her temptation. Like too much perfume, her attention was cloying. He couldn't afford to marry yet, and he wasn't about to have a child on the way before he was ready.

Perhaps that was why he desired Hattie. Of course that was it, he decided, sighing as a weight was lifted off his shoulders. He was just needing a woman, and who was safer to lust after than the unattainable Hattie Colfax? If he went to Bessie Jane needing loving, she'd give it to him, and Lord knows what the consequences might be. But panting after Miss Hattie, who'd doctored his scraped knees and could remember having to order him to wash his face and hands, was about as safe as a man could get.

That was what Reed tried to tell himself. But memories of Hattie's sweet kisses spoke otherwise. She didn't seem such a big sister any longer. Even friendship could be heated to the boiling point. The only thing to do was to refocus his thoughts on Bessie Jane. He'd still have to try not to bed her, but there was no reason he couldn't imagine it.

Carrying the proper S connectors and bolts back to the swing, he let his mind wander to that long-ago night with Bessie Jane. He hadn't undressed her, he remembered that. The lack of privacy in her father's barn had precluded even partial nudity. But he'd unbuttoned her blouse and pushed her camisole up to her neck to taste the abundance of her bosom. Pulling up her skirts, he'd discarded her drawers back over his shoulder.

Later it had taken them half an hour and lighting a lantern to find them again. He'd been so hurried, so eager, it had been over almost before it had started. Bessie Jane had touched his body in ways he wouldn't have thought nice girls knew about. Afterward she had cried so. That was the most vivid memory, her tears.

It did no good to remember if what he remembered was tears. Fantasizing about the next time with Bessie Jane instead, he'd sworn he'd take his time, do it right. Determinedly, he concentrated on the taste of her nipples, the slick hot welcome of her entryway. He allowed his mind to wander in lustful revelry, hardening with desire as he dreamed of the purposeful thrusting, the moans of pleasure in her throat, the breathy rush of her kisses. But as he envisioned pulling away from her sweet lips, he saw that the face beneath him, the body that closed around him with such eagerness, was not Bessie Jane Turpin's.

The moon was high and the night clear as Ancil Drayton walked Miss Hattie to her porch. She'd tried to follow Millie's advice and watch what she said. She'd found it easier to talk about Ancil's children and his past, subjects he obviously knew more about than she.

As they stepped onto the porch, she knew he was going to kiss her. She was ready. A wild flock of fluttery moths seemed to have made a home in her stomach, but she was excited about kissing Ancil. She wanted that strange, pleasantly anxious sensation she'd felt with Reed to happen again. Thinking about the feel of Reed's lips against her was distracting. It made her pulse beat rapidly and an uncustomary giddiness steal through her. By kissing Ancil, she thought, all her imaginings would soon be about him.

Ancil's monologue on his years of youthful rabble rousing stopped abruptly as he placed his hands on her shoulders and pulled her close. Slowly, as if he expected her to run away, he leaned down and placed a kiss on her lips.

Almost immediately he began to straighten, and Hattie was disappointed. A peck was nice, but was that all? Perhaps because of her previous hesitance he didn't think a peach would be welcome. Before her courage could desert her, she wrapped her arms around his neck, and opening her lips, just as Reed had showed her, she gave him a warm, eager peach.

Ancil obviously liked it. Sucking in his breath with a hiss, he pulled her tightly against him. Instead of answering her gentle suction with like tenderness, though, he ground his mouth against hers, shifting it back and forth like an unlatched gate. The taste of snuff was unpleasant, but the rough and forceful grasp on her shoulders was worse. Feeling choked and pressured, Hattie jerked away from his unpleasant kiss.

"Well, well, well," he said, smiling smugly. "You are full of surprises, Miss Hattie." Wrapping his arms around her waist, he jerked her back to him, pressing her against his chest. "Still waters run deep, huh?" he whispered against her neck.

Managing to disengage herself from his arms, Hattie was not sure exactly what to say, but for some reason she very much wanted to slap that self-satisfied expression off his face. She resisted, however, and said haughtily. "I think it's time you should go home, Mr. Drayton."

Still smiling broadly, Ancil wasn't offended by her change of heart in the slightest. "Yes, ma'am," he answered, his politeness clearly pretense. Doffing his hat he added, "It's been a pleasure."

Hattie thought that was to be the last of it when to her horror he reached around her and gave her backside a big possessive pinch. She cried out in pain and alarm, but he only chuckled.

" 'Night, Miss Hattie," he said as he stepped off the porch and walked cockily to his horse.

She stared after him with her mouth open in disbelief until he was out of sight, then reached back and rubbed the bruise he'd bestowed on her left buttock.

Twelve

THE wind blew against the barren top of the hill overlooking the church, billowing the women's dark skirts and whisking away the sound of voices raised in song.

> "Could my tears forever flow,
> Could my zeal no languor know,
> These for sin could not atone;
> Thou must save, and Thou alone . . ."

Hattie kept her voice strong and steady as she gazed at the young blond man who stood staring sightlessly at the plain pine box that contained the body of his father, now free from the pains of flesh.

It was Preacher Able who had come by with the bad news. Following Hattie's advice, he'd gone to the Leege shack to check on the old man. Drawing each breath was a challenge to Jake, and the dying man's contact with the here and now was completely broken. He spoke only to his lost wife and occasionally his long-dead mother. It was obvious he was seeing his last, and the preacher decided to stay beside the brave and frightened young man who took such tender care of his father.

"He wasn't a bad man, Preacher," Harmon had insisted during the long night. "It was the drink that took away his dignity, his hope."

The preacher nodded, and Harmon continued to talk, sharing memories of his childhood, before his father lost his direction and headed so far away from his friends and family.

Harmon had spent the bulk of his grief by the time Jake Leege drew his final breath, just before dawn. His son lovingly closed his eyes. Jake Leege had only stopped breathing that night. He'd lost his life years before.

As Preacher Able related the bare bones of the story to Hattie, she was already mobilizing to help Millie prepare the funeral dinner. "There won't be many that show up," Hattie said frankly. "But the young man deserves to see a spread to rival any in town."

Preacher Able agreed, but leaving the logistics of the occasion to the womenfolk, he turned to wave as Reed drove up, carrying a brand-new porch swing in the back of his wagon. "Morning, Preacher," Reed said. "What brings you out here so early?"

"Actually, I was looking for you, Reed."

Jumping down from the wagon, Reed asked with curiosity and concern, "What's happened?"

"Jake Leege passed away last night." The preacher paused to allow a moment of reflection. "With the heat like it's been the past few days, I think we'll probably need to bury him first thing tomorrow morning."

Reed nodded, thinking about Harmon. Jake Leege was no big loss to the earth, or so Reed would have thought a couple of months ago. As Harm's friend, though, he grieved. "Do you want me to be a pallbearer?" he asked the reverend.

Preacher Able nodded. "I asked Harmon who he wanted, and you were the only one he could think of."

Nodding sorrowfully, Reed thought of the irony that such a fine hardworking man didn't have enough friends to be pallbearers at his daddy's funeral. "I'll get my father and brothers," he said, already formulating plans.

"Hattie is going to help Millie set up the dinner," Preacher Able told him, "so I suspect everything will turn out just fine.

Somebody ought to be with Harmon tonight when he sits with the body."

"I'll stay," Reed said. "I'm not much good at talking, but I can sit up as late as the next man."

The preacher nodded.

Reed looked at Hattie, still standing on the porch. "I'll go find the pallbearers this morning and then go over to Harmon's shack. Is he making the coffin himself?"

"Yes," the preacher said. "He told me he could take care of it."

Reed turned back to Hattie. "I'll stay over there tonight, then have my father come over early in the morning while I go back to the house to change. You get all your cooking ready, Miss Hattie, and I'll come by and pick you up about eight o'clock."

Hattie opened her mouth in surprise, but before she could say a word, Preacher Able piped up. "Hattie can take care of herself, Reed. Besides, you'll be needing to pick up Bessie Jane."

Reed looked at the preacher stupidly, then realized what he'd just said. Of course Reed would take Bessie Jane to the funeral. She was the woman he was to marry. For a moment, he was speechless with his own foolishness. He'd forgotten Bessie Jane's existence completely. "Sure," he said finally. Glancing at Hattie, he shrugged. "I don't know what got into me. I'll be picking up Bessie Jane, of course."

Hattie nodded, furious with herself for the rush of excitement that had flashed through her.

"I'll send my brother Andy over to help you," Reed added. "I know you'll be fixing a ton of food, and you can't manage that by yourself."

"I could ride over to Drayton's place and ask him to help you," the preacher suggested.

"No!" Hattie answered much too quickly. "He didn't care much for Leege," she added lamely, "and if he went, he'd have to get all the children ready."

So Reed's youngest brother had loaded the buggy for her, and now she stood next to him as the last words of the graveside hymn faded away.

She couldn't see Reed, who stood to her right about four or five people down. She had seen him when they'd driven up. He was incredibly handsome in his dark suit, but he looked tired and worn from his long night without sleep. Bessie Jane was beside him, and if possible, she looked even more drawn and pale than Reed. Hattie was surprised. She couldn't recall ever seeing Bessie Jane less than lovely.

Harmon never glanced up at any of them, his gaze firmly focused on the coffin as the preacher intoned about eternal life and giving up the body. He'd already said good-bye to his father. In the long last nights of his life, Jake Leege had without a word between them parted amiably with his only son.

It was not his grief over the past that kept Harm staring at the coffin, but his fear of the present. If he raised his head and looked across the grave, he would see her. Bessie Jane was within his line of vision, as beautiful in grief as in joy, and he could not risk even glancing at her. If they exchanged just one look, the whole community would know how it was between them, how it had been, how it would be again with half a chance. Allowing himself that one look could ease a lot of his pain, but what was in his heart was not for public display. He would not have the love they shared become another morsel for gossipmongers. He kept his eyes down, and in his heart he pleaded with her for love and comfort.

After the final benediction, the crowd began to move away. Most stopped briefly to give their condolences to Harmon. Having both the preacher's wife and Miss Hattie meant that Jake Leege's funeral would not be stinted. Many of the church members now filed past Harmon, offering in death the kind words they'd never offered in life.

With Andy at her side, Hattie hurried to the buggy and then to the Leege shack. She'd been there earlier in the morning to leave the victuals. The place needed a good scrubbing, but she hadn't been able to do that with a room full of mourners and a body laid out on the table. She hoped to have time to make a few cosmetic changes before the funeral dinner.

Enlisting Andy in her plan, she soon had the place swept out, the windows washed, and the furniture dusted. Flowers that had been left with bowls of butter beans and steaming yeastrolls now brightened the drab corners of the room, papered in newsprint.

Harmon arrived in the preacher's buggy with Millie and Able. The Tyler family pulled in right behind them, then Reed and Bessie Jane with her parents in the Turpins' two-seater surrey. Hattie went immediately to Harmon as he stepped on the porch. She gave him a motherly hug for courage, then handed him a glass of lemonade.

Harm smiled, embarrassed but pleased by her gesture, and followed her orders to take a seat on the porch and drink his lemonade.

Within minutes, nearly everyone who'd been at the graveside had arrived to partake of the meal. Hattie was too busy serving food to look up but remembered to keep sending glasses of lemonade to Harmon. In her vivid memories of the funerals of her parents, she recalled needing to do something with her hands to keep control of her feelings. Sipping lemonade was the best occupation she could offer the young man.

Glancing up once during a lull, she found Bessie Jane at her side. "You look ill," she told the young woman.

Bessie Jane seemed startled by her observation. "I just hate funerals," she said.

Hattie found her reasoning curious. To her knowledge, Bessie Jane had never lost anyone close to her. Shrugging, she assumed that death, like most of life's realities, had not yet come home to roost for the young woman. "You can scrape these dishes if you've a mind to," she said.

To her surprise, Bessie Jane charged into the work, not just scraping the dishes but washing and drying them also. Truth to tell, Hattie had always thought Bessie Jane to be a bit on the lazy side, but she threw herself into the kitchen work, taking most of the cleaning burden off Hattie's shoulders.

Grateful for the respite, Hattie wended her way through the shack, speaking first to one person then the next. When she saw Reed on the porch, her first instinct was to go to him. However, she realized he was out there to offer support to Harmon. The younger man was not used to being accepted at community social occasions, and being the center of attention while still in shock over his father's death was more than most could have handled. Harm seemed to be holding his own, but Hattie was glad Reed was there to fill in the lags in conversation.

"Well, it's quite a sight, isn't it?" Arthur Turpin said from behind her. At Hattie's quizzical look, he enlarged on his statement. "I never thought I would see the day when decent churchgoing folks would waste an entire afternoon mourning a worthless drunken sinner who is better off dead than he was alive."

Hattie felt her spine stiffen. Bessie Jane's father was well-known for his rigid opinions and holier-than-thou Christianity. For the most part, folks just accepted it as part and parcel of the man. He was wealthy, by local standards, and his very prosperity frequently led him to maintain the most inflexible of religious convictions. Since the Bible stated that it was easier for a camel to go through the eye of a needle than a rich man to enter heaven, Turpin excused his riches on earth by his unstinting adherence to the straightest part of the straight and narrow. Though only, of course, when it didn't interfere with business.

"You know yourself, Mr. Turpin," Hattie said, "that a funeral is more for the living than for the dead."

"It's for that boy, you mean," Turpin replied. "It seems to me that you and the preacher's wife both fell victim to a spawn of Satan with a pretty face." The man shook his head disapprovingly. "Grown women ought to know better."

"Harmon is not a spawn of Satan," Hattie said, her chin coming up defiantly. "He is a hardworking young man who took care of his sick father and is now grieving. Nothing could be more Christian than helping him through this time of trouble."

"You don't know this boy like I do," Turpin insisted. "He's no good clear to the core, and he's going to cause a peck of trouble someday. I'm just hoping that he's far away from here when he does it."

"If you feel so strongly about this, Mr. Turpin," Hattie asked, plainly irritated, "then what are you doing here?"

"Reed was going to come, no matter what I said about it. And if he was going to bring Bessie Jane, I had to come to make sure she was safe."

" 'Safe'?" Hattie repeated, then added with mocking gravity, "You certainly have cause to worry about your daughter's safety at a funeral dinner among thirty members of the church with her betrothed beside her." Hattie was downright angry now. "I'm sure safety was your main concern, Mr. Turpin"—she gazed pointedly at his full plate of food—"but feel free to eat all you can while you're here protecting your daughter."

It was late afternoon before the crowd departed. Bessie Jane had taken care of the worst of the cleanup, but Hattie stayed to sort the array of borrowed dishes and pots that would have to be returned to their owners.

Harmon came in and seated himself at the table, watching her.

"Would you like some lemonade?" she asked him.

A wide smile flashed across his face. "No, ma'am. I've had enough of that to drown a less hardy man."

She smiled, glad that he was holding up so well. She knew a lot of men would have turned to the whiskey bottle at a time like this. She was grateful Harmon hadn't seen the need.

"I want to thank you for the dinner and all," he said sincerely.

"It wasn't me," she said. "The whole church—"

"The whole church would never have thought to even show up at my father's funeral, let alone give him a dinner, unless you'd made a point of it."

It was true, so Hattie didn't try to deny it. She simply shrugged it off.

"I won't be forgetting it, Miss Hattie," he said quietly. Looking around, he commented on the changes inside the shack.

"Oh, it just needs a woman's touch," she said. The change on his face was not a bright one, so she hastily added, "There are a lot of very nice young girls in this county, Harmon. Most of whom have the good sense to fall in love with the man and not his past."

Harm's smile was halfhearted. "I'm sure that's true of you, Miss Hattie. If old Drayton has the good sense to snap you up, he'll be a lucky man."

She looked away, flustered by the compliment.

A step was heard on the front porch, then Reed poked his head in the door.

"I thought you'd gone," Harmon said.

"I took Bessie Jane home. Thought I'd best come back for Miss Hattie."

"There was no need," Hattie said, but couldn't still the well of joy that had suddenly sprung up inside her. "I knew I could handle this myself or I would have asked Andy to stay."

"Andy had every intention of staying, until I sent him home," Reed said. "You want me to start loading those things in the buggy?"

With the help of the two men, Hattie soon had the rest of the dishes sorted, marked, and ready to go. Reed helped her up onto the seat, then turned to Harmon. "You going to be all right here?"

Harmon nodded. "I appreciate all that you two did," he said. "I feel like Daddy knows somewhere that we did right by him and that we mourned him.'' His tender words embarrassed him, and he gave a disparaging duck of his head. "Pretty fanciful thinking for a junkman.''

Reed embraced him like a brother, patting him heartily on the back. ''I'll be flooding the rice field in the next couple of days. I'd like you to be there to help me work that pump if I need it.''

''I'll be there,'' said Harm. ''I want to see Miss Hattie's face when we cover up all that pretty rice with water.''

As Hattie's buggy trundled down the road toward the colorful sunset, she felt ill at ease in Reed's presence. She was sure it was nothing Reed had done. It was her own foolishness that made her remember his kisses instead of Ancil's.

''I thought everything went well,'' she said finally, needing to break the long silence.

''What? Oh, yes, I think it was very nice,'' Reed replied. He'd obviously been deep in his own thoughts and completely unaware of the silence between them. ''I want to thank you for all you did, Miss Hattie,'' he said, smiling at her. ''The spread was really fine, and I know that was more your doing than Millie's. And I know what that house looked like when we left for the funeral. I asked Andy how you'd performed such a miracle, and he said you worked like a whirlwind.''

She laughed lightly. ''He probably said I worked *him* like a whirlwind. He did most of the sweeping and scrubbing.''

''I'll have to tell Mama,'' he said. ''She can't get him to even pick up after himself around the house.''

When their laughter faded and Reed spoke again, his voice was more serious. ''I guess I'm about the only friend Harm has. That's plenty surprising, since he's lived in this town all his life and I'd hardly talked to him two months ago. But that's the way it is. It should have been Bessie Jane taking care of the dinner and such. Since she's my future wife, it was really her job, and I'm sorry the whole burden fell on you.''

Hattie was surprised and a little perturbed at his attitude. ''I helped because I wanted to, Reed. It had nothing to do with you.''

''I didn't mean that you didn't,'' he said hurriedly. ''I was just thinking that Bessie Jane should have been more involved. She doesn't care for Harmon much.''

"She did help," Hattie said. "She was in the kitchen for over an hour, willing to do her share. I don't know much about her opinion of Harm, but I sure didn't care much for her father's."

Reed raised a curious eyebrow, and Hattie related Turpin's diatribe against the younger Leege.

"He is thickheaded," Reed admitted. "He's really set against farming rice and gives me an earful of advice every time I see him."

"I can't imagine what he has against Harmon."

"I do know that Harm was interested in courting Bessie Jane."

"I'd heard that, too, but nothing ever came of it."

"I'm sure Turpin gave him the boot before he even got up to the house. He probably wouldn't be the only father with that reaction, but it seems a bit long to hold a grudge."

When they reached Hattie's place, Reed pulled up in the yard and helped her down. They made several trips carrying the contents of the buggy into the house.

"I'll go unhitch the horse and give her a rubdown," Reed said when they had finished the unloading.

"Thank you," Hattie said. "Do you want a glass of lemonade? We've still got some."

He shook his head. "I've had a gallon of that today. But I could go for a cup of coffee if you've a mind to brew some."

Hattie was surprised at the request but eagerly complied as he headed out to the barn. By the time the scent of coffee was wafting through the house, she heard Reed moving around out on the porch. Curious, she stepped outside to find him sitting on the porch floor next to the swing he had hurriedly unloaded the day before.

"You ready for coffee?" she asked.

He looked up and smiled. "Yes, ma'am. Have you got a lantern in the house?"

"Yes, there's one here in the kitchen."

"Bring it out here, and I'll hang this swing for you."

Hattie poured the hot coffee into their usual breakfast mugs. Lighting the lantern, she hooked the handle on one arm so that she could carry everything in one trip. She'd just reached the door when Reed was on his feet opening it for her. He took his coffee and the lantern.

After managing the lantern on the nail on the front post, he took a deep swallow of the coffee and made a noise of appreciation. "Is this the best place to hang this thing?" he asked, indicating the far end of the porch.

"Yes, I think so," Hattie replied, studying his choice. "It will get the sun in the morning and the shade in the afternoon. I couldn't ask for more than that."

He smiled at her choice of words. "You really don't ask for much, do you?"

She glanced away, slightly embarrassed at his admiration. "I guess I didn't get around to thanking you for the swing. Things were so jumbled yesterday, I really didn't even think about it. But I like it a lot."

Shrugging off her gratitude, Reed tried to explain himself. "I just thought that with you courting these days . . . well, every woman needs a courting swing."

"Is that what this is!" she exclaimed, then giggled. "I was thinking it was someplace to rest my tired bones after you nearly work me to death in that rice field."

Laughing with her, Reed found he was very glad he'd made the swing. It was such a little thing, he should have built one for her years ago. He'd just never thought of it, not until he'd imagined her with Drayton.

"Swings were invented by fathers," he said. "It's the most uncomfortable place for sparking you can imagine. With Drayton calling on you and no menfolk or chaperone around, I was thinking you'd need kind of a safe place."

"Men don't like to sit in swings?"

"Well, it's better than sitting across the porch from each other, but it's not good for much else but hugging and kissing."

"Well, that's certainly enough," Hattie said, slightly shocked. What else did courting couples do? she wondered.

Reed heard the hint of outrage in her voice and cursed himself for a fool. Was he trying to make her afraid of Drayton? Did he want her to send him packing? "Hand me that drill, Hattie," he said, stepping up on a stool to reach the porch ceiling. "Can you hold that light a little closer?"

Watching as Reed pounded along the wood with his fist until he found the sound that indicated a beam on the other side, Hattie's gaze was drawn to his well-muscled arms and the strong masculine curves of his body. The memory of his kiss, his touch, flooded her, and she steeled herself to maintain her nonchalant manner.

Handing him the hardware and tools as he requested them, she countered the strange longings in her body by chattering incessantly. The strangeness of her behavior caused Reed to look at her curiously, but he made no comment. Within a few minutes they had the swing hanging properly.

"It looks wonderful!" Hattie exclaimed, standing back to observe his handiwork.

"Try it out," he said, and she seated herself hesitantly, like a queen. Her smile was so warm, so open, Reed had to look away. "I'm going to get some more coffee," he said. "You want some?"

She didn't, and Reed immediately disappeared inside the house. Sitting there alone in the lantern light, Hattie felt foolish. She still hadn't changed from her black silk dress, and she knew the severe style made her look older than her years. She was a dried-up old spinster, she thought, with an equally old gentleman caller. Now she had a courting swing like a young girl, and she suspected she might well be the funniest piece of gossip in the county.

Reed returned with the coffee in hand. "How does it sit?" he asked.

"It's perfect," she said as he seated himself beside her. They sat quietly for a moment. Their proximity brought to both their minds memories of the two of them on this porch, and they grew slightly disconcerted. Reed took a big gulp of his coffee, then got up.

Hattie thought he intended to leave and was surprised when he lifted the globe of the lantern and blew it out. "The light draws insects," he explained as he sat again, casually draping his arm along the back of the swing. "Besides, with the light on, you can't see the stars."

She leaned forward to see that indeed there were some tiny lights high in the sky watching over them. The breeze fluttered lightly, and Hattie tried to relax and ignore the arm that lay so close to her shoulders.

The silence between them lengthened interminably, until she couldn't stand it. What was becoming of their friendship that they could no longer talk? "I did kiss Mr. Drayton," she blurted out. She immediately wished she could call the foolish declaration back, but it was too late.

"Oh?" Reed's voice was coolly indifferent.

"Well, I thought you'd want to know," she explained, struggling to preserve what small measure of dignity she had left. "That I didn't make a fool of myself or anything. It was easy, just like you said. I don't think he suspected a thing."

"I'm sure he didn't," Reed replied, trying valiantly to forget the sweetness of Hattie's kiss, the heat that it had churned inside him.

"He kisses differently than you do," she added, hoping to sound blasé and impassive.

"Better or worse?" Reed couldn't keep from asking.

Worse was the word that came to mind, but Hattie didn't utter it. Ancil was the one who was courting her, after all. Surely she owed him some loyalty. "Neither," she replied diplomatically. "Just different."

"Did you give him the peck, like I told you?"

"Well, yes, at first. That's what he gave me, actually, but I wanted to try the peach, so I kissed him a second time the way I wanted."

She wasn't sure, but she thought she heard a hiss escape through Reed's teeth.

"The worst part was that he pinched me on the bottom," she said. "Why would a man want to do that?"

Reed didn't answer, but she could sense that he was displeased. She shouldn't have told him about the kiss, she realized, but it was too late now. She tried again to mend his feelings. "I just wanted to tell you that I did it. I'm not sure if I would have been able to go through with it if you hadn't shown me how. I know that normally a lady wouldn't talk about such things, but I wanted to tell you so you would see how very grateful I am for the time you took to teach me."

To Hattie's amazement, Reed slammed his coffee mug angrily against the arm of the swing. The mug shattered, sending a splash of hot coffee and shards of porcelain over both of them. He held the disembodied handle in his hand for an instant, then cast it onto the wood floor with the rest of the broken mug.

Hattie gave a cry of fright.

"Are you burned?" he asked anxiously.

"No," she answered, shocked and confused.

"Then why did you scream?"

"Because you broke the cup," she said, thinking it obvious. "What is wrong with you?"

"Nothing! There is nothing wrong with me!" His voice was mocking and angry.

"Then why are you acting this way?'' she asked, losing her temper also.

"Do you think I enjoy hearing about some man pawing all over you?''

"Nobody was 'pawing' me.''

"You let him put his hands on your behind.''

"He pinched me!''

"Same thing.''

"I was just trying to tell you how grateful—''

"Would you stop being so damn grateful!''

"Don't you curse at me!''

"Right. I can't curse you, but I can kiss you. If I kiss you, you'll be very grateful and will flaunt yourself all over the county, practicing what I've taught you.''

"I . . . you . . .'' she fumbled for words as Reed stood, kicking aside pieces of the broken cup.

"Good night, Miss Hattie,'' he said, his tone still rough with fury. "I'd better leave now before I do anything else that you might be grateful for.''

Thirteen

DUSK was creeping through the overhang of trees that edged the river behind the Leege shack. Harmon sat on the small dock he'd built, staring out at the water. One bare foot rested on the dock, his knee tucked tight against his chest, the other on the nose of his boat.

He heard the flutter of noise behind him but ignored it. An animal making its way through the grass was of no interest to him tonight. It was only when he felt the weight of a step on the dock that he turned to look behind him.

She was not dressed as she'd been earlier, so proper in black, so somber and controlled. Her pale blue cotton dress was obviously one worn around the house, clean and tidy but meant only to clothe, not to decorate.

"I had to come, Harm." Her voice was barely a whisper. "I knew you'd be leaving, and I had to say good-bye."

He continued to gaze at her for a moment, then he moved, dangling both legs over the dock, making room for her beside him. He patted the spot gently with his hand. "Come sit with me, sweet Bess."

Hesitating only an instant, she walked to the front of the

dock and with the grace that was second nature to her, seated herself at his side.

"At the funeral," she said, "all I kept thinking was that now that your father is gone, you'll leave also."

Harm didn't answer, or even acknowledge her words.

"You've always talked about leaving," she went on. "You've said yourself that you're no farmer and you want to work with machines. Now there is nothing to keep you here."

As he remained silent, Bessie Jane watched him out of the corner of her eye and wrung her hands nervously. "I remember you used to talk all the time about Detroit and all the factories for automobiles. Do you think you might go to Detroit? Reed says your ability with engines is a gift, like singing or playing the piano."

He turned to look at her then, his face void of expression. His blue eyes focused on her intensely, as if she were some strange object he was trying to understand.

"I'm real sorry about your father, Harm," she said finally. "I didn't know him, but I know you loved him a lot. I was glad I got to go to the funeral. If Reed hadn't wanted it, I'm sure Daddy would never have approved."

He spoke at last. "Thank you for coming, Bessie Jane. I needed you beside me, but just having you there was more than I'd hoped."

She flushed at his words. There was nothing she could say to that. They sat together for several minutes, his bare feet dangling so close to her shiny new brown leather high-buttons. It was like times remembered, but different, so sadly different.

"Take your shoes off," he said quietly.

She took a deep breath, garnering her courage. "I can't. I only came to say good-bye."

He reached for her chin and forced her to look at him. "I thought you'd already said that to me months ago."

As tears welled up in her eyes, she jerked her chin out of his grasp and looked away. "You're not going to make this easy for me, are you."

His light chuckle had no humor in it. "No, I'm not. If you're going to throw away everything that's between us, I want it to be the hardest thing you've ever done."

Quickly wiping away the evidence of her emotion, Bessie Jane forced herself to meet his challenge. "I've tried to explain it to you. It just wouldn't work."

"Because I'm not rich!" he said, anger coating the words. He gestured to the shack behind him. "You want a fine house, not my old shack. I understand that, Bess. I want better too. And I'm going to get it. I have plans, plans to make something of my life." He stared back out at the river, at the water moving ever so slowly out of their lives forever. "All my plans, sweet Bess, included you by my side."

"It's not just the money, Harm."

"Then what else is it?"

"Well, there's Reed."

"Reed didn't even know you were alive when you walked out on me. I'm not sure he knows it now. He's all wrong for you, Bess. Surely you see that."

"Reed loves me!"

"He may say that he does, he may even think that he does, but you're not right for him. He talks to you like a sister—no, like a daughter. You're just some child he's going to take to raise. That's no way to make a marriage."

"I thought he was your friend."

"He is. He's about the only friend I have, but being his friend doesn't make me blind." Harmon looked at her steadily. "Reed Tyler is not the man for you, sweet Bess, and we both know it."

Bessie Jane made no comment, then she shrugged as if to put that subject aside. "It's my family. My father—"

Harm raised his hands to stop her. "I know all about your father. That old man has had no use for me since I was a kid."

"It's not that he doesn't like you," she insisted.

"No, that's exactly it. He doesn't like me, because I know things about him that he'd like to forget."

"What kind of things?"

Harm opened his mouth, about to answer, then seeing something in her face—trust, vulnerability—he closed his mouth abruptly. "Forget it, Bess," he said. "The old man just never liked me."

Shaking her head as if she didn't believe it, she defended her father. "He only wants what's best for me."

"That's exactly what I want for you, Bessie Jane. And *I* am what's best for you! No man will ever know you or love you the way I do. Bess, use your heart as well as your brain."

He reached out for the first time to touch her. She flinched slightly, then allowed him to take her hand. "Your father only knows about needs like food, clothing, and shelter. He worries about those because he doesn't understand the other needs you have, sweet Bess.''

He lifted her fingers to his lips and kissed them, sending a current of gooseflesh up her arm and a rush of breath from her lips. "I know about those other needs." He slipped his arm around her back, bringing her closer. "You need a friend, someone you can talk to, the way we've always talked.''

"Yes," she whispered, their faces close, her eyes watching his lips as they inched toward hers.

"You need love, sweet Bess. The kind of love that a man can give only one time and forever. My heart, my life, is yours, and you've known that for years.''

"Yes," she repeated, as if in a trance. "We have always loved each other—so totally, so secretly.''

Pulling her tight against him, he pressed her breasts against his chest. He could feel the hard, distended nipples rising eagerly against him. "And you need a man who can make you scream with pleasure," he murmured, his mouth only inches from hers, his breath hot with passion. "Do you remember how I made you scream with pleasure?''

She closed her eyes. "I only wish I could forget it.''

"Oh, no, Bess, never forget it. I can't let you forget it. I've got to always remind you.''

His lips were on hers then, demanding, practiced, and she succumbed easily to the temptation, opening her mouth, eager for plunder. He filled her, leaning back until she lay at his side on the worn wood-plank dock. He ran his hands knowledgeably along her body. Remembering with pleasure all the hills and valleys of Bessie Jane Turpin, he refamiliarized himself with all of her, lovingly, tenderly, as his mouth continued its reunion with hers.

He released the buttons at the back of her dress and pulled it down, exposing a creamy shoulder. He could not resist the expanse of tender flesh and slid his mouth down her neck.

As he tasted her skin, he could hear her breathy protest in his ear. "I mustn't, I mustn't," she whispered, even as she grasped the delicate pink lace that covered her and bared her breast for him.

Accepting her invitation, he suckled her, not gently, releasing a hoarse cry of desire from her lips. Jerking up her skirts and pulling her thighs apart, he thrust his own thigh high against her, and she squirmed eagerly upon it.

"Sweet Bess," he whispered. "My sweet Bess, I would taste you tonight. Will you let me taste you again?" His request was punctuated by tiny lovebites on her tender breast.

"Yes, oh yes," she moaned as he rolled her onto her back. Bringing her knees up, he spread her wide before him, and she was unashamed in her desire. Harmon ran his hands along the inside of her thighs until he found that hot eager place that was already wet for him. He touched her there, and she arched against him.

"You are mine, sweet Bess!" he declared. "No other man will ever touch you the way I do."

Bessie Jane opened her eyes at those words and saw his hands move to the ribbon of her drawers. Reality abruptly intruded. "No!" she screamed, in near hysteria. "I can't. We can't." Sitting up, she thrust herself away from him, pulling her skirts down. She curled up like a frightened child, trembling, her eyes wide with horror at her actions.

He moved toward her, grasping her arm. Passion glazed his eyes as he refused to relinquish her. "You can't stop now, Bess, not now. I can't stop."

Her gaze went to his trousers and the hard evidence of his desire. "I'm sorry," she said, tears flowing from her eyes. "You make me forget who I am. I can't let you touch me like that again, Harmon. Never."

He didn't allow her to get away. Wrapping his arms around her, he held her close in a firm but tender grasp. "You don't want my mouth? What would please you, sweet Bess? I love you. How do you want me to show you tonight?"

"You mustn't do anything," she said, trying to pull away.

"Bess?" His arms tightened around her, and she jerked back, as if frightened. "Easy, Bess—you know I wouldn't hurt you."

"But I can hurt *you*. We can't do this, Harm. I can't do this. I am promised to Reed and . . ."

Harm stared at her for several minutes, passion and pain warring with intellect. "You're right. Reed is my friend. He's our friend. It isn't right for us to share this while he thinks you're still his. Tomorrow, we'll go together and talk to him. We'll make him understand that we have to be together."

"No."

"If you want to talk to him yourself, that's fine. But I must talk to him too. I want him to understand."

"No, Harmon," she said her bottom lip still trembling. She was unable to meet his eyes. "We can't tell him, because I'm not breaking it off with him. I will marry Reed Tyler in the fall."

Harmon was surprised by her statement but shrugged it off. "You can't marry him, Bess. Not with the way you feel about me. Do you still doubt that you love me? Do you doubt that you want me? After all these months of seeing him, it's still the same with us." Running his hand down the bodice of her gown, he teased the nipples that had hardened against the pale blue fabric. "Try to deny that you still feel the same for me!"

"I can't deny it." She pushed him away and covered her face with her hands. "I can't deny it, but I can't have it either."

"Sweet Bess—"

"No! You mustn't call me that anymore, and you must listen." She raised her head determinedly and looked at him as squarely as she could manage. "I love you and I want you, the same as before," she said quietly. "I admit that. It's because I'm weak, Harmon. With you, I've always been weak. From that first time, I never said no, never hesitated to follow your lead. The touch of your hand was all it took to convince me to forget everything my parents tried to teach me."

He started to move toward her, but she held up her hand to stay him. Taking a deep breath, she continued. "No one has ever made me feel as you do. With you I'm so alive and so free. You never look at me like a dressed-up doll, or a dessert to be sampled, or a toy to be owned. I can take off my mask with you. I can just be Bess and know that you won't be disappointed."

Looking at him, she saw that his handsome face was open, his sparkling blue eyes alive with hope. She swallowed nervously as she set her course to dash it. "That is a powerful weapon, Harmon. Love is something that is very hard to fight against. When I knew we could never be and I promised Daddy I would marry Reed, I still realized how easily you could change my mind. How quickly I would break my promises."

She studied her nails as sorrow gathered in her throat, making her voice low and hoarse. "I can't give myself strength to deny you, but I can give you strength to never desire me again."

Harmon frowned, anxious and confused. "What do you

mean? Bess, nothing you could ever do, nothing you could say, would ever change the way I feel about you.''

She tucked a stray hair behind her ear and smoothed her skirts—anything to put off the moment of her doom. Looking up again, she gazed deeply into the eyes of the man she loved and measured her words, her voice even and controlled. "I tried to think of a way to keep you from wanting me, to keep you from ever thinking to have me in your arms again.''

"Sweet Bess, having you in my arms again is all I ever think about. Only having you again at last will ever change that.''

Willing, eager even, to take his censure, his pain, she spoke quietly and with cold finality. "I have been with Reed Tyler.''

Harmon looked at her quizzically, at first not able to comprehend, then blanched. His mouth opened as if he found it difficult to catch his breath. Staring at her, pain distorting his face, he shook his head in disbelief. "You wouldn't,'' he said forcefully. "Never, Bess. I know that you wouldn't.''

Her silence was her answer. He folded his arms across his chest as if protecting a wound. "No!'' His cry was harsh and primitive, like an animal's. He closed his eyes and slowly lay back on the dock, moaning in pain.

Bessie Jane watched as tears leaked from the corners of his eyes. "Good-bye, Harmon,'' she said quietly, then got up and walked away, her step as forced and heavy as an old woman's.

The wheel on the floodgates was turned, and Hattie watched as the water from the river flowed in a rush across the field of sprouted rice, barely six inches tall. Neither of the two men working the gates had offered much more than a civil word to her, but she was determined to be at her rice field, despite bad-tempered men.

The days since Jake Leege's funeral had been busy and confusing. Reed's irrational anger had apparently persisted. He hadn't shown up for breakfast the rest of the week, and he seemed to go out of his way to avoid her.

Harm was no better. He'd made himself scarce for three days, then returned without a word of explanation. He did his job with a cold, quiet efficiency that was almost frightening.

Hattie had decided that the best way to handle her partners these days was just to steer clear of them. With that in mind, she'd kept away from the rice field and tended to her stock. On

Sunday, Ancil and his children had come to dinner. Her garden was well on its way, and she filled the children up on butter beans and fried okra. Ancil seemed pleased and captured her hand under the table to give it a friendly squeeze.

She enjoyed the day with the children. She and Ancil sat with Cyl and Ada making clover chains as little Buddy followed Myrene through the yard like a shadow. The boys were trying to get their kite up, and much of everyone's attention was focused on their efforts. The wind was never quite right, and time after time, just as the boys began to holler with success, the kite would make another fatal dive to earth.

Cyl laughed at their failures with such enthusiasm, Fred finally lost his temper and stormed over to their shady patch of clover. "Okay, Cylvia Drayton," he said, his cracking voice hoarse with frustration. "You think you can do better? I dare you."

Immediately accepting, Cyl ran eagerly to the kite. To the chagrin of Fred and the others, the bright blue kite was high in the air within ten minutes.

"Cyl can do anything," Ada told Hattie, her eyes wide with wonder.

Hattie nodded her agreement but added, "You do some amazing things too. Look at this chain, Mr. Drayton. I think your daughter has a real talent."

Ancil gave a halfhearted glance at the green-and-white necklace of clover blossoms. "It'll be dead in an hour," he said.

The young girl's face fell.

"But it's very pretty now," Hattie said, trying to save the day. "Look how carefully she's cut through the stem with her nail to weave in the next blossom."

Finally hearing the meaning in Hattie's words, Ancil actually took note of his daughter's handiwork. "It looks real nice, Ada," he said. To his amazement, Ada squealed in delight and flung her arms around his neck. Ancil stared at Hattie, clearly appalled at the child's behavior. He received a smile of encouragement that helped him live through the strange outpouring of affection.

Mary Nell was not interested in anyone or anything. She spent the entire afternoon sitting on the porch swing—or lying on it might be a more accurate description. With her head on the armrest and one knee up in the air, she kept a foot on the ground to rock herself back and forth. She was totally uninterested in anything that went on around her, but then, she'd already sown her crop of evil words that morning.

They had been leaving church when Hattie had found herself by Mary Nell's side.

"They say you're such a good person," Mary Nell said, "because you took care of your mother until she died."

Hattie was slightly taken back by the statement. "I'm not sure that makes me good," she replied. "My mother needed someone to take care of her, and there was no one else."

Mary Nell smiled broadly. "That's what I thought too. It's not that you're so good—it's that you didn't have any choices. Nobody wanted you, but I'm pretty. Everybody says so, and now that I'm getting my girlish figure, I suspect I'll be running off to Memphis to marry pretty soon."

Hattie's eyes widened in shock. "Oh, Mary Nell, you mustn't do that. You're much too young to think about marriage."

"Well, I'm sure not waiting around until I'm old like you and somebody marries me to take care of his younguns." With that, Mary Nell had flounced away. All through dinner she'd been obnoxious, so much so that Hattie would have loved to box the young lady's ears. Ancil had called her down a couple of times, but he clearly didn't want trouble, so Hattie had to let it go. The young girl's distance and anger were a barrier she wasn't sure she'd ever be able to overcome.

At dusk they ate a light supper, and afterward she and Ancil sat on the porch swing as the children played "potatoes." Buddy had snuggled up between them and fallen asleep with his head on Hattie's lap. She felt such contentment. This was what she had always wanted—a little family, quiet times spent together, and a husband. She looked over at Ancil.

He smiled at her. "Mary Nell!" he called. "Come take Buddy. The rest of you get your things and get on out to the wagon."

"You have to go?" Hattie asked, handing the sleeping child to his sister.

"Not right yet," he answered, and slipped his arm around her to gather her close. "I'm sending the kids to the wagon so we can get a little smoochy-smooch."

Blushing at the statement and inwardly cringing at his description of kissing, Hattie nevertheless managed a tight little smile.

"That's my girl," he said, sliding closer. "You've decided that you like me enough for a bit of smoochy, haven't you?"

"I do like you," she answered noncommittally.

The answer pleased him well enough, and he pulled her into his arms for a rather sloppy wet kiss. Hattie instinctively tried to pull back in distaste, but he held her fast. She made noises of protest. Ancil was either ignoring her or had mistaken the sounds for passion. When he finally released her, it was all she could do not to wipe her mouth.

Remembering that kiss the next morning as she watched the water spread through the rice field, she did raise her arm and wipe her lips on her sleeve. At least he hadn't pinched her. Marriage to him might be all right if he didn't want to kiss very much. She tried to imagine having to bed with him, but her mind kept straying from the idea.

She heard the men closing the floodgates, and the water began to settle. Only a few inches of the plants would peek above the surface, just enough to get sunlight. As the plants grew, the water level would be increased. The next time this field would be dry was harvesttime, four months away.

Hattie heard raised voices but couldn't make out a word. She looked toward the levee and saw that Reed and Harmon were obviously having an argument. With both of them acting like bears with a toothache, she figured she'd better go down and see if she could help. She'd just taken a couple of steps when she saw Harm come across with a hard right to Reed's jaw, felling him to the dirt.

Hattie broke into a stumbling run, hurrying to get between the men. Neither had moved an inch by the time she got there, though. Both seemed paralyzed, staring at each other as if they couldn't believe what had happened.

"What is going on here?" she asked, her hands on her hips.

"Don't ask me," Reed said, sitting up to feel the damage to his jaw. "This man is either drunk or crazy."

"Don't call me a drunk, Tyler, or I'll shut your mouth permanently!" Harm said.

"He's not calling you a drunk, because you aren't one." Hattie said. "But something is the matter with both of you. I thought you were friends."

"We are friends, dammit!" Reed replied.

"Don't you curse at me—" Hattie started, but was interrupted by Harm.

"That's right. Don't you dare curse at Hattie Colfax, or I'll knock the rest of your teeth out. You want to curse at someone, Tyler, make it me 'cause I'm ready."

Harm assumed a fighter's stance, and Hattie looked at him in exasperation.

Reed jumped to his feet, clearly ready to take up the challenge.

"Stop it, both of you!" Hattie's voice rang with authority. She gave each of them a cold, hard look. When she spoke again, they both listened respectfully. "I haven't seen such ridiculous behavior since I left the schoolroom. Perhaps you both need a good dose of tonic. I won't have you breaking into fisticuffs in my presence."

She turned first to the man she knew best. "What do you have to say for yourself, Reed Tyler?"

"He started it!" he protested.

"You have been crabby and disagreeable for a week," she said. "Now if you've got a bug up your craw, let's hear about it. Harm has a right to be a little confused right now. He just buried his father last week. You're supposed to be his friend. I'd think you would remember that."

Before Reed had a chance to comment, she turned to Harmon. "I have not known you very long, but I consider you a friend of mine and a fine, good man. As my friend, you should know that I do not approve of fighting. I don't think that breaking someone's jaw ever solves anything. If you feel the need to vent your anger by knocking someone down, I'd ask you to do it someplace other than my farm."

Harmon looked genuinely distressed. "Miss Hattie, you've been real good to me. I . . . you and Reed are the only friends I have." He looked at his adversary, and although there was still anger in his face, his voice was controlled. "I shouldn't have hit you, Reed. I'm sorry."

Reed, still rubbing his jaw, accepted the apology with a shrug. "I've not been thinking real straight the last few days. You're probably right about the canals. I think we should leave them just as they are."

Harmon looked surprised. He'd forgotten about the canals completely. "Your idea has some merit," he said to Reed.

"Maybe we could do a few of them that way to see how it works. If we see it's better, we could change them all."

"Fine," Reed answered, and the two began to discuss the changes they could make.

Hattie walked away slowly, not feeling quite right about the situation. They were both acting as if everything were fine, but underneath she could sense things were still bothering both of them.

The long summer day found Reed working late in the cotton, chopping and thinking. Motion was typical of his life, so he never stopped the rise and fall of the hoe as he worked, the hot sun plastering his shirt to his back like a second skin.

The bruise on his jaw was big and ugly and purple. It would take some explaining, but he wasn't concerned about that. Other thoughts were torturing him.

The rice field had been so important to him, he'd wanted it so much. He remembered thinking that once he had rice growing, he would be a happy man. He wondered why he wasn't. He was sure it had something to do with Hattie, but it didn't take a wizard to figure that out. He was trying to understand what had changed between them and when it had happened.

She was his friend, just as she'd always been. He told himself it was natural for him to worry that Drayton might take advantage of her. Any friend would feel the same concern. But that couldn't explain the unreasonable jealousy that had assailed him—still assailed him—at the thought of her kissing old snuff-smelling Drayton.

Bringing his hoe down sharply into the hard black dirt, he remembered the lightning-like sting of envy he'd felt when she'd spoken of Drayton. On no occasion in his life had he ever felt the slightest wish to be Ancil Drayton, but he had found himself wishing he was the one making calls to Hattie's front porch.

Did he care about Hattie? he asked himself. Of course he cared. She was like a sister to him. But he didn't care about her *that* way. Or maybe he did. Memories of the past few weeks flittered across his mind like a magic-lantern show. Hattie laughing in his arms in the pigsty, so flushed and embarrassed. A glimpse of pink rickrack on her drawers and her bodice covered in mud, amply displaying her charms. Hot sweet kisses in the fog . . . All were evidence that his feelings were not entirely brotherly. Even the memories brought a lick of fire to his loins, and he cursed his lack of control.

He was promised to Bessie Jane. That was the reality. A man promised was as good as married, some said. Reed didn't always believe that. But when a man had bedded a woman, that was a promise as sacred as any spoken in church. It made no matter what his father had said about making choices. Breaching a woman's innocence was a decision made. Momentarily, though, he wondered. No blood, no pain, an easy entry . . . Slamming the hoe roughly into a patch of crabgrass, he cast the doubt away. It was unworthy of Bessie Jane. It was unworthy of him. Looking for a reason to do wrong, a man would always find one. What he needed to be doing was resolving to do right.

Bessie Jane was young and sweet, and trusted his honor. She was flighty, but she had a good heart and a depth of feeling in her soul, he knew. She deserved better than a bridegroom with his mind on another woman.

And the other woman deserved better too. For the last eight years, he had talked with her, laughed with her, and worked with her. He probably knew Hattie better than anyone else in the world. Not once during all that time had it occurred to him to be interested in her as a woman. It was as if he'd had blinders on, looking at her every day and never seeing her.

Stopping to wipe the sweat from his brow, he thought that the old saw must be true: You really can't see the forest for the trees.

Hattie finally had a beau of her own, and he was singing sour grapes, jealous where he had no right. He should be wishing her well, yet he selfishly wasn't. He couldn't have her for himself, so he didn't want anyone else to have her. He wasn't being fair, but as he plied his hoe in the row of cotton, he didn't know how to stop.

Letting his mind wander through the past, he tried to recapture the feeling of that night, that one night with Bessie Jane. It eluded him. There had been desire and eagerness, but he couldn't remember passion, and certainly not love. That was it, he thought as he stopped to look back on the row he'd just completed. He didn't remember if he loved Bessie Jane. Lots of people married without being in love. He knew that. Bessie Jane would be a good, devoted, and faithful wife, always pretty and always by his side. A wife was someone who helped you in the field, cooked your meals, washed your clothes, birthed your children, and warmed your bed. Bessie Jane could do all of that, he told himself determinedly. But then, the devil in him pointed out, so could Hattie. And she could be a friend besides.

In disgust he stared across the field of nearly full-grown cotton to the impeccably clean white farmhouse in the distance. Bessie Jane would be his wife, and Hattie would be his friend. It was best that he resign himself to those facts. A man could have only one woman, and he'd already chosen his.

There was no second chances for second choices.

Fourteen

B Y the time the heat of July had settled in, the cotton crop
was laid by. Good weather had helped the cotton grow tall
and strong, and all that was left was for the bolls to blossom
and the pickers to pick. The word was that cotton was thin in
the Deep South but the weevils were thick. That meant a higher
price per pound and good news for Arkansawyers. The mood in
the county was light, and the need for laughter and music was
in the air. It was a special time of year, between chopping and
picking, when all the other farm chores were caught up and
neighbors who had barely had time to pass a word together since
spring gathered for fun and celebration.

Hattie had a brand-new dress for the July Fourth picnic, white
lawn with a pleated bodice and a sash of bright blue satin. In
honor of the holiday she pinned two bright red poppies to her
hat. For the first time in her life, she would be attending a
community outing on the arm of a man, and she couldn't keep
from smiling and humming as she packed the last of the huge
basket of victuals. Feeding eight on the ground was no small
task, but she took it on gladly.

The last few weeks had seen improvement in her life and her

outlook. Reed had finally begun to act like himself again, although he had still not returned to their former breakfast ritual. Harm would disappear for days at a time but kept returning to do his share. He was quieter now, yet he seemed to have formed a truce with Reed.

And Mr. Drayton—no, Ancil, she corrected herself. She had decided to start thinking about him on a first-name basis. Ancil had been a prince and a gentleman. He continued to call upon her two nights a week, and she had become increasingly relaxed in his presence. His "smoochy-smooches" were still not quite what she would have hoped, but she rebuked herself for wasting a thought on such trifling. She had put her foot down about the pinching, and he had acted the perfect gentleman since.

As she heard the wagon pull up in the yard, she hurried out to meet him. The last evening she had seen him, he had spoken with great seriousness about the future. She felt confident that he was going to declare himself soon. The very idea of it made her nearly light-headed.

By the time she reached the porch, Ancil had pulled the team to a stop. "Well, good morning, Miss Hattie," he called out. "Don't you look like a flag yourself."

She accepted the statement as if it were a compliment and asked the boys to come get the picnic basket.

"Daddy says there's going to be fireworks and I can stay up and watch!" Ada told her excitedly as Ancil offered her a hand into the wagon.

"Fireworks?" Hattie asked, looking at Ancil with almost as much excitement as his daughter.

"That's what I hear," he said. "Preacher Able told me they sent all the way to Memphis for 'em. Should be something to see." His wide gap-toothed grin was infectious, and Hattie found herself smiling back as they headed down the road.

Picnicking was not all that was involved in the July Fourth celebration. There were games for the children—sack races, horseshoes, tag, and hide-and-seek.

Just downstream a mile or so, there were cockfights in progress too. Although the practice was illegal and considered immoral by many, Preacher Able, the community conscience who heartily disapproved of gambling, was enough of a Southerner to relish a good cockfight. The women pretended not to know the feathered battles existed, and most of the children honestly didn't know, but the men would slip off to spend some time betting on the life of the best-looking rooster.

Hattie and the Drayton family spread their quilts under the shade of a huge water oak. Seating herself sideways on her knees, Hattie spread her skirts around her in an attractive swirl, modestly covering her limbs. Ancil stood behind her, leaning against the tree with a proprietary air and dipping snuff.

Enjoying the role of the lady of the house for the first time, Hattie cheerfully greeted friends and neighbors as they came by to visit a spell. Ancil Drayton had never been a particularly popular fellow, but Hattie was well liked. And because the two of them were the subject of much gossip and speculation, the stream of acquaintances was unending.

Mary Nell, for once, was on her best behavior. Apparently seeing the advantage of the notoriety of her father and his lady-friend, she sat most of the day with Hattie.

"Did you make that dress, Mary Nell?" Hattie asked her at one point, admiring the pale blue gingham.

The young girl, lacking an audience for her good behavior and seeing her father had stepped away to talk to one of the farmers, gave Hattie a half sneer for an answer. "It's one of my mama's that I cut down," she said finally. "You don't think my skinflint pa would buy me cloth, do you?"

Hattie was startled. That was exactly what she did think. A father took care of the needs of his children, and one of the needs of a young girl reaching maturity was pretty clothes to give her confidence.

With questions still in her mind, Hattie's attention was drawn to Emma Tucker, Reed's sister, walking toward them on her husband's arm. "Hattie," she said brightly. "Now don't you just look fit to be tied." Turning her head, Emma regarded the younger girl. "I see you're putting your hair up. Isn't that something, Sidney? Before you know it, all these children will be near grown."

It was obvious that Mary Nell didn't appreciate being considered only "near grown," but she preened under the attention of the Tuckers, one of the county's most well-to-do families.

"I haven't seen Andy here today," she said, abruptly interrupting her elders.

Emma gave the girl a speculative glance. "Oh, he's here. He would never miss that fiddle music tonight. I never saw a boy who loved dancing as much."

Ancil moseyed back to the group at that moment. "Never cared for dancing myself," he said. With a glance to Hattie, he added, "My ma was hard-shell Baptist. She didn't approve a bit. I never quite got the hang of it myself."

"I don't usually do much dancing myself," Hattie said, not bothering to point out that it was due more to lack of partners than lack of interest.

Emma and Sidney moved on to visit with the Howleys, and Mary Nell shortly made herself scarce on the pretext of checking on her brothers.

Farming was the subject of the day, and speculation on how high cotton prices might go was everywhere. Several farmers inquired about Miss Hattie's rice field too.

"It's just growing beautifully," she assured them, smiling. "Why, it's already nearly a foot tall, and we've got near half of the growing season still to go."

"Don't know why you bother with all that work," one man said. "With cotton doing so well, it seems like a wasted effort."

Hattie continued smiling, undisturbed by her neighbor's lack of enthusiasm for the project. "Cotton is doing well this year," she agreed. "But who knows what will happen with the next crop. I'm looking toward the future, and I believe the future in eastern Arkansas is rice."

The men generally gave her a tolerant look and wished her well. "Cotton is our crop," a farmer from near Hadley told her unequivocally. "This rice growing is just a flash in the pan."

Ancil continued his vigil beside her, visiting with all those who stopped by and occasionally speaking to Hattie, forcing her to crane her neck awkwardly to meet his gaze. It was during one of those personal interchanges that Ancil suddenly looked beyond her.

"Morning, Tyler," he said evenly.

Hattie quickly turned her head to find Reed and Bessie Jane standing in front of them. Reed already had his jacket off and slung over his shoulder. He'd rolled up his shirtsleeves, and the crisp white cotton contrasted starkly with his well-tanned arms. But what captured Hattie's attention were his warm cinnamon eyes.

"You look very pretty today, Miss Hattie," he said, his words strangely soft on the breeze.

Feeling a pleased flush stealing over her cheeks, she laughed self-consciously. "So you like my new dress," she said, choosing to misunderstand.

Reed smiled broadly at her confusion. As a fellow farmer Miss Hattie was undaunted, but gussied up in her finery, she was as subject to flattery as the next woman. "The dress is nice too," he said, not allowing her to mistake his meaning.

"Well, for new dresses and pretty ladies," Ancil said, "you ain't going to have to look far." He gave Bessie Jane a low, clumsy bow.

Belatedly, Hattie glanced over at Reed's intended and nearly blanched in mortification. Bessie Jane was a confection of pink and rose chiffon. Her hair was painstakingly arranged with pink and white ribbons, and a pink and rose parasol completed the outfit. It had obviously come straight from St. Louis, and Hattie's new handmade paled pitifully in comparison.

"That is the most beautiful outfit I've ever seen," she said with as much goodwill as she could muster. It was annoying enough to be compared to a woman both younger and prettier, she thought, and having clothes made by a modiste surely bordered on the unfair.

Bessie Jane acknowledged the compliments, then added with a shrug, "Mama thought I should save it for my trousseau, but I didn't want to wait that long to wear it."

"Well, I'm certainly glad you didn't wait," Ancil said. "It's just not fair for all your pretty clothes to be wasted on a man who will already be your husband."

The little group all laughed politely, as if Ancil's joke were actually funny.

As the afternoon wore on, the fresh summer dresses wilted, and the children's excitement was subdued by the heat and the good food. As the youngsters found shady spots to play marbles, tell tales, and speculate on the evening's fireworks display, the afternoon became more relaxed and informal for the adults.

Bessie Jane was alone for the first time of the day. She'd told Reed she wanted time to visit with her friends, but she had quickly become bored by the gaggle of giggling gossips, and a sense of exhaustion nearly overwhelmed her. Stealing away, she headed for the river to take a short respite in the private sanctuary created by an aged weeping willow. Wishing she could drop to the ground and stick her feet in the cool water, she stood, careful not to damage her gown, and gazed at the river. She was watching the water go by, but she was not seeing it, not thinking about it. She was trying not to think at all.

A light touch on her hand abruptly drew her back to the present. Automatically decorating her face with the winsome smile she forced herself to maintain, she turned to face the intruder.

Her pretense of girlish sweetness faded instantly as she faced Harmon Leege. "What are you doing here?" Her whisper communicated both anger and anxiety.

"I saw you slipping in here," he said. "I wanted a word with you alone, so I followed you."

"Someone could have seen you!" she exclaimed, glancing hastily through the willow's leafy covering to assure herself that no one was watching. "You've got to leave right now. Do you have no care at all for what people will think of me?"

"No one saw me," Harm said with a sigh of disgust. "Don't you think that it's time, Bess, that you quit worrying about other people and start worrying about our future?"

" 'Our future'?" Her tone was incredulous. "I thought I'd made our future perfectly clear down by the dock." Turning away from him, she stared out at the river again. "You're leaving here to go up north and get rich, or you're staying here and making a living as a junkman. You can do whatever you want. You have no one here to tie you down."

"Is that what you want, Bess? Do you want me to leave?"

Refusing to examine her own heart, she avoided the question. "It's what you've always wanted. To go someplace where you can be accepted for who you are, not who your parents were. I'll be staying right here. In the fall I'll marry Reed Tyler, we'll buy Miss Hattie's land, build us a little place, raise a house full of children, and go to church on Sundays."

"Is that what you want?" he asked her. "To spend the rest of your life with a man you don't love?"

"Reed Tyler is the best catch in the county," she answered, carefully repressing her feelings in the matter. "He's good-looking and hardworking, and he'll make a fine husband."

"Well, I hope Reed and your father will be very happy, because you won't."

Spinning to face him, she stared at him with disappointment. "You don't wish me happiness?"

"Yes, I do wish it for you," he said. "But you'll never find it with him."

Tears sprang to her eyes at his words. "I suppose some would say that it's exactly what I deserve."

"I wouldn't say it." His tone was gentle, consoling.

Bessie Jane wanted his sympathy even less than she wanted his ill will. "I told you I've been with him," she said, holding her head high in a refusal to be cowed by her emotions. "Did you think I was lying?"

"No," he said quietly. "I believe it."

"Then why are you here?" Her voice was louder now, shrill with pain.

"Because I love you."

Stunned by the declaration that was so uncalled-for, so humbling for him, she chose to twist the knife in the wound. "It doesn't matter to you that I've been with another man?"

"Yes, it matters. I wanted to drown him, drown myself. But it would make no difference, Bess. What's happened has happened. I can't stop loving you just because I hate what you've done."

Running both hands through his thick hair, Harm sought words to express the way he felt about his woman, the depth of the betrayal he tried to understand. "If you had loved him, it would be easier. That isn't how it was, I'm sure of that. Maybe you want him, maybe he gives you pleasure, but you don't love him. You lie with him to get away from me, Bess, but that won't work."

He pulled her into his arms. She resisted for only a second, then he spoke to her, his words a warm whisper against her cheek. "We are one, sweet Bess. I pledged you my love, my life, so long ago. You remember, don't you?"

Though she shook her head in denial, Bessie Jane remembered all too clearly.

"I've waited for you to realize that," he went on. "All these long months I've waited while you've dallied in the grass with Tyler." Impatience colored his voice, and a tad of anger. "I'm not waiting anymore. I've decided to help you remember. I'm not letting you go so easily. I'm going to fight for what is mine."

She looked up at him, her eyes wide with fear. "What are you going to do?"

"Don't look so scared. I'm not calling Reed out," he said

with a humorless laugh. "I've already tried to break his jaw, and he didn't have the vaguest idea why. The person I'm fighting is right here in my arms."

He pressed a tender kiss on her lips, followed by a sally of the tongue that sparked the dormant embers inside her to flames. "I'll be here all summer, sweet Bess," he whispered against her mouth. "Whenever you turn around, I'll be watching and waiting for you. I'll be at your window at night and everywhere you look in the day. When you get to that church to marry, I'll be waiting for you on the front steps. We belong together, Bess. I have no intention of letting you go."

Her body melted against his as a thirst for his touch, his caress, surged inside her. Then she heard the distant chatter of voices and jerked away from him.

"You must let me go," she said, and fled from him, hoping that leaving her love for him behind would be as easy.

Dusk was slipping across the picnic grounds when the lanterns were lit and the erratic notes of tuning fiddles was heard. Hattie laid the sleeping Buddy on one corner of the quilts, tenderly stroking his curly blond hair. Ada was already dreaming on the other side of the quilt, but she had made Hattie promise to awaken her for the fireworks. Carefully removing its pins, Hattie took off her hat and laid it on top of the picnic basket for safekeeping. The red blossoms were still vibrant, and she touched them, thinking what a nice memory they would make. A nice remembrance of fun and laughter and children in her arms on July Fourth. Smiling, she gave another loving glance to the two sleepy heads. No matter what happened, she would never forget the sweet emotion these children evoked in her.

Glancing up, she saw Ancil striding toward her, a disgruntled Mary Nell at his side. Drayton's eldest had also had a busy day. After watching the young girl cavorting with her friends, Hattie had determined that she suffered from the nonlethal pyrexia common to females of her age commonly known as boy-crazy. It was no excuse for her bad manners and surly attitude, but it did explain a great deal about why her family and father seemed to exist only as temporary annoyances.

"Mary Nell is going to watch the children for a while," Ancil told Hattie, ignoring the girl's angry look. Reaching for her hand, he helped Hattie up, then offered his arm in a gesture more natural to gentlemen than cotton farmers. "Have you enjoyed the picnic?" he asked conversationally as they strolled away.

"Yes. It's been such fun, and the children have been delightful."

He nodded, pleased. "I told them to be on their best behavior for you."

Hattie nearly said that she thought the children knew her well enough now to be themselves but decided against it. Surely he could see his children liked her, and that was enough.

"Nearly everybody in the county showed up," he said.

"I would imagine that most folks were in as much need of a picnic as we were."

He smiled down at her and patted her hand.

Thinking they were headed for the dancing, Hattie was surprised when Ancil made a detour toward a darkened copse of trees. She suspected he wanted a moment alone with her to steal a kiss and glanced around anxiously. Their kissing was vastly improved, but she wasn't willing to risk her reputation for it. "Perhaps we should stay with the others," she said primly, stopping dead still.

Ignoring her balk, Ancil slipped an arm around her waist and urged her into the shadows. "For this, Miss Hattie, I think it's quite proper for us to be alone."

Once they were safely concealed, Ancil stopped and released her. He simply looked at her for a moment, not touching her in any way. The "smoochy-smooch" that Hattie expected was not forthcoming, and the farmer seemed ill at ease as he shifted from one foot to the other. Removing his hat, he placed it over his heart and cleared his throat. "Miss Hattie," he began finally, "we've only been courting a couple of months now, and I guess some would say I'm speaking too soon."

In the darkness he couldn't see Hattie's face pale as she realized the import of his words.

"Lula's been gone the better part of a year," he said. "I cared a lot for that woman, but all the grieving in the world ain't going to bring her back, and I'm thinking to go on with my life."

He waited then, as if expecting some response from Hattie. She was too paralyzed with anticipation to speak.

"We are not children, Miss Hattie. We both know what we are about. And I see no call for spending months on end trying to decide on what we already know."

He swallowed hard and looked directly into her eyes for the first time. "I suspect you know what I'm asking. Them children of mine, they need a mama. And I'm needing a woman, Miss Hattie, not just for smoochy-smooch on the porch, but a real woman to share my life with. I think you'd do just fine for both tasks, if you're willing."

Hattie's heart was pounding so vigorously, she could hardly hear what he was saying. At last, at long last, it was happening to her. Hattie Colfax was being asked for her hand.

Her mind flashed back to those times when she had believed it would never happen. The foolish dreams of her childhood had been harvested in the disappointment of her twenties. She had struggled to make a life for herself without a husband, without children, without the familial love that so many woman accepted casually and treated frivolously. Here it was—a man to marry, a family of her own, the end of her loneliness.

Inexplicably the image of Reed Tyler at the plow, drenched in sweat but with a smile on his face, flittered through her mind. She dismissed it. It was a girlish, romantic notion to think that a husband should be young and handsome, always smiling. Reed was a young girl's fantasy—strong, handsome, noble, and determined. But he was only a fantasy, and a real husband was standing beside her. His hair might be sparse and his shoulders a little stooped. He might give smoochy-smooches instead of peaches, but he offered security, stability, a home, and a houseful of children to raise.

There was no more to consider, no more to imagine or wish for. Here at last was her chance for happiness, and she would be a fool to ignore it or let it slip away. "Yes, Ancil," she answered softly. "I'd be very pleased to marry up with you."

He hesitated a moment, as if to make sure he understood what she'd said, then his gap-toothed smile broke across his face. "You're willing then?" he asked unnecessarily.

She nodded, smiling back at him. He pulled her into his arms, planting a wet, happy kiss square on her lips. They giggled like children for a minute as he kissed her twice more.

"We're going to do just fine, Hattie," he promised her. "We got differences, lots of couples do, but we're going to make a go of this thing, I'm sure."

"I think so too," she said, resolving to make it so. "I think I do well with the children. I'm even beginning to understand Mary Nell."

"Don't you worry about those younguns," he said, allowing his hand to slide across her midriff. Hattie brought her arms down, effectively cutting short his exploration. Accepting that good-naturedly, he kissed her again.

"Let's go tell 'em," he said, indicating the crowd of people gathered farther down the hill near the river. The music had begun, and the sounds of fiddles, laughter, and dancing filtered up to their quiet enclosure.

Hattie hesitated, feeling almost shy with her new status. She wondered how the neighbors would take the news. Her courtship had been the most widely spread gossip of the summer. Would they think her fast to accept the first time Ancil asked? Would they tut-tut over the length of time since Lula Drayton passed away? Hattie was nervous, but she refused to let those thoughts intrude on her glorious moment of betrothal.

"Whatever you want, Ancil," she said sweetly, and was rewarded by a very lover-like kiss from her intended.

Delighted in her malleability, Ancil pulled her close again for a squeeze, then gave her an enthusiastic pinch on the derriere. At her cry of pain, he remembered his promise and tried to make up for his error by gently rubbing the injured spot. "I forgot," he said sheepishly. Hattie slapped away his hand and headed for the dancing. Ancil followed in her wake, a naughty grin plastered on his face.

Long before she reached the crowd, Ancil was at her side, his arm possessively around her waist. As they hesitated on the edge of the crowd, Hattie couldn't meet the eyes of her friends. She knew her color was high and hoped no one had seen them stepping out from the secluded glade.

When the tune finished, Ancil propelled her through the people until they were standing in the center of the dancing area. He held up his hands to capture everyone's attention, then pulled Hattie close against his side. "I've got an announcement to make," he said loudly. They all hushed to hear his words. "To put it short and sweet," he said, grinning down at Hattie, "Miss Hattie Colfax has consented to be my new bride."

A murmur of delight rippled through the crowd, punctuated by squeals from several females. Suddenly Hattie was surrounded by her friends and neighbors. As the women hugged her and laughed with delight, the men slapped Ancil on the back and joked.

"I knew it from the very first," Millie Jessup declared to anyone who would listen. "I just knew these two were perfect for each other. Why, I practically brought them together myself."

All around her there was excited talk about weddings and dresses and holiday proposals. Hattie felt almost divorced from what was happening. Her dream had come true, yet somehow it didn't excite her. Glancing up over the faces that surrounded her, she saw Reed standing next to a wagon. He was alone, watching her.

He was smiling, but something in his expression was sad.

Fifteen

THE dancing continued after Ancil's impromptu announcement. Hattie was snatched up by several of the farmers for a turn around the floor in honor of her upcoming nuptials. Reed watched her laughing and twirling in the arms of his friends and neighbors. In all the years he'd known her, he didn't remember ever watching her dance.

He was standing beside Arthur Turpin near the fiddler's wagon, along with a group of men, many of whom were smoking and all of whom were avoiding the ladies. When Ancil walked up, the backslapping continued unabated for a minute, until Arthur spoke. "This must be your lucky day, Drayton," he said. "I heard you won twenty-five dollars at the chicken fights."

Ancil shrugged good-naturedly. "When Lady Luck and a good rooster are on your side, it ain't no time to question."

"Both the damn birds I picked didn't have the spirit of a prissy-pants sissy," Arthur complained. "If there's one thing I can't stand, it's a gamecock that's scared of the sight of its own blood."

"Heard you lost a bundle," Ancil said. "What's your wife going to say about that?"

"My wife don't run me," Arthur boasted. "I run her." Looking to the other men, he jokingly added, "If she gives me trouble, I run her off."

With the bluster of male camaraderie supporting them, all the men found it easy to join in the joke.

"That's something you're going to have to remember," Arthur said, "now that you're tying the knot, Ancil."

Ancil scowled in annoyance. "You ain't talking to no green kid. I been married before, and I know exactly how to handle a woman."

His bragging was accepted amiably by the other men. He wasn't going to allow any teasing about being a new bridegroom, so Arthur decided to see how he'd do with teasing about his new bride. "So you are really marrying Miss Hattie?"

"Yep, sure am," Ancil answered easily. "I suspect it's about the smartest move I ever made."

Arthur nodded. "I guess with all those children to raise, you would need a woman of some kind."

Ancil laughed. Something about the sound of it caught Reed's attention. "My Mary Nell could raise those kids right enough. That ain't my reason for marrying up."

Arthur chuckled. "Got a lonely bed up there on the hill, you saying?"

"Oh, I don't expect Horseface Hattie to be much of a thrill in the blankets," Ancil said. "Though to my way of thinking, you put a bag over her head, you can't tell one woman much from another."

A roar of laughter burst from Arthur Turpin, and the other men followed suit. "Now, I don't wholly agree with that," Arthur said. "Some women is like holding a bag of sticks, and others is more like squeezing a tub of lard."

That comment was met by hoots and agreement.

"Hattie ain't neither of those," Ancil said boastfully. "I checked it out as best she would let me." Glancing at her as she spun in Cal Tyler's arms, he stated, "There ain't no bustle in the back nor ruffles in the front. What there is of her out there, fellows, are honest-to-God body parts."

Reed stood frozen in shock, as this group of dirty-talking men that he had always considered friends gaped at Hattie, assessing her as if she were some brood sow at the livestock show. He was tempted to run over and throw his coat around her, to hide her from the gaze of his fellow farmers turned reprobates. "Drayton," he said finally, "I don't believe that's any way for you to be talking about the woman you hope to marry." The anger in his voice was unmistakable.

Ancil flushed at the criticism. He hadn't realized Tyler was there. The other men also suffered a moment's embarrassment, knowing that Reed considered Miss Hattie another one of his sisters.

"I didn't mean no disrespect," Ancil said.

Reed couldn't imagine how his words could mean anything else. "Miss Hattie is a fine, gentle Christian lady, and you're talking about her like she's some hussy from Memphis."

Ancil was bent on defending himself. "A man doesn't marry up with a woman without having a carnal thought or two. I suspect those little walks you take with Bessie Jane wouldn't bear close scrutiny."

"Now wait just a minute there," Arthur Turpin said, ready to do battle over his daughter's good name.

"I don't mean nothing, Arthur," Ancil said soothingly. "What I'm saying is just the truth. A couple is going to do a little sparking, a little spooning. There ain't nobody would be surprised at that."

"A man doesn't talk about his woman in front of other men," Reed said. "Not if he's got feelings for her."

"Wasn't that what I was just talking about, feeling for her?"

An explosion of laughter ripped around him, and Reed felt the cold anger settle more deeply in his bones. He wanted to rip Drayton's self-satisfied snaggle-toothed grin off his face, but he held his peace. Taking deep breaths, he tried to remind himself that this man was Hattie's intended.

"So Miss Hattie is all woman?" Arthur said. "I often wonder about those quiet hardworking types."

"She's woman enough," Ancil said. "I'm sure everyone was curious about why I would marry old Horseface when there are plenty of younger, prettier women around."

Reed blanched at the man's casual use of the nickname. Seeing in his mind Hattie's tears when she'd told him about the boys' cruelty to her, he clenched his fists.

"Her name is Miss Hattie," he said between gritted teeth.

Ancil glowered at him. "She's my intended, Reed. I can call her anything I please, and it's nothing to you."

"I might make it something," he threatened.

"Reed, come on now, boy," Arthur intervened. "People have been calling her Horseface since she was a girl. It ain't like Ancil made up the name."

"I don't like it," Reed said quietly, dangerously. "I don't want to hear it."

"There's no call to get yourself stirred up," Arthur began. But Ancil interrupted him.

"It's okay, Arthur. I understand why Reed's got a burr up his butt, and it ain't got nothing to do with Hattie's nickname." Ancil smiled at Reed with snide confidence. "It seems that Reed is the only one that's already figured out exactly why I married Hattie."

"What do you mean?" Arthur asked him.

"You tell them, Tyler," Ancil taunted. "What in the world could a long-in-the-tooth old maid have that a man could want?"

Reed stared at him dumbly, not knowing what he was getting at.

"You claiming you don't know?" Ancil snorted in disbelief. "You been nice to that old maid for years for the very same reason."

Glancing around the group, he announced in a tone that stated the obvious, "Horseface owns the finest piece of ground in this county."

The men stared back at him, silent and stunned. Miss Hattie's land was some of the best, none would question that. But the suggestion that the kind, friendly woman they'd all known for years was being wed for a piece of real estate didn't sit well.

Ancil correctly gauged the tenor of the group and threw the unwanted criticism elsewhere. "Tyler's wanted that land all his life. He's worked his fingers near to the bone on it for years now and nearly sweat blood trying to buy it."

Letting the words settle around him, Ancil looked at Reed and shrugged unkindly. "Sorry, Tyler. When Hattie Colfax says 'I do,' that farm will be mine, no money down."

Now the men stared at Reed. He hadn't thought about the land. Hattie had promised to sell it to him, and he'd never given it a thought again. All the time she'd been courting, it hadn't occurred to him that a husband might not be willing to let him have it. He should have realized it, but he hadn't. He had Hattie's word on the sale, but he knew Drayton was right. Once they were married it would be his decision, and what Hattie had agreed to wouldn't mean a thing. Drayton would never sell it. It was twice as good as the land he now held, and putting the two together would make him one of the bigger land owners in the county. He'd be a fool to let it go.

As Reed's silence dragged on, the suspense got too much for Arthur. Slapping Reed on the back, he said, "I know it's a disappointment, boy, but that ain't the only land in Arkansas. Besides," he added, speaking more to the crowd than to Reed, "I've been trying to get him to give up farming and go into business with me. Bessie Jane is all I've got. I need a man with a good head on his shoulders to take over the store."

"I'm a farmer, Arthur," Reed said, his brain still spinning from Drayton's revelation. "I've worked the land all my life, and I'll continue to do that."

"If you're thinking to get her to sell it to you before we're wed," Ancil said, "I'd ask you not to. I'll not have her without that land, and breaking off the engagement would be a big embarrassment for Miss Hattie."

Reed paled at the threat, imagining the humiliation Hattie would face. "There's other land," he said calmly.

"I thought you'd see it that way, Reed." Ancil's tone was conciliatory. "I have great respect for Miss Hattie. My children like her, and she's a hard worker. I see no reason why we shouldn't have a fine marriage."

The men around him nodded solemnly in apparent agreement. Reed felt a cold pit of anger open up in his gut, but he fought down the feeling and purposely kept his voice even and reasonable. "Will you be wanting me to stay on another year to tend the rice?" he asked. "The crop is new to you, but I expect you could learn enough to handle it yourself in a growing season."

"Rice?" Drayton laughed. "Good Lord, Tyler, you don't actually expect somebody else to take up that crazy scheme of yours?"

"It's not a crazy scheme," Reed said. "Rice is the crop of the future. They've learned how to mechanize the growing and harvesting so that one man can farm a hundred acres. That's what we need, a crop that doesn't take an army of hands to tend it."

Ancil scoffed. "Hands may be a problem to a bachelor like you, Tyler. But us married men grow our own." Smiling, he glanced around at the other men, then added, "I've done got seven out of my first wife, and I suspect Miss Hattie's still young enough to whelp a brat or two."

The image of Hattie swelled with child filled Reed's mind, but he tamped it down. "That may be so," he said, "but the canals and levees have already been built. Miss Hattie's invested a goodly amount of money in the crop already."

"Like pouring water down a rathole," Ancil said, then rephrased it, attempting a joke. "Like pouring water down a rice hole!"

The laughter was weak, several of the men still concerned about Reed's temper.

"I'll be draining that nasty rice swamp you've made, Tyler," Ancil told him. "I'm planting cotton in that field."

"Cotton?" Reed was incredulous. "You can't plant cotton in that silt."

"It'll grow there just fine."

"Sure it will for a year or two. But it won't hold the ground. Ten years from now, that whole field will be clogging up somebody's bayou down past New Orleans."

Ancil shrugged, unconcerned. "That's the way of farming. You use the land until it's used up. Nothing stays the same forever."

"Not the same," Reed agreed, "but you don't have to destroy it. Don't you read the *Farmer's Bulletins*?"

Ancil bristled. "I done forgot more about farming than the sassy city slickers that write them bulletins will ever know. I don't waste my time on newfangled ideas from back east somewhere."

Silence widened around him as the men in the crowd mentally switched to Reed's side. The *Farmer's Bulletin* was widely read and revered, second only to the Bible.

"Does Miss Hattie know you plan to plant her rice field in cotton?" Reed asked.

Scowling with unspoken menace. Ancil said, "What is between my woman and me is none of your concern, Tyler."

Reed hesitated for a moment, then gave an almost imperceptible nod. Drayton was right. It was none of his business. Without another word, he walked away.

He could hear the men's continued conversation as he strode toward the woods, but it was over the roaring of his blood. He was more angry than he'd been in years, and helpless to do anything about it. When he was out of sight of the dancers and the crowd, he stopped in front of a scrub oak. With all the force of his right hand, he slugged the ungiving tree trunk, splintering the bark and sending a scream of agony through his arm. He shook his hand twice, throwing off the tiny bits of wood that clung to it. Gazing down at his bleeding knuckles, he tried wriggling his fingers. Nothing was broken, he thought in gratitude, and leaned against the tree, absorbing the pain that still encompassed him. It was better to hurt for a reason than to hurt for something that couldn't be helped.

He stood staring into the darkness, trying without success not to think at all. He belonged to another woman, and Hattie belonged to another man. He asked himself how he could let her marry someone who would never understand her tender feelings. A man who could use that awful nickname as if it were a joke, who could publicly state that he would get children off her by covering her face with a bag, who would never in a million years deserve the love that Hattie Colfax was capable of giving.

There was nothing that he could do, though. Breaking them up would not be impossible, but it wouldn't solve anything, either. She wanted a husband and children, and she should have those things. He couldn't offer them to her. He'd made his commitment to Bessie Jane, and there was no going back.

At least, he thought, he wouldn't have to be there to watch it. The realization gave him pause. He should have been thinking about his future, his land, that had been so abruptly stolen from him. He'd not given it more than a passing thought. His concerns were for Hattie. He shook his head in disbelief. All those years of dreaming and working to own Colfax Farm, and now losing all chance of ever having it had slipped his mind.

The meaning of that didn't bear close scrutiny, so holding his injured hand, he headed back toward the festivities. He had to find Bessie Jane. She was his. Losing Colfax Farm would affect her as much as him. But even if it didn't, when a man was troubled, he sought the comfort of his woman.

Deliberately pushing thoughts of Hattie and Ancil out of his mind, he scanned the crowd for Bessie Jane. He saw her before she saw him. She was standing on the edge of the woods alone and kept looking behind her as if expecting someone to step out of the trees.

She'd been looking for him, Reed thought as he hurried his

step. Pretty, sweet Bessie Jane. No man could want more, he admonished himself. This keeping her at arm's length was hurting their relationship. It was time they let nature take its course.

She was staring back into the woods to her left when he laid his hand on her right shoulder. She jumped.

"I didn't mean to startle you," he said, surprised at her frightened expression.

"I thought you were down by the fiddlers," she said unexpectedly.

The statement puzzled him. She'd obviously been watching for him. He put it down to coyness and smiled warmly as he took her arm. "Come with me back to our blanket," he said. "I've got something we need to talk about."

She glanced guiltily at the woods again, then whispered, "We can't just walk off together in the dark, Reed. Someone will see."

Ignoring her protest, he led her away. "Everybody in this county knows we're engaged. No one would say a word about us catching a minute or two alone." He gestured toward the crowd. "Nobody's watching us anyway."

Without another word, the couple made their way up the hill to a small piece of ground under a maple that was covered by the new pink and white picnic cloth Mrs. Turpin had made to match Bessie Jane's dress.

The sound of distant fiddle music floated up the hill. The moon hung low on the distant horizon, the area was shrouded in darkness and privacy. Reed kept his arm around her waist, reminding himself that she was his.

With his assistance, Bessie Jane lowered herself to the cloth. "You wanted to talk?" she asked. Her eyes were wide, and her lips were trembling slightly with a nervousness that sat ill on her usual carefree face.

She was beautiful tonight, Reed thought. Beautiful and vulnerable, and talk was suddenly the furthest thing from his mind. Dropping to his knees in front of her, he wrapped his arms around her waist and pulled her close for a kiss. "I want you," he whispered. "I don't want to wait another day."

Surprised by his sudden move, she resisted momentarily, but he ignored her hesitance. As he pressed his mouth to hers kissing her urgently, she parted her lips in invitation for his tongue. Usually this resulted in his immediate attempt at self-control, but tonight he didn't hesitate to accept her offer, delving instead into the hot sweetness of her mouth. Holding her tight against him, he rubbed his groin suggestively against her.

"Reed? What . . . ?" she asked in a panicked whisper before he pulled her down beside him on the cloth.

"I'm tired of waiting," he said hoarsely, his mouth against the tender skin of her throat. "I need a woman. I need a woman tonight. Are you mine, Bessie Jane?"

His hands were everywhere, exploring her breasts, caressing her backside, stealing up underneath her dress. "I won't wait anymore," he whispered. "You've been right all along. We need each other. We need this release."

His movements were mechanical and desperate. "I deserve this," he said through clenched teeth. "It's my right." He brought his knee up between hers, and she eased her legs apart for him. Allowing his fingers to wander the length of silk-covered leg and thigh for only a moment, he brought his hand up to clutch her womanhood.

Her involuntary gasp seemed more shock than desire. There was no trembling flesh or dampness to welcome him. After an instant of hesitation, she arched against his hand. Reed stilled. He knew her reaction was more duty than passion. His touch had not sparked her to flame. Biddable and loyal, she would allow him his way, satisfy his need, and give him her body as his due. He groaned in frustration, remembering her tears at their former mating. He could not accept such a gift.

Removing his hand, he lay down between her legs, his head resting against her breast.

The silence between them stretched on for several minutes. Bessie Jane tentatively stroked the thick black hair that lay against her bosom. "Have I done something?" Her voice trembled with fear. "People see things they don't understand and can misinterpret them."

As his breathing slowed, Reed raised his head to look into her eyes, glassy with unshed tears. "It's nothing you've done, Bessie Jane," he assured her. "It's me. I . . ."

Pulling himself off her, he lay at her side and absently helped her straighten her skirts. His feelings were muddled. Desire, disappointment, anger, fear, and incompetence all warred for dominance in his thought. "I injured my hand," he said, holding it up for her inspection. "I guess the pain distracts me."

Whether Bessie Jane believed this strange explanation of his behavior he didn't know, but she accepted it with a nod.

"I heard some bad news tonight, sweetheart," he went on. "And I think it's best that you hear it from me."

She raised herself up on one elbow, her face pale in the moon's faint glow. "What have they told you? Is it about Harmon?"

"Harmon?" He looked at her quizzically. "What's happened to Harmon?"

Realizing her mistake immediately, Bessie Jane sat up, smoothing her skirts unnecessarily. "Oh, I haven't heard anything," she said, grasping for an explanation. "I just assumed if it was bad news it would surely be about Harmon Leege."

Shaking his head in disapproval, Reed sat beside her, crossing his legs Indian-style. "I know you don't like him, but I've told you several times, he's a friend of mine."

She sighed deeply, then nodded, and Reed thought the strange expression on her face might have been relief. "It's not about Harm," he said. "It's about us."

"Oh?"

"I guess you heard about Miss Hattie's engagement to Drayton," he began.

She nodded scornfully. "Everyone heard. I assumed that was the reason to announce it now and avoid the expense of an engagement party."

Taken aback by her observation, Reed wondered momentarily if that had been Drayton's motivation. Grimacing with disgust, he continued. "I was just talking with Drayton and your father down by the fiddlers." He paused, trying to find the least hurtful way to tell her. "It seems that Drayton wants to keep the Colfax farm, so it won't be up for sale."

He waited for her reaction, but she continued to look at him expectantly. "And?" she asked finally.

Dumbfounded at her lack of understanding, Reed felt anger begin within him. "And I won't be able to buy the farm. I've worked fifteen years for that land. I wanted it, but now it's gone forever to a no-account mushbrain like Drayton."

Bessie Jane sighed in exasperation. "It's too bad that you didn't get the land, Reed. But I never cared about that land." Her tone was blunt with honesty. "I don't even want to farm. That was your dream, Reed. I'm sorry for you, but to me it's nothing."

"Is marriage to me nothing also?" he asked coldly.

She stared at him, the color draining from her face. "This

shouldn't affect our marriage," she said, trying to keep her voice steady while an inexplicable trembling seemed determined to set in.

"I can't marry you if I haven't got land, Bessie Jane. It wouldn't be right."

"It wouldn't be right?" she repeated. "We must marry, Reed. We must marry, and it has to be soon. I don't care whether you have land or not. I need a husband. My father would be happy to take you into his business, and then we could live in town. Maybe it's the best thing that could happen to us."

"I'm sorry, Bessie Jane, but it just wouldn't work."

"Are you saying you don't intend to marry me?" she asked, not able to look at him.

"Of course I intend to marry you," he said, wrapping his arm around her shoulders. "I just can't do it right now." Giving her a small squeeze of consolation, he tried to reassure her. "I've taken you as my woman and asked you to be my wife, Bessie Jane. A man never goes back on a promise like that." Both staring straight ahead into nothingness, he continued. "It will just take me a little bit more time. My uncle Ed has a piece of rice ground near him that I can probably buy. He's going to help me get ahold of it."

Her eyes widened with enthusiasm. "That would be even better, to go somewhere else, to start fresh."

He smiled. "I never thought you'd want to leave town," he said with surprise.

"I do. I hate this town with all its gossip!" she said vehemently.

It crossed Reed's mind to mention that Bessie Jane was the town's major source of gossip, but he kept his peace.

"How soon do you think we can marry and move?" she asked.

He hesitated. "A couple of years, I guess."

"Two years!" she was clearly incredulous. "That's impossible. I can't wait that long."

"The time will fly—" he began, but she wouldn't hear of it.

"We have to get married in the fall," she stated. "You promised that we'd marry in the fall."

"That was when we were getting Miss Hattie's land," he explained. "I'll have to continue to work for Miss Hattie until we get the rice in, at least. I may stay on until she marries.

After that, I'll have to get together the financing for the land near Helena, and then I'd want to try it by myself at least one season to make sure it's fair enough to support us.''

"I can help you work the farm,'' she said. "It'll be my home, too, and I'll need to be there beside you.''

"That's very nice of you to want to help, sweetheart, but you don't know a blame thing about farming, and I won't have time to be catering to you.''

"I wouldn't expect you to,'' she said.

But Reed was adamant. "I'll work at least one season by myself to assure myself that I can make a living on the place.''

"Well, then you should get started right now. Between what you've saved and Daddy and your uncle Ed, we'll be able to raise the money to buy the new place, and you'll be there for the harvest. That's what will tell you whether the land is good or not.''

"I can't leave Miss Hattie.''

"Of course you can,'' Bessie Jane insisted. "She'd be happy to take your crop in lieu of your not finishing out the year.''

Reed jerked up a sprig of grass, then cast it down angrily. "I bet Drayton would love it. He's probably praying that I'll do something stupid like that. But I'm not doing it. I've planted Miss Hattie a rice field, and she's going to have it this year, if never again.''

"What are you talking about?''

"I promised Miss Hattie a rice field. I'm going to see that she has one.''

"You promised to marry me!''

"And I'm going to, Bessie Jane. You just have to have patience. We'll wed in time.''

"I don't know how much time I have, how long I can hold out,'' she said, desperation evident in her voice.

"What are you talking about?'' Reed asked, completely baffled.

"Reed, I can't wait any longer for you. I want to marry soon, this fall or sooner.''

"Sweetheart, I'm sorry, but without Miss Hattie's land, there just isn't any way.''

"There is a way!'' she said resolutely. "There just has to be.''

Sixteen

I T was Thursday afternoon when Miss Hattie unexpectedly pulled her buggy into the yard at the Drayton place. Her typical smile was nowhere to be seen, and lines of worry were etched in her face.

In the two weeks since she'd agreed to marry Ancil, she'd gotten used to the idea of being somebody's wife, somebody's mother. She'd almost forgotten that she was the undesirable old maid, the woman nobody wanted. That memory had come home to roost that morning, and she'd decided the only way to deal with her doubts was to face them squarely.

The children hurried out into the yard. Little Ada called, "Miss Hattie! Miss Hattie!" as she waved the corncob doll Hattie had given her for her birthday just last week.

"Go get your daddy for me, Ada," she told the child, and watched her scamper off to the field. Her gaze fell on Cyl, whose expression was wary.

"What's happened?" the young girl asked, sidling up to the buggy. "What fool thing has Daddy done now?"

Hattie wanted to answer, "Nothing, nothing at all," but she was afraid that wasn't true.

Bessie Jane had arrived just after breakfast. Hattie had been more than a little surprised to see her drive up. She couldn't remember seeing the young woman out in a buggy unaccompanied.

"Has something happened?" she asked Bessie Jane anxiously. "Reed's raising the water level in the rice, but I can fetch him right away."

"Oh, no," Bessie Jane answered, glancing in the direction of Colfax Bluff. "I've come to talk to you, Miss Hattie. There are some things I think you ought to know."

Relieved but curious, Hattie invited the younger woman into the house for coffee.

"I'd prefer tea if you have it," Bessie Jane said.

Stoking up the fire, Hattie said, "I don't have a spot of tea on the place. Mama used to drink it, but I never cared for the stuff myself."

"Coffee is fine, then," Bessie Jane assured her.

Glancing at Reed's intended sitting so uneasily at the kitchen table with something clearly bothering her, Hattie was struck by her youth. She was really little more than a child. Idly she wondered if Bessie Jane was treated like a child because she persisted in acting like one or if she persisted in acting like a child because she was treated like one.

"I've got cool buttermilk if you want some," Hattie said.

"Buttermilk would be wonderful," the young woman replied, and Hattie poured her a tall glass before filling her own mug with coffee.

Seating herself at the table, Hattie watched Bessie Jane take a long appreciative drink of the buttermilk, then daintily wipe her mouth. "What did you want to talk to me about?"

Bessie Jane looked down, studying the checks in the tablecloth for a moment, then taking a deep breath for courage, she spoke. "I don't know if Reed has told you that our wedding has been postponed."

Hattie raised her eyebrows at the news. Reed had not breathed a word to her. "Why is that?" she asked. "Is there something wrong with the crop?" It was hard to imagine any other reason for a postponement.

Bessie Jane shook her head. "The crop is fine, and Reed is staying to finish it out, so you don't have to worry."

" 'Finish it out'?"

"Yes. He won't be leaving until after the cotton and rice are in."

" 'Leaving.' " Hattie breathed the word in disbelief. "Reed is leaving?"

Nodding solemnly, Bessie Jane said, "I had a feeling you didn't know."

"Why would Reed leave here? This is the best piece of ground in the county, and he's always planned to build his rice crop here." Hattie groped for understanding. "Surely you're mistaken, Bessie Jane. What earthly reason would Reed Tyler have for leaving?"

Bessie Jane looked her straight in the eye. "Because Ancil Drayton told him that the Colfax Farm was not for sale."

Hattie stared at her, her mind aswirl with thoughts she couldn't control. "I don't believe it," she said finally.

Bessie Jane sat quietly for a moment, then said, "It's true." The young woman continued to talk, explaining Reed's plans, how he would try to start over again and how long it might take him to make a go of it. Hattie only half listened. Her ears heard every word, but her heart, her dreams, were drowning in unshed tears.

"Miss Hattie," Bessie Jane said, "Reed has every respect for you, and he wants you to be happy. So much so that he's willing to sacrifice our future so you can wed Ancil Drayton. If Mr. Drayton only wants you for your land . . . well, it hardly seems like it's worth it."

Hattie looked up sharply. The tactlessness of that last statement obviously surprised even Bessie Jane.

"I didn't mean that like it sounded," the younger woman said quickly, trying to take back the hurtful, unfeeling words.

Waving away her apology, Hattie forced a brave smile that didn't reach her eyes. "No use beating around the bush, Bessie Jane. You're absolutely right. If he only wants my land, I'd be a good deal better off without him." As she spoke, she hoped it was true.

They parted amiably, although Bessie Jane seemed a bit frightened. "I really shouldn't have told you," she said with sincerity.

"No, no, Bessie Jane. The truth is always the best. The Bible says it will set you free."

"That's what I'm afraid of," Bessie Jane replied with another nervous glance toward the bluff.

"Reed will never hear a word of this from me," Hattie said, understanding her concern. "This is between me and Ancil now, and no matter what happens, you and Reed are another matter entirely.''

Bessie Jane began to cry. "You are too nice to me, Miss Hattie. I don't deserve it. I came out here knowing what I had to say was going to hurt you.''

"You came out here to see me do right by your man,'' Hattie corrected her. "A woman goes as far as she has to on that account.''

Now, sitting in her buggy in front of Ancil Drayton's house, Hattie wondered how far she would go. She didn't love Ancil, at least she knew that much. She wanted marriage and a family, and Ancil was a means to that end. If it was true that he only wanted her land, her heart wouldn't be broken. The injury to her pride, however, might be just as severe.

"He's done something to ruin it?" Cyl's words penetrated her thoughts, and she glanced down at the girl. The usually smiling mouth was drawn into a thin, angry line.

"I just want to talk to your father on some private business,'' Hattie said, hoping the words didn't sound as cold and hopeless as they felt.

"I knew it was too good to be true,'' Cyl said, kicking the dust. "Figured he'd be bound to do something stupid before he managed to get you to the altar.''

Hattie swallowed hard, her personal feelings warring with her loyalty to her intended and love for his children. "He hasn't done anything stupid, Cyl,'' she said finally. "You father is basically a good man who's lived a hard life. We have some disagreements about things. That's only human.''

She saw Ancil walking in from the fields then, Ada hurrying at his side. His straw hat was worn and scraggly, his overalls were tattered, and he was covered in sweat and dirt. His face was dark as a thundercloud. "Take Ada and make yourself scarce,'' he said roughly to Cyl. The young girl stared at him defiantly for a moment, then with a glance at Hattie, she took her sister's hand and headed toward the barn.

Ancil watched them go. When he turned his attention back to Hattie, looking up at her in her buggy, his expression was anything but welcoming. "You going to say your piece in the buggy,'' he asked, "or you coming down to sit on the porch?''

With only the slightest of hesitations, Hattie held out her hand, and he helped her down. They stepped up onto the front porch, seating themselves on a couple of milking stools that were the worse for wear.

"I'd offer you some lemonade," he said politely, "but I doubt if there is any. Mary Nell don't take to doing that sort of thing, and Cyl is too busy taking care of the animals like you taught her."

"She takes care of them by herself?"

"Ada helps her a bit, I suspect, but mostly it's her. She likes you a whole lot and wants you to be proud of her, I guess."

"Well, I am," Hattie said calmly. "She is a clever, loving little girl. I'm sure you and Lula have always been proud of her."

Ancil rubbed his chin thoughtfully. "I always wanted boys myself. Lula—hell, I don't know what she wanted or cared about. Don't imagine I ever asked her."

Hattie accepted this bit of telling information without comment. They sat quietly together for several minutes, each planning what to say.

Ancil spoke first. "You come out here on your high horse about something, I guess you'd better spit it out."

She met his eyes bravely. "Did you tell Reed Tyler that I wouldn't be selling my farm?"

Ancil pursed his lips and winced in self-disgust. "I woulda swore that boy wouldn't say a word to you about it."

"He didn't. Bessie Jane told me."

Ancil sighed fatalistically. "I shouldn't have shot off my mouth like I did. I was feeling pretty good that night, and I guess I wanted to brag a little."

"You wanted to brag about marrying the best piece of bottomland in the county."

Straightening his shoulders at her sarcasm, he attempted to deal with her honestly. "It ain't that I got no feeling at all for you, Miss Hattie. I think you're a right fine lady, as decent and hardworking as any I know. And you been good to my young-uns. That's a real mark in your favor."

"But," Hattie said, "all that is just gravy for you. What you really want is my farm, and you'd take me no matter what I was like to get it."

Ancil hesitated only a moment. "It's a dandy little farm, Miss Hattie."

The sound of something crashing within the house startled

them. Ada immediately fell out the front door, Cyl right behind her.

"These two brats are spying on you, Pa," Mary Nell said, appearing in the doorway. "You ought to take a switch to the both of them!"

Ada started to cry, but Cyl jumped up and took off running.

"You come back here, you little she-devil!" Ancil yelled after her, but the girl kept running.

Reed and Harmon were on the levee, carefully raising the water level in Miss Hattie's rice field. The river was down from lack of rain, and Harm was operating the noisy pump to draw the water up into the field. The two men, whose relationship continued to be strained, worked quietly beside each other. They were polite, but there was none of the comaraderie of earlier times.

Both men were startled by the unexpected arrival of a young girl dressed in torn, too-big overalls. "Mr. Tyler! Mr. Tyler! You gotta do something quick!" she called as she ran toward them.

Reed and Harm exchanged worried glances before both hurried to meet her.

"What's happened?" Reed asked. He caught the youngster in his arms and kneeled down to get a look at her. "You're one of Ancil Drayton's girls," he said.

Cyl, having run the better part of four miles, gasped for breath and could only nod.

"Is somebody hurt at your house? Somebody injured?"

She shook her head, then managed to catch her breath. "It's Miss Hattie. She—"

"Something's happened to Hattie!" Reed paled visibly, and his eyes widened with fear.

"No, mister," Cyl assured him. "Ain't nothin' happened to her exactly. She's havin' a set-to with my daddy."

Reed's expression turned to puzzlement, then just as quickly to anger. "Has your father hit her?"

Cyl was annoyed at the suggestion. "It ain't my daddy that hurt Miss Hattie. It's you and that Bessie Jane."

"Bessie Jane?"

"Yep." Cyl folded her arms across her chest. "That gal done tole Miss Hattie that Daddy is marrying up with her for the land and that you're getting gypped out of the deal."

His mouth falling open with disbelief, Reed stared at the girl for several seconds. "Bessie Jane told Hattie that?"

"That's how Miss Hattie explained it to Daddy, and now they're sure enough gonna be busted up over it. Marryin' Miss Hattie is the best idea my daddy ever had. It's your gal that caused this trouble. I suspect you're the only one can fix it."

Reed was at a loss. Glancing back at Harm, he asked, "What can I do?"

Harmon shrugged. "You can talk to Miss Hattie. That's about all. Tell her about that place you might get next to your uncle. Think of something. Lie."

"Miss Hattie can ferret out a lie at twenty paces."

"Well, you'll have to do something," Harm said.

Reed agreed and taking Cyl's hand in his, started toward the Drayton farm.

Harm watched them walk away, his mind whirling over what Bessie Jane had done. Returning to the pump, he continued to observe the water level in the rice field. Finally, when the water level suited him, he shut off the pump, slammed his hat on his head, and turned determinedly toward town.

Bessie Jane was sitting under a shade tree doing embroidery when Harmon walked into the backyard. Startled, she jumped up so quickly, her chair tumbled behind her. "What are you doing here?" she asked in a panicked whisper as she glanced back at the house. "What if somebody sees you?"

Harmon's expression was not at all gentle, and his voice was significantly above a whisper. "Oh, they're going to see me, all right. They're even going to hear me today."

"Harmon!" She desperately tried to shush him.

"Did you tell Miss Hattie about Drayton only wanting her land?"

Bessie Jane raised her chin defiantly. "I only told her what was the truth."

"It may have been the truth, but that's not why you told it. You told it selfishly, trying to make sure that nothing interferes with your plans for marrying Reed."

There was no way for Bessie Jane to defend herself against the facts. With a prideful silence, she waited for him to finish.

"How many lives are you willing to ruin?" he asked her. "Already you've decided to destroy your own and mine. You added the unnecessarily honorable Reed Tyler to your plan. Now Miss Hattie and even poor old pitiful Drayton and his ragged kids. Are everybody's dreams at risk so you can try to please your selfish, short-sighted father?''

"I don't have to discuss this with you," Bessie Jane said with as much haughtiness as she could manage.

She turned to go, but Harm grabbed her arm, spinning her to face him. "It's crossed my mind more than once today to turn you over my knee and blister your fanny," he warned. "The only reason I don't do it is because I think it's high time someone treated you like a grown woman."

"Reed—" she began.

"Reed thinks you're a pretty child. And that's what you are as long as you let Daddy and Mama make all the decisions for you. I love you, and you love me. With that in mind, a *woman* would make the decision to marry me. Only a pretty child would do what Daddy says."

"He only wants what's best for me!"

"I only want what's best for *us*." He drew her into his arms, slowly, slowly bringing his lips down to meet hers as she whimpered in anticipation. Warm and proficient, his mouth promised bliss and recalled rapturous heights she had vowed to forget.

Bessie Jane melted against him. Memory and desire leading her, she kissed him as if she were starved for his touch, thirsting for his taste. She wrapped her arms around his neck, pressing her bosom against his chest and clinging fiercely to him. Her tiny moans of desire convinced him more of her love than her previous denials of it had ever convinced him otherwise.

Harmon continued to kiss her, but allowed his hands to roam down her slender back. Rediscovering the gentle slope of her hips, his hands finally met at her buttocks where he clutched her and pulled her up hard against him.

With a tiny choked sob of desire, she whispered against his neck. "I love you.'''

"I know, sweet Bess," he answered as he reluctantly released her and stood back.

She looked confused for a moment, then caught sight of her father's house only twenty yards away. "I forgot where we were," she said breathlessly. She reached for his hand. "No one can see us down by the pond." She turned and started off. When he didn't move, she looked back, startled. "Let's hurry."

He shook his head. His breathing was still labored, and his

blood still surged through his body, but he was determined. "No more for me, sweet Bess," he said evenly. "No more green grass, hidden bowers, or deserted buildings. I want nice clean sheets and curtains on the windows. I want a marriage bed with a woman of my very own."

"Harmon, I . . ."

"No more excuses. You are my woman, and I want you openly and honestly. And I intend to have you, make no mistake."

"I've tried to explain—"

"Yes, you've tried to explain, but explanations mean nothing. The truth—isn't that what you mentioned earlier? I'm a great believer in the truth. You used the truth with Miss Hattie, so perhaps I should use it with Reed. I bet he doesn't have an inkling that he wasn't the first."

She slapped him. With a cry of horror, she watched the bright red imprint of her hand appear on the side of his face.

"What's going on here!" Arthur Turpin was striding toward them, his expression dangerous.

"Hurry! You must leave," Bessie Jane told Harmon, gently touching the cheek she had treated so harshly. "I'll calm him down and meet you later, and we'll talk."

"There is no more need for talk," he said, taking her hand and bringing it to his lips. "I would never tell Reed, I'm sure you know that. You are going to be my wife, and your reputation is mine also."

"Get your hands off my daughter, Leege!" Turpin ordered as he reached them.

Harm looked the older man in the eye, then brushed another light kiss on the back of Bessie Jane's hand.

"Go pack your things, Bess," he said calmly. "I'll tell your father all about our plans."

" 'Pack'? 'Plans'? What are you up to, Junkman?" Turning to his daughter, he added, "Little girl, don't you move a muscle until I get to the bottom of this."

Bessie Jane was frozen in place, frightened for herself but more terrified for Harmon. Her father's words crystallized in her brain. He ordered; she obeyed. Harmon was right. She was a woman, but if she stayed with her daddy, she would always be a little girl. "I'll be ready in fifteen minutes." She spoke quietly, looking directly into Harmon's eyes. "I just need to get a few things and say good-bye to Mama."

Harm nodded, and Bessie Jane turned and walked to the house.

"Now wait a minute—" Turpin began, but Harmon stopped him from following his daughter by laying a hand on his arm.

The older man glared at him, his face black with anger. "Keep your hands off me, you filthy little bastard, or I'll tear you apart."

Harmon was unmoved. "You've wanted to tear me apart for a lot of years, Turpin. You should have done it when you still could."

"Why, you—" Turpin jerked his arm away and assumed a fighter's stance. "I ain't lettin' you have my baby," he said through clenched teeth. "I'll fight you if I have to, to keep you from ruining her life."

"It's not her life you're concerned about," Harmon said calmly. "I've known all along what this is really about."

Turpin's look grew wary, but he kept his fists up.

"You know what has finally brought your daughter and I together today?" Harm asked. "The truth."

The old man hesitated. "What truth?"

"Just the truth, between us. Are you worried, old man? What truth are *you* thinking of?"

"I ain't thinking of nothing," Turpin said, but he swallowed hard and watched Harm carefully.

"The truth is," Harm said, "that you don't want Bessie Jane to love me. But not for the reasons you've told her. Oh, you're right, I don't own my own land. I can't support her in fine fashion. My family isn't the cream of society. That's all the truth. But it's also the truth about Reed Tyler. Even Bessie Jane could see that and couldn't understand it."

"What lies have you told Bessie Jane?" There was a note of desperation in Turpin's voice. "She'll never take your word over mine."

Harmon hesitated for a moment, choosing his words. "You've always wondered if I knew, haven't you? You saw me that day at the dock when the two of you were making your plans. You've always wondered if I overheard."

"I don't know what you're talking about." Turpin's voice was hoarse with bluster, but he had paled at Harmon's words.

"I'm talking about when my mother left us. You were going to Memphis on business, or so you told your wife. But you told my mother you would take her to St. Louis. You told her you loved her, that you wanted a life with her far away from your spouse and children.''

Turpin was sweating now. ''It was a craziness that just overtook us. We didn't mean to hurt anyone. It was just that what we had was so powerful, so unexpected, we had no control over it.''

''I was a respected member of the community. I had a prosperous business, a pretty wife, and a wonderful little girl. Can you imagine how much I loved your mother to give all that up?''

Harmon stared at him for a moment, the old childhood pain warring with adult understanding. ''But you didn't give it up,'' he said quietly.

''No.'' Turpin stood before his inquisitor with no defenses left. For him, too, it seemed the truth was the only recourse. ''The bliss lasted about a week before the guilt took over entirely. We spent two more weeks trying to talk it out, trying to find a way that we could have it all, before we decided that we just flat didn't deserve happiness.''

Turpin chuckled, but there was no humor in the sound. ''I came back, but your mother wouldn't. She said she'd betrayed your father, and even though she was sure he'd forgive her, she'd never forgive herself. It was probably best that she didn't come back. Living so close and not being able to touch, it might have been more of a temptation than either of us could stand.''

Pausing in his narrative as if to sift through the past and wonder if there had been another solution he could have tried, Turpin looked at Harm. ''I know my wife suspected something, but she never said a word. I was completely safe. It was like what I'd done had never been, except for you. I did see you that day at the dock. I wondered what you heard, how much you understood, and when you might be able to put it together . . . put it together and hurt me, hurt my daughter. That's what you've finally done, isn't it?''

Harmon looked at Arthur Turpin, loud-mouthed, sure-of-himself Arthur Turpin, now broken and frightened that an evil deed done in darkness so long ago would now come to light. ''I've known all along,'' he said. ''I understood that my mother left with you, and I realized that I was the only one who knew. When you came back, I kept waiting for her to walk through the door too. Night after night, Jake lay drunk on his cot while I waited for Mama. She never came back.''

Turpin gathered up the last of his strength, raising his head with as much pride as he could muster. "So you've decided to turn the tables on me. You're taking Bessie Jane away, and she's never coming back, so I'll suffer the same way you did."

Harm shook his head, his expression almost pitying. "I am going to marry Bessie Jane. We've been in love since we were children. There was something between us from the moment we met. We didn't ask to love each other, we both tried not to, but we couldn't stop the loving."

His voice was sincere, with no intent to hurt or lay blame. "Mr. Turpin, we're not children anymore. We intend to marry and be happy. If you choose not to be a part of that, it's your choice. Bessie Jane loves you a lot and wants your approval. If you decide not to give it, you'll only be cheating yourself."

The back screen door slammed, and Bessie Jane came walking toward them, traveling bag in hand. Her mother fluttered along at her side, seeming stunned at the unexpected turn of events. Her head held high, Bessie Jane walked straight to the man she would marry, whether her father approved or not. When she reached Harmon's side, she glanced warily at her father before saying, "I'm ready to leave."

Harmon slipped a protective arm around her waist and took her bag.

"I just don't understand what is happening," her mother said, wiping her eyes with the corner of her apron.

"Don't worry, Mrs. Turpin," Harmon told her. "We'll send you a wire when we get to Memphis to let you know where we'll be." He held out his hand to her father. "Good-bye Mr. Turpin."

Bessie Jane's father just stared at him.

Harmon withdrew his hand and indicated to Bessie Jane that is was time to go.

"Good-bye, Mama. Good-bye, Daddy," she said simply, and turned to follow her heart and the man who was to be her husband.

They had gone only about ten paces when Arthur Turpin found his voice. "Little girl!" he called. Bessie Jane turned to look at him. "Don't you two stay gone *too* long. I got a business to run, and I'm going to need help. Besides, I'd hate to travel to here and gone just to watch my grandchildren grow up."

Tears smarting in her eyes, Bessie Jane ran back into her father's arms.

"Thank you, Daddy. Thank you so much for understanding. You're going to love him, I just know you are."

"Why do you think so?" her father asked, trying to blink back the moisture in his eyes. "Just because you do?"

She nodded and gave a tearful little chuckle. One more hug for her mother, and they both wiped their eyes on her mother's apron. Then she ran back to Harmon.

With a glance over her shoulder, she added her final parting words. "Tell Reed the wedding is off."

Seventeen

B Y the time Hattie went to church on Sunday morning, the story of her difficulties with Ancil Drayton was just making the rounds. It did not, fortunately, spark inordinate attention, being plainly overshadowed by the news that Bessie Jane Turpin had run off with Harmon Leege.

Millie had hurried out to her house on Saturday to let her know. Hattie had been shocked. That morning Bessie Jane had passionately pleaded for an expedient wedding to Reed, and in the afternoon she'd left for Memphis to marry up with his business partner.

Confused, her heart aching for Reed, Hattie sat in her usual pew at the Sunday service and listened as Preacher Able made the announcement. "Arthur and Maude Turpin want to announce the marriage of their daughter Bessie Jane to Harmon Leege."

In the ensuing silence every eye was turned on Reed Tyler, watching for his reaction.

"The couple was married on Thursday in Memphis," the reverend continued, "but they plan to return to this community to make it their home."

Not giving his neighbors the satisfaction of knowing his feelings, Reed kept his gaze on the preacher, an expression of indifference on his face.

"I'm sure," Preacher Able concluded, "that the entire church community will be eager to welcome this new couple into our midst."

Hattie had her doubts. Bessie Jane's capriciousness would not be soon forgotten. And the church members, if it was deemed necessary to choose sides, would pick Reed, a well-liked regular church member, over Harm the junkman without much deliberation.

Sighing quietly, Hattie hoped it wouldn't come to that. Harmon was a fine fellow, just making a place for himself in the community. Who would have thought he would run off with Bessie Jane, though? The girl had never given any indication of even liking Harmon. In a small way, Hattie felt that part of it may have been her fault. While Bessie Jane was being lured away, Reed had been at her house trying to talk her into marrying Ancil Drayton.

She had met up with Cyl and Reed on the road between her place and Drayton's. "You'd best go home now, Cyl," Hattie had said as she stopped the buggy beside them. "I think your father is pretty much over his anger, but it won't do you a bit of good to stay away from your chores half a day."

The young girl had nodded fatalistically, then turned to Reed. "You'll talk to her?" she asked.

After assuring the young child that he would, Reed stepped up into the buggy and seated himself beside Hattie. She didn't offer him the reins, so he leaned back, clasping his hands behind his head in a relaxed pose. "So," he began with almost light-hearted teasing, "I guess you got your feelings all hurt and broke your engagement."

Silent for a moment, Hattie tightened her jaw with anger. "Yes, I suppose I did," she replied stiffly. "It was silly of me, I guess, to even imagine a man might want me for myself instead of my farm."

Reed straightened immediately, his expression contrite. "That's not at all what I meant."

"What exactly did you mean?" she asked. "Now that I know how Ancil really feels, I'm just to shrug and say, 'Ain't it a sight,' and go ahead and marry him?"

"The point is, Miss Hattie, that what you heard isn't necessarily how Drayton feels."

"He did say it, didn't he?"

Reed shifted uncomfortably at that question. "Sometimes men say things in a group, Miss Hattie, that they would never say if they were thinking straight. Believe me, a bunch of men laughing and joking are going to go for boasting over honesty anytime."

With a strangled little laugh, she asked, "Is it normal to boast about marrying a woman for her farm?"

"Lots of men find their gentler feelings for a woman a little embarrassing. A fellow may say he likes her looks or he thinks she'll be a good helpmate, 'cause he don't want to say that she makes his hands shake like a green boy and that he's lonesome with all his friends around because she's not there."

Hattie felt a sudden stab of irrational jealousy that other women had men who felt that way about them. "You don't need to stir yourself to make excuses for him, Reed. I asked the man straight out, and he said his interest was in the farm."

"Idiot!" Reed spat the word like a curse beneath his breath. "Miss Hattie, I don't like to take up for the man," he went on after a moment. "You know I don't like him. I think he's a lousy, careless farmer, and I'd hate to see him put your rice field in cotton. But I don't want to be responsible for breaking you two up. I'm not willing to let you sacrifice your future for me."

The chords of the closing hymn interrupted Hattie's thoughts, and she stood for the benediction. She wondered about sacrificing her future. Had Reed already known that Bessie Jane was leaving him? Was that why the land was no longer important to him?

Perhaps she had been hasty giving away her only chance to be a wife and mother because of hurt pride. Had she truly believed Ancil was in love with her pretty face? Maybe Reed would go down to Helena now. That would certainly be easier on everybody, if Bessie Jane and Harmon did come back there to live. He wouldn't want the land, and then where would she be? No husband, no children—and looking for a new sharecropper.

It was wrong of Ancil to want to marry her for her farm, but the words Millie had spoken in her kitchen drifted back to her: "Ten years from now, do you want to be right and alone or right and married?"

Speaking politely to various members of the congregation,

Hattie left the church. Ancil was waiting for her beside her buggy.

He tipped his hat and smiled his usual gap-toothed smile. "May I drive you home, Miss Hattie?"

It took her only a moment. She shook her head. "I need some time to think about this, Ancil. I'll drive myself today, thank you."

He looked disappointed, but his smile faltered only slightly. "I was hoping I might call on you again," he said. "I know I've been a mite clumsy and I've tread upon your feelings, ma'am, but I would like to share a glass of lemonade with you sometime. Perhaps I can redeem myself."

She looked at him, wondering if she was really willing to give up her newfound role as wife and mother. She wasn't sure.

"You have my permission to call," she said at last. "However, we are no longer engaged. I'll need time to reconsider."

Ancil's smile widened as he helped her up into the buggy. "You take all the time you need, Miss Hattie. Why, pickin' season ain't even started."

The next two weeks were busy ones for Hattie. Her garden was at its peak, and she was frantically trying to get everything put by. Bushels of corn lay about the kitchen and porches waiting to be shucked, but the baskets of tomatoes, huge red orbs, were what had Hattie's attention today. Two big cauldrons of tangy tomato stew were already on the stove, and Hattie sat at the kitchen table ripping the peels off a huge pile of the blanched fruit.

Ancil showed up two or three times a week. Mostly they sat on the porch swing and drank lemonade, but she had invited the family over for dinner last Sunday. The boys had built a Flying Jenny on an old stump not far from the house. Hattie had wondered about digging that stump out, but now she thought that perhaps there was no need. It was nice having all the children around, and she imagined what it would be like to have them living in her house permanently. But Ancil was still Ancil, and despite what Reed had said, it hurt to think that a man wanted her only for her farm—although she was convinced that he did take great enjoyment in stealing "smoochy-smooches" on the porch.

She'd hardly seen Reed since that day in the buggy. He kept to himself, working in the fields and, Hattie guessed, healing his wounds.

Harmon and Bessie Jane had returned to town the previous Saturday, and nearly everyone had expected something to happen at church the next day. They weren't disappointed. Reed walked out to meet the Leeges when they arrived. In front of the whole congregation, he offered Harm his hand and congratulations. He gave Bessie Jane a chaste kiss on the cheek. If some wondered about his sincerity, none doubted his intent. Reed accepted the new couple, so no one else could have any reason to shun them.

Hattie smiled as she dumped the dishpan full of peeled tomatoes into the colander and headed out to the back porch for more. Reed was the same kind of man that he was a farmer: Whether it rained too much, didn't rain enough, or was just about perfect, you took what you got and made the best of it.

She paused on the back porch and sniffed the air. The fresh odor of new-mown hay broadened her smile—immediately followed by a look of horror. "Oh, no!" she cried. Grabbing up a bucket and clean dishcloth, she raced across the yard to the cellar. She pulled the door open and hurried down the steps to the darkest corner where the ice crate stood. She peeled back the burlap, grabbed the ice pick that was hanging on a nail above her, and chopped off a large chunk of the cold clear ice.

As she wrapped it in the dishcloth and ran out of the cellar, she realized she'd forgotten her bonnet. She didn't take the time to retrieve it, though. Assuring herself that the ice was secure in the bucket, she slung the handle over her arm and raced toward the fields as swiftly as a young girl.

At the hay meadow, she saw exactly what she had suspected. The team had already made several runs, leaving a ring of mown hay around the tall growth that stood ready to cut. Determinedly she strode straight to the team that pulled the mower and the young man who drove them. "What's the matter with you," she shouted, "not telling me it was time for the mowing?"

Reed turned to look at her. At least she thought it was Reed. It was his body and his hat, but the puffy face was unrecognizable. His complexion was bright red, his eyes mere slits. She wasn't even sure he could see.

He pulled up the team and jerked a handkerchief out of his

pocket. After blowing his nose rather loudly, he looked up and said in a nasal voice, "I didn't want to bother you."

Hattie sighed with exasperation. "And you don't think it 'bothered' me when I smelled this hay and knew you were out here?"

Ever since he was a child it had been understood that the perfume of haying that delighted most caused an agony for Reed Tyler. For that reason, Reed rarely even got near the field during mowing and raking. Hattie had been hiring it done for years and paying it equally out of her and Reed's shares.

She stared at him. "I can't believe you are so unwilling to have a conversation with me that you wouldn't even tell me when it's time to hire a hay hand!"

"I just wanted to do it myself," Reed said. "I forgot it was this bad."

"Well, get down from there. I've got some ice in this bucket and you're going to need to lie down."

He managed to set the brake on the mower but was unsteady getting off the rig. Hattie wrapped her arm around his waist and allowed him to lean on her as they walked away.

"This is fine," he said. "I can lie down here."

"You're not lying in that hay. We're going to walk up this rise and get you under that shade tree. If I thought I could do it, I'd take you up to the house and put you to bed."

He managed a choked laugh. "I've thought about your bed a time or two, but I don't think today is the day."

"It would be the best thing in the world for you," Hattie said, completely misunderstanding, "but I just don't think you have the strength to make it."

When Reed hooted with laughter, she feared the heat and hay were making him daft.

She helped him to lie down under the shade tree, then seated herself beside him and began chipping the ice in the bucket. As she wrapped the small pieces in the cloth, Reed surprised her by shifting around so he could rest his head in her lap. A small sigh of contentment escaped him, and she was grateful he was able to relax.

She carefully placed the ice-filled cloth on his face, pressing the healing coolness lightly against the swollen sinuses. "Is your throat raw?" she asked. "Do you want an ice chip?"

"Yes, please."

She fished one out of the bucket. Finding it the right size with no sharp points, she brought it to his lips. Her intent was to slip the piece of ice carefully inside. Before she had a chance to ask him to open his mouth, his tongue snaked out and captured her fingers, curled around the ice, and drew it inside. The unexpected contact sent a strange quivering sensation through her entire body.

Making tiny sounds of appreciation deep in his throat. Reed luxuriated in her gentle ministrations. After a while, the sounds ceased, and Hattie assumed by his even breathing that he slept.

As she continued her tender care, her gaze was drawn more than once to the wide expanse of his chest. He had undone the buttons on his shirt. It now lay in crinkled heaps on either side of his chest, and his nakedness was a sore temptation to her.

The only man's chest she could recall ever seeing had been her father's. It had been considerably more barrellike than that of this lean-waisted, slim-hipped man. Her father's hair had been brown and gray, in great mats all over his chest. Reed, she noticed, had considerably less hair, but it was jet-black and curled in an attractive trail down the length of his torso. She could see where the sun fell every day and where it only occasionally visited. As her gaze followed the direction of the curly black hair, she discovered a tiny strip of pale flesh just above his belt and caught herself wondering about that area the sun never visited.

Forcing herself to look at his face again, she berated herself for allowing her gaze to wander over him so blatantly. Reed was a good friend and her partner. It was wicked of her to have such carnal thoughts about a man who had always been like a younger brother.

Still, she glanced again at his exposed flesh and wondered if the slight breeze might give him a chill. With perfectly respectable reasons, she reached out to touch him to measure the temperature of his skin. She didn't know if it was cold or hot, but it was incredibly smooth and silky. Her hand cruised lightly across him, feeling the delicious softness of those swirls of black hair. Her fingers were determined to try to make some order out of it, carefully untangling the silky black mat only to have it curl eagerly again, this time around her fingers.

Discovering his nipples, like shiny pennies in the curly black forest, she ran her fingers lightly across them. So different from her own, she mused, yet so similar in the way they sprang to attention. The vision of his hand against her breast that night so long ago flashed through her mind. The memory spawned an odd quiver inside her, and she squirmed.

Her movement must have awakened Reed, for although he didn't speak, he moved his head restlessly. She jerked her hand away from his chest as he continued to seek a comfortable position on her lap. To her dismay, he seemed determined to wedge his head as firmly as possible into that secret womanplace, which was just as unchastely determined to throb against him.

Panicked that she might lose control of this strange new lustfulness, Hattie focused her gaze on the hayfield and the two poor mules standing patiently in the hot sun. Grateful for her mother's stern belief in the recitation of Bible verses, she whispered to herself the entire St. Matthew's version of the Sermon on the Mount. The warmth didn't completely go away, but she gained control of her breathing and resolved to keep her hands to herself in the future.

Reed was snoring lightly now, and she eased his head from her lap. The team had been standing in the heat for the better part of an hour and needed tending. Having left her bonnet at home, Hattie picked up Reed's hat and headed down the hill with the intention of watering the animals.

Reed awakened slowly. The melted ice had dripped in runnels onto his temples and into his hair, leaving the wet cloth in a soggy heap on his face. His head was not clear, but it was better. Finding the bucket, he dampened the cloth and wiped his face and neck.

As he sat up, he began buttoning his shirt. He remembered that it was unbuttoned. He remembered everything . . . When sweet, caring, gentle Hattie had run her hands across his chest, he had wanted to moan aloud with pleasure. But he hadn't. He had been surprised but pleased by her touch. Too pleased, he thought wryly. When she'd touched his nipples, it had been all he could do not to take her hand and lead it to the area where it could really do some good. He was glad he hadn't. Her whispered Bible verses had been a sure sign that she wasn't ready to accept lustful gestures.

Assuming that she had returned to the house, Reed was taken aback when he stood and glanced down at the hayfield. Most of the sweet grass was cut, and the team was making another round under the leadership of a driver in a dress and apron, sporting his straw workhat. He grinned in appreciation as he watched her. Hattie Colfax was not a woman to be taken lightly.

In fact, Reed had spent a good deal of time in the last few weeks thinking about Hattie. Grabbing up the bucket and cloth, he headed down the hill toward the meadow. Bessie Jane's defection had stunned him. The embarrassment of being jilted, he'd decided, could be measured only by the sorrowful expressions of his neighbors and acquaintances, and the kind words and pats on the back from his friends and family. It was a horrible experience, knowing everyone was watching, looking for signs of heartbreak, hoping for emotional outbursts, then conversely thinking him brave and noble when neither occurred.

Those first few days he'd merely tried not to think at all. He'd been angry at Bessie Jane, puzzled by Harmon. Remembering the blow he'd taken from Harm down on the levee, he didn't doubt that something had been going on between those two for some time. He felt cheated by his friend, betrayed by his intended, but creeping stealthily on the edge of those emotions was relief.

He could no longer remember what he'd ever seen in Bessie Jane. All his memories of her seemed vague and out of focus. He hadn't been able to fathom it until last Sunday when they arrived together at church.

Having already decided to put the best face on everything, he had been stunned nonetheless by the sight of the two of them together. Bessie Jane had never looked happier, and Harmon had seemed more carefree and animated than Reed could remember. When he and Harmon had clasped hands, the feeling of goodwill between them had been genuine.

Thank God he hadn't married, Reed had thought. Bessie Jane could never have made him as happy as she made Harmon. A buoyant feeling had overtaken him in the churchyard, and he almost shouted out loud, "I'm free!" The thought ricocheted through him joyously.

At the edge of the hayfield he caught Hattie's eye and waved to her.

"Stay right where you are, Reed Tyler!" she called to him. "I'm almost finished here, and I don't want your sniveling to start up again."

" 'Sniveling'!" he hollered back in mock outrage. "I'll have you know, woman, that I do this swelling-up on purpose, just so I don't have to do haymowing!''

Her laughter floated to him across mown grass, and he remained there watching as she finished the field. The wind was coming from behind him, so the worst of the dust was blown away from him. The pungent odor still tickled his nose, and within a few moments his eyes had begun to run again.

Hattie raised the blade and drove the team out of the field, heading them for home. Reed caught up with her and jumped up beside her on the crosstongue. "You didn't need to mow my field, Miss Hattie," he said gravely. "I'd already decided to ask Cal and Andy to come help me tomorrow."

She glanced at him and answered with almost a teasing flirtiness. "I don't always need to get your permission, Mr. Tyler."

His grin widened. "I can see that. But who gave you leave to go wearing my worst beat-up straw hat?"

Hattie jerked off the hat and slammed it none too gently upon his head. The motion threw her off-balance, and Reed steadied her with a strong arm around her waist. To Hattie it seemed he was holding her unnecessarily close. She failed to complain, however, and traveled the remaining distance to her barn with the strong arm of her sharecropper around her.

At the barn they parted company. Reed stayed to unhitch the team while Hattie hurried to her kitchen to check on the forgotten stewing tomatoes.

By the time Reed got up to the house, Hattie had relit the fire in the stove, washed the worst of the field grime off, and traded her hay-strewn dress for a fresh cool calico one.

"Now don't you look pretty after a hard day in the field," Reed said, coming in the back door.

Hattie blushed at the compliment, then harshly reminded herself that a kind word from a friend was not the same as the truth. "Well, you're looking a little better too," she said. "When I got down to the meadow, I wasn't sure your face would ever look human again."

"I *feel* a lot more human than I did then," he said, and took her hand in his. "Thank you, Miss Hattie. These hands of yours could heal a lot of hurts."

Feeling herself about to tremble and trying to will away the sudden inexplicable desire to lift his hand to her breast, Hattie stepped back.

"Would you like some more ice for your eyes?" she asked, keeping her voice impersonal. "It does seem to work better than anything else."

"It certainly felt good today," he admitted. "Could I put my head in your lap again?"

Her eyes widening in shock, she opened her mouth to speak but had no idea what in the world she could say.

Reed took a step toward her, and she immediately backed away, right up against the kitchen table. Her expression was like that of a cornered animal. Hesitating, he moved away to give her more room and was rewarded when the hint of fear in her eyes drained down to mere wariness.

Glancing away from her, he tried another tack. "Something sure smells good, Miss Hattie."

"It's just tomatoes," she said. "I completely forgot about them, but thankfully the fire went out instead of scorching them."

"You know, I hear all over the county that you're a fine cook, but I swear, Miss Hattie, I don't believe you've ever invited me for supper before."

She frowned in puzzlement. "Why, Reed, we've eaten breakfast together a million times. You know exactly how I cook. You can come here for supper any time you've a mind to. You know that."

"How about tonight?" he asked cautiously.

"Tonight?" Hattie was almost at a loss for words. "Reed, you know I'd enjoy having you over, but truthfully, having worked in the field all afternoon, I haven't got a thing cooked for supper."

He laughed. "Okay, my fault. I can't come for supper tonight, because there is no supper. How about later on this evening, Miss Hattie? I could come over, and we could sit a spell on that porch swing I built you."

She stared at him. It sounded suspiciously as if Reed Tyler were asking to court her. But surely he wouldn't be asking such a thing. Should she ask him straight out if that's what he had in mind? Casting out the idea as altogether too risky—if he said no, he had never considered such a wild idea, she would undoubtedly need the earth to open up and swallow her—she decided just to agree and see how it went.

Then her memory snagged on an important detail. "Tonight might be a bit crowded," she said, hoping her lightness and humor would protect her from making a fool of herself. "Ancil will be here a little after dark."

Reed's smile dimmed appreciably, but he shrugged in understanding. "I didn't realize you'd become engaged again."

"We haven't," she said quickly. "He's simply calling on me like before. There is nothing understood between us. We're just courting."

Accepting that with a nod, Reed grabbed his hat and turned to the door. "Well, I guess I'd better be going." Annoyance was clear in his tone.

"Good-bye," she said.

"Good-bye."

He stepped out the back door, and Hattie sighed heavily. What had he wanted? she wondered. What was he saying? She would probably never know. Just as she turned back to her stove, the screen door was jerked open, and Reed walked back in.

"Is Drayton calling on you tomorrow night?" he asked.

"No."

"May I come sit on your porch then?"

"You can come for supper."

"Fine."

"Fine."

Eighteen

CASTING a quick glance at her face in her hand mirror, Hattie paused to smooth her hair back before heading to the kitchen. She was certain there had never been a longer day than the one she had just lived.

Everything was ready for her supper with Reed. A succulent pork roast was keeping warm on the top of the stove, yeastrolls were in the breadbasket, green beans and new potatoes simmered patiently, and the okra was ready to fry. A peach cobbler sat cooling on the windowsill, and Hattie was dressed once again in the summer lawn dress Reed had admired at the July Fourth picnic. All that was needed now was the gentleman caller. At that thought, Hattie trembled with nervousness.

Since Reed's departure the previous evening, she could only describe her erratic behavior as "in a tizzy." Again and again she'd warned herself that she was making far too much of Reed's request to sit on her porch. "He's hurt and lonely," she would say aloud. "It's only natural that after being jilted, he would seek the companionship of a close friend."

But even her sensible words couldn't still the feverish anticipation she felt. Her visit with Ancil the night before had been a disaster. He had caught her wool-gathering more than once and had left early, obviously irritated.

She had been able to think of nothing but Reed, though. The sight of him—laughing beside her in the pig sty, holding her as she cried on the porch, the strip of naked pale skin she had glimpsed at his waist—and the taste of those wondrous sweet kisses they had shared. "Peaches," she whispered dreamily to herself. Raising her head in startled surprise, she stared in horror at the cobbler cooling on the windowsill.

Peaches! Would it remind him? Would he think she *meant* to remind him? Glancing nervously at the back door, she grabbed the square cobbler tin and covered it quickly with a clean dishtowel. Opening first one cabinet then another, she finally deposited her embarrassing dessert on the top shelf of the pantry. With a hand over her heart and a sigh of relief, she assured herself that the oven was still warm enough to bake a batch of cookies and hurried to mix her sweet substitution.

Time and time again as she mixed up the substitute dessert, she glanced at the back door, waiting for him to make his usual appearance. He would give a tap on the screen and let himself in, then sit at the kitchen table and begin talking about his day and asking questions about hers. It was this certainty about his behavior that led her to assume that the knock at her front door must be either a peddler or a neighbor passing by. Displeased by the interruption, she couldn't quite keep the annoyance out of her expression as she answered the door.

Reed stood on Miss Hattie's front porch, feeling distinctly uncomfortable. He wore his Sunday dress suit but had discarded the tie before he'd gone even a hundred yards from his house and now sweated in the unseasonable coat. His hair was still damp and slicked down tightly to his head. Clasped in his fist was a handful of marigolds and dahlias. The cheerful flowers contrasted sharply with his expression, which was distinctly uneasy.

"Reed!" Hattie exclaimed when she saw him. "What a surprise."

He caught his breath at her words, and his heartbeat accelerated with anxiety. "You did invite me for supper this evening?" he asked quickly.

"Yes! Oh yes, of course," she said. "I just didn't expect

you at the front door. I mean . . . '' Feeling increasingly foolish, Hattie finally opened the door. "Please come on in.'' Her voice sounded formal and distant even to her ears.

Reed stepped into the little parlor and stood ill at ease for a moment. Glancing at Hattie he saw she seemed equally at a loss. As if suddenly recalling his purpose, he thrust the flowers at her. "These are for you.''

Taking them, Hattie felt a flutter of pleasure. Unsure what to make of it, she made a hasty retreat. "Let me put these in water,'' she said as she turned to the kitchen.

Alone in the parlor, Reed couldn't decide whether to continue standing and wait for an invitation to sit or simply sit. Remaining at the edge of the room for a couple of minutes, he finally realized how stiff and awkward he must appear. Immediately he sat down in a cane-seat rocker covered by needlepoint pillow and back. Rocking back and forth, he barely had time to get comfortable before he changed his mind and moved to the settee, seating himself at the far end to give Hattie plenty of room to join him.

Through the day, he had become increasingly unsure of himself. Eyebrows had raised all around his family's table that morning when he'd ask his mother about the flowers in the garden.

"They're not too many left,'' she said, an unspoken question in her voice.

"I just need enough for a bouquet,'' he said.

"You going courting already?'' his father asked with calculated nonchalance.

Reed nodded and concentrated on his breakfast as if it were really no one's business.

"I was beginning to wonder if he was just going to pine away forever,'' his brother Cal teased. "Who's the young lady?''

Reed gave his brother a sarcastic look. "Since when have you been interested in the ladies I call on, Cal?''

"Not interested, just curious.''

"I bet I know who it is,'' Andy piped up. Everyone looked at the handsome teenager with the infectious grin. "Eva Lynn Holmes swears that God answered her prayers when Bessie Jane set you free.''

"Eva Lynn Holmes!'' Reed said incredulously. "She's just a schoolgirl.''

"She's the same age as Bessie Jane,'" Andy said.

Reed shook his head and chuckled. "I remember when Mrs. Holmes would ask all us kids to keep watch on Eva Lynn 'cause she was prone to eat dirt." The rest of the family joined him as he laughed. Turning to his youngest brother, Reed added, "I'm not very likely to ever feel the desire to call on a female I remember as a dirt eater."

Andy nodded.

"So who are you calling on?" his father asked finally.

Reed carefully finished chewing his bacon and swallowed. "Hattie Colfax."

The silence was deafening.

Clive cleared his throat. "I think that's a fine idea, Reed. Miss Hattie is a lovely woman. Your mother and I both like her a lot."

This wholehearted endorsement by their parents didn't squelch his brothers' surprise. "You're serious?" Andy asked, appalled at Reed's interest in a woman Andy considered strictly a part of the adult world. "She's a lot older than you."

"Only five years," Reed said.

Cal couldn't resist the obvious tease. "You see, Andy," he explained, "Reed doesn't want a woman if he can remember when she used to eat dirt. He wants a woman who can remember when *he* used to eat dirt."

Reed had blushed fiery red at that statement, and even thinking about it now in the comfort of Miss Hattie's parlor embarrassed him.

All afternoon he had wondered about the nature of his friendship with Hattie. They had been friends for so long, but he had always been the younger one. Did she remember those years when she used to order him to wash his hands before he sat down to her table? How about the time he'd smashed his hand on the cotton planter and she'd put the ice on it while he cried like a baby? She dried his tears and held her hanky for him to blow his nose. When she looked at him, did she remember that? Running a nervous hand through his hair, he desperately hoped not.

Could a woman entertain romantic illusions about a man she'd known in kneepants, a man she'd splashed in the face with buttermilk when he'd gotten too big for his britches?

"The flowers are just lovely, Reed," Hattie said as she reentered the room. She hesitated by the cane-seat rocker, glancing over at the space beside Reed on the settee. He moved slightly as if making room for her. With her eyes focused on her feet, she crossed the room to sit next to him.

They smiled politely at each other in the uncomfortable silence that followed.

"It's rather late in the year for marigolds," Hattie finally managed to say.

"They were the last in my mother's garden," Reed said, shifting over to make sure she had plenty of room.

"The very last? Well, it was so kind of your mother to share them with me."

"Well, I asked her for them, actually. I told her I was coming courting."

Hattie's eyes widened, and she quickly looked away. He was courting her! That was what he'd said. She was sure of it. Daring a glance back at him, she almost asked him to repeat it.

Watching the expression on Hattie's face, Reed was daunted. She hadn't realized his interest. It obviously had never occurred to her that his call was anything but friendship.

They both sat in an increasingly awkward silence, struggling for something to say. After several abortive attempts at the weather, the crops, and the neighbors, Hattie excused herself to get supper on the table.

The moment she left the room, Reed knocked his forehead with the heel of his hand in self-disgust. He was making a fool of himself, and he didn't know how to stop. His experience with women had generally been positive. He was always calm, always in control, even in his teen years, and the girls he'd called on had always seemed subordinate. They were eager to please him, and if there was any timidity and awkwardness to be overcome, it had never been his. Now, suddenly at twenty-four he was with a woman who was his equal, and he felt as clumsy and insecure as a schoolboy.

Supper wasn't much better. The flowers sat in a vase in the middle of the table, a glaring reminder of his presumption. Reed tried without much success to retake some of the ground he was sure he'd lost. "The rice looks real good," he said. "I think we might do better than we originally thought on that little field."

"That's wonderful," Hattie replied.

"I've been able to keep the water level pretty steady. If the depth of the water is uneven, the crop won't all ripen at the same time."

"You still think it'll be ready for harvest in September?" she asked as she passed him another roll.

"The way I've got it figured, I'll drain it about the time the pickers get here. By the time we've got the cotton at the gin, the rice field will be dry enough to get the binder in."

"How is the pump working?"

"Pretty well. Harm was out a couple of days ago and had a look at it. He thinks it will make it through the season with no problems."

Hattie smiled with pleasure. "So you and Harm have resolved your differences."

Reed hesitated. In his current rather defensive state of mind, Hattie's words sounded maternal, even condescending. Bessie Jane's ill treatment of him still rankled at times, and he hated being the recipient of sympathy. He especially didn't appreciate gracious motherly concern from Hattie.

"Harmon Leege and I have no differences to resolve," he said with more sternness than was called for. "Harm is my friend, and my former relationship with his wife is a thing of the past."

Reed's refusal to be brokenhearted about the faithlessness of his intended struck Hattie as cold-blooded, but she steered away from that. "I think you've been brave about the whole unfortunate incident. And I was so proud of you at church when you shook Harmon's hand, as if to let bygones be bygones. I think it will really help the community accept them."

"I didn't do it to get the community to accept them," he said with exasperation. "I shook his hand because he's my friend. I maintain the highest regard for Bessie Jane, but what's over is over."

Again, Hattie found his apparent callousness unsettling. "Well, it sounds to me as if your feelings for Bessie Jane were fairly shallow, for a man engaged to be married."

Reed bristled at the criticism. Did she think he was so young and easily hurt that he would come to her like a child to cry on her shoulder? "Sometimes people marry for other reasons than tender feelings," he said, then asked pointedly, "How is Drayton?"

"He's fine," Hattie replied, her blood roaring through her veins at his reference to Ancil's contrived interest in her. The hurtful insinuation made casual conversation almost impossible.

"He was here last night?" Reed asked.

"We had lemonade on the porch."

Continuing to stir the food around on his plate, Reed asked the question that was uppermost in his mind with as much nonchalance as he could muster. "Are you still thinking about marrying him?"

Hattie hesitated. Somehow, thinking about marrying Ancil Drayton was inconceivable at this particular moment. "Perhaps," she answered, her head high.

"Do you think he loves you?" It was an unfair question, and Reed could have bit his tongue as soon as he heard his own words. Still, he wanted the answer.

"He doesn't love me, no," Hattie said honestly. "His interest is in the farm. I am aware of that."

Reed nodded. It surprised him that she could speak of it with such detachment. A woman like Bessie Jane would take to bed in a grieving fit over something like that. Of course, he knew Hattie was different. She was so mature, perhaps the personal things that hurt young girls no longer bothered her. Maybe she didn't really care if a man loved her or not.

She'd told him she wanted to get married. It was possible that the security of marriage and the hope of children were all that really interested her. "Drayton isn't much of a farmer," he said, "and he isn't interested in your rice field."

"So?"

"So I know how to grow that rice for you. And I'm twice the farmer Drayton will ever be. If you're looking for a husband who wants your farm, well, I want it."

"What?"

Reed felt clumsy and awkward, but having stated his position, he was determined to follow through. "I want this farm, Miss Hattie. You know I always have. I planned to buy it, and I still want to if that's what you'd like. But I thought to myself, why should Drayton get this farm and you too when he doesn't even know you and knows even less about this plot of ground?"

Hattie stared at him, obviously dumbstruck.

He continued. "To be honest, I never considered marrying you. I guess I just never thought about you that way. You were simply my friend, a spinster lady. When Drayton started to call on you, I began looking at things differently, but I was already engaged to Bessie Jane. Now that I'm free . . . well, I'm free to ask you to marry up with me."

Hattie continued to stare at him, opening her mouth to speak, then shutting it again, unsure of her words. Finally she started to sort everything out. "So," she began hesitantly, "you say you're not upset about losing Bessie Jane, because now you can marry me and get my land."

"I want the land," he said. "And I'm willing to buy it, just like always. But if we married up, we could take the money I've been saving to pay you and put it into irrigation for more rice. Miss Hattie, you'd be surprised what we could do with this farm in, say, the next ten years or so." His eyes were on her, but she could see that he was visualizing a distant dream. "You know what kind of farmer I am. What you want is a farmer for this land, and I'm a far better one than Drayton."

"I'm looking for a farmer?" she asked, her voice barely more than a whisper. "I thought I was looking for a husband."

The two stared at each other for a moment. Hattie felt as if someone had reached inside her breast, grabbed her heart, and twisted it out of her body, only to discard it in the slop bucket. Tears welled up behind her eyes, painful burning tears, but she bit down fiercely on her lip and would not allow them to disgrace her. "Let me get you your dessert," she said, rising from her chair. By the time she reached the kitchen, she was holding her pain in with anger. Grabbing the plate of sugar cookies, she walked back to the table, chin high and shoulders straight.

"Here are your cookies," she said calmly, handing him the plate. "why don't you just take them with you?"

"Miss Hattie, I . . ."

Retrieving his coat from the rack, she all but threw it at him. "I believe you know your way out."

Reed stood, coat in hand, floundering for the right words. "I'm sorry, Miss Hattie, I didn't mean . . ."

Ignoring him, Hattie began clearing the table as if he had already left. Reed watched her for a moment, then let himself out the front door.

Hattie continued to carry the dishes to the sink, calmly, serenely, as if nothing out of the ordinary had occurred. When all that was left on the table was her mother's milk-glass vase holding the beautiful bouquet of bright flowers, she reached out to caress the delicate petal of a red dahlia. A tear spilled from the corner of her eye. She jerked the flowers from the vase and opened the front door. Throwing them out, she spoke to the silent evening. "And take your stupid flowers with you!"

Slamming the door shut, she leaned against it, no longer able to stop the tears. She allowed herself the luxury of private grief and wept for several minutes. Finally she wiped her eyes with her handkerchief and washed the dishes, though a teardrop occasionally fell into the soapy water. By the time all evidence of the supper was cleared away, she felt better. As she washed her face and readied herself for bed, she came to grips with her feelings. "It's not as if he was dishonest about it," she told herself aloud. "Ancil does just want me for the farm. So if Reed wants the farm, it's really the same thing."

Sighing, she stared at her wide-jawed face in her hand mirror. "Maybe I should be glad I have a farm to offer!" she declared. Setting the mirror down, she blew out the light and crawled into bed.

Her mind was a whirl of confusion, and it was her nature to try to bring order to it. When a problem cropped up in the fields or with the animals, she always forced herself to restrain her reaction until she'd sorted out all her options and reached the best decision. In the quiet darkness of her room, with only the sounds of the crickets outside her window to distract her, Hattie reviewed the possibilities.

Things remaining exactly as they had been was an alternative. Of course, a person could never truly retrace her steps, but Hattie was fairly sure she could go back to being the hardworking, self-supporting spinster she had always been. Unfortunately, she didn't particularly long for the tranquil sameness of the past. The excitement of a man in her life could not be underrated.

Marriage to Ancil would be a reasonable decision. She'd acquire a fine man and a houseful of precious children. Reed was right—Ancil was not so good a farmer. She could teach him to be better, though. He didn't love her, but she didn't love him either. They were equal in that. The neighbors already expected a marriage, so the entire community would be behind it.

Or she could marry Reed. He would make some woman a fine husband. Hattie had every confidence that he would provide for her and care for her. They had been friends for years, so there was no question about their ability to get along. The community would be scandalized by their marriage, however. They might suspect that Ancil had married her for her land, but they would know that Reed had. He didn't love her.

Why did that truth sting so much more with Reed than with Ancil? Because her feelings for Reed were more than they should be, she answered herself, and she well knew it. He was young, virile, handsome. Was it so unreasonable that a woman, even one of her age, would find that appealing.

Without conscious thought, her tongue ran along her lips, as if to taste Reed's sweet kisses again. Moaning softly, she ran her hand across the breast that he had touched so fleetingly, and the memory, more than the caress, sparked her to flame. She felt the familiar throbbing of urgency between her legs, and she pulled her thighs together tightly against it. How long must a woman bank the fires inside her? Would a lifetime of self-denial be worth it?

Sitting up in the bed and wrapping her arms around her knees, she knew that it would not. Wanting a man, his touch, his children . . . Those were not evil things. It was something most women took for granted. She would not deny herself anymore. Maybe neither man loved her, but she was sure both could bed her and give her children—now, before it was too late to bear any.

"Mrs. Hattie . . . ," she said aloud. She hesitated in her thought, but only an instant. Given a choice between peaches or smoochy-smooches, a decision was easily reached.

Nineteen

T HE loud pounding on the front door awakened Hattie with
a start. It was still dark, very dark. Fumbling for a match,
she lit the lamp by her bed and hurried to the parlor. With a
hasty glance at the clock, she saw it was two-thirty, and her
heartbeat quickened. Only a tragedy would bring someone to her
door at this time of night.

Slipping back the bolt, she opened the door to see Reed
standing on her porch, his coat gone and his hair mussed.

"What's happened?" she asked anxiously.

He stared at her for a minute, then the urgency in her voice
made him realize how late it must be. "Nothing. I just wanted
to talk to you."

She gaped at him in disbelief. "Are you drunk?"

He ran a hand through his hair and shook his head. "You
know I don't drink, Hattie. But if I were a drinking man, you're
right, this would be a night for it."

"Well, the night will be morning before you know it," she
said sternly. "You'd best go home and get some rest."

"Not before we've talked," he said, then sighed with disgust. "I doubt I could sleep with this on my conscience. I know I hurt you, Hattie, and I'm sorry."

"It's not important," she lied.

"It's important to me, and I want to talk about it, explain it."

Hattie wasn't sure she could live through further explanations. "Oh, I think you made yourself clear at supper."

"No," he said, a strange inflection in his voice. "I think I just muddied the waters."

She watched him for a moment, then realized his eyes were focused on her chest. Glancing down, she saw that in her haste she'd forgotten her wrapper. Laying her free arm protectively across her bosom, she asked, "Are you sure you're not drunk?"

He gave a little snort of derision. "I only wish I was. I have plenty of faults, Hattie, but a fondness for liquor isn't among them."

"Well, apparently your faults include waking decent people up in the middle of the night for no good reason!"

He nodded. "It's not a habit of mine, but tonight is a special occasion, I guess." Hesitating a couple of moments to gather his courage, he finally said, "May I come in?"

"Absolutely not," she answered, scandalized that he would even make such a suggestion. "It is very much past the hour for a gentleman to be calling, and inviting you into my house would be unquestionably improper."

"Well, can we talk on the porch?"

"I'm not dressed," she said, then wished she hadn't mentioned it because it drew his gaze back to the thin cotton nightgown that covered her.

"Get your wrapper."

"I'll not sit on the porch with a gentlemen while dressed in a wrapper!" She was shocked that a decent man would even make such a suggestion.

"Take your time. Wear whatever you feel comfortable with. I'll wait on you."

As Hattie turned to go back to her bedroom, it occurred to her simply to send him on his way. But he was right. They did need to talk. She knew she'd never get back to sleep tonight. They might as well go ahead and get things settled between them. "It will take me a few moments to dress."

Reed watched as she retreated back into the house. Slipping

his hands in his pockets, he sighed loudly and walked over to the porch swing. Stretching his long legs out before him, he arched his tired back and yawned.

He hadn't bothered to go home. After Hattie had practically thrown him from her house, he'd followed the trail to the rice field. As he walked, he called himself every low, no-good name he could think of. Drayton was a weak-minded pig-brain, but Reed was no less a cad, and he knew it.

He'd felt so uncertain, so off-balance with her tonight. Whether it was the teasing of his brothers or the knowledge that Hattie was different from the other women he'd known didn't matter. He'd been anxious, and he'd handled it badly. No woman had ever made him feel quite so vulnerable, though. She had been appalled that he had thought to court her, as if he were some callow youth too immature to be considered. Then she had to remind him that another man, a younger, less experienced man, had just stolen his girl, and she offered sympathy. It was the straw that broke the camel's back.

He'd approached the idea of marriage in a businesslike manner, knowing she respected his business acumen, even if she thought him too young to wed. He'd hurt her with his cold speech, and that was the one thing he hadn't wanted to do.

It had taken him hours, gazing at the dark river as it flowed southward in the moonlight, to figure out what went wrong. When the answer finally came to him, he couldn't wait until the next day to test his theory. Hattie treated him like a boy, he decided, because he had never treated her like a woman.

Remembering her breathy moans the night he'd taught her to kiss and the sight this night of her high full breasts not quite invisible beneath her thin cotton nightgown, he doubted that being man to her woman would be much of a chore.

As Hattie at last stepped out on the porch, Reed stood in his most gentlemanly manner, smiled, and thanked her for agreeing to sit with him.

The fancy white dress of earlier in the evening had been discarded for a sturdy calico workdress. It was obvious to Reed that she intended to go straight from the swing to the hog trough.

Aware of his perusal, she said, "I don't wear my Sunday best for gentlemen that pay calls in the middle of the night."

His smile broadened. Her defiance was a good sign. He'd hate to think of her crying over his thoughtless words. "You look fine to me. I do regret you putting your hair up, though. How long is that braid exactly?"

She ran her hand over the neatly wrapped coil at the nape of her neck, surprised at his words. "Not quite to my waist," she said. "My hair just doesn't grow to the floor like some women's."

He reached for her hand, and she didn't pull away. He settled her on the swing, then sat beside her, his arm draped loosely along the seat back.

"It's thick, though," he said, casually caressing the braid. "And the color is real pretty."

"It's the color of possum fur," she said quietly. He laughed as if she had told a fine joke, then she felt his hands smoothing the tightly pinned braid.

"No possum ever looked this good. The color is wonderful. You don't see it in the sunshine like I do. It picks up the light and shines gold and red and brown." He fingered the braid gently as if to loosen it. "It's so soft, Hattie. Let me see it down."

"What?"

"Take your hair down for me, Hattie."

His words were barely a whisper, but something in his voice was so demanding, she felt compelled to obey. "It's a lot of foolishness," she said tartly but began removing the pins that held her hair in place.

Reed turned sideways, and his new position gave him an unrestricted view of Hattie's breast as she sought the pins in her hair. When she held them all in her hand, she unwound the coil so that the braid lay over her shoulder and breast.

In the dim light of the moon, she could barely see Reed's eyes, but she could feel his hot gaze on her. As an uncomfortable heat shot through her, she resolved to finish the task as soon as possible and hastened to undo the plait.

"Let me," Reed whispered, and before she could respond, his hands were there.

He gently began separating the three strands as his hands edged up the front of her body. His knuckles brushed her breast, bringing the nipple to immediate attention. Recognizing her reaction, he moved his hand against the nipple itself, teasing it as if accidentally with the hank of hair.

"Reed . . ."

He heard a thread of fear in her voice and carefully continued his task, freeing her hair from the tight bonds. When the plait was undone, he ran his hands through the silky strands, separating and stroking them, then spread the hair about her like a shawl.

"It's beautiful, Hattie," he told her.

Refusing his flattery, she replied, "You'll have it wild, running your hands through it like that."

"Wild? Is that a promise?" He leaned closer to her, his breath soft on her cheek.

She jerked back, but he stayed her with his hand, and his voice was comforting, his lips only inches from hers. "Remember what I told you when I gave you this swing? As long as you stay on the porch swing, a man can only go so far."

"How far is that?" she asked, her voice quivering with both excitement and anxiety.

"Not nearly far enough," he answered as he barely touched her lips with his own.

Reed heard her catch her breath and moved closer, sliding his arm around her back to her waist and pulling her against him. Again he touched her lips, then her throat, listening for the sweet sounds of her pleasure. He kissed her eyes, her cheek, the edge of her jaw beneath her ear, her neck, her throat.

"No," she moaned. "No, Reed, no."

He stopped abruptly, banking the fires that sparked within him. "You don't want my kisses?" he asked, his hot breath against her neck.

"Peaches," she whispered.

"What?"

"Peaches, Reed, not pecks. Alone at night in my bed, it's peaches I dream about."

His eyes widened in surprise, then he grinned with delight as he lifted her onto his lap. "I have bushels of peaches, Hattie, and they're all just waiting for you."

Their lips met with an eagerness and familiarity that was unique for two who had never been lovers. The teacher was delighted in the innovation of the student, and the student reveled in the expertise of the teacher.

Peaches, such peaches, were mixed with pecks and wicked malvalvas, and they all took Hattie's breath away. She hated to let his lips leave her own, but when she learned how good the kisses felt against her skin, she allowed him to make an occasional foray, only to pull his mouth back to hers, eager and sweet.

When he touched her breast, it seemed so wonderful, so right. She pressed against him, urging him to take what liberties he would.

Reed gasped at the sensations she evoked. He'd planned to make her see that he was a man. He realized that with her squirming on his lap, she would quickly be able to testify with certainty to that fact. He wondered with amusement if she understood that the big hard lump she was sitting on was not typical of his anatomy. He wrapped an arm tightly around her waist to hold her in place, then pressed up against her buttocks. She wiggled in response but seemed more concerned with the touch of his hand on her breast.

As if taking her compliance as a suggestion, he quickly released the buttons at the back of her dress and began uncovering her bodice. Hattie cried out in surprise as the cool air stroked her bare skin, but she offered no protest.

He skimmed the calico down to her waist and began covering the exposed skin with kisses as his fingers sought the tiny ribbons that held the gathers of her chemise. "Do you like peaches, Hattie?" he whispered against her skin.

"Yes, oh yes, you know I do," she answered, squirming against him even more.

He gently pulled away the cotton batiste that covered her bosom. "How about here, Hattie?" he asked, gently stroking her breast with his fingers. "Would you like peaches here?" Her answer was a strangled cry as she pulled his head down to her breast. His tongue licked the pouty nipple. "Malvalva is nice here too," he told her in a hot whisper.

Her breasts were high and firm, the nipples pointing upward as if eager for his lips, one still glistening from the attention of his tongue. They were beautiful, he thought. Sweet, hardworking Hattie, so plain with her long face, had the most beautiful bosom ever admired by a man, he decided.

"Please . . ." She begged only once before Reed took the nipple into his mouth to suckle it. Hattie threw her head back, moaning with pure lust. She wiggled provocatively on his lap for a moment before she found it necessary to squeeze her thighs tightly together to keep from exploding.

Reed, luxuriating in the sweet taste of her breast, was not unaware of the tensing in her thighs and understood her need.

Jerking the calico up to her knees, he allowed his hand a slow and careful exploration of her black cotton stockings. Her knees opened unhesitantly to his crusade, and when he persevered to the tender bare flesh between her stockings and drawers, they both gasped with delight.

"I could put peaches there too, Hattie," he whispered, his words bringing a tremor to the skin he caressed. "Peaches for all your secret places," he added when she sighed enthusiasticly. "But not on this damn swing."

His frustrated humor lightened the mood slightly, and Hattie found herself better able to breathe. "What are you doing to me?" she asked, her eyes glowing with passion.

"I'm sparking you," he replied as he lowered his head to give her nipple another caress of his tongue.

"Oh!" was her reply to that, but when she captured her breath, she added, "I don't feel like sparks. I feel like a prairie fire."

"Really? I guess I could describe my feeling as kind of like the Yule log," he said, and held her tightly in place, one hand still on her inner thigh as he pressed his taut erection against her backside.

She let out a little gasp of surprise. "Is that . . . I mean, do you . . . ?" She ran her hand gently across his face, then threaded her fingers in his thick black hair. "Do you want to do *that* with me?" she asked quietly.

His hand traversed the last forbidden inches across her cotton drawers to cup her gently. "Oh yes, Hattie—I want to do *that* with you."

She hardly heard the words because of his touch. Throwing her head back, she softly called his name. Reed looked at her, his vision clouded by the desire that assailed him. "Don't worry, Hattie," he choked out, trying not to look at her eagerly parted lips and the beautiful breasts she held before him like an offering. "Nothing will happen. I swear nothing will happen." His breathing was labored as she squirmed on his lap, attempting to settle his hand more firmly against her. "Nothing will happen, Hattie. Nothing, I promise."

"Are you sure?" she asked him as she lowered her head, her lips hovering above his, her fingers desperately seeking the opening on his shirt.

Reed was nearly strangling with his desire. "As long as we stay on this swing, Hattie, I promise you nothing will happen."

"Then let's get off the swing!" she cried as she finally ripped off the last buttons on his shirt to find his naked chest.

Reed gaped at her, but she didn't have to ask twice. Removing his hand from the warm haven of her femininity, he caught her up and rose to his feet, intending to carry her into the house to a nice soft bed. When she ran her tongue across the hardened nub of his nipple, he promptly forgot his plan and dropped to his knees, gently laying her on the hardwood porch. If he was surprised that the flowers he'd brought for her table lay around her in sweet splendor, he said nothing. It seemed only right.

He leaned over her, planting tiny pecks on her face, her shoulders, her breasts. She pulled his suspenders out of her way, tried to relieve him of his shirt, and finally succeeded as he continued his foray across her body. Pulling him against her, she reveled in the contrast of the dark coarse hair of his chest against the softness of her bosom.

"Peaches, peaches," she whispered to him, and he complied. Then he thrust his tongue into her mouth, startling her. But as they began the strange duel of tongues, she found she liked it. It affected her potently, and instinctively she raised her pelvis, trying to press against his thigh.

"Easy, Hattie," he whispered, bridling her with peaches and pecks. "I know you feel it there, but we're going slow tonight."

He slid a hand down to clutch her aching mound, and she ground against it eagerly, a plea of desire falling from her lips. She was hot and wet and throbbing against his hand. He wanted to rip down her drawers and plunge himself inside her . . . deep inside her. He threw his head back and sought cool air. She was fresh, a virgin. He couldn't go tearing in with the wild recklessness of a Hampshire boar. With determined gentleness, he undid the ribbons on her drawers and mentally began reciting the multiplication table.

He lowered the cotton drawers from her hips, her ankles, and laid them aside. When his hand returned to the mat of light brown curls, she arched against him once more.

"Nine times eight is seventy-two," he murmured against her breast as he again worshiped the pouty nipples. Working his way to her lips with a sweet trail of hot kisses, he allowed his hand to explore the hidden secrets of her depths. When he placed his mouth over hers, she thrust her tongue eagerly inside him, and he answered her silent request gratefully.

Capturing a knee with each arm, he bent them back, holding her legs high and wide, and positioned himself between them. "Twelve times seven is eighty-four," he said hoarsely as he eased himself slightly into her. She was so hot, so tight. He gritted his teeth to hold himself back.

"Oh!" she exclaimed breathlessly as he found the guardian of her innocence.

In truth, he had little experience with virgins. Bessie Jane had felt nothing like this. He tried to move forward slowly, gently. The shield didn't budge. The barrier was an annoyance. He became more forceful and heard her catch her breath. "Shhh . . . ," he cooed to her. "It's just because you're innocent."

"I'm not innocent anymore," she whispered.

The blood was roaring in his ears, and he wasn't sure of her meaning. Her words were so final and so sure, though, he feared there was regret in them. "You're still innocent," he said against her lips. "I haven't breached you yet—that's why it still hurts. Do you want to move back to the swing?"

"Move back?" Her breathless whisper was incredulous. "No, never, never. Please move forward, Reed," she pleaded, wrapping her legs around his waist. "Move forward now!"

And he did.

Hattie's cry of pain rang loud in his ears, and he braced himself on his arms to hold back, plying her lips with peaches until he felt the tension ease from her thighs. He was throbbing with the need to have her quickly, and the tight warmth that surrounded him had caused him to lose his place in the multiplication table. Gritting his teeth and resuming his silent recitation, he asked, "Are you all right?"

"Is that it?" she asked, her tone rife with disappointment.

His grim expression dissolved into a smile, followed by a light laugh that helped him gain control. "Oh, there's more," he promised. "But the part that hurts is all over."

He kissed and caressed her, holding back as she grew accustomed to him. Slowly, so achingly slowly, he began to move inside her. She pressed up against him timidly. But timidity was not what he desired. "Are you afraid, Hattie?" he asked quietly.

"Only of not pleasing you."

He raised his head to look at her. "You do please me, very much, my Hattie," he said. "I think we should work on pleasing you."

To her complete astonishment, he rolled over on his back, pulling her on top of him. She gave a startled cry of exclamation when the new position lodged him more deeply within her. "You can do this with the woman on top?" she asked, her eyes wide with wonder.

Rolling his hips provocatively and smiling with devilment, he replied, "At least we can try."

Little by little, Hattie began her own motion, fascinated by the pleasure and the power.

"Do you like it?" he asked.

She nodded as a sweet sigh of delight escaped her lips.

"I like it too," he said, loving the look of her swaying body in the moonlight. "I like to watch you."

"Watch me what?" she asked, her eyes half closed with passion.

Her faded calico dress rode high on her thighs, and the bare flesh between it and her dark cotton stockings glowed in the silvery light. The bodice was bunched around her surprisingly small waist, and the chemise, its ribbons all undone, lay wide open, caught only by her elbows. The breasts that he'd so admired were full with the eagerness of desire, the nipples luscious and erect.

"I only wish you could see yourself as I see you now, Hattie," he whispered. He watched her eyes darken in distrust. She would never be able to see her own beauty, he realized. He would have to make her feel it.

His hand disturbed one of the dahlias as he lifted it to touch her, and he grasped the flower. With a quick assessing glance he brought it to his lips. "I'm sending you a kiss, Hattie." He extended the flower until it brushed her mouth.

She smiled against it. "Are you so far away, you can't bring them yourself?" she asked.

"Sometimes it's best to send an emissary." As he spoke, he slid the blossom slowly across her cheek, following the path of her smile and traveling farther to her sensitive ear.

Hattie's smile faded, her lips parting in anticipation as she realized his intent. She wriggled enticingly upon him as he eased the gentle petals down the warm flesh of her throat. Ever so slowly, he trailed the flower to her breasts, teasing them. He flicked her distended nipples with the silky red petals until desire shuddered through her and she arched her back, eagerly offering her bosom to more caresses.

He continued to toy with her as she writhed with building arousal, seating him more strongly inside her.

Perspiration beaded on Reed's upper lip as he watched her. He was hot and throbbing inside her now. The teasing dalliance with the flower had spawned a wild lust, but he would not permit himself the indulgence of giving in to it alone. Allowing the dahlia to drift from her alluring breasts, now tender and aching with want, he watched as Hattie's hands replaced the flower, clutching and caressing herself wantonly.

Resuming his determined recitation of the multiplication table, he dusted her belly with the fiery magic that fell from the soft red flower. When the bunched yards of calico got in his way, he moved to remedy the situation. Jerking up the offending skirt, he caught his breath at the sight of himself buried inside her. His hand trembled as he lowered the flower to its final destination, an aching, eager nub, nearly hidden in the small triangle of brown curls.

Her cry as he caressed her there sent fire coursing through his veins. Clenching his jaw, he increased the friction against her flesh. He would have her with him, he vowed.

Slowly, slowly, the pretty dahlia cajoled her cooperation. Her head thrown back and gasping for breath, she moved vigorously upon him, and he met each rhythmic thrust with one of his own. Passion glazed his eyes as he watched the rapid bouncing of her breasts and listened to her deep-throated moans of desire.

"Reed! More! Yes, Reed! I want more!" she pleaded in a litany that her lover could no longer ignore.

Pulling her into his arms, Reed rolled her onto her back and thrust into her wildly, his powerful movements scooting them across the floor.

Hattie's fingernails dug deep into the flesh of his buttocks as she screamed her fulfillment and Reed cried out her name as the hot thick power of his passion flowed into her.

When he could breathe again, he raised himself on his elbows to keep from crushing her and kissed the end of her nose. Her eyes opened, and a smile of satisfaction spread across her face. They lay entwined for several minutes, not talking but occasionally touching, kissing, still connected in the ancient fusion of male and female.

Finally Reed rolled over to lie beside her, holding her close, not yet willing to release her completely. Contented, she sighed and kissed the fingers that reached over to wipe the hair from her face. With a possessive sense of pride, Reed lovingly ran his hands along her body, leisurely reminding them both of the secret geography they had learned.

When he reached the juncture of her thighs, he picked up a flower that lay there. The red dahlia had been crushed and flattened between them. He brought it to his lips for a tender kiss.

"Will you marry me, Hattie?" he asked, offering the much-abused blossom.

She took it.

Twenty

I T was nearly midmorning when Reed stopped the buggy in front of the parsonage. After setting the brake, he turned and gave Hattie an encouraging smile before jumping down and reaching a hand up to her.

Dressed in his suit, with two buttons hastily resewn on his shirt and the previous night's wrinkles carefully pressed out, Reed looked especially handsome to Hattie. She was wearing a prim shirtwaist and a short summer jacket, and felt distinctly plain in her wedding garb.

"Are you all right, Hattie?" he asked as he took her arm. "You look a bit nervous."

She blushed. "Well, shouldn't I be?" she asked. "Having to face the preacher first thing in the morning?"

Reed's smile faded slightly. "Do you have regrets?"

Hearing the concern in his voice, Hattie smiled wryly. "Like most sinners, I regret the doing much less than the atoning."

Reed gently placed his fingers beneath her chin and raised her face to his. "I'll try to make it a sweet atonement," he said, and dropped a playful peck on the end of her nose.

They had not quite made it to the front door when Preacher

Able strode around the house, a bent disk blade in his hand. "Reed! Miss Hattie! What a surprise," he said, reaching out to clasp hands. "I'm glad you're here, Reed. I've been putting off fixing this disk since the harrowing, and I decided that today is the day."

"I think you'll have to put it off again," Reed said lightly. "I'm hardly dressed for blacksmith duties."

The preacher, prodded to attention, perused the couple, then raised his eyebrows in surprise. "You two are looking mighty slicked-up this morning."

Reed gave Hattie a quick glance and saw that she was pale, her smile too frozen to be natural. "Miss Hattie and I are here to be married."

Preacher Able's mouth dropped open, and he stared at the two as if they had suddenly sprouted antlers. Regathering his composure, he leaned the disk against the edge of the house and wiped his hands on his handkerchief. "Well, this is certainly a surprise," he said at last. "When did you decide this?"

"Last night," Reed answered calmly. "I asked Miss Hattie, and she accepted."

Nodding, Preacher Able glanced back and forth at the two of them. "Marriage is a very serious decision," he said solemnly. "It isn't the kind of thing folks do on the spur of the moment."

Having anticipated resistance, Reed showed neither concern nor annoyance at the preacher's words. "Miss Hattie and I have known each other for more than fifteen years. I think we're both aware of what we're getting into."

Folding his arms across his chest, Preacher Able wasn't so easily convinced. "Seems to me, Reed, it was only a few weeks ago that you were betrothed to Bessie Jane Turpin. And you, Miss Hattie—didn't I hear at the July Fourth picnic that you were marrying Ancil Drayton?"

Flushing with embarrassment, Hattie attempted to stammer an explanation, but the preacher cut her off. "Now, I know you two have had your problems. Reed, you're probably still feeling a bit of a sting over your broken engagement, and Miss Hattie, Ancil has spoken with me about the misunderstanding you've had. Let me warn the both of you, when your feelings are all stirred up like this, it's no time to be making rash decisions."

"It's not a rash decision," Reed said emphatically, and turned to Hattie. "Why don't you see if you can find Millie?

We'll want her for a witness, and I'm sure you'll want to see to your hair or something.''

Accepting her dismissal gratefully, Hattie headed for the door.

"She's probably back in the kitchen, Miss Hattie,'' Preacher Able called after her. ''You just go on in and make yourself at home.''

The two men watched her go, and when she was out of earshot, the preacher spoke. "What is this foolishness about, Reed Tyler?''

"It's not foolishness, Preacher. Miss Hattie and I want to get married. We know each other, care for each other, and we want to run the farm together.''

"That farm!'' the preacher exclaimed in exasperation. ''I almost wish Old Man Colfax had left her penniless. You fellows all scrambling for that piece of ground.''

"Well, he didn't,'' Reed answered practically. "It's Hattie's farm, and she can do with it what she will. And what she's decided to do with it is share it with me.''

Preacher Able pressed his lips together in disapproval. "There is a heap more to being a husband than just sharing the farmwork.''

"I know that, Preacher. I admire Miss Hattie, and I truly care for her. That's a good deal more than Drayton could say.''

The older man frowned. "Drayton made some mistakes, but he's older and more mature than you. I still suspect he'll make Miss Hattie a good husband.''

"And you think I won't?'' Annoyance tinged Reed's voice. "You didn't have any objections to my marriage to Bessie Jane.''

"Your engagement to Bessie Jane was based on entirely different reasons. Two attractive young people . . . well, it's expected that they'll want to marry. But a lusty young man tying himself to a old maid who's more than a little long in the tooth . . .'' Preacher Able shook his head. "It just don't sit well with me.''

Reed stared at him for several moments, regaining his patience before he spoke. "Preacher Able, I've always had the greatest respect for you. But if you think I'd have been happier with Bessie Jane than I will be with Hattie, I tell you, you're about as smart as mud.''

The preacher stared at him, dumbfounded at Reed's discourtesy.

"Miss Hattie is a fine, gentle, lovely woman,'' Reed continued. "She is the kind of woman any man would be proud to have by his side in sickness or in health. Preacher, I consider myself blessed and honored that she is willing to marry up with me. As for your ill-mannered reference to her age—" Reed frowned, "correct me if I'm wrong, but isn't twenty-nine the same age as your wife? Are you getting ready to put *her* out to pasture?"

The preacher had the good grace to flush, but he wasn't going to be won over that easily. "You've made your point, Reed," he admitted. "Perhaps you and Miss Hattie could make a good life together. But I still see no reason to go off half-cocked. Why don't you start courting her? Spend some evenings together, get to know each other. That way, you can truly make sure you're evenly matched and suited for each other. 'Marry in haste,' they say, 'repent at leisure.' "

Reed gnawed on the inside of his cheek as he considered his next words. "We can't wait around, Preacher. Miss Hattie and I need to get married today."

"What on earth for? A few months won't make any difference. If you're both really of sound mind and believe you can make a future together, there's no reason why you can't begin it later rather than sooner. If, after the harvest is in, you still want to marry, I'll be happy to perform the ceremony. I know that the church people will want to throw you a big shindig. Why, even Miss Hattie would probably want a big fancy wedding with all the trimmings." Preacher Able was smiling broadly now, assured of the quality of his advice. "After harvest is always a better time for weddings, anyway."

Reed sighed with exasperation, shifting from one foot to the other. There were some things a gentleman just didn't reveal, but telling the preacher wasn't quite like spilling the story at the billiard parlor. Looking the older man squarely in the eye, Reed spoke with quiet sincerity. "Preacher Able, I spent the whole of last night at Miss Hattie's farm. Her reputation will be in shreds if anyone hears of this."

Momentarily knocked off guard by the statement, Preacher Able was silent for an instant before he waved away the statement as ridiculous. "I don't think you need to worry about any untoward gossip, Reed. Nobody in this community would ever believe that Miss Hattie could do something wicked or improper with a man."

Raising an eyebrow, Reed allowed himself the slightest hint

of a smile. "Then I'd say this community is a bunch of damned fools."

The first afternoon of Hattie Tyler's married life was a busy one. They visited Reed's parents, then arrived home rather late to do the chores. Hattie gamely threw herself into the work, but her thoughts continued to flit through the jumble of events that had irrevocably changed her life in the past twenty-four hours.

After she'd accepted the battered blossom and his proposal of marriage, she had lain comfortably in Reed's arms, kissing, cuddling, and waiting for dawn.

"We can go in the house," she'd told him. "It's foolish to sleep out here on the porch when there is a comfortable bed inside."

He scooted down a little and rested his head comfortably against her breast. "Aren't you the same woman who said just a couple of hours ago that inviting me into your house would be unquestionably improper?"

She ran her hand adoringly across his cheek and pressed him lightly against her. "I suspect it's a bit late to be thinking of the proprieties."

Reed continued to anyway. "The night I sleep in your bed will be the night I'm your husband. My mama would be scandalized to think I had compromised you."

Hattie sighed pleasantly. "I should be scandalized myself. I just never imagined being compromised would feel so wonderful."

He laughed at that, and then kissed her playfully in appreciation. They vacillated between sparking and sleeping until dawn crept over the horizon.

"I'm starving," Reed said as the gray light illuminated their nakedness and they searched the porch for discarded clothing.

"Me too," she said. "What do you want for breakfast? Sausage? Biscuits?"

Watching her as she carefully rearranged her chemise to cover her newly revealed charms, Reed had other ideas. "How about peaches?" he answered. "This morning I have a powerful craving for peaches." He pulled her into his arms, kissing and caressing her until she nearly forgot what she was about.

"None of that, now, Reed Tyler," she said firmly. "There is work to be done this morning, and we can't just be lying around all day."

"It could be fun," he said, tempting her.

She shook her head with determination. "Myrene's going to be up here bawling to be milked any minute. And there are chickens to feed and hogs to slop. We've got a lot of work to be done if we're going to be married this morning."

Reed raised an eyebrow. "You want to be married this morning?"

Hattie blushed at her own presumption. "Well . . . yes. I mean . . . I thought . . ."

"You're right, Hattie," he said, gently brushing a lock of hair from her face. "The sooner we're wed, the better."

They sat looking at each other, both trying to grasp the rapid change of events. Hattie reflected lovingly on his tenderness and blushed at her own behavior. But how could any woman maintain decorum when kissed like that?

Realizing what she could serve for breakfast, she actually giggled. "I have the perfect breakfast for us," she said, then jumped up like a young girl and ran into the house. Moments later, she returned with a cobbler tin and two spoons. Setting the pastry between them, she handed Reed a spoon, and he eagerly dug into the pie.

Holding a spoonful up for inspection, he smiled wickedly. "Peaches?"

Rushing through the last of his chores, Reed was happily aware of the spring in his step and the cheery tune whistling through his lips. He was married! And to Hattie Colfax. Managing that in one day of courting was a good deal more than he'd hoped for, and he was certain the rest of the world had expected it even less.

After the hasty ceremony in the church, they'd headed to his parents' house to give them the news. He'd left Hattie with his mother and made his way out to the field where his father and brothers were working.

His father had seen him coming and walked out to meet him, purposefully choosing to confront his son alone. "When a man goes off courting and doesn't return until the next day, he causes a whole lot of speculation," Clive said before any word of greeting or welcome.

Reed stood face-to-face with his father, respectful but unwilling to be cowed. "Miss Hattie and I were married this morning," he said.

Clive studied his son for a few moments, then gave the barest of nods. He opened his mouth to speak but thought better.

"What?" Reed asked.

"I was going to ask if she was all right, to ask if you'd hurt her. But I think I know you better than that."

"You're right. You know me better than that."

The elder Tyler held out his hand. "You've got a fine woman, Reed. Congratulations."

Reed accepted the handshake, then threw his arms around his father for the hug that felt more natural.

"We'd best go tell your brothers," Clive said. "They're all about to bust from curiosity." The two men laughed, knowing the truthfulness of that statement.

By the time Mary Tyler had dinner on the table, the Tyler's felt relaxed and almost at home with the newlyweds. When Reed walked up behind Hattie, wrapped his arms around her waist, and planted a kiss on her neck, she squealed more from surprise than embarrassment. It endeared her to the family.

She was seated next him, and Reed took her hand as Clive said grace. The "amens" were barely said before the teasing began.

"Reed, pass the potatoes," Mary said.

Before he could reach for the bowl, Cal lifted it off the table. "Let me do this," he said with mock solemnity. "It's Reed's wedding night. He'll have to keep up his strength."

The hazing went fast and furious throughout the meal. Hattie's cheeks blazed, but Reed managed to parry it all. He was grateful for the good humor.

When the meal finally concluded, Hattie assisted with the dishes while the men helped Reed load his possessions in the buggy. Without the gentling influence of the women, the jests became nothing less than bawdy. Reed's face heated to bright red more than once.

"Reed!" his mother called from the back door. "Come here. I want you to get something for me in the cellar."

"I'll do it," Andy answered. He was his mother's usual errand boy, and he thought to spare his brother fetching duty on his last day at the Tyler farm.

"I want Reed!" Mary said.

Raising an eyebrow, Reed followed his mother down the cellar steps to the musty interior. Shelves covered all four walls and were lined with jars and bins. Barrels of foodstuff took up most of the floor space.

"Take some of this pickled okra," Mary said, indicating the top shelf on the left. "Nobody in this family likes it like you do, and I suspect Miss Hattie didn't put up much of it."

Reed began unloading a few jars from the high shelf. "I'm not taking all of this, Mama. Hattie's already put up enough food for an army, and I suspect she knows what I like."

"The question is, young man, do you know what she likes?" His mother sounded so vexed, Reed immediately turned in surprise.

"I've heard all I want to hear about Miss Hattie's farm," Mary declared. "What I want to hear about are your feelings for Hattie. Marrying a woman for a piece of ground is about the biggest insult a man could make to a woman. If that's what you've done, then I'd say you've got a lifetime of making-up to do."

His mother's words made Reed blush more fiercely than any of his brother's jests. "It's not like that," he said. "There are other pieces of land. I'd already decided to go for that place down near Uncle Ed."

"Then you married her for love?" Mary asked with a hint of skepticism.

Reed lowered his gaze. "I care for Hattie. I always have, you know that. She's kind and hardworking and fun." He smiled, as if recalling a cherished memory. "She's really fun, Mama. Sometimes it's just like being a couple of kids on the farm." More seriously, he went on. "I know she's not pretty in the way you normally think of that, but she's got her own ways. It wasn't so much wanting her land. It was more that I didn't want Drayton to have it." With a look of puzzled realization on his face, he gazed at his mother, curious at his own thoughts. "I didn't want Drayton to have *her*," he said quietly.

Mary watched the play of emotions on her son's face for a moment, then a tiny pleased smile crept across her mouth. "You take this pickled okra," she said. "Everything is going to be fine."

•   •   •

Making a last cursory glance around the barn to assure himself that he'd forgotten nothing, Reed hurried back to the house.

Hattie had a dinner of ham steaks and corn bread ready when he walked in the door. He'd taken the opportunity to wash up at the well and seated himself beside her in a clean shirt, smelling of her clove-scented soap.

To Reed's mind, Hattie was strangely quiet, and he worried she might be having second thoughts about their hasty nuptials. "What you thinking about?" he asked.

"About Ancil, actually," she answered. Seeing the shock on Reed's face, she hastened to explain. "I mean, I really should have gone to tell him about our marriage. I'd hate for him to hear it from somebody else."

"He already has," Reed said, his voice edged with a hint of coolness. "I asked Preacher Able to let him know, and he said he would."

"I still should have faced him," she said. "That's the only thing I faulted Bessie Jane on—not talking to you directly."

"It didn't make any difference hearing it from Bessie Jane or her father," Reed said. "And it won't make any difference for Drayton, hearing it from the preacher or you."

"You're right, I know. Still, it seems like the coward's way, and I am sorry about the children."

"The children?"

"They really need a mother, Reed. I feel so sorry for them."

Swallowing hard to dispel the knot of inexplicable anger that had settled in his throat, Reed controlled his voice carefully. "I'm sure they do need a mother, Hattie. And I'm sure Drayton will find one for them. But I'm very glad that it won't be you. I hope you feel the same way."

Something in his voice captured Hattie's attention. Glancing up at him, she could see that Reed was displeased, but she couldn't imagine why. It occurred to her that he sounded almost jealous, but she dismissed that idea as too farfetched. Reed Tyler could never be jealous of Ancil Drayton. It was impossible. "Of course, I prefer being married to you," she said, finding it strange that clarification was necessary. "I did choose you after all."

"I seduced you," he reminded her quietly.

Hattie choked sightly and took a sip of water. "I'd already

decided to accept you," she said, and was surprised to see an expression of stunned delight across his face.

"You'd already decided to marry me?" he asked, wanting to assure himself there was no misunderstanding.

"Yes. I'd made my decision before you came back."

Letting her words soak through him like spring rain on a parched afternoon, Reed was pleased with himself. He fought down the desire to crow like a victorious rooster and took a big bite of corn bread instead. "You are the best cook in this county, Hattie," he said cheerfully.

Her modest reply was almost inaudible.

"The cotton is coming along real well," he went on. "I suspect the pickers will be getting close to a hundred bales if the blight don't get us."

"Do you really think so?" Hattie was astounded. "It would be the biggest crop ever brought in on Colfax Farm."

Reed smiled slightly. Something unusual in his expression struck her, and she recalled her own words. "Oh!" she whispered as if realizing a terrible social blunder. "I forgot it's not the Colfax farm anymore. It's the Tyler farm."

Reed watched her consider this additional change in her life. She didn't appear upset or resistant. "It sounds funny," he said after a moment.

"I suspect we'll get used to it," she answered. Her smile was unconcerned, and it pleased him.

"It's our farm, Hattie, no matter what we call it."

"I know." Her smile broadened. "Your family really made me feel at home today, Reed. I don't mind calling it Tyler Farm because I already feel like a Tyler."

His grin wide and open, Reed surprised her by leaning over to plant a peck on her throat. "I'm thinking, Hattie," he said as he lazily pushed his plate aside, "that people will always think of it as Colfax Farm and if we call it Tyler, folks will just get confused about it and my daddy's place."

She nodded. "Why don't we just be the Tylers of Colfax Farm?"

"Fine. So you like being one of the Tyler women?" he asked as she stood to take his plate.

"Yes, I think I do," she answered with a slight blush. "Do you want some dessert?"

He took the dishes out of her hands and set them back on

the table. "There are a few rules that Tyler women have to follow," he told her, snaking an arm around her hips to pull her closer.

" 'Rules'?"

"Yes. One of the rules for Tyler women is that frequently they forget dessert and leave the supper dishes to go to bed early with their husbands."

Twenty-One

HATTIE raised her eyebrows in an expression of pure skepticism. "What I heard today in church were vows, Plowboy, not rules," she said. Grabbing up the dishes again, she headed to the sink. His eyes alight with devilment, Reed was right behind her, bringing a handful of his own.

"What are you doing?" she asked.

"An extra pair of hands will make short work of this little bit of dishes," he replied, scraping the leftovers into the slop dish for the hogs.

"You're going to help me in the kitchen?" Her voice was incredulous.

"If you're in the kitchen," he said, grinning, "then I want to be there too." He leaned over and laid a noisy teasing kiss on her cheek.

She pulled away from him. "You're keeping me from my work," she protested. But as she finished clearing the table and mixed the hot water in the kettle with cooler water from the pump, Reed was everywhere, touching and teasing her, even though she constantly tried to avoid him.

Drying the dishes and hastily putting them away under Hattie's direction, Reed refused to let his wife linger over an already clean kitchen. Placing a hand on each of her hips, he hauled her up against him, then wrapped his arms around her and shared with her a sweet sultry peach.

He heard the little moan in her throat, yet she pulled away from him. "Hattie, what is it?" His voice was gentle with concern.

"I . . . Well, I don't know."

"Are you frightened? I promise it won't hurt again like it did last night."

"It's not that, exactly. Last night was, . . . so unplanned. It just happened. Tonight, it seems wicked to rush to that bedroom as if I couldn't wait for something to happen."

He smiled. "Is something going to happen, Hattie?" he asked, pressing his lips to her hair.

"It is if we go into the bedroom," she said with certainty.

"How about if we stay in the kitchen?" he asked, leaning down to kiss her. He held her tight against him so that she could feel his arousal.

Her shocked intake of breath indicated she was not totally unmoved by his naughty suggestion. "Maybe we *should* go to the bedroom," she said, attempting to move away from him.

Reed would have none of it. Sliding one arm under her knees and the other around her back, he lifted her.

"Reed!" she exclaimed. "Put me down!"

He feigned dropping her on the floor, and she squealed with fright before he pulled her close.

"I think this is a tradition," he said. "Or at least it's our version of it."

The sunlight crept across the tangled sheet as Hattie opened her eyes. She was not surprised to wake up in Reed's arms. It felt as natural as breathing. He awakened as she did, and she felt his sweet sleepy kiss in her hair.

"Good morning," she said, purring like a contented cat before turning to him. She winced slightly, and he noticed it.

"Sore?" he asked with concern.

"A little, I guess," she admitted.

"I think you've got a right." His hand caressed her naked body beneath the sheet. "I think we overdid it a bit for the wedding night."

"Married people don't normally do it that many times?" she asked with innocent curiosity.

Reed's grin was half pride, half delight. "Not if they expect to live long enough to farm the next day."

Hattie joined his laughter and eased herself closer to his body. She already loved the tenderness and warmth of being near him. "Does that that mean we won't get to do it again for a while?" she asked.

"If you're sore, Hattie," he said seriously, "I think we should wait."

"I'm not that sore!" she assured him quickly. When he still looked hesitant, she sighed in resignation. "How long do we have to wait? A week?"

Reed looked genuinely alarmed. "No, not a week. Surely not a week."

"How soon?"

He shrugged. "Maybe tonight?" It was more a question than a statement, but Hattie was delighted.

"I think I can wait until tonight," she whispered, then leaned down to nip his nipple with her teeth.

"Stop that, Hattie," he ordered with feigned sternness. "If we're going to wait until tonight, you've got to help me."

"Why should I help you? Waiting is your idea, after all."

He rolled her over onto her back. "You're trying to tempt me, you little wench. I already wasted half a day in your bed. The chickens are starving, the hogs are losing weight, and Myrene gave up banging on the door an hour ago. And still you want to keep me here." He took a playful bite out of the corner of her lip. "Do you know what I think, Mrs. Tyler?"

"What do you think?"

"I think you *like* this naughty-things-you-do-in-the-bed stuff."

"That's your fault," she complained. "If you didn't make it feel so good, I wouldn't like it at all."

Reed's laugh was heavily laced with old-fashioned male pride. No strutting rooster had ever been more self-satisfied. "Well, I bet you're glad this morning that you didn't wake up with old Ancil Drayton," he said without a pretense of modesty. "He would have never given you what I did last night."

Hattie raised an eyebrow at his conceit. "If I'd married Ancil, I would have seven children. That's something you didn't give me last night."

His mouth dropping open in shock, Reed's flash of jealousy made him forget his vow. "You want children, I'll give them to you," he said, then spread her knees with his own and slid inside her.

She cried out sharply, and he stopped immediately. "Hattie, did I hurt you?" he asked anxiously, and would have withdrawn if she hadn't wrapped her legs around his waist.

"Not too much," she answered. "It hurts a little, but it feels so good too."

Gently, easily, Reed began to rotate his hips, striving to give her pleasure without causing her the slightest twinge of discomfort.

"Would you really give me children, Reed?"

"That's what this does, Hattie. You know that."

"Yes, I know how it works," she whispered. "But would you want me to have your children?"

He visualized her swollen with his child and found himself strangely intrigued with the idea. "Yes, Hattie, I want children, and I'd want no one else to be their mother."

She moaned as she squirmed beneath him, the rhythm drawing her away from the conversation. "I want a big family," she murmured. "A big family like your mother has."

Reed began to plunge more forcefully within her. "If Drayton would have given you seven, then I'll give you eight."

She lifted her hips to meet his thrusts, and her head began to flail back and forth on the pillow.

"Would you like that, Hattie?" he said against her ear as his tempo quickened. "Eight children? Is that what you want?"

Hattie no longer listening to him as she arched her back, her nails digging into his shoulders.

"Eight . . . is that what you want, Hattie?" he asked again as her eyes glazed over and she threw her head back in sweet agony.

"Eight, Hattie? Eight?" he cried out as he felt her wild contractions pulling him over the edge with her.

"Yes! Yes!" she screamed before they both fell through to the near side of heaven.

When their senses recovered and breathing became less of a task, Reed gently kissed her forehead before collapsing beside her. His hand covered his eyes for several minutes as the two lay in respite. Then Reed's lips curved into a wide grin. "You know," he said with adequate solemnity. "It's a good thing you like this, 'cause if I'm going to give you eight children, we'll have to do it a lot.''

The production of eight children became the Tylers' private joke during the first week of their married life. Reed took every opportunity to touch, taste, and kiss his wife, claiming it a necessary prerequisite to the production of offspring. Too dazed to protest, Hattie found her husband's ardor much to her liking. Rather than discouraging his constant advances, she goaded him with his hasty promise, then willingly left the evening dishes while he labored to fulfill his pledge.

Before dawn one morning Reed woke her with words of congratulation. With his protesting bride still dressed in her nightgown, he carried her out to the barnyard.

"Have you lost your mind?" she asked him, not sure whether to laugh or knock him over the head.

"You want eight children, Hattie," he said. "Well, I've been up half the night getting them for you."

"What are you talking about?"

Reaching the pigsty, he made his way inside and strode to the farrowing house.

"Mabel's had her litter!" she exclaimed delightedly. "Why didn't you wake me?"

"I didn't know, myself. I woke up about an hour ago and thought I heard something outside. By the time I got here, she'd already had three. I had to stay to make sure that while she was still laboring, she didn't wallow around and roll on one of them."

They ducked into the door of the dry, well-ventilated building, and Reed at last stood Hattie on her feet. Mabel was lying on her side, resting from her ordeal, her breathing heavy with weariness. The tiny little pigs lay like a row of mewling sausages along the belly of the huge black-and-white sow.

"They're wonderful!" Hattie said, her voice breathy with awe as she dropped to her knees beside the farrowing nest.

Placing his hands on her shoulders, Reed unconsciously kneaded the muscles as he watched his wife's delight in her new additions to the barnyard. "I'm sorry there's only eight," he said. "I know you expected more."

"Eight is perfect. Why, this is Romeo's first try. I'm sure he'll get better with age."

Reed dropped to his knees behind her, wrapping his arms around her waist and resting his head in the crook of her shoulder. "So you think older males are better at this?" he asked with feigned annoyance.

Pursing her lips as if genuinely considering his question, Hattie finally replied, "I don't think it's age so much as practice."

" 'Practice'?" Reed considered the statement for a moment. Cupping her breasts in his hands, he said, "Yes, I firmly believe in practice."

The workweek at Colfax Farm was both busy and idyllic. Long hot looks and suggestive references to sundown enhanced the weeding of the garden, the tending of livestock, the cleaning and repairing of buildings and fences, and the field work.

Although Reed had carried a dinner bucket with him for years, Hattie found that her day was not quite so long when she packed a basket and carried it out to Reed in the fields. They would talk and plan and laugh together as they ate, then both would return to the task at hand—she with a lighter step and he with a cheerful whistle.

One afternoon, as they sat beneath the cottonwood tree that overlooked the rice field, Hattie lazily leaned back against the trunk and watched Reed as he talked about rice.

"The South is changing, Hattie, and the cotton culture is going the way of the old plantation. Once the land is broken up and the fields planted, one man can manage three or four hundred acres of rice until harvest. It doesn't take gangs of pickers or whole communities of sharecroppers to make it work. If we were to go into rice exclusively, we could double or triple the size of this farm and still handle it ourselves."

Hattie found his dreams exciting and his enthusiasm infectious. "What about the harvest? How will we handle that?" she asked.

"Rice is a modern crop. That's one thing that really impressed Harm when we were in Helena. While sugar and cotton planters still rely on strong backs and good mules, the rice farmer is ready for the new century."

His eyes sparkled as he described the wonder of the industrial age come to the farm. "They've got binding machines, Hattie, that cut the grain stalks and tie them in bundles without the touch of a human hand."

She giggled at the idea. "This machine has little fingers that tie the rice up in knots?"

"Wait till you see it work, Hattie. It's a marvel of modern agriculture."

"How are we going to get a machine like that for our field?"

"Uncle Ed's got one. He'll help us get the rice shocked and braced, so we'll be ready whenever the threshers head through this way. His rice will probably be in before ours is ready, so I asked him to come up and help us with the harvest."

Hattie smiled with delight. "That would be wonderful! He'll stay with us?"

"I'll ask him if you want me to, but he'll probably be stopping over with my folks, catching up on his visiting and such."

"Of course, you're right. It's probably a good opportunity to see your family."

Reed nodded. "I don't know if I'll be ready for company that soon anyway." His voice became husky and smooth as warm molasses. "I'm kind of enjoying having all these private evenings with my wife."

Hattie couldn't keep the grin of pride from her face. His desire for her was separate from his love of the farm, and she was just selfish enough to encourage it.

"What are you smiling at, Mrs. Tyler?" he asked, pulling her closer to him.

"I was just thinking."

He chuckled, and his eyes danced with mischief. "Were you thinking what I'm thinking?"

"What are you thinking?"

"I'm thinking that we're newly married and all alone," he answered as he reached a big calloused hand to the tiny buttons of her shirtwaist.

"Reed!" she pushed his hand away and folded her arms protectively across her breasts.

"Sorry, Hattie," he said with genuine sincerity, but his smile never wavered. "I didn't mean to scare you. I just wanted to see you in the daylight."

"What do you mean?"

"Have I told you that you've got a really pretty bosom?"

She stared at him in shock. "Reed Tyler! I've never heard of such a thing."

He clucked his tongue with feigned reproof as he barely held back a wicked grin. "Well, I'm not surprised," he said. "I

doubt seriously that many in this community have had an opportunity to observe your bosom as closely as I have.''

"Nobody else has seen me!'' she declared unnecessarily.

When he laughed at her outrage, she continued her tirade.
"Woman don't have pretty *bosoms*! A pretty face or pretty hair,
but not . . . People just don't speak of such things.''

"Don't worry,'' he said, laughter dancing in his voice. "I'd
never mention it around town. Don't want the other fellows
getting curious.''

"You!'' She punched him hard in the belly, but his hard
sinewy muscles deflected the blow, and she elicited only a slight
rush of air.

Raising his hands to the heavens, he implored divine intervention. "I tell the honest truth and give my wife a genuine
compliment, and she beats me for it.''

"I should beat you on the head where it could do some
good!''

"My head is much harder,'' he warned her. "I wouldn't
want you to hurt your hand. Then you'd never open your dress
and show me your pretty bosom.''

His grin was infectious, and despite her embarrassment, she
couldn't help but smile back at him. "You are a shameless
husband,'' she said, trying without much success to keep from
giggling.

"Yes, that's true. Reed is shameless, and Hattie has a pretty
bosom.'' He raised a hand and gestured across the empty horizon. "There's just me here, Hattie, and I'd like to see my wife
as intimately in sunlight as moonglow.''

"It seems so wicked,'' she whispered.

Capturing her fingers in his hand, he brought them to his lips
for a kiss. "Nothing between us is wicked.''

"Because we're married?''

His brow furrowed as he considered her words. "That's true,
I suppose. But even that night on the porch, when we were
blatant sinners, somehow it still felt right.''

After a moment's hesitation, she nodded. "It felt that way
to me too.''

They stared at each other, remembering the sights and sounds
and tenderness of that first time. For that moment there were no
secrets between them.

"Please, Hattie,'' he said, and reached toward her. Holding
up a hand in protest, she stopped him. Though she was blushing

furiously, she managed to keep her hands from trembling as she worked the buttons on her shirtwaist.

Scarcely breathing, Reed rested his hands on his thighs as he watched her progress, ignoring the nervous sweat that beaded on his upper lip.

When the dress was open to her waist, Hattie glanced hastily at him before focusing her attention on the ribbons of her chemise. The delicate ties, usually so simple to manipulate, were as hesitant as Hattie herself. She almost wept in gratitude when she managed to loose them.

Looking up at Reed, she saw the expectation and desire in his gaze. To bolster her courage, she took a deep breath. That had the incidental consequence of raising her breasts, as if taunting him. She watched as Reed's lips parted and he swallowed, choking back his passion.

Grasping the sides of chemise and dress, she pulled the parted fabric back to her shoulders, baring the firm white globes with their pink-tipped crowns already taunt and waiting.

Reed's look was as thorough as a touch, and she longed to close her eyes and moan with the feel of it. But she wasn't willing to give up the sight of his appraisal. Her breathing quickened, his gaze followed the gentle sway of her breasts. When he moistened his lips with his tongue, she was sure she was melting. "Is my bosom pretty in the sunlight?" she asked, her voice quivering with desire.

"No, Hattie," he answered. "Not pretty. Beautiful."

If Hattie had needed confidence in her attractiveness, that afternoon under the cottonwood gave it to her. In the marriage vows Reed had said, "with my body I worship thee," and the exquisite passionate love they had made in broad daylight had been nothing short of worship.

That night at the house, Reed grudgingly admitted that the dalliance had resulted in sunburning his buttocks. They giggled together like naughty children as they lay on the bed and Hattie tenderly applied salve to his red-tinged behind.

"It's all your fault," he declared.

Her snickering got out of control. "Next time," she said, "I'll let you wear my hat."

The image of her big straw hat riding his buttocks had them both laughing hilariously.

When they were able to catch their breath, Reed spoke with soft sincerity. "You know, that night I came courting . . . I was really uncomfortable about being younger than you and maybe appearing foolish." He shook his head at the memory. "The idea that you might tease or laugh at my lovemaking just plain unmanned me."

"How could I have laughed at you?" she asked in surprise. "You were the teacher, the one who knew what to do."

"But you knew me when I was just a kid. You used to dry my tears and blow my nose." Grimacing in self-derision, he added, "That night I was thinking that you'd probably changed my diaper."

She lightly grazed her hand across his crotch. "I don't think this thing ever fit in a diaper."

Nursing time was over then as he grabbed her and pulled her beneath him to kiss away her amusement. Returning his kisses with equal fervor, Hattie wrapped her legs around his waist.

"Careful with me, woman," he said as her knee brushed his bottom. "Remember my injury."

"Does that mean you'll be too sore to do this for a while?" she asked innocently as she wriggled against him.

"Absolutely," he said, then gave her sensitive ear a malvalva. "I'll be unable to husband you for at least the next ten minutes."

Actually, it was five.

Twenty-Two

B Y Sunday, Hattie and Reed were as relaxed and intimate with each other as many couples who had been married years longer. The friendship they had shared so long had now expanded to include passion. Knowledge of each other's strengths and foibles gave them an uncanny intuition.

It was that intuition that made Reed slow the mare from her brisk pace as they were in sight of the church.

Hattie looked at him quizzically. "Why are we slowing down?"

He answered her question with one of his own. "What's wrong today, Hattie?"

She glanced away. "I don't know what you mean."

"For some reason, you don't want to go to church today. And I'd like to know why."

"Of course I want to go to church," she said with more vehemence than necessary.

He turned to get a good look at her. "You've been stalling all morning. Since the minute we finished the morning chores and started getting spiffed up for church, you've been dawdling."

"I never 'dawdle'!"

"That's what makes me so sure that something is wrong. I don't mind being made to wait a good ten minutes by the buggy because you can't decide what to wear. But I do mind you being troubled and not talking to me about it."

Hattie couldn't quite look him in the eye. At her hesitance, Reed transferred the reins to one hand and took her hand in his. "Is it Drayton? Are you worried about having to face him?"

She shook her head. "No, not really. I expect Ancil to be annoyed and to have maybe a few cross words to say. That doesn't bother me. I do want to talk to the children, though, explain that I still care about them." She sighed. "They really do need a woman in that house to love them."

His expression grave, Reed brought her hand to his lips and asked quietly, "Are you having regrets, Hattie?"

She jerked her head up, startled at his question, then grinned. "Do you have to ask that, Reed?" She grasped the hand that held her own. "I'm sorry for them, but I am very happy for me."

His smile returned, but a hint of concern lingered in his eyes. "So what are you worrying about this morning? If it's not Drayton, what can it be?"

She eased her hand free. "Reed," she began nervously, keeping her gaze lowered, "do you think everyone will know what we've been doing all week?"

He looked at her blankly for a moment, then quickly smothered his humor and answered as seriously as he could. "You mean taking care of the livestock and working out in the fields?" he asked.

Her head popped up, a look of exasperation on her face. "Of course not! You know exactly what I mean!"

It was impossible to keep the grin from his face at the sight of his wife's discomfiture and irritation.

"Oh," he said. "You mean does the whole congregation know that we've been going to bed right after supper and not sleeping until after midnight?"

She nodded anxiously.

"And you're wondering if they know about me putting my hand under your skirt when you were bent over, picking okra in the garden?"

She gasped and covered her pink cheeks with her hands.

"And maybe," he went on, "they know about that afternoon under the cottonwood or that evening I bent you over the kitchen table."

"Reed!" Hattie's face was burning with mortification.

He pulled into the churchyard. Hattie had made them late, and the sounds of voices raised in joyful hymns floated toward them as he set the brake and gave his wife a long, thoughtful look.

"Hattie, they don't know a thing," he said quietly. She visibly relaxed and took a deep, grateful breath. Reed allowed her a full minute to regain her composure before he added, "But I imagine they suspect exactly what we've been up to."

When her eyes widened in horror, he couldn't hold back the laughter another minute.

His humor infuriated her, and she sputtered with anger as he drew her lovingly into his arms.

"We're married people," he said. "We haven't got to answer to a soul in that church."

She didn't struggle from the comfort of his arms, but she did respond petulantly. "It's easy for you. Men just get a pat on the back and congratulations. But women . . ." She sighed with dismay. "Oh, Reed, I don't think I can bear to have every eye in that church focused on me, looking to see if debauchery is written on my face."

He kissed her brow, then released her and jumped down from the buggy. As he held up his arms to her, she grudgingly went into them. To her surprise, he didn't immediately set her on her feet, but eased her down the length of his body. The sensual contact didn't stop when she was finally standing on the ground.

Holding her close against his body, he whispered, "They probably will imagine something like this."

He brought his mouth down on hers, and she opened for him. Gently, lovingly, they met the passion of the other, interspersing sweet kisses with tiny pecks, until heat flared between them and their tongues imitated the goal of such desire.

Moaning in the back of her throat, Hattie pressed herself more tightly against him, rubbing lustfully against the evidence of his appreciation.

When he abruptly separated them, she gave a little cry of dismay and attempted to return to his arms before she became aware of her surroundings. "In the churchyard!" she gasped as she turned away from her husband. "I really have no shame when you touch me, Reed."

He touched her cheek, silently urging her to face him. "I wouldn't have you any other way," he said.

She smiled shyly and started to speak, but he held up a hand to stop her. "What those people will see," he said, "when you walk beside me into the church and your place next to me in the Tyler pew is a woman who looks happy, fulfilled, and content with her marriage."

His warm gaze captured hers, and Hattie felt a fluttery tenderness stealing through her. The words *I love you* sprang to her lips, but she held them back. Her eyes, however, spoke very clearly. Reed's lips curved into a smile and he caressed her soft cheek until she turned her head to kiss his hand.

"I'm ready to go in now," she whispered. "I have you beside me, and I don't care what they think."

Obviously pleased with her words, Reed nevertheless gave her a wry look. "You may be ready to go in," he said, "but I think I'd better wait a couple of minutes."

At her quizzical expression, he glanced downward. Her gaze was drawn to the front of his trousers, and she blurted out a naughty giggle.

The final hymn before the preaching was in its last chorus before Reed and Hattie Tyler walked down the center aisle of the church. The high color in the newlyweds' cheeks only added to the speculation about their late arrival.

When the benediction was pronounced and the last "amen" declared, Reed took Hattie's hand. If he'd planned to steal her out of the church, though, he was doomed to be disappointed. The Tyler family surrounded them, offering hugs and kisses. After they had each had a turn, the rest of the congregation approached with congratulations and curiosity.

As they slowly made their way to the back of the church, Hattie saw Ancil waiting at his pew, his children looking lost and confused. Her step didn't falter, partly because of the warm surge of strength she drew from the feel of Reed's hand at her waist.

"Good morning, Ancil," she said. Her gaze was direct and without any pretense of concern or challenge. "Preacher Able brought the news of our wedding to you?"

"Well, sure he did," Ancil replied crankily. "But I think you owe me an explanation yourself."

She paused, determined to find the right words to account for her actions, but was prevented from doing so as Reed stepped between them.

"I'll straighten this all out with Drayton," he said casually to her. Taking the older man's arm in a not too gentle grip, he turned Ancil to the door. "Hattie would like a few minutes alone to talk with the children."

The rest of the congregation had filed out the door, and Hattie found herself alone in the church with seven young faces looking up at her.

Their expressions, curious and sorrowful, put her at a loss how to begin. As she hesitated, the heavy silence dragged on. The deadlock was finally broken as the youngest threw himself against her legs and begged to be picked up.

Hattie eagerly pulled the child into her arms and hugged him. "I've missed you, Buddy," she said. "Have you been a good boy?"

Buddy nodded vigorously, though his devilish smile made his answer questionable. She smiled at the child, delighted and saddened. Buddy needed a mother, and soon he would have one, but it wouldn't be Hattie.

"You married Mr. Tyler?" The question came from Ada, who was sitting in the end of the pew between her sisters.

"Yes, I did," Hattie answered.

"Does it mean that I have to give my doll back?" she asked anxiously as she eyed the rag-filled toy in her arms.

Smiling warmly, despite the sharp shard of steel that pierced her heart, Hattie started to assure her, but was interrupted by Cyl.

"Don't be dumb, Ada," she said, her voice rough with anger. "Of course you can keep the stupid doll. She doesn't want it." Rising from her seat, Cyl sidled out of the pew, stopping only for an instant to stare Hattie in the face. "She doesn't want it, and she doesn't want us," the girl spat out. Her fury was mighty, but she was unable to hide the tears in her eyes as she turned and ran out the door.

Ada looked like she might be likely to cry, too, but Mary Nell shushed her immediately. "Don't be a baby. Cyl's just having a fit over nothing. We'll be getting another mama, and that's a certainty."

Ancil Jr. stood up and took his little sister's hand. "I'll take Ada to Cyl," he said. "They ain't hardly never parted, and they maybe need each other now. Congratulations on your wedding," the young man added with stiff politeness. "We're all hoping you'll be right happy."

"Me too," Luke said simply, and followed his brother's retreat.

Fred stood also. His bewildered expression revealed his mixed loyalties. "I always liked Reed Tyler," he told Hattie.

She tenderly ruffled the thatch of reddish-blond hair that was sorely in need of cutting. "He's a fine man, Fred, and I really love him," she said, surprising herself at her own admission.

The young boy shrugged with acceptance. "Well, I guess it's all right, then. Is it true he's young enough to be your son?"

Hattie blanched at the comment, and Mary Nell's giggle quickly turned her face from white to scarlet. "I am older than he is," she said, "but not old enough to be his mother."

The boy nodded, reassured, then held out his arms for his brother. "Come on, Shorty," he said to Buddy. "You can't be hanging onto the women's skirts forever."

Delaying the inevitable, Hattie hugged the child one more time and planted a soft kiss in his curls, then turned him over to his brother. She watched as the two walked hand in hand out of the church and down the steps before breaking into a run. The toddler tried without success to keep up with his older long-legged brother. Briefly Hattie mourned the loss and offered a quick prayer that someday her own boys would go running down those steps.

"I don't see what the big fuss is about." Mary Nell's voice broke into Hattie's reverie. "It's not like you're the last woman on earth. Preacher Able is already settin' up an introduction to the widow Blackburn from over at Carson's Flat." Sighing loudly, Mary Nell shook her head with dismissal. "To my way of thinking, one stepmother is pretty much the same as another."

"And you don't want one, no matter who she is," Hattie said.

"I want one, all right," Mary Nell answered, surprising Hattie. "Believe me, it was nothin' personal. I want someone to take over the housework and minding the kids. I'm deathly sick of it, for sure." The young girl's exasperated sigh was telling. "It weren't that I didn't like you, Miss Hattie. I just wanted you to understand, right off, that I'm plumb grown and I don't need no mothering and I don't take no orders."

"So you don't mind if your father remarries?" Hattie asked.

"Oh, it really don't matter much to me," the young girl said lightly, rising to her feet and cocking one hand on her hip. At that point Hattie noticed her dress. She was clearly attempting to portray herself as a woman several summers older than thirteen years. "I'm plannin' to marry up pretty soon, by next spring anyway, so I'll be gettin' out of that house for good."

Hattie was appalled. "Mary Nell, you are not near old enough to marry."

The young girl raised her chin defiantly. "I most certainly nearly am. I got my woman's curse last winter."

"You're so young," Hattie insisted. "You have years of fun and friendship before you need to settle down to marriage."

Mary Nell shook her head. "I'm marryin' soon. Do you think I want to wait around like you did and be passed over by every man in town?"

The cruel words caught Hattie unaware. In the months that she'd been courted and during the last few days of marital bliss, she'd already forgotten that she was nobody's first choice for wife.

Some of her self-doubt must have shown in her face. Mary Nell walked over to her and patted her consolingly on the arm. "That's all right, Miss Hattie. You got you a man anyway. And believe me, I couldn't agree with you more."

"Agree with me about what?"

"If I had two men itchin' to marry me for my land, I'd choose the young stud over the old geezer myself."

Reed led Drayton gently but persistently away from the church, conversing about the weather. Given a choice, he wouldn't have wasted an extra breath on Ancil Drayton, but he wanted Hattie to have her private moment with the children.

"I think I gotta right to be riled," Drayton said, finally shaking free of Reed's grip and stopping. "I spent a couple of months there softening her up, and you just came in and nabbed her."

Reed raised one shoulder in a careless gesture, unconcerned about Drayton's annoyance. "Sometimes that's the way it happens. I'm sure you'll find someone else."

"Well, sure," Drayton replied, making it clear that he was not suffering from his loss. "I'm goin' to start calling on the widow Blackburn next week, though her land ain't much. Not like Miss Hattie's. I sure had my heart set on that piece of ground."

They had reached the shade of one of the scrub oaks near

the buggies, and Reed figured they were far enough away for Hattie to be spared any annoying comments from Drayton.

"I'm sure you'll make do with the widow's acreage," he said as he turned to leave, eager to get back to Hattie.

Drayton nodded. "Sure I will. And it ain't all bad. Widow Blackburn's a fine-looking woman. Even with that good piece of ground, marryin' up with Horseface Hattie didn't set too well with me. I suspect you feel about the same."

Reed turned back, his face white with anger. His eyes narrowed dangerously, but his voice was deceptively quiet. "I do not want to hear my wife referred to by that name ever again."

Drayton laughed. "It ain't like I made it up, Reed. Folks been callin' her that since she was a schoolgirl."

"I know." Reed's words were even and controlled. "But I don't want to hear her called that ever again."

Unaware of the depths of the other man's anger, Drayton attempted to counter his unkind words. "I ain't saying she's not a wonderful woman. Lord knows, she works harder than a dozen of these young gals and she's real kind. She was real kind to me," he emphasized. "From the neck down, she's passable, but facts is facts, boy. That woman's got a face that would curdle milk."

Drayton gasped as Reed suddenly grabbed him by the shirt-front, lifted him off the ground, and slammed him into the trunk of a tree.

Reed's eyes were no more than slits, and his words were released between clenched teeth. "Don't *ever* call my wife by that name again, Drayton. I'd hate to have to beat up on an old man like you."

A crowd immediately formed around the two men, with Preacher Able struggling to get through.

Eyes bugged out, and strangling on his own fear, Drayton was eager to accommodate. "Whatever you say, Reed. From now on, I'll call her Hattie."

Pulling his victim forward slightly, then slamming him against the tree trunk again, Reed said, "You call her Mrs. Tyler, and tell your friends to do the same."

Reed felt a hand on his shoulder and turned to see Harmon beside him. He glanced around at the wide-eyed crowd, shocked by his own actions. He was not a man prone to brawling or displays of temper.

He released his captive, abruptly, and Drayton might well

have fallen to his knees had Harmon not propped him up. Before a word could be spoken between Drayton and Reed, Harmon threw an arm around Drayton's shoulder and hustled him away.

Reed heard his friend telling Drayton in a most amicable tone, "I agree with Reed one-hundred percent, and if I hear you speaking cruel of Miss Hattie, I'll try to get to you before Reed does."

As his friend and former rival left, Reed found himself standing beside Bessie Jane. Casting a disdainful glance in the style that had made her the belle of the county, Bessie Jane froze the gawking crowd with one look. As the churchgoers quickly discovered other interests and moved on, she turned to face Reed. "Are you all right?" she asked.

He looked down at the sweet heart-shaped face with the determined little pointed chin and wide blue eyes, and smiled. "I guess I lost my temper," he admitted.

"Sometimes that's the best thing to do. At home I was taught that a lady never shows her temper. But Harm has convinced me that coming right out with what you think and feel is a much more honest approach to life."

She looked so serious, so thoughtful, that Reed found himself intrigued by this new Bessie Jane. "Are you happy?" he asked, surprising himself with his curiosity.

She nodded, smiling. "Yes, I'm very happy. I know it must have seemed irrational to be engaged to you for so long and then suddenly run off with another man. But Harm and I have really known each other for a long time."

"He was the one, wasn't he?" Reed asked. "The man before me."

She looked puzzled for a moment, then bit her lip. "You knew?" she asked incredulously.

"No," he assured her. "Not until Hat—Let's say I finally figured it out."

"It was terrible to use you like that, Reed," she said. "Daddy hated Harm and wanted me to marry you. I thought if we did that, I—I could forget the man I really loved."

He shrugged. "It doesn't work out that way."

"You were so gentle with me, Reed, but it's just not the same as when you love someone."

"I know." The certainty in his voice startled Reed, but Bessie Jane seemed to find nothing amiss. "Bessie Jane, about that other, I want you to know that I would never say or do anything to compromise your reputation. What happened between us was so unmemorable, it's completely forgotten.''

"You don't have to tell me that,'' she said. "I would feel safe to trust you with my life, not just my secrets. Besides, the only person who really matters to me is Harm, and he already knows.''

Reed's face paled. "He knows?''

"I told him so he would give up and leave me alone, but he didn't. He loves me enough to forget the past.''

Reed stared at her, absorbing the words before understanding dawned in his eyes. "So *that* was the jawbreaker punch.''

"What?''

"Never mind,'' he answered, and screwed his face into an expression of grave concern. "Just do me a favor, Bessie Jane. I'm sure Hattie is as forgiving as Harm, but let's not put her to the test, okay?''

She giggled at Reed's feigned terror. "So you *are* happy with Miss Hattie,'' she said. "I'm so glad. It bothered me to think of you alone, and you've always just thought she was wonderful.''

"She is.''

"Everything has turned out for the best, hasn't it?''

Reed couldn't help but agree.

"I'd best go rescue Harmon,'' she said, "before old Drayton talks his ears off.'' She turned to go, then hesitated, looking back. "You'll always be special in my heart,'' she said, and impulsively threw her arms around his shoulders.

His sweet little kiss was one strictly reserved for sisters, and Bessie Jane accepted it as offered. As she hurried off to find her husband, Reed glanced up and saw Hattie coming down the church steps. Her face was pale and troubled.

Hattie's expression was as cloudy as the Arkansas sky in a rainstorm as the buggy kept a leisurely pace back to the farm. On both sides of the road, as far as the eye could see, cotton was lush and ripe, the bolls just beginning to burst. Reed surveyed the prophecy of a good harvest dispassionately. His mind was focused on the woman at his side.

When he'd taken her arm to escort her to the buggy, she'd smiled sweetly. Still, it was obvious she was troubled. And unlike that morning, when he'd been sure he could help end her worries, he was now concerned that he might be the cause of them.

The little peck he'd given Bessie Jane had been impulsive and foolish. Married men did not going around kissing other women, even if they had been engaged to them for several months. *Especially* if they had been engaged to them for several months!

His visage grim, Reed berated himself. He had threatened Drayton with bodily harm to keep him from hurting Hattie's feelings. Then he had immediately done something potentially much more hurtful. Glancing over at Hattie, he captured her attention, and she smiled at him. She didn't appear angry or hurt. It was concern that lined her face. Reed didn't know how to smooth those lines away. Drawing her close, he wrapped an arm around her shoulders. Maybe he couldn't make it better, but he could hold her.

Melting into the comforting embrace of her husband, Hattie tried to forget the words ringing loudly in her ears: *If I had two men itching to marry me for my land, I'd choose the young stud over the old geezer myself.* Hattie was aware that the truth could be a good deal more painful than the most hideous lie. Reed had offered her no more than Ancil had. He'd spoken no words of love, no vows of undying devotion. She had agreed to marry him for exactly the reasons that Mary Nell suspected. She desired his body and felt like a woman in his arms.

Snuggling closer to him, she sighed deeply. The scent of Reed Tyler, her Reed Tyler, filled her nostrils and made her mouth curve in a smile. She was wanton with him, there was no way to avoid that truth. But was it simple lust and animal instinct like Romeo and Mabel, or was it more? It wasn't lust that made her laugh a dozen times a day at his wit and charm. Nor was the pleasant companionship she felt working by his side base or wanton. Her feelings for him were not easy to describe, not easy to label.

He was her friend, her closest friend, but he was more. From the moment her eyes opened in the morning to his last kiss before she drifted off to sleep, Reed Tyler was primary in her thoughts. What he felt, thought, wanted, or needed filled her mind as surely as her own concerns. Not as a mother or sister cared about the hurts and joys of a man but as the woman who shared those hurts and joys, as the woman who loved him.

She loved him. As clearly now as they had been obscured

before, she saw that her feelings were not lust or friendship. Safe in his warm embrace, her head on his shoulder, she realized that she loved Reed Tyler. When had this come about? What day had her childhood friend turned into the man of her dreams? And why had she refused to acknowledge the truth? It was not something that had happened yesterday or the day before, not even on her wedding day. Her love for him had existed for months, maybe years, when he was not free, when there was no hope in her heart of ever having it returned.

Her love had been like an embarrassing secret, and she'd hidden her own face from the reality. Her land, the only thing she thought she had to offer, had been his for the taking since her mother died. Ignoring opportunities to better her life and increase her stake, she'd held steadfastly to her decision to sell the land to Reed. If he had her land, he would have a part of her, and she would always be in his life. As the realization wafted through her, she closed her eyes in shame. How vainly she had prided herself on her independence. It had been a ploy, a ploy to keep her close to and dependent on the man she loved.

Reed pulled the buggy up to the back door, and Hattie disengaged herself from his embrace, but not before he'd planted a gentle kiss on the top of her head. "You do trust me, don't you, Hattie?" he whispered against her hair.

Surprised at his words, she looked up at him quizzically. "Yes, of course I do."

"And you know that I would never break my marriage vows to you. That I would never even want to." His eyes were dark with concern and she felt herself melting.

Gently she ran her hand along his cheek and jaw. She had watched him shave that very morning, but still she could feel the slight roughness that made his face so different from her own. "I know you are kind and honorable and true, Reed Tyler. You wouldn't speak a wedding vow that you didn't intend to keep."

"Then you're not upset about Bessie Jane?"

She raised her eyebrows. "What about Bessie Jane?"

Reed hesitated. If she hadn't seen, why tell? But someone else may well have seen. Better to hear it from him lips than from someone bent on spitefulness. "I was talking with Bessie Jane after church," he said nonchalantly as he jumped from the buggy and reached up to help her down. "I guess we were kind of sorting out our apologies."

As he set her on the ground, Hattie nodded. "Sometimes that's the best way. I hope that Bessie Jane and Harmon will be our friends. I'd hate for the past to hang over us." Her decision made, she patted him on the arm reassuringly. "I'm glad you talked with her, Reed."

He was tempted to let it go at that, but his conscience overruled his caution. "There's more, Hattie."

"More?"

"I kissed her."

A wave of green jealousy almost swamped her as she gaped at him. She stepped away, walking up onto the porch as if distance might give her perspective. "You kissed Bessie Jane out in the churchyard?"

"Just a little kiss," he said quickly. "A very little, very sisterly kiss."

"A peck?"

"Yes, a peck. It was exactly the kind of peck I would have given Mama or Marybeth."

Hattie looked at him for several moments. As the jealous fear ebbed, she saw before her the husband she loved, contrite and honest. She nodded, smiling faintly. "Just don't be giving away my peaches, Plowboy. You know how partial I am to them."

She giggled at the thunderbolt of surprise that crossed his face, then walked into the kitchen. She'd left most of the dinner cooked and warming on the stove, and all that was needed was to stoke the fire and mix a batch of corn bread.

She'd barely put her apron on over her good dress when Reed stormed into the kitchen. "Is that it?" he asked, annoyance plain in his voice.

She shrugged. "I believe you, Reed. You kissed Bessie Jane like a sister."

He continued to stare at her, not quite believing her. "You're not even the slightest bit jealous."

"You just told me there was no reason for me to *be* jealous, so I'm not." She spoke with some truth, merely failing to mention that moment of blazing female fury she'd managed to contain. "I should think you'd be glad I trust you."

"I am!" he answered, but the anger in his voice belied his words.

She turned to the stove, but he stayed her hand. "If this ain't the beatenest thing I ever saw," he said. "I'm driving home worrying myself into a early grave because I'm thinking my

wife has seen me kissing another woman. In fact, she hasn't
seen a thing. But I, in my shame and despair, confess the truth
to her, and you know what she does? She laughs at me!''

His wild, improbable fury and his logical explanation was so
silly, Hattie couldn't stop the burst of laughter that escaped from
her lips.

For a moment Reed was stunned, then realizing how foolish
he must look and sound, he could hardly blame her. "You're
still laughing at me!'' he exclaimed, wrapping his arms around
her and lifting her off the floor to shake her, his anger now
obviously feigned. "I come before you like a repentant sinner,
and you make jokes.''

Hattie could hardly catch her breath. "It's no joke,'' she
managed to say. "I believe that you only gave her a peck.''

"That's right,'' he said sternly. "I only gave her a peck, and
you don't care about the pecks as long as you get the peaches.''

"It's not that I don't care about them,'' she replied, swallowing her giggles with difficulty. "I just forgive you.''

Reed was still not satisfied. "You forgive too easy, Hattie.
You're supposed to make me suffer.''

"All right,'' she said cheerily. "Nothing for you but bread
and water for a week.''

He nuzzled her neck and nipped her ear. "If it's your bread,
that's not even a punishment. You know it's the best-tasting in
the county.''

Her heartbeat quickened as he left a fiery trail of lovebites
on her neck. "Then what should a wife to do to her errant
husband?'' she asked breathlessly.

His hand finding its way to her breast, he kneaded her soft
flesh as his lips returned to hers. "Make me beg, make me plead
for your forgiveness,'' he whispered against her mouth.

"Yes, oh, yes.''

To her surprise, Reed immediately released her and dropped
to his knees in front of her. His hands clasped together, he raised
them in supplication. "Hattie, precious Hattie, my devoted wife,
I have wronged thee. Can you ever forgive me?''

"I forgive you,'' she answered between giggles.

"No, can you ever *really* forgive me?''

"I do forgive you.''

He maintained his show of disbelief. "What can I ever do
to make it up to you?''

She giggled again. "I'm sure you'll think of something.''

"You're right. I'll think of something." He grinned wickedly. "I already have an idea."

"I don't like that look," Hattie warned him.

"But you're going to like my idea. You say you like peaches. I'm going to show you a new kind of peach."

"A new kind of peach?"

"Uh-huh," he said, pure devilment in his husky tone. "I call these nasty peaches."

Without another word he grabbed the hem of her dress and pulled her skirt over his head.

Hattie shrieked his name as he grasped her buttocks and pressed his face against the crux of her drawers. "Reed Tyler! What are you doing?" she asked, her legs trembling at the intensity of this new sensation.

His answer was unintelligible as he was preoccupied with undoing the drawstring on her drawers with his teeth. When the drawers had dropped around her ankles, he backed her against the kitchen counter. Balancing her on the edge, he raised her legs off the floor and eased her thighs apart. Slowly, ever so slowly, his lips sweetly gave her the most succulent of peaches. Hattie's words were lost in whimpers as she clawed the curtains at the kitchen window behind her. Desperately she sought something to grasp to hold her to the earth.

Arching her back, muscles taut almost to the point of pain, she screamed his name as her husband's questing mouth introduced her most thoroughly to the erotic delights of nasty peaches.

Twenty-Three

THE bulging bolls of cotton had burst into white puffs that filled the fields as Hattie and Reed awaited their turn for the pickers. The harvest was going to be exceptional and the price high. Low yields in the Deep South were added to bad luck in northern Arkansas and Missouri.

Just before the cotton had been fair to pick, rains had stalled over the farms upstream, and much of that crop was rotting before the farmers' eyes. The ground was too wet to save the cotton that had survived.

Reed and Hattie, as well as most of the farmers in the county, shook their heads in sorrow at the bad luck of their neighbors, then offered a quick prayer to heaven asking that the same fate not befall them. And it seemed that it wouldn't. Rains threatened, but held off. If the river was running faster and higher than the old-timers had seen for quite a spell, at least it was taking its trouble downstream.

Pickers, unable to work in the soggy northern fields, surged into the community with their haggard wives and hungry children, eager for the backbreaking task of pulling the gauzy white fiber from the sharp sticky bolls.

Though the cotton now garnered attention, the rice had also grown tall. The stalks of cultivated grass bent low with the weight of the grain. Even before the picking crew finished up at Clive Tyler's and moved their camp to the Colfax meadow, Reed and Harmon had gone to work in the rice field.

As soon as Hattie could escape the kitchen, she hurried to join them. "It's beautiful," she said as she surveyed the abundance of grain the few acres had produced.

"It's looking good," Reed agreed, but his gaze strayed from the ripe field to the noisy water pump and the high, fast-moving river. "We can't drain it with the floodgates," he said. "The river's higher than the water in here. We're going to have to pump every drop of it out."

Harmon heard the worry in his partner's voice and offered his own optimistic appraisal. "It's just takes time and fuel," he said to Hattie. She smiled, then left the men to wander along the levee. "This pump's a goodun," Harmon continued. "It's going to do the job, Reed. I'm real sure of that."

"I'm counting on that, Harm. I just hate the extra time it takes. My uncle'll be here by the end of the week, and we need this field not just drained but dry." He surveyed the area again skeptically. "That machinery is heavy. We can't have it bogging down in the mud."

Harm nodded his understanding, sliding his hands into his two back pockets. "All we need is a few good hot days, and it'll dry right out."

"But first we've got to get it drained, and I've got fifty pickers ready to go into the cotton."

Harmon shrugged. "I haven't got any pickers, Reed. I've got a stake in this, so let me worry about getting this field dried out. You go ahead and pick your cotton."

"No," Reed said. "You've got your own business to take care of, and I hear you've been working with Arthur Turpin at the store. You don't have any more time to nursemaid this field than I do."

"Reed," Harmon said with mock gravity, "I know you'll understand what I mean if I tell you something on the sly."

Turning to his friend, Reed offered his complete attention.

"If I had a choice of fighting alligators bare-handed or working with my father-in-law at the store, I'd choose the alligators five days out of seven."

Both men burst out laughing and managed to attract the attention of Hattie, who'd moseyed down the levee to survey the beauty of her first rice crop. "What kind of awful tales are you men a-telling?" she called out.

"You know that all men ever talk about is women, Hattie," Reed answered. "You best not be asking questions you don't want the answers to."

Hattie wasn't so easily placated. As she walked back to them, Reed, in a movement that seemed more natural than deliberate, wrapped his arm around her waist and pulled her close. "Harmon's going to be keeping an eye on the rice for us while we're busy with the cotton."

Reaching out to the other man, Hattie grasped his hand in friendship. "I knew I was thinking right when I took you on as a partner."

The following days were busy ones for Reed and Hattie. He was in the fields with the pickers from dawn to dark, and Hattie sweltered in the kitchen providing food for every man, woman, and child working on Colfax Farm. At night they snuggled together, happy and hopeful as they talked about their dreams, their plans, their future, and rice.

The cotton crop was more than half picked when Harmon unexpectedly showed up at the house after supper one night.

"How's it going?" Reed asked, a nervousness stealing into his tone.

Harmon glanced at Hattie as if deciding whether to speak plainly in front of her. Concluding that the truth was best, he sighed and said, "I think we've got some troubles, Reed."

"Are you not going to be able to get it drained?" Reed asked.

"No, that's pretty near done. I expect to get the last of the water out tomorrow."

"Then it'll still have time to dry."

"Yep, I think so," Harm said. "But I think we've got worse worries than that."

Reed raised an eyebrow questioningly, and the younger man continued. "The river's not crested yet from all that rain upstream, and it's really high. It's a good five feet up the levee."

Reed's expression showed concern but not surprise. "I was

thinking the other day that maybe we hadn't built it high enough.''

Harmon nodded, then defended their decision. ''It was as high as any we saw, Reed. All this rain upstream is just a fluke. Surely it'll crest by tomorrow.''

Grabbing a lantern, Reed quickly lit it with a reed from the stove. ''Let's go out and take a look,'' he said, then turned to give Hattie a hasty peck on the lips.

''Be careful,'' she said unnecessarily.

''Don't wait up,'' Reed told her as he headed out the door. But she did.

It was the middle of the night when he finally shucked his clothes and lay down beside her on the bed. ''I won't lie to you, Hattie,'' he said. ''It's bad. Who would have believed that water could come up that high, that fast?''

''Is there anything to do?''

He curled up close to her, resting his head on her breast, and she lightly stroked his hair. ''If it hasn't crested by tomorrow, Harm and I are going to try to reinforce the levee. Make it higher if we can.''

''That sounds like it might work.''

Reed sighed, rubbing his cheek against her bosom. ''I don't know how much we can do, working at night, but I'll just have to try.''

'' 'Working at night'?'' she repeated in surprise. ''Why in the world would you have to work at night?''

''I can't be over there until the cotton is in. And I'm not about to let Harmon do all that himself. He came in as a partner, not a slave.''

''Why can't you be there to help him? It's not like you're taking off to go fishing. It's still work, Reed, even when you enjoy it.''

He laughed at her little joke, hugging her, then spoke seriously. ''The cotton's got to come in, Hattie. It's our cash crop— we depend on it. If we lose the rice, that's a shame. But to lose the cotton would be a disaster.''

Knowing he was right, Hattie still searched for an alternative. ''Couldn't somebody else handle the rice? One of your brothers or . . . I can do a lot, Reed. You remember that first crop we brought in. You didn't do that by yourself, you know.''

He rolled on top of her, bracing himself on his elbows. ''Hattie, nobody knows your value more than me," he said, smiling down at her moon-shadowed face. "But somebody has got to cook, or the pickers will drop in the field."

With a deep sigh that admitted the truth of his statement, she reached up to run her hands along his strong arms and shoulders. "Let me help you, Reed," she whispered.

"Oh, Hattie, just having you in my life is more help to me than you can ever imagine."

He kissed her, and she responded lovingly. They made the slow, lazy love of two people who were too tired for sex and too enamored for abstinence.

Having thought the matter settled, Reed was surprised to look up from the huge cotton-laden hampers and see his wife striding across the field, determination in every step.

"I know what you're going to say," she told him before he'd opened his mouth. "But the truth is, I'm not needed at the house. Bessie Jane is doing the cooking, and I'm free as a bird today."

"Bessie Jane? Bessie Jane can't cook, and why in the world would she even want to?"

"She showed up with Harmon this morning and wanted to know what she could do to help, so I told her. She wants to do it, Reed. It's important to her to be a help to Harmon."

"Hattie—" he began, but she interrupted him.

"I'm here to work, Reed," she said flatly. "Now you can let me take over here at the weigh-in, where I am vaguely familiar with what to do. Or I can go over to the rice field, where I haven't the faintest idea of how to reinforce a levee, and Harmon and I can muddle through the best we know how."

Reed gazed at her long and hard, before handing her the scales. "Don't wear yourself out," he warned. Then with more of a peach than a peck, he added in a lusty whisper, "See you at suppertime."

It was past suppertime when he came in. It was past bedtime.

Hattie awakened with a start to hear him washing up on the back porch. She hadn't meant to fall asleep, but the unusual physical labor in the cotton fields added to her lack of sleep the night before had conspired against her. Slipping out of bed, she hurried to the back porch. "Reed? Are you all right?"

"You shouldn't still be up, Hattie. I'm fine, just tired."

"Let me fix you some supper," she said through the screen.

"If you've got some leftover corn bread and milk, that'll be fine."

She only half listened to his request as she retrieved the ample portion of the evening's meal that she'd saved for him in a pie plate in the oven. It wasn't hot, but it was at least somewhat warm. Adding to it a big hunk of leftover corn bread and a jug of milk, Hattie set her husband's meal on the table.

He came in, barechested, with a towel draped around his neck. He glanced at the meal on the table, then looked at her, sighing with appreciation. "It looks so good, Hattie, I swear I could eat it tablecloth and all."

She laughed "You best not eat my mama's tablecloth, Plow-boy, or you'll be taking your meals in the barn from now on."

He answered her teasing with a warm but weary smile. "Let me get a shirt," he said, turning away.

"Don't waste your time. Sit down here and eat."

Raising an eyebrow, he said, "A man doesn't eat his dinner in front of a lady without his shirt."

"There is special exception to that rule made for wives," she said primly. "Besides, the sight of your chest doesn't ruin *my* appetite."

When he smiled, she added, "I've already eaten."

"Oh, Hattie," he said as he dug into his meal. "You do make me laugh."

Deciding that a bit of laughter might do him some good, she set out to entertain him. "If you think I am normally a caution, you should have seen me in the fields today. I thought I would remember all about bringing in the cotton, but I must have forgotten more than I ever knew. Thank heavens for the pickers. I explained what was going on, and they all pitched in to help me do it right."

She rambled on about her foibles and foolishness until he'd consumed most of what was on his plate. Then, with an arm around his waist, ostensibly as an embrace but actually because she feared he might fall over in exhaustion, she helped him to bed.

"I love you, Hattie," he whispered as he drifted off to sleep.

"Of course you do," she replied, stroking his hair as tears stung the back of her eyes and she wished with all her heart that it was true.

Wishing, however, did not get the cotton in, she told herself the next morning as she walked with the pickers to the fields. Reed had been up before her, laughing and joking as if everything were fine. The dark circles under his eyes were plain, however, and she'd wondered if she looked as worn out as he did.

As the pickers moved through the fields with their sacks, pulling the cotton from its prickly holdings, Hattie waited with the scales at the end of the rows. The pickers would bring her their full sacks, and she would weigh them to determine if they merited a marker. Most of the pickers were experienced enough to know when the sack was heavy enough to exchange for a marker. Only the children were frequently weighed short and sent scurrying back for more cotton.

Row by row, marker by marker, the fields were slowly denuded of the bright white balls. By midway through Hattie's second day on the job, all the fields had been picked over, and the second walk through for the late-blooming bolls commenced.

The wind slapped the clothes wildly as Hattie hurried to retrieve them from the clothesline. Off to the northwest, the sky was so dark it looked almost purple, and the smell of rain hung heavy in the air.

"I hope Reed gets back before this cloud lets loose," Hattie said to Myrene, who followed in her wake.

The pickers had finished just after noon the day before. The cotton—"some of the finest I've ever seen," Reed had declared—had been loaded into wagons that morning and taken to the gin. Hattie had felt a surge of pride at Reed's words. She'd brought the cotton in. She was Reed's partner in more than just name, and she'd proved it that week with hours of backbreaking toil.

Uncle Ed and the rice crew had arrived at the Tylers', and Reed and Harm had worked frantically shoring up the levee so that the rice field would be dry on schedule.

After two weeks of hectic activity and crowds of people, Hattie, alone on her little farm, had found the afternoon strangely quiet. Unexpectedly the memory of her former life and the solitary future to which she had resigned herself years before crept into her thoughts. She wondered how she could have imagined herself content with such loneliness. Today, after only a few hours of her own company, she looked forward eagerly to her husband's return.

After dropping the last of the clothes into the basket, Hattie shooed Myrene out of her way and scurried into the house, the ominous sound of thunder loud on her heels.

Reed and Harm had done some early celebrating the previous evening, congratulating each other on the growth of the rice and the anticipated harvest. "The field is dry now," Harmon had said excitedly. "I don't think we'll have any trouble getting that machinery in there in a day or two."

"It's going to be rich harvest, isn't it?" Reed asked, already knowing the answer.

Harmon laughed. "Turpin tells me nearly every day that it's a waste of my time and the foolest dumb notion you ever had to try growing rice in good cotton country."

"That old man has been telling me the same thing for years," Reed said laughing with Harmon. "He just refuses to believe that things can ever change."

"Well, I expect he'll get used to it," Harmon replied. "Bess and I have come as quite a shock to her father. I don't think he's quite as sure about anything anymore."

"I know," Reed said confidently, "that Turpin and the rest of this community are going to be laughing out of the other side of their mouths when they see what we'll make on this little patch of rice."

"It does feel good to have everybody say you're wrong and be able to prove that you're right!"

"Shame on the both of you," Hattie said as she set plates of cobbler before them. "What a pair of boastful sinners you are. Showing off before the neighbors is what little boys want to do. Men and women don't need such childishness."

Harmon blushed at her words. Only nineteen, he was sensitive to aspersions on his youthfulness. Reed, however, suffered no such mistaken impression of the maturity level of his new bride.

Grabbing Hattie around the waist, he pulled her to him, her hip tight against his shoulder. "Do tell us, Mrs. Tyler," he said, looking up at his wife expectantly, "exactly what you're going to say to Mr. Ancil Drayton, who believed your interest in rice to be a bit of female foolishness and vowed to drain that field and plant it in cotton."

Placing her hands together as primly as a matron, Hattie gave each man a serious look before replying. "I will simply look Mr. Drayton in the eye and say to him what any rational adult would say. 'Nanny-hanny-poo on you. Stick your head in chicken-do!' "

A burst of laughter escaped Harmon, and Reed squeezed her tight.

Hattie smiled now at the memory. It was a sin, no doubt, to want to be proven right to the whole community, but she was just human enough to want that little taste of "I told you so." As another bolt of lightning sent eerie shadows through the house and thunder crashed loudly enough to make her jump, she wondered if their feeling of victory had been a bit presumptuous.

By the time Reed arrived back at the house over an hour later, Hattie was dismally watching the rain fall in buckets.

Water cascaded from Reed's hat like a waterfall as he crossed the yard to the back door. He didn't even bother to hurry his step since he was already soaked to the skin.

When he reached the porch, Hattie was there to meet him, a towel in her hand. "Don't even bother to come in," she said bossily. "There's no need for you to track up the house."

"You want me to stay outside till I dry out?" he asked in disbelief.

Her laugh was a cheery light in the gloomy afternoon. "That won't be necessary. Just take off those wet clothes and drop them in the washbucket. I've got a nice hot bath waiting for you in the kitchen."

His expression turning to one of delightful appreciation, Reed tossed his hat on a nail and began undoing the buttons on his shirt. "I'll tell you the truth, Hattie," he said, a teasing lilt to his voice. "If I'd have known that married men have hot baths waiting for them when they get caught out in the rain, I'd have married up years ago."

Dropping his sodden shirt into the washtub, his suspenders dangling at his sides, Reed reached for the buttons on his pants. He stopped abruptly and looked up at his wife, who continued to stand in the doorway. "You're going to watch?" His words were as much a challenge as a question.

She leaned against the doorframe and folded her arms across her chest. "Uh-huh."

The two looked at each other for a moment, teasing smiles on both faces. Reed's fingers made quick work of the buttons at his fly, but he had to squat to remove his workshoes before he could divest himself of the water-logged britches. When they lay in a dripping heap atop his shirt, he stood before her in his underwear. His summer balbriggans clung damply to him like a second skin, displaying his form rather than concealing it. Quickly he unbuttoned the undershirt and slung it into the washtub. The swirls of damp hair on his chest captured Hattie's attention, and her fingers itched to touch him.

As if sensing the change in her scrutiny, Reed slowed his hands as he fingered the buttons at the front of his drawers. With deliberate leisure, he eased the first button through its housing, intently watching Hattie. Her eyes were fixed with hot expectation on his body, and her gaze had the unanticipated result of arousing him.

He bent forward, hiding the effect she had on him, and stripped the wet cotton from his buttocks, thighs, and legs. Discarding the balbriggans in the washtub, he glanced back at her. She still watched him, unashamed.

"Hattie, what have I done to you?" he asked as he straightened, revealing his swollen erection. "You're acting downright scandalous for a farmer's wife."

Her smile revealed only delight. "Do you really think so?"

Reed Tyler stood buck naked on his back porch in the pouring rain and stared at his wife, his hands on his hips. "Positively indecent, Mrs. Tyler," he said, then walked toward her until his cold nakedness was pressed against the warm softness of her gown. "And, Hattie," he whispered, seeking warm sweet peaches from her lips, "I thank the Lord for it every night."

Tenderly, lovingly, Hattie returned his kisses as she wrapped his loins in the soft dry towel. When she finally broke the kiss, she gazed into his teasing cinnamon eyes and offered her own snippet. "Your bath, O noble yeoman farmer, awaits thee in the kitchen," she said with great pretense of submission.

His grin widening, Reed slipped an arm behind his wife's

knees and lifted her high against his chest as he stepped across the threshold of his house. "I do believe, O pliant and meek helpmate," he said, enjoying her little game, "that it is due time to ascertain if yon bathtub is big enough for two!"

Hattie began to laugh, struggle, and protest. The sounds of a shriek and a splash a moment later were drowned by the torrent of rain and thunder overhead.

Twenty-Four

WHEN Reed rolled out of bed at dawn the next morning, his mood was less playful. He gave Hattie a gentle pat on the bottom as she passed him on the way to the kitchen, but it was obvious his thoughts were elsewhere. Although it was past sunup, the clouds and the rain left the kitchen as dark as a cave.

Hattie lit the lamp, producing a strange glow in the gloomy morning. "It's been raining all night," she said, question in her tone.

He was clearly concerned. "This is going to slow us down a lot. With a frog-strangler like this, it will take a week to dry that field."

"Your Uncle Ed won't appreciate being stuck here another week."

"He won't like it any more than me, but he'll stay around, I reckon. I just hate to have to wait."

Understanding his disappointment, Hattie left him to his own thoughts as she stoked the fire in the stove and put the coffee on to boil. When that was done, she headed for the back porch, reaching for her slicker.

"Where do you think you're going?" Reed asked, walking up behind her as he adjusted his suspenders on his shoulders.

"Myrene will be slogging through the rain in another fifteen minutes if I don't get down to the barn and milk her."

Taking the slicker from her hand, he shooed her back into the house. "I'm going to have to go out there anyway, and there is surely no reason for both of us to get wet this morning."

Hattie put her hands on her hips, as if ready to argue. "You're just hoping that if you get wet again, I'll give you another bath."

His grin was wide and wicked. "I'd roll in pig manure if I thought I get another one like last night!"

As she watched him hurrying to the barn, Hattie felt a peculiar fluttering inside her. "I love you, Reed Tyler," she said aloud for no one to hear. "I don't care if you just married me for my land. I'm only glad I had it, 'cause I can't imagine ever being this happy without you."

She and Reed had barely finished their breakfast when someone pounded on the front door. "Harmon!" Hattie exclaimed when she saw the half-drowned man on the porch. "Come in the house and get dried off."

Harm peeled off his oilcloth and draped it across the porch swing before carefully wiping his feet and stepping into Hattie's parlor.

"You've been down to the levee?" Reed asked. Harm nodded. "How bad is it?"

"It's bad," Harmon said gravely. "The river's running almost as high as before, and if it doesn't stop soon, it's going to start seeping through the levee."

Hattie's jaw dropped open in shock.

"If that levee goes," Harmon added, "we'll lose the whole crop."

To Hattie's dismay, Reed nodded in agreement. "We'll just have to make sure the levee doesn't go." Turning from them, he headed for the back porch. "Just let me get my slicker, and we'll see what we can do."

As Hattie watched the two men disappear into the gray morning, rain pouring steadily down upon them, she couldn't shake the despondency that engulfed her. Reed had worked so hard for this rice field! she thought frantically. He couldn't lose it now.

•   •   •

It rained all that day, that night, and the next morning. Hattie spent virtually all of that time alone. Reed came home only to eat and sleep, tired to the point of exhaustion and chilled to the bone. Hattie fretted and prayed for a letup in the rain but never asked him to stay home. She knew how much the rice field meant to him.

By noon the second day, she finally gave up on being the long-suffering wife at home and gathered her things together. A big kettle of stew, appropriate dishes, spoons and a knife, two loaves of bread, and a jar of butter were placed in her largest laundry basket. She covered those with several towels, a half-dozen good-sized chunks of dry wood, and several pieces of kindling. A length of rope and an old tarp from the shed finished the load. Pulling on her slicker and hoisting her heavy burden, Hattie slowly made her way through the rain and mud to Colfax Bluff and her husband in the rice field.

It was a wet, cold, and miserable walk, but Hattie felt better than she had for two days. This was important to her husband, and she was going to help. She had a sneaking suspicion he wouldn't appreciate it, but she wasn't about to let that stop her.

Arriving at the rice field, Hattie's first sensation was despair. The river was running wild and high, the swirling muddy water looking menacing and beyond control. The two men, with shovels and wheelbarrows of dirt, had set an immense task for themselves.

Hattie shook her head to clear it. Thinking defeat was no way to join the fight, she admonished herself. Carefully making her way down the side of the bluff, she found the perfect place for her camp between a couple of blackjack oaks.

She had hardly begun to sort out her things when she heard her husband's voice. "Hattie Colfax! What in the name of heaven are you doing out here!" She turned to see him hurrying up the incline toward her, anger in every movement.

"My name is Tyler, Plowboy," she shot back in the same belligerent tone. "This is *my* rice field, and I came here to do my part to keep it from becoming a fish pond."

He reached her then, and she stared at him, starved for the sight of him. His hat was missing, and his hair was plastered to his face. Water ran in rivulets down his cheeks and off the end of his nose. He looked worn-out and disgusted, and she felt a sudden urge to take him into her arms and comfort him.

Instead she braced her hands on her hips and stared him

down like her worst enemy, unwilling to let him use her tender feelings against her. "I've got work to do here. I don't know a whole lot about reinforcing a levee, but I can sure provide a hot meal for those who do."

They scowled at each other for a minute, the rain beating down on them. Hattie waited for his reply, poised for more argument. With a sigh of defeat, though, Reed shook his head. "You want this tarp up?" he asked.

Without waiting for an answer, he turned and called to Harm to come help him. The two men hung the tarp between the trees as Hattie retrieved the dry wood and kindling. Soon she had a small fire going under the canvas. Reed cut a long green limb from a nearby elm and wedged it like a pole in the middle of the tarp, forming a pitch to keep the rain from collecting.

By the time the men had their temporary shelter set up to their liking, Hattie had the stew bubbling hot on the fire and insisted that they sit, rest, and eat. She didn't have to ask twice. Both men nearly collapsed on the soggy ground, eager for the hot meal but almost too tired to consume it.

Reed scooted over beside her, sitting just close enough to touch her thigh with his knee. The contact seemed to give him some kind of strength or pleasure, so Hattie leaned closer, increasing the contact.

Neither man had much to say, and Hattie didn't urge them to talk. She understood that there were times when it was better not to speak fears aloud. Her heart was in her throat as she watched Reed continually turn to glance once more at the river that was rising steadily to consume the fruits of his labor.

Wanting to take him in her arms and comfort him, love him, she sat quietly beside him until, with a sigh of determination, he planted a tiny peck on her nose and headed back down the bluff to fight his watery enemy.

It was late in the afternoon when Hattie finally returned to the house. An old buckboard with a jury-rigged cover sat in the yard, and she quickened her step to meet her company.

"Miss Hattie?" a man called from her porch. "Where in the world *is* everybody in this rain?"

The man waiting for her was a stranger. In his middle years, he had the sun-browned face and neck and sturdy arms and chest of a farmer. As she came closer, the handsome Tyler visage was easily discernable. "You must be Reed's uncle Ed," she said.

The man's smile was an open, familiar one. "That's who I am, Miss Hattie. I swear I'da known you anywhere. I came over to have a talk with that boy. Where's he got himself off to in this weather?"

Hattie stepped past her visitor and opened the door. Discarding her slicker, she urged Uncle Ed to do the same. "Reed and Harmon are at the rice field. The river is very high and they're trying to reinforce the levee."

It was impossible to miss Uncle Ed's surprised expression, and Hattie hurriedly explained. "Our rice field sets right next to the river, and it's been very high for the last couple of weeks, and now this much rain . . ."

Uncle Ed's smile became strained.

"You did know about the river?" Hattie asked as she led him into the kitchen.

"Sure I knew about the river," he answered, sitting at the table as she put on some coffee. "It's been flooding upstream for a couple of weeks. I almost didn't make the trip at all 'cause I figured Reed had already lost that field."

Uncle Ed scooted his chair back from the table and crossed his legs in a relaxed position. "Truthfully, I came over to tell him we'd just be heading back."

"Oh, you can't do that!" Hattie said. "The rain is bound to stop any minute, and the fields will dry up in a day or two. The rice is beautiful, so tall and heavy. It's the most beautiful crop I've ever seen. You can't just let it go!"

Uncle Ed ran a hand through his heavy thatch of silver hair. "Now, ma'am. I know this rice means a lot to you. That's all that Reed talked about when he was with me—growing rice right here on Miss Hattie's farm. But farming is not a sure-thing business. It's a gamble with nature that never ends. Bad years come along—floods, droughts, plagues—and you just have to take your licks and try again next year."

Knowing his words about farming were the truth, Hattie didn't comment on them. The risks of farming were a part of life that she'd accepted long ago. She'd seen lifetimes of plans wiped away by the hand of God. But something in the first part of his statement captured her attention, and she quickly corrected him. "The rice means a lot to *Reed*. I only want it because he wants it."

Raising an eyebrow skeptically, Uncle Ed took a long look

at the woman Reed had married. Finally he decided to trust her. "Reed can grow rice anywhere, Miss Hattie. I've tried a half a dozen times to get him to buy good rice land down near me."

When Hattie's eyes widened in surprise, Ed continued. "It don't matter how good the deal or how much I try to sweeten it, that boy's been determined from that first summer he came to work for me that the two of you were going to grow rice."

"The two of us?" Hattie's asked in confusion.

"Yes, ma'am. After you all did that first cotton crop together, he was convinced you were the best farming partner anywhere." Uncle Ed smiled as if recalling a spark of humor from the past. "He talked night and day about that crop. You made a real impression on the boy. Still bowed down in grief and with the responsibility of your mama, you just dove right into what had to be done. And you turned to him for help. He was little more than a kid, but his opinions held value for you, and that made him feel grown-up." Laughing lightly, he added, "I guess it was more than feeling. That summer he really did grow up."

Noting his nephew's wife's stunned expression, Ed leaned an elbow on the table and continued his tale. "When Reed decided that rice was a better crop for the future, he just became downright determined to bring it up to this prairie. That was the only way you two could farm it together."

Hattie stared at Reed's uncle in stunned disbelief. "Are you telling me that Reed could have had land elsewhere? He didn't need Colfax Farm?"

"Miss Hattie, I'd never say one unkind word about your daddy's ground. It's fine land. But it'll take a heap of time, work, and money to turn it into rice country. I'm sure you and Reed are up to the task, but there is plenty of better, easier rice land all over this part of the state to be had for less than this piece of cotton was going to cost him."

"I'm sure if Reed stayed here at Colfax Farm, he had his reasons," Hattie said.

The older man smiled. "Yes, ma'am, and the main one is sitting across the table from me right now. My biggest worry was that the boy wouldn't grow up fast enough to be able to see that he already had exactly what he wanted."

"But why . . . ?"

Uncle Ed laughed. "I told you why. There's plenty of other good land in this state, but none with you sitting on it."

Confusion stymied Hattie, making it impossible for her to reason out Uncle Ed's words. The smell of coffee pervaded the room, and she poured them both a cup. After setting a plate of cookies on the table, she sat down and took a sip of the hot black coffee to settle her nerves. Questions were bombarding her brain, but she couldn't seem to get a handle on any of them.

Uncle Ed didn't need urging to speak. He dipped one of the cookies into his coffee and said, "I've known Reed a lot of years. He's almost like one of my own boys." Ed stopped and took a hefty bite of cookie before he continued. "Since I've been here, I've heard a lot of talk about what a surprise your wedding has been." He leaned back in his chair and eyed her across the table. "The truth is, it weren't no surprise to me, ma'am. That other gal, well, I don't even remember hearing her name from him. But everything that happened, everything that he did or saw, he'd say, 'Wish Miss Hattie could see that' or 'Wonder what Miss Hattie would think of this.' A blind man could see that he had his heart set on pairing up with you."

Hattie felt a blush of embarrassment stain her cheeks. Surely Uncle Ed was mistaken, or perhaps he was just being kind. "Reed's feelings for me have never been more than friendship," she said.

Uncle Ed shrugged. "I suspect he wasn't even aware of how he felt. You're an older woman, after all. I doubt it ever occurred to him to think of you like a sweetheart. Sweethearts are what we have as schoolboys. It takes a lot of years for a man to realize that wives are a different crop altogether."

Hattie analyzed that statement. "Oh, I see what you mean. A man should marry for practical reasons rather than some silly romantic notion."

Uncle Ed shook his head, indicating that she had missed the point. "A man learns to let his silly romantic notions follow his heart."

Unwilling to believe what he was telling her, Hattie quickly sorted out the facts and the evidence. Why would Reed have thrown away good opportunities elsewhere just to stay a share-cropper on Colfax Farm?

Hattie was sure he'd been in love with Bessie Jane, but he *had* gotten over her pretty quick, and she remembered Bessie Jane's complaint about the delay in their wedding. He hadn't been willing to leave with his intended until he'd brought in Hattie's rice crop. Could Uncle Ed be right? Could Reed's feeling for her be more than a friend's? Were his reactions more those of a lover?

Hope and excitement bubbled brightly in Hattie's heart, but she consciously forced them back down. Reed liked and cared for her; he was gentle and tender with her and so conscientious in bed. She would not wish for or covet more. Her mother's bitterness and dissatisfaction were never going to color her life. She would be happy with what fate had handed her, not stew in dissatisfaction for those things she would never have.

"Uncle Ed, I'm sure that you believe what you're saying, and I see no sense in arguing with you." she smiled. "I think Reed and I are going to be happy together.

"However," she added, raising her chin with a hint of challenge, "the problem right now is not marital bliss, but flooded rice. That's where we're going to need your help."

The next morning, hours before sunup, it was still raining steadily as Hattie loaded the wagon. She hadn't slept much, but she felt energy surging through her.

"Hattie! What in the blazes are you up to?" Reed called to her from the back porch. He stood shirtless, his trousers riding low on his hips, his suspenders lying purposeless at his thighs.

Smiling at the appealing sight, Hattie steeled herself for his disapproval and lack of cooperation. Casually she walked to the back step, heedless of the rain, as if on a carefree summer jaunt. "I've got your breakfast in the warming oven," she said, "and the rest of the food is ready to load."

"Load for what?" he asked as he helped her out of her slicker.

"To take to the river," she said, walking into the house. "I see no reason for me to carry lunch clear down there when I can cook it and help at the same time."

Reed stared at her, dumbfounded, for a moment, then the import of her statement became clear. "Hattie, you've got no business working on that levee," he said flatly.

She retrieved his breakfast from the warming oven and set it on the table, then turned to him, hands on her hips in a defiant stance. "I think it'd do you good to remember, Plowboy, that it's *my* levee."

He crossed his arms stubbornly in reply. "It's *your* levee,

but you're *my* wife. That river is getting wilder and more dangerous every minute, and I don't want you out there.''

Feeling an undeniable thrill at his protectiveness, Hattie still
held her ground. "If it's too dangerous for me, then it's too
dangerous for you."

"Somebody has to keep the river back. I'm not about to let
a whole season's work got to waste if I can avoid it."

"I'm not about to either. I talked to Uncle Ed yesterday. He
says it's too big a job for two men."

"Well, of course it is, but two men is all we are, and believe
me, one extra person, even if that person is yourself, isn't going
to make a difference."

"How about a whole crew, Plowboy? Could a whole crew
make a difference?"

Reed looked at her quizzically for a moment before guessing
her intent. "Uncle Ed and the rice crew are coming to help?"

She grinned. "Sure. Along with just about everybody else.
I sent word to Millie that we need help."

A smile spread across Reed's face as he pondered this new
development. "By gawd, with more men, Hattie, we just might
be able to hold it off."

The river was high and wild when they arrived at the rice field.
Hattie set up a cook camp at the top of the bluff and was shortly
joined by Mary Tyler, her daughters-in-law, and young
Marybeth.

Since Uncle Ed's rice-cutting crew had come to help, it had
seemed only normal for Clive Tyler and his sons to join them.
Cal, George, and Andy all showed up, and even Emma and her
husband, Sidney were there, bringing with them the employees
from his cotton gin.

Preacher Able and Millie arrived about eight o'clock, and
Millie eagerly told Hattie that they had been driving around the
area telling everyone what was going on.

"I'm sure they all said, 'I told you so,' " Hattie replied.
"Nobody believed that we could raise rice here."

"Maybe not," Millie said. "But most told the reverend they
would be here to help this morning."

Millie's words proved to be true as wagon after wagon pulled
up to Colfax Bluff and men scrambled down with shovels and
tools to see what they could do to help.

Bessie Jane showed up a few minutes later in the company of her parents. Arthur Turpin brought a load of lumber to help shore up the sagging earthwork, and Harmon directed the men to unload it.

"Harmon had this idea last night," Bessie Jane explained to Hattie, "about how a frame might help brace things. He was saying all the things that he'd need and wondering how we could get them and if his idea might be worth the cost."

The young woman straightened her shoulders. "I just walked into Daddy's store this morning and told him that I hadn't got my wedding present yet and I wanted it today."

Hattie found herself smiling at this new independent and free-thinking Bessie Jane, and hugged the young woman.

The most surprising arrival, to Hattie's mind, was Ancil Drayton. He'd barely pulled his wagon to a stop before the kids jumped out of the back. Ancil, carrying an enormous umbrella, escorted a large, full-figured woman to the tarp-covered camp.

"Mrs. Tyler, ladies," he addressed the women. "I want you all to meet Mrs. Maimie Blackburn from over to Carson's Flat." Ancil's color was unusually high as he added, "The widow Blackburn has graciously consented to become my wife."

The big woman punctuated his words with a giant "huh-ruh," and the women all voiced their congratulations.

"Somebody needed to take a hand to those little heathens he's a 'raising," Widow Blackburn said, "and that's the truth of it." Glancing over her shoulder, she hollered like a referee at a hogcalling. "Mary Nell! Git them children under this tent afore I find a switch and take it to your hind end!"

Mary Nell, who was back to girlish skirt lengths, her hair in pigtails, quickly did as she was bid.

Turning back to Hattie, the Widow Blackburn added, "Them children of Ancil's are a pretty good bunch if the truth be told. Along with my four, it makes quite a family." Smiling at Mary Nell's haste to obey, the widow confided, "That oldest little gal got a little too big for her britches. But I raised three sisters afore I was wed, and I know all there is to know about takin' the starch out of a sassy stitch."

Cyl and Ada raced to Hattie's side. "What can we do to help, Miss Hattie?" Cyl asked anxiously. "Ma Blackburn said we's comin' to give you and Mr. Reed a neighborly hand."

Hattie reached out to touch the sweet friendly face she had missed so much. "And so you can," she told the girls cheerfully. "Do you know how to make camp biscuits?" When both girls shook their heads sadly, Hattie smiled. "Good, because I want to teach you how to do it just the way I like them."

Working with Cyl and little Ada, Hattie left the Widow Blackburn to help with the cooking and Mary Nell to watch Buddy and the widow's two youngest.

"She's nice," Cyl whispered in Hattie's ear.

Hattie smiled with pleasure. "I'm glad."

"She's not you, of course," Cyl went on. "But she's got real set ways of gettin' things done and she don't allow for no shirking." With the wisdom that rode so strangely on the youngster, she added, "I think she's good for Pa." She giggled. "And she sure lit a fire under Mary Nell!"

Morning wore into afternoon as more and more neighbors, friends, and even some of the pickers out of work from the weather showed up to see if man could stop nature at the edge of Colfax Bluff.

With the crowd of men working against time to brace the levee, the women had their hands full. Hot coffee and plenty of soup and camp biscuits were ready every minute. There was no stop in making meals. Voluntarily, some men would make their way to the tent while others continued to dig and shovel, raising the height of the levee in some places, repairing small breaks in others.

Hattie watched worriedly as her husband worked longer and harder than the other men. Finally, filling a plate and grabbing a cup of coffee, she apprised the other women of her mission. With their encouragement and warning to take care, she crept down the muddy slippery slope to the levee.

Reed was using the back of his shovel to pound a mud poultice on a small but persistent crack in the levee when a word from another man caused him to look up. Seeing Hattie, he cursed under his breath and handed his shovel over. Slogging over to her, he took her arm and escorted her from the dangerous mud embankment. "Damnation, Hattie!" he said angrily. "I told you to stay off this levee!"

"Don't you curse at me, Plowboy," she snapped back. "I'd be content to stay under that nice dry tarp if I had a husband who had enough sense to come in out of the rain once in a while!"

She was right, he knew, but he doggedly tried to present his side of it. "It's my field."

"No, it's *my* field, and I'm not even allowed on the levee." Gesturing to the mud-splattered crew, she added, "These men wouldn't be here if they thought you were too lazy to do your own work. You've got nothing to prove, Reed Tyler, except that lack of nourishment will lay you low as quickly as any other man."

Despite being exhausted, soaked to the skin, and dispirited, Reed found himself smiling at his wife. Taking the tin plate from her hands, he looked under the sodden dishcloth at the damp, already cold fare she'd brought him. "This would undoubtedly lay me low quicker than the other men," he said. "It could be a major embarrassment for us both, Mrs. Tyler."

His teasing prompted her to mock outrage, and he slid his arm around her waist as if to make up to her. Arm in arm, the two made their way back up the slope. Beneath the tarp they sat together near the fire and shared a meal.

Hattie watched as the men worked frantically. The river had risen quickly in the night, and salvaging the drooping water-logged rice seemed more and more remote. To Hattie it looked impossible that so few men could fight off such a mighty onslaught of water.

"I can't believe all these folks turned out to help us," Reed said as he finished his meal.

"I guess they know that we'd do the same for them. They're just glad we don't have to."

He gulped the rest of his coffee, kissed her quickly, then was gone. Hattie watched him head back to the fight and couldn't help but worry. The rice was so important to him. *Please let him win,* she prayed silently.

Ancil appeared for a quick meal also, and Hattie couldn't help but make comparisons. Ancil looked like a drowned rat, his thin hair lying in disorganized strands across his head, his clothes plastered to his long, lanky frame. Momentarily, she thought of the warmth of her husband's embrace and the sweet taste of his hot passionate peaches. She made the right choice, and she knew she would never regret it.

Out of the corner of her eye she caught Ancil taking a healthy pinch at the widow's ample buttocks, and she thanked heaven for her reprieve.

Forget what I said about the rice, Lord. I've already had more favors than I deserve.

Twenty-Five

DUSK brought discouragement to the tired and overworked men. Harmon's bracing system might have worked in a lesser flood or if it had been built sooner, but it was obvious that the valiant efforts of the men, mud, and two-by-fours were not going to hold back the onslaught of nature.

Wagon by wagon, their friends and neighbors began to leave.

"It's too dangerous down here for my boys," Ancil told Reed. Glancing at the boisterous youngsters trying to do a man's work on the muddy levee, Reed agreed. "It's too dangerous for all of us," he said. Speaking loudly enough to capture the attention of most of the men, he called, "I thank you all for coming, but I don't want anybody hurt down here. That far north end is not going to make it through the night, and there won't be any joy in saving the south cuts if we lose a man to the river."

Murmurs of agreement went up and down the line as the workers gathered up buckets, rakes, shovels, and other tools. Taking their leave, man after man stopped at Reed's side to offer a handshake, a word of consolation, or a ray of hope. Reed accepted each stoically and with the good grace that was intended.

Slowly the men made their way up the slope, joining their women and adding a word of comfort to Hattie as they headed out. The press of wagons, buckboards, and teams disappeared quickly, leaving only bent grass and muddy tracks as witness to the outpouring of neighborly spirit.

It was nearly dark by then, and Hattie began packing her wagon. She could barely make out Reed's form as she watched him working mechanically to reinforce the south bank and heighten the ridge between the cuts.

She hurt inside, the kind of angry hurt when you want something so bad for someone and know you haven't the power to give it. Was a good crop of rice so much to ask? Apparently it was. The rain showed no signs of letting up, and praying for a miracle was about the only solution left.

Stowing the last of the camp gear on the wagon, she glanced at the levee again to see if her husband was on his way. He continued to work steadfastly. A wave of tenderness washed over Hattie as she watched Reed gamely continue the struggle as if unaware that he was alone in the fight with night settling around him like a dark blanket of hopelessness.

Blinking back tears that stung her eyes, she headed down the slope to help him. If Reed thought there was still a chance to save the crop, she would not dissuade him but would stay beside him.

The river raged wildly and slapped against the top of the levee, occasionally spilling over in a persistent reminder that victory over the forces of nature was hard-fought and rarely won. She took up a shovel that leaned against a tree. Her intent was more to keep herself steady on the muddy slope rather than work on the levee.

Picking her way carefully to the levee, Hattie noticed a widening crevice in the north bank. Water was beginning to rush in, and she realized it needed to be stopped immediately. The small break would quickly become a gulf, and the muddy river would spill into the rice. It was not a sight she wanted to witness.

Having watched the men for two days, she knew exactly what to do. She dug up a shovelful of mud, then pounded it into the widening crack. Her immediate success encouraged her, and she quickly went after the other cracks that were forming up and down that part of the levee.

In just a few minutes, though, she saw that the levee was

dissolving faster than she could daub it back in shape. With a glance at the roaring river, suddenly so close on her left, she realized she was in trouble.

"Reed!" she shouted. He glanced up. Their eyes met for an instant, but it was like a lifetime. Before she could call out for his help, she felt the ground shift beneath her and water rush across her shoes. She watched Reed's eyes widen in horror, but his cry was lost to her as the levee fell away below her and she was pulled down into the wild, muddy torrent of the river.

Clawing and kicking frantically, Hattie strove to find the surface. But where was up? *Which way was up?* She fought the current that pulled against her as her lungs burned like fire, craving air. In a vortex of water and debris, she struggled against the heavy clothes that encumbered her. Flailing pointlessly in the water with energy born of panic, she was disoriented by the dark torrent that engulfed her. She knew only that she must find air. Her head suddenly broke through the surface, and she was just able to catch another breath before the raging river pulled her into its depths once more.

Gathering her strength and will, she rallied her senses and exhorted herself to remain calm. *You're a strong swimmer, Hattie. Panic will kill you, but swimming will get you to the shore.*

Determinedly, she forced her legs to kick and her arms to stroke. *You can swim,* she assured herself. *You can swim out of here.*

The violently rushing water and the fallen tree branches and wreckage that struck and impeded her said no, but she continued the calm, deliberate strokes. *You can swim out of here. You can swim out to Reed.*

It was working. Again she broke the surface and glanced quickly toward the bank. It was a long way, but she wasn't deterred. She didn't see Reed yet knew he was there. He was waiting, arms open to hold her and comfort her. Sweet peaches and tender words were only a watery distance away.

Just as her confidence rose, a hidden branch gouged her thigh painfully. She cried out as pain stormed through her body and she submerged, grabbing her injured leg. The fallen tree enveloped her like the tentacles of a malicious river monster. Ignoring the eerie ambience, she massaged the screaming agony in her leg and assured herself that she was all right.

Throwing off the fire that seared her thigh, she swam again for the surface. Her progress was abruptly halted. At first she was merely startled by her immobility. Her torn dress was caught in the branches that enveloped her so closely. Annoyed, she jerked at it. As precious seconds passed and the dress remained entangled, she realized she was hopelessly trapped by the underwater limb. Frantically she pulled at the wet sturdy calico, but the vicious talons would not release her.

"Hattie!" Reed screamed as he saw his wife being swept into the river. A cold chill of terror spread through his body as he jumped onto the levee and ran down the bank. Ceaselessly he searched for some sign of the woman who had been his friend from childhood, the woman he had married, the woman he had pledged his life to, the woman he loved. Nothing in his life had prepared him for the cold shaking horror of his helplessness. In the back of his mind he saw her wide toothy grin and heard the echo of her warm artless laughter. *Hattie!* Wild-eyed, he raced up the south levee and tore through the underbrush as field turned to untouched riverbank.

"Come up, Hattie," he whispered as he ran, his gaze never leaving the whirling water. "You've got to breathe, my Hattie. Come up now!"

When he saw her head surface a good hundred yards downstream from the rice field, his joy was balanced by the practical realization that he could never catch up with her at the rate the river was carrying her downstream.

Racing along the bank, his eyes ever watchful, he begged feverishly that she somehow get hold of a rock, a branch, anything so that he would be able to get to her. "Take my farm, my future, my life, Lord, but don't take my Hattie farther downstream," he prayed.

The reality of his love for her, his need for her, the void that would be his life without her enveloped his entire being, and he fervently stared at the water as if to draw her to him with his will.

He saw her come up again. She was farther downstream but closer to the bank. Hope blazed brightly in Reed as he ran on. She was trying to make it to shore. She was coming to him.

"Swim, Hattie!" he screamed over the torrential sound of the turbulent river. "Swim!" If she could get closer to the shoreline, she'd find something to hold on to.

His breath rushed from him in frightened gasps as he ran

onward. Like a racehorse in the last furlong, he no longer thought of the pain of the run, only of the victory at the end.

He saw her again, closer now. "Hattie!" he called, but his breath was stolen by his efforts to reach her.

Suddenly he saw her jerk strangely, and a cry of pain floated across the water to him. "Hattie! Hattie!" he screamed as she sank from sight.

He ran on. She didn't come up. He scanned the swirling water, frightened, shaking, sweating with fear.

"Hattie!" he screamed again to the roaring river, his arms outstretched in a plea to nature. "Hattie! Where are you!"

Hurrying back to the place where he'd seen her go under, he jerked off his workshoes and without a thought for the futility or the danger, dove into the wild water.

Immediately he gashed his brow on a fallen tree hidden just below the surface. Dazed, at first he nearly allowed himself to be pulled downstream. Then, with a gasp of understanding, he desperately clawed for a hold on the tree. She was here. She was trapped on one of these limbs. He knew it.

Groping blindly in the muddy water, he clung to the submerged branches as he searched for his wife. Hattie was here, and he would find her. He couldn't allow the waters to pull him away. He would never let anything keep him from Hattie again.

When he felt the sparkly light-headedness of lack of oxygen, he surfaced quickly, keeping a grip on a tiny branch to hold him to the tree. *She's here*, he told himself, *and I will find her*.

Hattie felt the fire in her lungs building unbearably as she acknowledged at last that she was not able to free herself. Anger surged through her. *Why me? Why now? I was finally so happy.* In a fit of temper, she struggled uselessly once more.

Relax, she told herself. *Fighting will only wear you out more quickly.* Pain was searing her lungs, and the dark muddy water around her turned blue, then green, as she slipped through consciousness.

Her life flashed before her in bits of nonsensical detail. A pretty bit of ribbon from Turpin's store. Mama showing her when to dig the potatoes by looking at their withered leaves. Her father's horsey grin as he spun her in the air like a whirligig. And Reed. Reed young, Reed now. Her mind filled with visions of Reed as she had known him. The sparkle in his eyes, the tender touch of his lips. Reed had made her laugh. Reed had made her love. For this sweet short time, she had known bliss. Could she ask for more than that? Happiness for only a day was worth more than decades merely lived.

She felt herself relax. The pain in her thigh was gone, completely gone. All physical sensation had disappeared, and she felt strangely unburdened by her body. Gently, without touching or feeling, she began to move through the maze of limbs that imprisoned her. She was no longer bound to the tree. She was tied to nothing on earth, and she surged upward, floating above the river, above the pain and danger.

The merciless flow of water was like a vision of mighty power in the moonlight. Watching it, entranced, she felt her fear dissolve as she admired its strength and majesty. It was so strange that she, who had thought herself plain and ordinary, should finish her life absorbed by something so wild, unfettered, and beautiful.

In that moment of peace and contentment her attention was captured by the sight of her husband's head breaking the surface of the water below her. Fear again poured through her as she watched the man she loved struggling to save her.

"Save yourself!" she attempted to cry, but she had no voice and knew that he couldn't hear her. He dove once more, and she watched anxiously. Surely he must see that the cause was lost. She could never live without breath for so long. *Stop, Reed. I'm not there anymore.* Her heart seemed to break as she watched him dive and surface only to dive again.

At last she understood. Reed Tyler loved her. It was as clear to her now as her love for him. Reed would not save himself. He would lose his life in this river just as she had lost hers. *Oh, no!* she pleaded to heaven. *He is so young! He's worked so hard. He deserves to see his dreams, his future, his children.*

But she knew he would not save himself. She must save him.

Reed's strength had almost given out. His arms ached from the frantic fight with the river, and a haze of tears and terror blinded him as each precious second slipped quickly toward a terrible end.

"Hattie, I love you, I need you," he pleaded to the river, and again dove into the dark blackness to see nothing, find nothing. Reaching, grasping, he silently begged the branches to relinquish the prize he sought.

Faint and disheartened, he was ready to surface for a hurried taste of the air when a hand suddenly grasped his leg. With unexpected joy, he reached down, touched the cold lifeless body, and pulled it to him. His hands swept eagerly over the tangle of clothes that held her. As if all the power of heaven were with him, he ripped the dress from the confining branches.

Immediately they were wildly coursing down the river. Hattie was like a bundle of sticks in his arms, as still as death, but Reed remembered the strength of her grasp on his ankle and promised himself that she would live. Not twenty feet down-river, a log lay as if in wait. Pulling himself and Hattie against it, Reed made it to shore, exhausted and gasping for breath, carefully holding her head above the water.

He rolled her onto the bank before dropping beside her. Ignoring his dizziness and fatigue, he turned her over on her stomach and worked to pump out the water that clogged her lungs.

Choking, coughing, and moaning in pain, Hattie rid herself of the horrific water, then lay panting beside her husband.

"Alive," Reed whispered to himself as he used the last of his strength to touch her brow, assuring himself that it was no dream.

"Reed? Reed, are you all right?" she asked, her voice hoarse.

"Am I all right?" He was too tired even to smile. "That's supposed to be *my* question."

They lay silently in each other's arms, weariness overcoming them as the darkness of the night settled around them. Reed pulled her more securely against him, suddenly afraid of not holding her close enough. Their eyes closed in exhausted slumber.

The night was pitch-black when Hattie awoke, wet and shivering in the rain. Startled at the strangeness of her surroundings, she moved too quickly. The searing pain in her thigh stopped her instantly.

"Hattie," Reed whispered groggily beside her. "You're fine, my love. You're safe."

She remembered the fall in the river and the odd dream that had puzzled and frightened her. Carefully turning toward her husband, she ran her hands over his chest, making sure he was alive and well beside her.

As reality slowly seeped back into her consciousness, she realized what had happened and sat up. She had fallen in the river, and Reed had saved her. Reed had risked his life to save her. Or had she saved him?

He sat up beside her and wrapped his arms around her, laying his head in the hollow of her shoulder. "I love you, Hattie," he said quietly.

"I know, Reed," she answered, caressing his cheek. "Because I love you too."

They sat together calmly, content, secure in their happiness and thankful just for the chance to touch.

Finally the reverence resolved to tenderness, and Reed sprinkled pecks on the mass of sodden muddy hair at the nape of Hattie's neck.

"I must look a sight," she said lightly.

"Why worry? It's pitch-dark."

Laughing, she turned in his arms and shared a sweet summer peach kissed with raindrops.

"I'll never worry about being younger than you again," he said, teasing. "I swear I aged twenty years when that levee gave way."

"The rice!" she exclaimed with sudden dismay.

"What?"

"The rice! The levee broke. Reed, we've got to get back. You'll lose all of your rice."

Reed pulled his wife into his arms, ignoring her consternation. "Hattie, darlin'. I don't give a damn about the rice!"

"Of course you do," she said. "You've wanted to grow rice on this farm for years. If you don't hurry back to that field, you're going to lose everything."

He tenderly cupped her cheek. "Hattie, today I almost did lose everything." He kissed her brow, then sighed. "You are everything to me, Hattie Tyler. All I have ever wanted, all the ambition I've ever had, has always centered on you. I love you, Hattie. That is the only thing that matters to me."

Rising to his feet, Reed Tyler lifted his wife into his arms and carried her home.

• • •

It was nearly a week before the sun finally shone and Hattie and Reed walked out to the rice field. The river had ebbed quickly but left sodden reminders in its wake.

Reed waded into the rice field. The standing water was little more than a few inches, but he sank in the mud up to his knees.

Hattie tied her skirts around her waist and silently followed him into the muck. In the days since their brush with death, she and Reed had opened up to each other. For the first time both were willing to look at the love between them and talk about it. Both marveled that the love they had searched for elsewhere had always been so close at hand.

"I think I'll always feel grateful to Ancil Drayton," Reed told her. "When he decided to court you, I was nothing less than jealous. It was the first time I'd allowed myself to think of you as a woman."

Hattie pulled him to her and kissed him. "I'll always be grateful to Ancil myself."

Raising an eyebrow, Reed waited for her to continue.

"If he'd never asked to court me, I'd never have learned about peaches."

"Humph!" Reed scoffed. "It's a good thing you came to me for lessons. Drayton probably knows less than you."

Hattie nodded in pretended seriousness. "I don't think he understands peaches at all. But he is quite fond of 'smoochy-smooches.' "

"What?"

"Never mind."

Opening their hearts added so much to what they already had, it was almost impossible to contain. They held each other in comfortable tenderness and confessed their truths both large and small. Thankful, grateful, they sat together and listened unconcerned to the rain running off the roof.

Their days of joy had been a time out of time, special moments of love and closeness that many married couples live a lifetime and never see.

But today, as they stood in the ruin of their former rice field, the things of earth again took precedence over higher concerns.

Reed reached down and pulled up a handful of full-grown, beautiful, but rotten and ruined rice. "Damnation," he cursed, then glanced back to see if Hattie was going to take exception to his language. She seemed to be of similar mind as she gazed upon the ungodly mess.

Slapping the sopping grain against the leg of his trousers, Reed was furious. "They all told me it wouldn't work," he said angrily. "But I didn't believe anyone. 'It's perfect for rice,' I said. Rice is the crop of the future. Isn't that what I said, Hattie? Just a few years from now, and the whole county will be seeded in rice, and they'll have me to thank."

Grabbing up another bunch of ruined grain, he threw it down in disgust. He slogged through the muddy field, searching for something—some answer, some small reason to continue to believe in his dream. Stopping at the cut bank, he surveyed the ruined field before seating himself on the wet grass that clung tenaciously to the slope.

"Facts are facts," he said, mostly for his own benefit but as if he were addressing Hattie. "Cotton is the crop that we know how to grow on this prairie, and cotton is what we're going to grow."

She walked closer to him, watching the play of emotions on his face.

"Hattie, I'm putting this back into prairie grass to see how much of this topsoil we can save," he said. "I hate to admit it, but when I'm whipped, I'm whipped."

Hattie silently surveyed the disaster around her, then she studied her husband as he stared out over the ruined field. She tried to recapture the future as Reed had always seen it. Suddenly making a decision, she raised her chin defiantly. "Wait just a minute, Plowboy!"

Startled, Reed turned to look at his wife.

She folded her arms across her chest and spoke sharply. "If you remember correctly, this is *my* rice field. I'll make the decision what we're going to do with it."

His smile was tentative. "Hattie, a joke is a joke, but this mess . . . Well, what else can I say?"

"You can say that you're going to repair that levee and as soon as it dries out a bit, you're going to get this field in shape so we can get a jump on the rice planting next spring."

He leaned back against the bank and folded his arms obstinately. "Hattie, I've failed. It's time we faced the facts. I've already wasted a lot of time and money on this witless idea of mine. Obviously we can't grow rice here. I was wrong all along, and it's finally been proven to me and everybody in the county."

"It hasn't been proven to me," she said tartly. "The old-timers say that this was the worst flood ever seen in these parts. Floods happen to everyone. If the cotton hadn't already been picked, we would have lost a lot of it on the lowlands too."

Reed shook his head. "No, Hattie, I've given up on rice. I'm out of the rice business forever. I'm a cotton farmer from now on."

"Plowboy, I want a rice field. If you aren't going to grow it for me, I'll find some other farmer who will!"

Reed leapt to his feet, ready to argue. The two faced off for at least a minute, holding themselves rigid. Then a hint of a smile tickled at Reed's mouth. Reaching out, he grabbed his wife and hauled her to him. They both tumbled into the thick murky black mud.

"Another farmer!" he exclaimed. "Miss Hattie, you've got more farmer than you can handle right now."

To prove his point, Reed pulled Hattie onto the gentle grass-covered slope of the cut bank, and there in the bright sunshine of midmorning, their bodies slick with the mud of the ruined rice field, Mr. and Mrs. Reed Tyler planted a crop of an entirely different kind.

Epilogue

R EED cranked up the tin lizzie and listened with a pleased expression to the well-tuned engine.

"Come on, Hattie, boys, Sally!" he called. "If you all don't hurry, we'll be late for church."

Three young boys raced out of the house. The eldest, a tall black-haired boy of ten, beat the others to the car. His handsome Tyler face was accented by a strong Colfax jaw.

"Daddy," the boy said, "Hershall asked me to have Sunday dinner at his house. Then we're going to take the raft out for a while."

"Do Hershall's folks know about this?"

"Yes, sir," the boy answered, nodding. "Hershall done asked. Mr. Leege said he'd be down at the dock anyway, and Mrs. Leege said one more child at their table would hardly be noticed."

Reed smiled at the truth in those words. In Bessie Jane and Harmon's brood of nine youngsters, another one more or less wouldn't make much difference. Harmon's business sense had paid off well for him. Machinery was all the rage, and Harm had been the first to bring modern farm equipment and light manufacture to the county. That and everything else. Leege Mill was the biggest this side of New Orleans, and after Arthur Turpin died, Harmon had expanded the dry-goods store to a whole streetful of shops. New people and businesses had started moving in right away. It was only natural that the town's new business district be called Leege Avenue.

"I guess it'll be okay," Reed said, "but mind your manners and do what you're told."

"Sure, Daddy," the boy replied, then clambered into the backseat.

The two other boys were chasing each other around the house, destined to get their clothes dirty before they made it to the door of the church. The long veranda they roughhoused upon was a far cry from the little porch of the old Colfax farmhouse. John and Sarah Colfax had never needed space the way the Tylers did. Reed had added a room here, a room there, until the porch began to looked dwarfed. Finally last year, he'd built around the old house, creating a big three-story Victorian-style home with a wide veranda on three sides.

"John!" Reed shouted. "You and Cole quit horsing around and get in this car." He stepped out of the car to help the two dust off their dirty knees. "What's keeping your mother?"

"Mama's sick," a small girl answered, jumping from the porch, to the ground.

"Sick?" Reed asked.

The child's black curls danced as she nodded. "She run out to the privy and I heard her throwing up."

"Snooping, snooping. You follow Mama like a shadow," Cole taunted his sister before silencing at his father's disapproving glance.

"Well, you just get in the car, Sally," Reed said, "and I'll go check on your mother."

Climbing over the door instead of opening it, young Sally joined her brothers in the back seat of the shiny black vehicle.

Before Reed could make good on his promise to check on his wife, Hattie came hurrying out of the house. "We're going to be late for sure this morning," she said with dismay as she settled in her seat.

"It won't be the first time," Reed said. Turning to glance at the children in the backseat, he made a grand pretense of making sure all were accounted for.

"One, two, three, four," he said, pointing at each one of

them in an old family joke that he couldn't keep track of his own children.

As the childish laughter in the backseat receded, Hattie took his hand and laid it gently on her abdomen.

"Five," she said.

"Five?" His eyebrows rose.

She nodded. Reed just sat looking at her for a moment. With a warm smile, he leaned over to give his wife a bite of peaches.

"Ew, mush!" the occupants of the backseat complained loudly.

Reed ignored them. "Are we still trying for eight?" he whispered.

"I hope not," Hattie replied, and the two giggled conspiratorially.

Giving her a tiny peck on the nose, Reed sat back up to put the car in gear, then hesitated. Leaning back toward Hattie, he said seriously, "I don't think I can face them at church today."

She frowned. "What *are* you talking about?"

"With five children, everybody *knows* what we've been doing!"

Hattie Tyler's laughter floated on the morning air as the shiny new car headed down the road toward church. The summer sun shone warmly on the fertile fields that surrounded them. On each side of the road, bright and green and stretching, as far as the eye could see, grew acres and acres of Arkansas rice.

ABOUT THE AUTHOR

PAMELA MORSI is a native of Oklahoma who now resides in Texas with her family. Winner of numerous awards, including two RITA Awards, she is the author of *Heaven Sent, Courting Miss Hattie, Garters, Wild Oats, Runabout, Marrying Stone, Something Shady, Simple Jess, The Love Charm, No Ordinary Princess,* and *Sealed with a Kiss.* A former medical librarian, Pamela Morsi has been praised as "the Garrison Keillor of romance" (*Publishers Weekly*) for the down-to-earth flavor of her delightfully romantic novels.

Printed in the United States
by Baker & Taylor Publisher Services